SHADOW OF THE EIGHTH

More tales of the Astra Militarum from Black Library

MINKA LESK: THE LAST WHITESHIELD
An omnibus edition of the novels *Cadia Stands, Cadian Honour, Traitor Rock* and several short stories
by Justin D Hill

THE FALL OF CADIA
A novel by Robert Rath

CREED: ASHES OF CADIA
A novel by Jude Reid

OUTGUNNED
A novel by Denny Flowers

CATACHAN DEVIL
A novel by Justin Woolley

STEEL TREAD
A novel by Andy Clark

KRIEG
A novel by Steve Lyons

VOLPONE GLORY
A novel by Nick Kyme

WITCHBRINGER
A novel by Steven B Fischer

VAINGLORIOUS
A novel by Sandy Mitchell

HONOURBOUND
A novel by Rachel Harrison

YARRICK
An omnibus edition of the novels *Imperial Creed, The Pyres of Armageddon,* the novella *Chains of Golgotha* and several short stories
by David Annandale

GAUNT'S GHOSTS: THE FOUNDING
An omnibus edition of the novels *First and Only, Ghostmaker* and *Necropolis*
by Dan Abnett

SHADOW OF THE EIGHTH

JUSTIN D HILL

BLACK LIBRARY

A BLACK LIBRARY PUBLICATION

First published in 2023.
This edition published in Great Britain in 2024 by
Black Library, Games Workshop Ltd., Willow Road,
Nottingham, NG7 2WS, UK.

Represented by: Games Workshop Limited – Irish branch,
Unit 3, Lower Liffey Street, Dublin 1,
D01 K199, Ireland.

10 9 8 7 6 5 4 3 2 1

Produced by Games Workshop in Nottingham.
Cover illustration by Marzena Nereida Piwowar.

A CIP record for this book is available from the British Library.

ISBN 13: 978-1-80407-361-2

Printed and bound in the UK.

---

*For Cris and Giles, and all those who I have rolled dice with.
And all of you for whom the pleasure is in our futures.*

For more than a hundred centuries the Emperor has sat immobile on the Golden Throne of Earth. He is the Master of Mankind. By the might of his inexhaustible armies a million worlds stand against the dark.

Yet, he is a rotting carcass, the Carrion Lord of the Imperium held in life by marvels from the Dark Age of Technology and the thousand souls sacrificed each day so his may continue to burn.

To be a man in such times is to be one amongst untold billions. It is to live in the cruelest and most bloody regime imaginable. It is to suffer an eternity of carnage and slaughter. It is to have cries of anguish and sorrow drowned by the thirsting laughter of dark gods.

This is a dark and terrible era where you will find little comfort or hope. Forget the power of technology and science. Forget the promise of progress and advancement. Forget any notion of common humanity or compassion.

There is no peace amongst the stars, for in the grim darkness of the far future, there is only war.

DRAMATIS PERSONAE

CADIAN 101ST COMMAND

Lord General Isaia Bendikt	
Colonel Baytov	Regimental commander
Mere	Bendikt's adjutant
Prassan	Quartermaster
Chief Medic Banting	
Captain Ostanko	First Company commander
Colonel Rath Sturm	Second Company commander
Captain Irinya Ronin	Third Company commander
Colonel Sparker	Eighth Company commander

SEVENTH COMPANY

Captain Arminka Lesk	Seventh Company commander
Colour Sergeant Tyson	
Lieutenant Sargora	First Platoon commander
Lieutenant Orugi	Second Platoon commander
Lieutenant Viktor	Third Platoon commander
Lieutenant Senik	Fourth Platoon commander
Lieutenant Grüber	Fifth Platoon commander
Sergeant Dreno	
Anastasia	Driver
Breve	Driver
Baine	Trooper
Blanchez	Trooper, sniper
Bohdan	Trooper
Hwang	Trooper
Jaromir	Trooper
Lyrga	Trooper
Maksym	Trooper
Nathanial	Trooper

Olek	Trooper, medic
Yedrin	Trooper
Yuriv	Trooper

WHITESHIELD COMPANY

Major Luka	
Ankela	Whiteshield
Juliar	Whiteshield
Renie	Whiteshield
Skyrin	Whiteshield
Thainne	Whiteshield

AERONAUTICA

Esting	Lighter pilot
Mesina	Lighter pilot

OFFICIO PREFECTUS

Chief Commissar Shand
Commissar Hontius
Commissar Knoll
Commissar Salice

MINISTORUM

Father Keremm
Confessor Talbeas

SCHOLASTICA PSYKANA

Sanctioned Psyker Valentian

PROLOGUE

CINNABAR'S FOLLY

Cinnabar's Folly had been governed by the Felhkom family for more than a millennium, and this palace, the Durondeau, had been the country seat of one of the family's lesser branches for nearly a thousand years. A tumbling mansion, whose grand wings formed an inner paved courtyard, it had once been a place of quiet and contemplation, with wide lawns and gardens, and extensive hunting grounds for the family's younger members. But that was before the war had come.

Now, the grounds were overrun with tank parks, fuel depots and miles of metalled bahns. In the gardens, the smooth lawns were pockmarked with craters, the flowerbeds overwhelmed by rampant weeds that trembled with each salvo of distant artillery fire, and the statue of one of the illustrious family members had been used for target practice.

Of the palace itself, rounds of military requisition had left the place looking distinctly down at heel. The emptied cellars smelt of urine, its tall sash windows were sandbagged, priceless murals had been boarded over, and hand-woven carpets were covered with flakboard walkways.

It was a grim sight, but as he stood in the Imperial Dining Room watching Lord General Bendikt examine the trench plans of the Tribulation Salient, Adjutant Mere knew one thing for certain: it was much better than being in the trenches.

All eyes were on Bendikt as the artillery barrage grew in volume, like a distant storm. The lights flickered.

He had worked for months to bring the battle for Cinnabar's Folly to the moment of culmination and it seemed that finally the trap was sprung. He had throttled the throat of the salient till he had threatened to encircle a whole third of the heretic forces. The enemy commander would have to deploy his best troops or lose the battle, and when he did, Bendikt would send his finest against them: fire with fire, anvil against stone.

Mere's gaze shifted to an unravelling scroll issuing from a scribe servitor. He read the words upon it as they appeared from the cyborg's sickly grey hand. His body language gave the game away before he spoke. 'Raiding parties have confirmed. Scourged warriors have been moved into the front-line trenches.'

There was a round of applause and congratulation.

Mere shook Bendikt's hand. 'Well done, sir. You have their neck upon the block!'

Bendikt closed his eyes. His fingers were shaking. They wrapped about the glass beaker on the desk before him. It was true. The enemy had been forced to bare their throat. All he had to do was swing.

He paused.

For some, the weight of command grew lighter with each passing engagement. But not for Lord General Bendikt. With each battle, the consequence of his orders weighed heavier and heavier, and he knew the enormity of what he was asking of his old regiment, the Cadian 101st: to assault across the hell of no-man's-land, in the face of fierce resistance.

The general took a deep breath. 'Colonel Baytov.'

The commander of the 101st stepped forward.

'You will deploy into the front-line trenches along the neck of the salient. Your orders are to strike at dawn. You will destroy the enemy and advance until relieved.'

Colonel Baytov made the sign of the aquila. 'Thank you, sir.'

Bendikt had to hold the tears back as the commander of the 101st strode to the varnished ironwood door. There were no words he could say.

Finally, he said, 'Baytov...?'

'Sir?'

Bendikt stared at the colonel, eyes red with emotion. In the end he walked to the door and took Baytov's hand and squeezed it.

'Good luck,' he said, and turned away.

Prassan was standing in the hallway with the rest of the command staff, who had gathered to see the colonel off. Baytov grinned at him as the dining room door clicked closed. He was buoyed up by the enormity of it all. He was proud of his troops. Damned proud.

'It's on,' Baytov said simply. 'We attack at dawn.'

Baytov's Centaur carrier was waiting for him at the steps of the palace.

The metalled bahns took them straight towards the front, a two-hour drive past acres of silent tanks, fuel depots, and mile upon mile of military camps sunk under the blasted ground. The wind was thick with drifting dust and the smoke of battle. But the closer to the front they drew, the more blighted the landscape. Stumps of trees, rank weeds, each blade of grass – everything was stained black by fyceline soot.

Despite the landscape, Baytov was in a fine mood. They had planned for this moment for months. He relished the chance to meet the Scourged warriors, gun-barrel to gun-barrel. The Cadian 101st were already on the move, pushing up through the darkness to the front-line trenches, ready to surprise the enemy at dawn.

Prassan could picture it all as Baytov stood at the front of the Centaur, the flicker of artillery playing on his face. The colonel was puffed up with responsibility and excitement. If he felt any trepidation, he did not show it.

There would be no week-long artillery barrage to alert the foe, just a sudden burst to keep the heads of the enemy down as the first wave of troops went over the top, and then the 101st would charge across no-man's-land. They would storm the trenches where the Drakul-zar's elite troops had been trapped, and they would crush them.

In a matter of weeks, the moon of Cinnabar's Folly would be theirs.

When the Centaur carrier arrived at Baytov's command post, the office staff came out to greet him: a tight huddle waiting under the single bare lumen hanging above the entrance. Soot stained the bulb, and the lumen flickered with the thunder of artillery, but it was enough to cast a sepia puddle of light.

Prassan stood back as Baytov stepped down from the Centaur. The colonel paused to shake hands with his staff officers waiting to congratulate him. At the end of the line, Baytov turned. 'You should all get some rest,' he told them. 'It will be a long day tomorrow.'

But of course, none of them would sleep. How could they? Not when the rank and file were risking everything in the assault.

When Baytov got to the end of the line, one of his officers offered him a lho-stick.

'Thank you,' Baytov said. He put it between his lips and bent forward to light it.

The las-shot hit the back of Baytov's head with the force of a punch.

The crack was almost drowned out in the thunder of the bombardment. No one could quite believe it. His peaked cap was no protection. The beam blasted through skin and bone, into the wet fat of his brain, and his legs went out from under him.

The colonel did not hear the shouts of alarm. Did not hear the cries of his staff for a medic to come at once. Like a smashed lumen, his life dwindled to darkness.

PART I

I

CINNABAR'S FOLLY

Minka's boots were misshapen lumps of thick trench mud. They weighed down each step like lead. They made moving slow and ponderous. They'd get her killed, she thought, as she pushed along the zigzag access trench.

Her platoon should have reached the front-line trenches an hour before, but this stretch had suffered ferocious counter-bombardment and it was hard to find their way when the trenches had been blasted apart.

A rocket screamed overhead, descending towards the heretic lines and erupting with an earth-shattering blast. 'The attack is starting in ten minutes,' Sparker shouted. He sounded as rattled as she was.

'We'll be there,' she told him as he led his squad left, and she went right. The trench before them had taken a direct hit and it was now a mess of broken earth. She put a muddy foot to the firing step and risked a look at no-man's-land.

The enemy's artillery bunkers were ten miles back from the

front, a forest of Earthshaker batteries, each one firing six times a minute, each shell's arching parabola a twenty-second flight over artillery lines, supply depots, communication and support trenches, saps, banks of wire and no-man's-land, before it smashed down into the mud of Cinnabar's Folly.

The air was full of whistling shrapnel, the landscape seething and tortured with eruptions of blasted earth, but she thought she could see the line of trench ahead.

'Follow me!' Minka shouted, but no one could hear a bloody thing.

She crawled forward, head buried into her shoulders, hands slipping on the broken clods of earth. She couldn't tell if the wet lumps were mud or flesh.

This land had once been red, but war had bled the moon of Cinnabar's Folly dry. It was a burnt and blackened corpse, stained black with oil and flesh and fyceline soot. But dead or not, Minka told herself through gritted teeth, this moon belonged to the God-Emperor, and the forces of the Imperium had come to reclaim it, crater by crater, yard by yard, inch by filthy inch.

In the hellish ruin, the only guide to the line of the trench was the length of razor wire, fixed in place by pigtail iron stakes. Curtains of smoke swept over the battlefield. They stank of sulphur and promethium. She felt the fizz as las-bolts and hard rounds stitched overhead.

A stray slug slammed into her canteen. She felt the impact, felt the water start to trickle down her fatigues as at last a line of sandbags came into view. Shells screamed earthwards as Minka dragged herself over the lip and tumbled into the trench on the other side, filthy water rising up to her elbows.

One by one, her platoon made it, skidding down the same slide. They lost two on the crossing.

Blanchez pushed her sniper rifle before her, and then tumbled after. 'Darin and Kastov,' she said. She looked shaken.

Minka checked her chronometer. Seven minutes left. They zig-zagged forward through the battlescape of razor wire, corpses and craters.

At the next intersection a signpost had been nailed to the flakboard panels. There were a series of names and arrows: Bastion Nine to the right, Death Run and Viper's Neck to the left.

A rotting trooper had been buried in the wall of the trench and pale maggots dripped into the filthy water as Lieutenant Minka Lesk stumbled past, one hand on the flakboard reveting. A mortar shell landed just above them. A fountain of filth splattered down. Another shell landed. Long as well. And then a third as Minka rounded the corner and half tripped over a body already sinking into the filth: dead trooper. Sniper shot. Half the head missing.

'We're nearly there,' she said, checking her chronometer. Six minutes until the attack.

Bastion Nine was a rockcrete pillbox that dominated a low ridge looking down across the blasted plains. Minka found the Forax Binary troops sheltering in the bunker, waiting for relief.

'Who is in command?' Minka demanded.

The captain came forward. Under his flak armour his greatcoat was ripped and torn, and one sleeve was missing, the stuffing pale where it had been torn away. His name, Iago, was stencilled onto the chest of his flak armour breastplate. His visor was pushed back, and his face was dark with stubble and mud. His eyes were hollow.

He was trembling as he spoke. 'You're the relief?'

'Yes,' Minka said. The 101st were what the Munitorum classed as 'fresh troops'.

Captain Iago was too spent to speak, but he couldn't hide his disappointment. He started to cry. The Forax Binary troops had been in the front-line trenches for a month, and the stress was starting to take its toll.

She pulled him up into the trench. 'Show me the front line.'

He still couldn't find his voice, so he pointed instead. There was a crude trenchscope. A hundred yards down the valley she could make out the zigzag of dark lines marked out with thickets of razor wire. She was almost surprised to see that the plans were largely accurate.

Her Swabian power sabre hung at her side. A memento from her last deployment. The basket hilt was smeared in mud; she wiped off the worst as she checked her lieutenant-issue Mauler-pattern bolt pistol, and the three barrel magazines clipped to the small of her back.

The Forax Binary troops were already pulling back as the Cadians hurried left and right, getting themselves into position. Minka risked another look. No-man's-land was a mess of matted razor-wire thickets, corpses and craters, flaring with explosions.

She paused, looking for the best route of attack as an Earthshaker shell roared overhead.

There were two minutes left before the assault. Minka closed her eyes and allowed herself a deep breath in. It was weeks since she'd seen the sun. Weeks since she'd had a good night's sleep. Months, perhaps... It was hard to remember and she felt like she'd fought a battle already, and all they had done was reach the starting line.

Vivran was right behind her, bowed under the weight of the vox-caster, hand-mic pressed to her mouth as she reported that they were in place and ready.

Minka went along checking each of the sergeants. They were

ready. As she came back to the bastion, Jaromir already had the heavy stubber in place, and fired off a quick salvo to check the workings.

'Ready!' he shouted.

Minka slapped his back. There was barely a minute before the attack.

She touched her pistol and the sword-hilt, pulled her water bottle free and tossed it into the mud, checked her magazines, and took another deep breath.

'Incoming!' a voice shouted.

The shell landed in no-man's-land. They felt the tremors through their boots as a fountain of filth billowed up and the mud slid down between the revetments. A gobbet of mud hit Minka's shoulder. It was black, but it had the sticky consistency of flesh. She knocked it off into the trembling bilge-water.

The warning shout went up again. A blunt projectile hit the ground twenty feet away and showered them all in another torrent of muck, but the distinctive screech did not end with an explosion.

'Dud,' Yedrin said.

A memory from Cadia went through Minka like a cold blade.

'Drop pod!' she roared as she leapt to the firing step, bolt pistol ready.

The adamantine tulip loomed up over the wire, the posts, the tilted tank traps and the corpses, the rifle butts scattered across the rotting devastation of no-man's-land. It sat at an angle within a flooded crater, steam and smoke billowing up from the superheated metal.

There was no insignia Minka could see. Just the heat-stripes and discolouring of its descent. But she knew what was inside, knew what was coming and her mouth was dry, her heartbeat thundering. In an instant she had gone from veteran trooper to hunted animal.

'Ready to repel!' she shouted as the petals slammed down.

Instead of Space Marines, a blizzard of frag shells blasted out.

The storm was as sudden and fierce as a monsoon shower, circling the drop pod with a ring of devastation. Grenades landed in the trench and tore through flesh and armour.

The air was full of shouts of pain and alarm. A rattling voice called for a medic. Bodies lay like dolls strewn about, bleeding and broken. Vivran's fingers were tight on Minka's arm. Her eyes were wide, like she had just woken from hell. She was breathing rapidly as she made a dreadful mewling sound.

'You're all right,' Minka said as she pulled a suture strip from her belt. Her hands were slippery with mud and blood. She looped it round the bloody stump of Vivran's leg and pulled it tight. 'Stay with me!' Minka hissed as she pulled the knot closed and tightened it.

Vivran nodded, breathing quickly.

'Get her out of here!' Minka shouted, and started to order the defence in depth. 'Stand ready!' she roared. 'One minute!'

Two of Yedrin's squad stripped the vox-caster away, then lifted Vivran, one at the shoulders, one by the remaining leg as someone else shouted another warning. Bohdan discarded his own backpack and pulled the vox-caster on. Another drop pod slammed down fifty feet ahead of them, with the same blunt, earth-shaking force. They threw themselves against the flakboard revetments as the frag shower passed.

Minka knew what was coming next.

'Get a heavy weapons team! Plasma, melta, anything!' Minka yelled.

Bohdan had one finger in his ear. 'Yes,' he shouted. 'We're in position. Raise the alarm. Space Marine intrusion! Bastion Nine.'

There was an observation trench that ran close to where the drop pods stood.

'With me,' Minka told Jeremias. She ran along the front-line trench, five troopers behind her. The duckboard was narrow, the flakboards pinned into place with iron stakes and lengths of rebar.

Jeremias nodded, easing the flamer shoulder-straps over his flak armour. He flicked the ignition stud and set the pilot flame alight.

They splashed through the wet, and turned right into the observation trench. They were halfway along when ash started to fall. It was dirty and grey. A flake landed on the back of Minka's hand and she realised it was snow. She felt the chill, saw the delicate and unique pattern of the ice flake, and she heard the crackle of static, smelled the stink of ozone.

Minka's skin goose-pimpled. She put her hand up for the others to slow.

Krail was pale. 'Something's behind us,' she whispered. 'And it wasn't there a moment ago…'

'I've got it,' Jeremias said, pushing to the front, flamer ready, and suddenly everyone was shouting and calling for reinforcements.

Over it all came the distinctive clunk of powered armour.

Jaromir half-crouched in Bastion Nine. He leant into the heavy stubber, stared down the gun-barrel, through the round metal spider-web sights, into the matted thickets of razor wire, pig-tail posts, corpses and craters – keeping the drop pod in view.

He blinked as the air beside the drop pod started to stir. It was like a heat wave, rippling from a hot road. But instead of rising, it was swirling in upon itself, till it was a blue-and-white vortex, then a sudden shaft of light, within which a figure took shape.

Jaromir was not a quick thinker, but there were times when you didn't need to think. 'Contact!' he shouted and started to fire, even as the figure emerged.

The heavy stubber kicked into his shoulder, the brass shell cases rattling to the floor. There was no way he could miss. The immensity of an Astartes Terminator appeared in the mud of no-man's-land, its size and bulk impossible in a space where there had been only air, its trophy rack rising five feet above its head.

It was so big the rest of Jaromir's squad could see it over the trench tops.

'Throne!' one of them cursed.

'Fire!' Jaromir shouted as he kept the figure within the circle of his sights, kicking off a long salvo.

The rounds slammed into the huge figure and... did nothing.

The Terminator barely seemed to notice. Jaromir kept tracking it as it stamped through the tangle of razor wire. The bullets shattered on the surface of its armour or slewed off into no-man's-land.

'I can't see it!' Jaromir called out as it dropped down into the observation trench – and then the Terminator's trophy rack appeared, jerking over the top of the sandbags, each ponderous step bringing it towards the trench he was in.

The squad were ready, in firing position, kneeling, lasrifles braced.

Everyone was shouting now. The las-bolts were useless. There was nothing they could do to stop it. 'Where are the frekking plasmas?' Jaromir shouted as the Terminator turned towards them with the clank of metal and the hiss of pistons.

The Terminator filled the end of the trench as an adult would fill a child's chair, making the space look preposterously small and cramped. Jeremias backed towards them, flamer spewing a roaring blast of fire.

Minka's squad were first in line.

'It's still coming!' Krail shouted as she caught a glimpse of the figure, striding through the flames.

There was the mechanical roar of a storm bolter and Jeremias came apart, his disintegrating body dancing as the rounds tore into him.

His promethium tank exploded. The fireball rolled down the trench towards where Minka stood.

'Stand firm!' Minka ordered as she scrambled back, bolt pistol raised.

The Terminator was a square hulking block of black-and-brass armour, ten feet tall. It strode through the storm of las-bolts as if they were snowflakes, patches of promethium flickering and burning on its slab-armour.

The Terminator's head was hunched into the middle of its chest, with vast armour pads rising on either side. Its size, and the terror radiating from it, stunned them all: spikes adorned its armour, each impaled with a human head, casually thrust onto the barbed tip. Attached to one arm was a chainfist, the opposite hand wielding the storm bolter, which clicked as it reloaded and fired again.

The troopers in front of Minka disappeared as bolt shells shredded flesh and bone, reducing them to ribbons of steaming flesh. A red mist hung in the air as the Terminator followed Minka. She kept backing away.

Minka felt the red targeting-light on her face, tripping on a dead body as she threw herself sideways, narrowly avoiding a furious salvo of bolt shells that tore chunks out of the trench walls.

It was all she could do to hold on to her bolt pistol, shake off the slime and wipe her eyes clear as she crawled forward, one hand trailing the trench walls.

Her helmet rang out as she slammed head first into a ferrocrete wall.

The blow dazed her for a moment, and she had to clean her hand on the back of her jacket before she could smear her eyes clear again. She had crawled into a dead end.

She drew her sword and held her pistol out, tried to pray through trembling teeth for the Emperor, or any of His saints, to come and help her as the Terminator came on with all the paralysing speed of a nightmare: colour-distorted gun barrels steaming with coolants, the cruel brass teeth of its chainfist starting to spin.

It turned its body towards her as if in slow motion, and Minka held her pistol out before her, hand firm and power sword raised.

'For Cadia!' Minka shouted, or was it, 'The Emperor Protects!' She could not tell.

The words died on her lips, she was so shaken with horror, as the Terminator took a huge stride towards her and opened fire.

II

'Holy Throne!' Jaromir exclaimed as the craft skimmed past his head.

It felt like a thunderbolt had grazed the top of the sandbags. The blunt-nosed Land Speeder scorched over no-man's-land, jet engines burning with a fierce blue flame, tracer arcs following desperately as it curved back round again.

On the second pass, Jaromir got a good view. It flew so close over the landscape it knocked the upraised hand of a dead man flat as bending lines of heretic bullets spat towards where it had been, seconds before.

'What the frekk was that?' Solanki hissed, as the skimmer swept back towards their trench.

Minka ignored the blinding light and emptied her magazine into it, the bolt shells ringing off the armoured ceramite like the tired knell of a cracked bell. She ignited her power sword for a last desperate swipe.

'It is dead,' a voice said.

Her gun swung round and up. A black-armoured figure stood behind her. He was nearly seven feet tall, but his face had a youth to it, despite his oversized jaw and heavy brows.

'Who are you?' she said.

'I am Scout-Brother Terseus.'

'What… what regiment?'

He almost smiled. 'My Chapter is the Black Templars. I have come for Brother Gunter.'

Minka followed his gaze. Another Black Templar lay in the mud behind her.

Gunter had been ripped apart by bolt shells, his stomach ending in a ragged skirt of intestines.

'He lives!' she said.

Terseus nodded. 'Yes. But not for long.'

Gunter was still breathing. A gout of blood came up from his lungs as he tried to push himself to his feet, but his arm ended in a stump, and he fell forward. His meltagun lay next to him, the superheated nozzle steaming in the mud.

'You did well to kill the traitor, Gunter,' the Scout said as Gunter tried to speak. 'Fear not, brother. The Apothecary is coming.'

A third figure dropped into the trench. This one was armoured in bone-white power armour stained with mud and blood. He knelt at the side of the dying warrior.

'You did well, Brother Gunter,' the Apothecary said. 'Your battle is done. You will sleep in the Peace of the Emperor, and your gene-seed will ensure that others will continue the fight.'

Minka felt as though she was witness to a sacred ritual as a metallic arm attached to the Apothecary's backpack reached forward over his shoulder. She expected a form of medication or healing, but as the arm came to rest upon the dying Space

Marine's temple there was an audible click as it drove a bolt of steel into the dying warrior's brain.

Minka had seen death enough to watch the moment, but even as gouts of blood started from his nose and eyes, Gunter still twitched, as if he could not let the battle go.

The captive bolt left a bloody, round entry wound. The Apothecary was already at work, his lascutter burning through the shredded flaps of carapace armour and exposing the dead warrior's chest. There was the whirr of an underslung chainblade as he cut through the wounded ribcage, flecks of bone and flesh whipped up from the spinning blade, then the Apothecary reached inside.

Minka could not look away even as the Apothecary pulled something from the wound with a wet, sucking sound. The bloody offal was slipped into a canister, which was then sealed and mag-locked to his belt.

Minka had seen Banting at work: a medicae's labours could be brutal, but this was more like butchery. The bone-white figure stood. Without giving Minka even a passing look, he put one hand to the side of the trench and leapt out, as if hurdling a fence.

Only Brother Terseus remained. He was dwarfed by the dead Terminator as he dwarfed Minka. She looked up at the dead monstrosity.

'What is this thing?'

'It is a traitor,' the Space Marine said. He looked towards the drop pod. 'But there will be no more. We have destroyed the teleportation transponder.'

Minka nodded, but she was so shaken she had no idea what he was talking about.

Without another word he jumped and caught the bar of the hovering Land Speeder, and hung from it as it sped off across the battlefield.

Minka remained alone with the butchered remains of the Space Marine. The Terminator's armour stood rigid before her, eye-lenses glowing a baleful red, stabilisers still humming with latent energy. The chainfist had stopped, the storm bolter starting to slip from the slackening grip.

A round hole had been burnt through the chestplate, the edges melted smooth – a neat circular bore-hole. The kind of wound a krak missile made in a tank's armour.

Minka had to steel herself to approach it. She was trembling like a child and barely came up to its waist belt. If she could have reached it, she could have put her fist into the hole in its armour, from which acidic blood dripped, hissing, to the mud.

The grand history of the Horus Heresy was little more than a parable to her. All she knew was that the Imperium faced down abominations like this and her hatred was deep and visceral. An ancestral emotion, indoctrinated into her blood, a hereditary loathing.

It was then she saw what it carried, stuck into its gory trophy rack, and she felt tears welling up.

'You frekking bastard!' she spat and kicked it and cursed it again.

She was so angry she was oblivious to the hissing of battle that filled the air about her. There was no way she could reach ten feet above her. She braced her back against the trench wall, and her boots to its armour, and shimmied up.

It took both hands to pull it free, but at last she did, and she fell back into the trench bottom.

She could barely believe what she held in her hands.

The standard had been shot and burnt and torn away; only the cloth hoop remained stapled in place, the edge frayed. But it was a Cadian banner-pole, the top bearing the proud crest of a golden aquila.

'I'm here!' she shouted as she heard her platoon call out to her, her hands trembling as she wiped the mud from the crest.

The regimental badge was scratched and chipped, steel showing through the gilt plating, but the number on the crest was clear.

She held the staff upright as Jaromir approached.

He was lugging the heavy stubber in his arms, ready to face down any terror. 'It's dead,' Minka told him. 'I'm fine.'

Jaromir's eyes narrowed. Even he could tell she was lying. Then he saw what she was holding. The gilt chipping, the golden aquila, the etched runes.

Minka nodded. 'The Lord Castellan's Own.'

Jaromir stood dumbfounded, working over memories he had not touched in years. He had tears in his eyes.

'Ursarkar E. Creed!' he said, as if that name were a prayer.

At that moment there was a sudden furious salvo of artillery. It was so fierce that the whole world felt as though it were shaking, and through the thunder came the shrill blast of whistles.

'Up!' Minka shouted, clambering up the side of the trench. 'Up!'

The attack was on, and they had a few moments of barrage to get across no-man's-land.

She stood on the parapet, standard in hand, voice drowned out by the cacophony of explosions, waving her platoon forward.

It was a scene from hell, with the air above her full of shrieking shells, las-bolts flaring, and great gouts of earth and debris fountaining about her.

'For Cadia!' Minka shouted as she found herself running wildly across no-man's-land towards the enemy trenches, banner-pole held high, and the Cadians charged after.

III

The 101st had gone over the top three hours ago, and Adjutant Mere stood on the flagstoned terrace and said a silent prayer to the God-Emperor of Mankind.

Bendikt was pacing alone.

Mere looked west towards the front lines. The Tribulation Salient was hidden behind a cloud of smoke and dust, the gloom lit with the flashes of battle, the dead garden trembling with the thunder of war.

Footsteps sounded behind him. A throat was cleared. The guards were edgy.

'Sir. We should really get him inside,' the Kasrkin sergeant said, 'after what happened to Baytov.'

Mere nodded and looked over to Bendikt, who was still pacing.

'I will speak to him,' he said.

Broad stone steps led Mere down to the gardens. The flagstoned path had once been lined with herbaceous beds. Thin weeds brushed against his boots as he strode out along to where Bendikt stood.

The lord general's head was down, lips moving, his hand chopping the air as he argued against himself.

'Sir,' Mere said.

Bendikt looked up. His face was pale.

'Tell me.'

Mere cleared his throat. News was sparse, but the first reports were in. 'Ostanko has taken the first line of trenches. Ronin's Kasrkin are fighting for Hymnal Ridge. A number of companies are already attacking secondary objectives.'

Bendikt nodded. 'And the losses?'

Mere pulled a sombre face. 'As expected.'

Bendikt nodded and turned his back. 'Such is war,' he said at last.

Mere felt he was being watched. He turned and looked about. Cadian engineers had cleared the nearby trees and buildings, and now the only feature was the ring of rockcrete defences and curled beds of razor wire. Kasrkin guards were spaced around the garden perimeter, their faces turned outwards, watching for any snipers.

Mere said, 'The sergeant asked if we could come back inside.'

Bendikt nodded but did not move.

After a pause, Mere said, 'They're a little edgy.'

Bendikt laughed. 'I'm sure if there was a sniper he would have shot me already.'

Mere half smiled. 'When was the last time you slept?'

'Yesterday,' Bendikt said, meaning over a day before.

It was the same for Mere. 'I think it would be good if you took a little rest, sir.'

Bendikt let out a long breath. 'Yes,' he said. 'You're right.'

News filtered in as the hours wore on: objectives seized, prisoners captured, officers killed or wounded. When Bendikt returned from his personal chamber, Mere brought him a platter of food and a second bottle of amasec.

The 101st had smashed through the enemy, and were already pushing through to their day-two objectives. The casualty lists were still coming through.

Bendikt stood over them, reading the names in silence.

At midday the astropathic dispatches were brought in. There was the usual range of missives from the Munitorum and the forge world of Rula.

'This one is gene-locked to you,' Mere said, handing Bendikt an adamantine cypher-sheath.

The tube was cold in Bendikt's hand. The cypher-scroll opened at his touch. He slid the roll of vellum out, putting his glass down as he broke the seal.

'Great news,' Bendikt said at last, but his voice broke as if he were in mourning. He handed Mere the paper, and turned away.

The message had come from Lord Militant Warmund himself. He had brought the heretical warlord to a pitched battle, and then bogged him down in a bloodbath of hive-war, trench and slaughter, finally stopping the Scourged advance in the foothill habs of Hive Ourtho.

'As Drakul-zar's forces were pinned down, my flanking forces swung around through Oukk and Malouri and Namarra. We crushed them. Rejoice! The heretic legions have been broken. Drakul-zar has fled with the remains of his personal bodyguard. The Scourged have been broken.'

Mere put the scroll down without speaking.

'Rejoice,' Bendikt said at last, emotion frogging his throat. He paused. 'I wish we had been a part of it.'

'We were,' Mere said. 'If we had not taken Malouri, the trap would not have been sprung.'

Bendikt nodded and took a deep breath. 'I know, I know. But

I always imagined the Hundred-and-First on the battle plains of Joalara.' He let out a sigh. 'We earned that right at Traitor Rock. To be the tip of the spear at Drakul-zar's throat.'

Mere nodded. It was true. The 101st had punched well above their weight.

Bendikt picked up the vellum again. 'Warmund instructs us all to remain vigilant.'

Mere forced a smile. 'Cinnabar's Folly is on the warp route.'

Bendikt nodded, but they could not get diverted by what-ifs. He pulled the chart of the Tribulation Salient towards him. 'The Scourged upon Cinnabar's Folly have not been broken, yet. Prassan, what news from the front?'

'Teogone's Point, reported captured,' Prassan said as one of the staff officers moved a counter up the chart. 'Servo-skulls have visual confirmation that supply trenches are already being overrun, here and here.'

Bendikt looked down. The 101st had smashed through the enemy reserve lines. 'It's revenge for Baytov.'

Mere nodded. The 101st were fighting like the possessed.

As the afternoon went on, they kept going, accelerating even, as they battled through the reserve and artillery units, plunging deeper into the guts of the enemy. They were turning a defeat into a rout. But at the end of the first day, more casualty lists started to come in from field stations and company dispatches. 'Heavy losses,' Mere said.

'Who's in reserve?'

'The Cadian Exiles, an ad-hoc unit of scavenged Cadian units, awaiting amalgamation. Mainly Cadian Nineteenth, and the Hundred-and-Ninetieth and Two-Hundred-and-Fifty-Fourth.'

Bendikt barely let him finish. 'Send them in at once!'

* * *

As the day wore on, Bendikt poured his reserves into the gap that the 101st had smashed open. Shock troopers eliminated any resistance as armoured assault units of Hellhounds and Leman Russ battle tanks pushed forward, cutting off the heretics, and incinerating them in furious gouts of burning promethium.

Behind them trudged tens of thousands of reinforcements. But throughout the engagement, the 101st remained at the forefront of the battle, pushing relentlessly forward, like an assassin, searching for the heart of the enemy.

A week after the assault had been launched, the decimated companies of the 101st finally stormed the ruins of Bastion Hab, completing the encirclement of the enemy forces within the Tribulation Salient.

And only then did Bendikt give the order for the 101st to be pulled back. 'Get stretcher teams forward,' he ordered. 'I don't want to lose any more than we have already.'

'Yes, sir,' Mere said, though he had already put those preparations into place. Once the order had been relayed, he paused. 'There's something else, sir.'

Bendikt looked up. 'It sounds bad.'

'Not bad,' Mere said and took a deep breath. 'Lieutenant Minka Lesk says she has found something impossible.'

'What?'

Mere stopped and cleared his throat. 'A banner-pole, from… from a lost Cadian regiment.'

Bendikt steadied himself.

Mere's cheeks coloured with an emotion he'd not felt in years. 'It's the Eighth's, sir.' He read the feeling in Bendikt's eyes and nodded. 'The banner of the Lord Castellan's Own.'

IV

A squadron of Bane Wolves rattled forward over the pockmarked landscape, their low profiles thick with slabs of extra armour, their pressurised vats of flesh-boiling chemicals sandbagged as well. No one spoke. The roar of the engines and the metallic rattle of their tracks carried over the bleak ground as they pushed past the ruins of Bastion Hab.

The rockcrete strongpoint was broken and fire-stained, the dead still lying where they had fallen.

The 101st had stopped in the shadow of their last victory.

Fresher units had pushed forward, and Minka was slumped against the revetments of rough-sawn pit-props as her platoon regrouped in a horseshoe Medusa emplacement littered with scraps of ration wraps, crudely opened tins and piles of empty bottles, half buried in the mud.

She had started with five squads, forty-two troopers; ten miles of fighting had reduced those to just twenty-nine still capable of fighting. The others had been carried back, or were lost to the mud. She did not know how many were still alive.

Those who sat with her were all as weary as she was, their faces smeared with filth and gore, their bloodshot eyes haunted. They sat in exhausted silence.

They were too tired to move as the battlefront pushed ever forward.

They ate and drank and some of them slept where they sat. Above them the banner of the Eighth stood.

The sight of it stirred up old memories. No Cadian could look upon it without being reminded of what they had lost, and why they were still fighting; where they had been when they listened to Creed's gravelly voice coming over the vox-casters, promising them victory.

As the hours of waiting dragged on, many of them went back to their past.

In their mind's eye they were sheltering in a rockcrete bunker; huddling in a crater; patching a wound; rationing out their last powercells; holding their last grenade; rolling a lho-stick, trying not to think of their best friend, who lay dead next to them; trying not to listen to the howl of the heretics, the thunder of bombardment, the fiery rain of drop pods, the whine of mortar shells lifting high into the air.

Minka and Jaromir sat shoulder to shoulder, the rest of her squad arrayed about them. A plasma shot had glanced his left arm high up, below the shoulder. It now hung in a rough sling, the wrappings stained and swollen, his face pale as he injected himself with another shot of stimms.

'We'll get you back,' Minka said.

'It doesn't hurt,' he said.

She didn't believe him, but what could the medics do? His arm was as cooked as a joint of slab.

Jaromir looked down at his arm and nodded. This injury would mean the end of his career. He had hoped not to survive.

Neither of them could bear to speak about it. Their talk was of anything else, and as the bloodless sun drifted across the sky, the shadow of the banner fell over them.

'Makes me think of Schola Five,' Minka said, speaking slowly as her exhausted brain struggled to order the memories that came bubbling to the surface, like a ship's anchor. 'On the blackboard. "Do not waste your tears; I was not born to watch the world grow dim..."' She paused. 'Yegor!' she said. 'Mordian. Booby trap. He got killed. Took the blast for me...'

Jaromir nodded slowly. After a long pause he said, 'I was in a hospital ship in orbit about Agripinaa.'

Yedrin said nothing. He'd only been a boy then, with his hopes of returning to Cadia being slowly dashed.

The last to speak was Blanchez. She had her sniper rifle lying across her knees. She'd also been a child when Cadia fell – just another orphaned camp-brat trying to stay alive.

'All we heard was the "War for the Obscurus Front". Never knew it was Cadia. It was years before we guessed. I knocked the bastard who told me down. I didn't believe it. He was lucky not to get his throat cut.'

Colour Sergeant Tyson picked his way along the craters. The veteran warrior was a bull of a man, broad-necked and broad-chested, but he went pale as he looked at Jaromir. The big trooper was asleep, his bandaged arm hanging across his chest.

'Plasma shot,' Minka said. 'Said it doesn't hurt. Dosed him up just in case.'

'Stretcher teams are coming up,' Tyson said. He looked up at the banner. 'So that's it?' he asked. His voice was breaking. In his mind he could hear the military band playing 'Flower of Cadia'. Creed. Cadia. The Lord Castellan's voice crackling over the vox making his evening addresses.

Tears welled up.

Minka had never seen him cry before.

He wiped them away before they dared to fall.

'He came to see us,' Tyson said at last. 'In a single Valkyrie, with Kell by his side. That was the only time I saw him, before Cadia fell.'

As he spoke a column of Rough Riders made their way past, power lances held upright, their gene-hanced steeds snorting as a flight of Thunderbolts roared overhead, descending on a strafing run.

Minka shook Jaromir. 'Come on!' she said. 'We're pulling back.'

Night fell like a blanket as the front line edged slowly away from the 101st, and the Cadians picked their way through what had been no-man's-land.

Jaromir limped along, Creed's banner in his remaining hand. As the thunder of the battle faded away it was replaced by the moans of wounded, who lay all about the battlefield. Here and there execution squads were steadily working their way through them. There was the snap of a laspistol as each heretic was dispatched, the shrill of a whistle as stretcher teams were summoned to recover Imperial wounded.

Throughout the night front-line troops tramped forward, and the Cadians stood aside. They were so tired they slept on their feet, and as the reserve columns passed forward, Minka had to go along the line, waking her troops.

As the night wore on they reached captured trenches filled with third-line troops who were busy burying the dead, repairing the trenches, playing cards. There were young faces, ill-fitting uniforms, slack discipline. When they recognised the Cadians, they stood and stared as before their eyes legend came to life.

At last, they reached a point halfway back to what had been

their front lines and the order went out for the Cadians to stop and rest, but there was no rest for Minka. Everyone wanted to come and see Creed's banner. Everyone wanted to touch it.

It was theirs as much as Creed had been, even Cadia itself: the land, the air, the water and the bruised nightmare of the Eye of Terror, hanging over them all.

Minka could not have stopped them, even if she'd had the energy.

Some cried. Others turned pale, stood in silence. Captain Ronin was too overcome. She stared up at it, but would not touch it. Captain Ostanko took it from Jaromir with both hands and held it up to the cheers of his First Company.

'Creed's banner!' he said as he held it in both hands. His eyes gleamed as he looked up at the top of the banner-pole with its gilded sigil.

Afterwards he said to Minka, 'I saw the remains of that bastard… How did you do it?'

'I didn't,' Minka said. 'It was the Black Templars.'

But that was not the story Ostanko wanted to hear. 'Heh! Look at what Lesk did!'

'I know!' Sparker said, waving a bandaged hand. 'One of my best.'

'I just saw it,' Minka said. 'That's all.' But no one wanted to know. It was not as good a tale as that of Minka bringing down a Heretic Astartes and claiming the prize.

That was the story they wanted.

That was the story Ostanko would have told.

Next morning the Cadians pushed on again, reaching what had been the front-line trenches. White flags marked out a narrow walkway, cleared of mines, across no-man's-land.

At one point a Samaritan-pattern Chimera rumbled past, the

vehicle so laden with wounded that the orderlies were sitting on top, holding the stretchers down as the medicae tank rolled over the craters.

Minka flagged the Chimera down. 'Jaromir,' she called and pointed.

'It doesn't hurt.'

'Get to Banting.'

'Let me walk back,' he said. 'This last time.'

Flakboard walkways carried them over flooded craters. The stench of death was all about them. Not the metallic stink of the fresh dead, but the foul, rotting stench of long-dead bodies blasted out of their graves.

The drop pods stood out from the blasted landscape like stone menhirs.

The white-taped paths ran alongside. As Minka approached, her heart started to quicken. They menaced them all as they pushed carefully through the beds of criss-crossed wire which had once fortified their trenches, the razor-sharp coils cut and bent back upon themselves, and down the flakboard steps.

Minka counted her troops through and stumping down the steps, as the next platoon came forward. Her boots were still caked up to her shins in the cloying mud. They slid on the flakboard steps.

'Steady!' Tyson said. The colour sergeant was standing in the trench. He put out a hand and helped Minka down.

'I'll catch up,' she said.

She could not help herself. She had to go and see.

Minka knew the trench. It still stank of promethium.

She moved along it, but as she did so she could feel her tension rising, remembered Jeremias' shouts.

The bodies had been cleared away, but the flakboards were charred, and the stink of blood remained. She paused at the last turning, but the sap was empty: Astartes, heretic. All gone.

Minka looked about, checking her bearings. She could feel the menace still hanging in the air, as if the ghost of the heretic hung in this place.

'Bastard,' she said, her hatred as fierce as a foundry-flame.

Never, she told herself, remembering the vow all Cadians made. They would never surrender to the enemy.

Never.

V

Dawn was breaking on the third morning when, at last, they reached the reserve camp: a rockcrete city sprawled out below ground with buried bunkers, medicaes, barracks, shower blocks and toilet-block trenches leading off from each bunker area.

Banting's team were triaging the walking wounded, Centaurs waiting to ferry the worst to the medicae, and Minka took Jaromir to the front of the queue.

Jaromir's arm was still hanging from the sling, but now the bandages were stained with infection.

'Throne,' Vasily cursed and called Staarki over.

'It doesn't hurt,' Jaromir said.

'He keeps saying that,' Minka said, and started to explain what had happened, but Vasily had no time to talk. He took the banner-pole from Jaromir without knowing what it was. Minka grabbed it from him as he forced Jaromir down and started to cut the bandage away.

It was Banting who came over.

'Why wasn't this man brought back?' Banting demanded, as the bandages came off the wound and they saw the mess underneath.

'Holy Throne,' Vasily cursed as Banting called for a Samaritan.

Within a matter of seconds they had Jaromir on a stretcher, a drip hooked up, one of the medics holding a bag of clear plasma above Jaromir's head.

The whole time Jaromir kept protesting that he felt no pain.

'This will knock you out,' Vasily said, and he removed a shot of stimms from its wrapping. Last to come off was the plastek sheath over the needle. He pressed the plunger enough that a clear liquid spurted from within, then he plunged the needle into Jaromir's arm.

Jaromir's voice faded away as the stimms kicked in.

'Can you save it?' Minka said.

Banting looked at her as if she were stupid. 'Of course we cannot save the arm. My concern is if we can save the man.'

Someone called Banting's name. He started to go. Minka wished she had said something to Jaromir now, but she was shattered as she turned back to her platoon.

'Lesk!' It was Colonel Sparker, shouting over the crowd. 'Chief Commissar Shand is looking for you. Said it was urgent.'

'Where is he?'

Sparker pointed and Minka started to go when Banting said, 'Let me check you.'

She lifted her arms to let Banting check her over. She had cuts and scrapes. Wire, fine shrapnel, just the usual. Nothing serious.

Minka was given shower tokens for her platoon. She handed them out and had a handful left over.

'Here,' she said, 'take two.'

Orugi had taken his helmet off. His hair was stuck down to his head. 'When is Seventh Company's turn?'

'Two hours,' she told him. 'Until then the canteen is open. Get in there and fill up.'

They sat eating their first hot meal in weeks, looking with envy towards the other companies as they came out of the shower block, towels hanging about their necks.

Minka was last to get her meal. Orugi was on seconds as she found a seat on a low bench of sandbags and rested her mess tin on her lap.

It was filled to the brim with boiled carbs and grey slab stew. She savoured each mouthful as she looked about. It was the best thing she'd eaten for weeks. No one spoke.

Afterwards, Orugi offered her a lho-stick. He took an igniter from his pocket. Cadian issue. They were starting to become rare these days. He flicked the flint, and the promethium hissed alight.

He lit hers first, then his own. They stood, sucking the rough fumes in.

'Not like you, sir,' Orugi said.

Minka took another drag. 'I know,' she said. 'It's been a long few weeks.'

They stood waiting for Seventh Company's turn, and as Tyson blew his whistle to call Sparker's company to the shower block, Commissar Hontius appeared.

'Lieutenant Lesk!' he called. 'I've been looking for you. Please, come with me.'

Minka pointed to the shower. 'Can't it wait?'

'No. You've been summoned to HQ.'

'And they want me to smell like this?'

'I don't think they care,' he said.

'Here,' Minka said as she slapped her shower token into Orugi's hand. 'Treat yourself.'

* * *

Hontius led Minka through the reserve trench. It was long and straight, with sandbagged dividers every fifty yards. Minka could feel troopers looking up and watching her pass, could hear her name being spoken.

Barracks and medicae facilities opened up on either side. Minka could hear the suppressed moans of the wounded, the low voices of the corpsmen as they ministered to the dying.

As she climbed up into a Centaur in black Commissariat livery, the distinctive whine of a buzz-saw briefly rose into the air. Just long enough to amputate an arm or leg, before fading away again.

Minka felt the tension long before she saw Commissar Shand and Father Keremm waiting for her. They made an incongruous pair. They had both been in battle, but only Shand had washed. He stood tall and clean-shaven, dressed in impeccable black while Father Keremm still wore his ragged wool gown, the hems of which were stiff with dried mud. His unkempt beard hung down to his rope belt, and he carried his eviscerator on one shoulder, the teeth still clogged with gore.

'Lieutenant,' Shand said as she stood and made the sign of the aquila. 'HQ have heard rumours that you have claimed an item of interest from the battlefield.'

She nodded. 'Yes, sir.'

'Where is this item?'

'In the company bunker, sir.'

One of the bats came from that way. 'We have it, sir,' he called out. 'They didn't want to let it go.'

'You're damned right,' Minka said.

Shand put his hand to her shoulder. It wasn't what she expected from a commissar.

He was almost conciliatory as he said, 'Don't worry. We shall take care of it. But please accompany us.'

'Where to?'

'The Durondeau.'

'Where?'

'Lord General Bendikt's command post.'

Minka nodded. 'How far is it?'

'An hour or so,' Shand said.

Minka sighed. She climbed aboard the waiting Centaur without waiting to be asked, conscious of the looks that she was getting. It was ominous when the commissars took a trooper away, and men and women were stopping to stare.

There was a row of fold-down metal seats in the back of the open-topped vehicle. She sat down without asking for permission as Hontius wrapped the banner-pole in cloth, then handed it to the chief commissar.

Father Keremm blessed it and attached seals of faith and purity, and after a brief prayer they pulled out. Another tank came in behind them, and then Cadian-pattern Sentinels fell in on either side as an honour guard.

'Not taking any chances?' Minka said.

'Not after Baytov.'

'What happened to him?' Minka said. She had heard battlefield rumours, but you could never trust them.

'It was an unfortunate accident,' Shand said. 'He served the Emperor well and his service is now over.'

'Who will lead the Hundred-and-First now?'

Shand did not know.

'You?' Minka said.

Shand smiled coldly. 'What an idea,' he said, as if he rather fancied it.

The trip took nearly three hours. A Leman Russ tank went ahead of them as an honour guard. It forced a passage eastwards, as everyone else was heading west, towards the front lines.

Bendikt was pouring all his reserves into the breach, and the roads were full of them: tanks, infantry, mobile artillery, logistic supplies stacked high on the backs of cargo-12s, and all manner of uniforms and pennants.

Minka dozed most of the time, waking only as the rough terrain knocked her sideways. At one point she overheard them talking in low voices of news from Joalara.

'Drakul-zar has fled?' she said, suddenly wide awake.

Shand's face was stern. 'The news has not been released yet.'

Minka nodded, but she felt a wave of disappointment run through her. Baytov had assured them that after victory on this planet, they would be called up by Warmund to help in crushing the arch-heretic. A promise that had died with him, she thought.

'So that bastard Warmund did it without us...' she said.

Shand nodded. He looked as disappointed as she felt.

VI

Prassan stood with the staff at the front steps of the Durondeau, with Adjutant Mere, waiting for the banner's arrival.

The first sign was the sound of a Leman Russ tank approaching at the end of the palace drive. The gun-barrel appeared first, swinging through the rockcrete pillboxes, then the tracks spun and it started down the long route towards the palace steps.

The commander stood high in the cupola, a Cadian 101st pennant flapping from the turret. Behind his tank rolled a Centaur, and then a second Leman Russ, while loping on either side was an honour guard of armoured Sentinels, hip-mounted armaments tracking for targets. The hiss and creak of hydraulics filled the silence as the rumble of the Centaur's engine steadily grew louder.

The hum of excitement increased as the convoy approached. The Cadians met it with an air of reverent respect. It was as if the body of Creed himself had been brought in honour from the front line. The Cadians removed their helmets and Prassan held his breath as the Centaur swung round to the bottom of the steps and stopped.

Father Keremm stepped down, mumbling prayers, and behind him Chief Commissar Shand descended, a wrapped banner-pole cradled in his arms.

The purity seals flapped in the wind as Adjutant Mere came down the steps to greet him. 'This is it?' he asked.

Shand nodded, and Mere put his hand out to touch the bundle with the reverence a man might touch a relic.

'Well done!' he said. 'Come, the lord general awaits.'

Prassan let the rest of the procession go inside and stepped towards the Centaur.

Minka was standing at the back of the vehicle's compartment, her armour and uniform stained with all the dirt of battle.

'Minka,' he said. 'Please. Come with me.'

Her eyes were hard. She pushed herself off the side of the compartment and as they followed the others inside, Prassan tried to think of something to say.

He ran through the list in his head and none of them felt right, but as they passed into the palace she looked about her in wonder. 'I would have spent more time in the scholam, if I'd known I'd get to live in a place like this.'

'You'd hate it here.'

'It's better than the trenches.'

'I'm sure,' he said.

They passed Cadians on either side – catering staff, officers, guards, attendants, all standing to attention.

Mere led them up a broad processional staircase. The silk wallpaper had worn bare where shoulders and hands had brushed against it, and there were dark squares where portraits had once hung. At last they paused outside General Bendikt's office.

'Please wait here,' Shand said to Minka, and she and Prassan were left outside. Kasrkin stood to either side, their gaze staring out over Minka's head.

'Will this take long?' she said.

'I don't know,' Prassan replied.

Minka cursed silently. She was dirty and tired and she felt uncomfortable standing exposed like this, as if she were still in battle. She kept waiting for the whine of an artillery shell, felt the need to crawl into the corner of the room, felt her hands looking for her pistol and the hilt of her power sabre.

She forced herself to concentrate. She was in the corridor outside Lord General Bendikt's private quarters. There was no safer place on the planet. And then she remembered.

'Baytov?' she said.

Prassan nodded and coughed to clear his throat. 'Yes.'

'An accident...' Minka said.

Prassan took her aside. 'It was a sniper,' he whispered.

Her face said it all. How, so far behind their lines?

'We captured a dozen of them but one of them got through. I was there. It was just as the assault started.'

'Did you get him?'

Prassan nodded. 'Yes,' he said. 'You might have seen him, hanging from a lumen-pole alongside the road.'

Minka shook her head. It should not have happened. Not to Baytov. He was a good man: hard, disciplined, ruthless. The kind of commander the Cadians responded to.

She said nothing for a long time, then asked, 'Who's taking command now?'

Prassan shook his head. 'I don't know. Ostanko?'

Bendikt's private chambers had been least affected by the requisition.

The barrel-vaulted chamber had survived the worst of the

damage that had been inflicted upon the rest of the estate. The walls were papered with dark silk velvet, and there was an alcove set into one of the walls with an icon of the God-Emperor, the Throne etched out with gold leaf that threw back the light of votive candles.

Bendikt was standing in the bay windows when Mere entered. He spun around and saw the look on Shand's face and knew in his gut that it was true.

The air of reverence was palpable as Bendikt stopped before the chief commissar. 'This is it?' he whispered.

Shand's cheeks were pricked with red. 'It is.'

Bendikt signalled for him to untie the thongs. As the last ties fell away, he pulled the canvas aside and set the brass foot spike down onto the aquila rug, and held the ironwood pole upright.

Bendikt took it all in, from the brass base-spike to the gilt-covered aquila at the top, with the numerals *VIII* etched into it.

The whole room stood in silence.

'Throne!' Bendikt said. 'Holy Throne.'

Bendikt had thought of a thousand reasons why this could not be the banner of the Eighth. But now he felt none of those doubts. 'Look!' he said, showing the power fist pressure-scars pressed into the ironwood shaft. 'This is where Kell held it.'

They all stood in awed silence. Bendikt stepped back to admire this hallowed object as Mere took it and then passed it along from hand to hand. Last to take it was Father Keremm. He had dirt and blood under his fingernails, and wiped his hands on his robes before he accepted it.

'I see the hand of the God-Emperor in all this,' he said as he felt the weight and the history of the object in his hands. '*This* is why we were not sent to fight on Joalara...'

The priest spoke with passion and belief. He looked at Bendikt and said, 'He had a special mission for us, for you! Just think!

There might be survivors, members of the Eighth, out there. Still fighting.'

Bendikt reeled. Those words hit him like a blow and he remembered the first time he had met Creed, standing on the viewing deck of the *Fidelitas Vector*.

In that moment, he could remember the smell of the old cruiser, the chill scent of the viewport, the stale scent of lho-stubs, the brown stains upon Creed's fingers. And he could remember the months stuck inside Sanctuary 9983 upon Cadia. The frustration of waiting.

Bendikt took the banner-pole back from Keremm and lifted it up, feeling the weight of it, before setting it down again.

'Mere. Has anyone thanked the Chapter of the Black Templars?'

'Yes, sir. I did so personally, on your behalf.'

'Good. And have they disengaged from the Tribulation Salient?'

'I believe so.'

'Shame,' Bendikt said. 'Do we know what they are hunting?'

'I cannot tell you what their mission was,' Mere said.

The arrival of the Black Templars strike cruiser above Cinnabar's Folly had been as much a surprise to Bendikt as it had to the enemy. Although they fought on the same side, the priorities of the Space Marines were as obscure as the plans of the enemy and Bendikt had not been so foolish as to attempt to command them.

Mere went on, 'Their last incursion there was three days ago. The augurs tell me that they have moved their operations to the northern polar ice caps.'

Bendikt looked up at the banner-pole. He appeared to be only half-listening. 'Let them know that if we can be of any assistance…'

'Yes, sir. Although, there appears to be a small Heretic Space Marine contingent upon Cinnabar's Folly. The ones, I believe, that Lesk confronted.'

'Yes,' Bendikt said. 'Where is Lieutenant Lesk? Bring her to me at once.'

Minka gave Prassan a look as the varnished door opened before her.

She was not used to the soft tread of carpet underfoot, but it was the opulence of the chamber that stunned her as much as the faces of the men before her.

'Lord general. I apologise. I was summoned straight from the trenches, and Chief Commissar Shand insisted that there was no time to waste.'

Bendikt looked older than when she had last seen him. 'Haven't they let you wash?' he said, without waiting for her to answer. 'No matter, lieutenant, please come in. It makes a nice change from the command staff. I've not been on the front lines since Malouri.'

Her eyes fell on the power sword that hung on the wall. Bendikt had been gifted that by Gerent Bianca. It was Saint Ignatzio Richstar's ancestral power sword, a fine duelling blade, with a jewelled hilt.

'I've been told that you took this item you retrieved from the body of the dead...' Bendikt said.

Minka didn't want to have to remember. She spoke quickly. 'Yes,' she said. 'The Traitor Astartes. It had a rack on its back. The banner-pole was there. I... I saw it straight away.'

A voice from behind her said, 'What else did it carry?'

It was Shand. The chief commissar was looking very serious.

She felt a cold sweat forming on her forehead, and her heart started to thud in panic. She willed herself to calm down. 'There were metal spikes. Each one had a head thrust onto it, sir. Why?'

Shand again: 'And did any of these have a helmet?'

'Yes, sir. There were two Astartes. I do not know what regiment–'

'Chapter,' Mere corrected her.

'Chapter,' she said. 'And there was a fresh unaugmented human head. The spike had gone through helmet and bone. It was fresh. I think. I mean, it had not yet started to rot. The others... It was hard to tell. They were all rotten or so old there was nothing left but bone.'

'Were there any Cadian skulls?'

She was shaking by now, putting herself back in that moment. She swallowed down a wave of nausea. 'No. It was a Krieg helmet.'

'But the older skulls,' Shand put in. 'What about them?'

'They were dead, sir,' Minka said.

'Did they–' Mere started, but Bendikt cut him off.

'Lieutenant. You are to be commended for your actions. But there is a chance...' He stopped. 'The thing that you fought... It carried the banner-pole of the Eighth. Tell me about the skulls. You're absolutely positive none of them wore a Cadian helmet?'

'No, sir.'

'But there were heads that did not have a helmet?'

'Yes. Most of them didn't.'

Bendikt paused. He and Mere exchanged glances. It took Mere to explain. 'Lieutenant. We need you to recall all the details.'

'I've given them to you. I saw the banner-pole. I had to get it back.'

'To repeat,' Shand said, 'there were no Cadians?'

Minka shook her head. 'Not that I could tell.'

'Thank you,' Bendikt said. He acted as if Minka were no longer in the room. 'And Mere. Try the Black Templars again. They must have the body.'

'Yes, sir.'

Bendikt frowned. 'It's of utmost importance. Communicate that urgency. Add our credentials... Have we fought with the Black Templars before?'

'I have asked the savants to check...'

Bendikt nodded. 'Good. Good.'

Minka was shown outside. 'What do you think?' Mere said, after Minka had gone.

Bendikt paused. 'Well. There is nothing conclusive. The banner-pole could have been taken from Cadia...' There was a mug of cold recaff. He took a sip and pulled a face as he swallowed. 'This sector once lay on the supply routes to the Cadian Gate. But what are the chances?'

Mere said nothing for a while. 'It is possible that the heretic fought on Cadia. But there are many who swore that Creed escaped from Cadia before it fell. If so... there's a chance the monster took that banner from somewhere else... A chance that there are elements of the Eighth still out there. Still fighting. Maybe even Creed himself.'

A long silence hung in the room.

Bendikt turned to the banner-pole as if seeking guidance. 'Shand. Wring her dry. I want to know everything. Everything she saw. Every tiny little detail.'

VII

Minka could have screamed.

She sat at a wooden table, the surface worn of varnish, the solid top engraved with initials and names and dates and regimental numbers, and repeated herself for the seventh time.

Shand tore the sheet of paper from his pad and laid it on the desk, face down.

'Again,' he said. He read her body language and said, 'We need to know everything about the thing that you killed.'

Minka ran her hand over her face.

'Lieutenant Lesk,' Shand said.

Minka had her fingers pressed to the bridge of her nose.

'I didn't kill it,' she said. 'It was like this...'

She closed her eyes and went back to that awful moment. She saw it again in her mind's eye. The shattered trenches. The scramble across no-man's-land. The preparation for the assault trench. Captain Iago and the Forax Binary contingent.

The drop pods slamming down.

'The heretic was not in the drop pod?'

'No,' Minka said. 'I've told you. There was a transponder thing. The Space Marine. He said he had destroyed it. Jaromir said he just appeared in the air. He said there was a swirl of light and then it was there. Ask him.'

'Jaromir is currently sedated.'

Minka sighed. She kept her eyes closed. She could hear the scratch of Shand's stylus on paper. He went through a series of questions he had asked before, and at the end he asked a new one. 'Why would a lone heretic appear?'

Minka's patience finally snapped. 'How the Throne should I know?'

There was a long pause. A nerve twitched in the corner of Shand's eye. His jaw tightened. He spoke quietly, but with great menace. 'I should remind you, lieutenant, that my rank is chief commissar.'

Minka opened her eyes, and sat up straight. 'Yes, sorry, sir. I'm just tired.'

Shand looked down at his pad, assessing the answers she had given. He made a low grunt, as if to say he was satisfied, then gathered all his papers together, closed the leather file with a snap, and slid his stylus into the inner breast pocket of his coat.

'Is that it?' she said as he stood.

'Remain here,' he said as he paced to the door.

'How long?'

'Do not raise your voice at me, lieutenant.'

'I'm not raising my voice, sir. I need to go back to my platoon.' They had been through hell together, and she did not know who was still alive and who was dead, who was wounded and dying while she sat here.

'You will remain here until we come back for you.'

'Can I ask one thing?'

He paused.

'Jaromir was taken to the medicae. Let me know when he comes round.'

'I will check,' he said, and shut the door.

She heard the click of the key being turned.

She stood to look around. They had taken her down to the cellar. The corridors had smelt of urine, but in this room the air was cool, the flagstone floors had a damp sheen, the white-washed walls had years of soot and dirt engrained in their surfaces.

A thin grey light fell into the chamber from a high barred window.

It had been screwed shut. She paced up and down, listening to the sounds that came through the door and the walls and the ceiling; she could hear muffled voices, footsteps, the creak of floorboards and door hinges.

Minka checked the door. It was locked. She banged on it with her fist.

'Food!' she shouted. There was no response. 'Can you bastards get something for me to eat?'

Nothing.

A wave of emotion rose in her. She willed it back. She was Cadian: born, bred, raised and trained. Still…

She kicked the door in her frustration.

Bastards!

The light in her window faded as the bloodless sun sank into the clouds of battle-smoke.

She found a dry corner of the room and curled up, ears alert to the sound of footsteps, the gurgle of pipes, the slow settling of the ancient house.

She had slept in worse places, she told herself, and at least no one was shooting at her here.

At last she slept – a deep, heavy, dreamless slumber.

Next morning the click of the lock woke Minka.

She was up in a moment. By the time the door swung open she was already on her feet. It was Commissar Hontius, looking smug and well rested.

'Lieutenant Lesk,' he said as a greeting. 'I trust you slept well?'

'No,' she said.

'Never mind. Are you ready to return to your company?'

'That's it?' she said.

He looked about the empty chamber and said, 'Yes. We could have made it a little less austere.'

'You could have fed me. Even a clean set of clothes.'

Hontius nodded. 'Ah. Yes. That we can deal with now. Come.'

He led her down a long corridor, paved with broad flagstones, to the quartermaster's office. The staff officer was a greying man with round spectacles, a short grey goatee and a stylus tucked behind his ear.

'Any word on Jaromir?' she said as she waited.

Hontius shook his head. 'I have heard nothing. Which is usually good news.'

The quartermaster brought her a Munitorum-issue towel and a spare set of fatigues, and waited till she had signed the chit, before pushing the pile towards her.

'Which way is the shower?' she said.

'I'll show you,' Hontius said.

The shower block was in the cellars, next to the kitchens. Minka's stomach grumbled as she smelt the odours coming from within.

Hontius stopped at a heavy flakboard door. 'I'll wait outside,' he said.

Minka went inside. Her bootlaces were caked in dried mud. She peeled off her jacket, undershirt, trousers and underwear. Her trousers were so stiff with dirt they half stood as she threw them to the side. When she'd stripped it all off, she stepped into the shower of water.

The water came straight from a pipe. It was lukewarm and smelt of purification chems. But it was a shower.

She closed her eyes, ran her fingers through her dirt-stiff hair, found a bar of caustic soap, rubbed a lather in her hands and scrubbed herself down. The water that came off her was brown with a week of battle filth. She kept washing herself down, and finding more dirt. It was under her arms, between her legs and toes, in the small of her back as well.

Afterwards, she dried herself and dressed in fresh clothes, ran her fingers through her hair to help dry it out. She felt almost human again.

Hontius was standing outside the door with his fingers linked behind his back. 'Right,' he said. 'Food?'

'Yes,' Minka said, her humour returning. 'I thought you'd never ask.'

A few minutes later, Minka sat in the empty mess hall watching as the kitchen staff laid out the trays for breakfast. There were real eggs, fried hard, and wide aluminium vats of slab and carb. It was a long time since she'd seen such a fine spread.

She filled her tray and spooned it all down. A little more of her humanity returned.

She thought about Jaromir. She'd have to go see him. He'd come to her when his former regiment of the Black Dragons had been disbanded. In another age he would have been retired.

Serviceable, his official report had said.

That word was branded into Jaromir. 'They left me with just enough brain to know what I've lost,' he joked.

But now? The Imperium of Man was not charitable. Who wanted a trooper who could no longer fight?

The savants occupied a chamber in the basement of the villa. The rooms hummed with the fans of cogitators.

Dawn was breaking as Prassan brought the results of their labour back up the stairs to Bendikt's office. Bendikt looked like he had been up all night. He and Adjutant Mere were standing over the charts. The encirclement was complete. This next part of the battle was all about logistics: engineering brigades were extending rail lines, and the vast reserves of ordnance were being dragged up to the new batteries. It would be a barrage such as Cinnabar's Folly had never seen.

The enemy were about to understand the cost of heresy.

He stood, waiting until Mere looked up and caught his eye. He gestured for Prassan to speak.

Prassan cleared his throat. 'Sir. I have the reports about the Black Templars. Marshal Amalrich led the Cruxis Crusade of the Black Templars during the Battle for Cadia. But this fleet has no history of us sharing a warzone since.'

Bendikt paced up and down as he considered the best way of requesting help. At last he had the form of words in his head and dictated it to Mere.

'Have that communicated at once,' Mere said.

Prassan took the missive and made his way to the comms room at the top of the house, a low, dusty attic chamber filled with the droning sound of case-cogitators, coding machines and servitor stations.

Vervens, the vox-operator, had a stylus stuck behind one ear. She had another stylus in her mouth, as she fed a series of field orders into the code scrambler.

'This is for the Black Templars,' Prassan said.

'I'll try,' Vervens replied.

The name of the Black Templars cruiser was *Fury of Lycur*. All previous messages had been acknowledged, but there had been no answer. 'Come on,' Vervens said to her team and they started the process of raising the vox-link to the orbiting craft.

There was a long pause, before one of the servitors spoke in lifeless monotone: 'Vox-link established.'

Vervens and Prassan exchanged looks as the cogitator fans whined, the broadcast equipment straining to establish a link.

Vervens entered the dispatch into the comms wafer. She fed it into the broadcast machine. There was a click as the communication came to an end. She turned to the vox-receiver. A servitor sat embedded into the machinery, vellum spooling from its grille mouthpiece.

Confirm: vox received, the automated message read.

There was a short pause, before the spool ran again.

Vervens stood back up, bent to read it and gave a short laugh. 'Delegation inbound,' she said.

Prassan found Minka in the canteen, sitting back and enjoying a mug of recaff.

'There you are!' he said.

She stifled a belch. 'Throne!' she said. 'Do you lot eat like this all the time?'

'Yes,' he said, laughing. 'Better be quick.'

'What?'

'I thought you should be there.'

'Where?'

He stopped as he realised he had to explain. 'The Black Templars. They're coming here.'

VIII

The Black Templars gunship roared just a few feet over the landscape. Auspex picked up its approach as it lifted over the defence line, the Hydra platforms tracking its blunt-nosed silhouette as it swept towards the palace complex.

Minka and Prassan arrived just in time to see it make its final approach, skimming over the beds of razor wire. They made their way to the side of Bendikt's delegation. All were transfixed, staring at the approaching craft.

Minka felt the roar of the engines in her bones as the craft lifted briefly and then settled onto the metalled front yard. Condensation steamed off its superheated armour plating, the metal reeking with the fire of planetary entry. The craft was bred for war, weapons glaring out from its nose.

Minka put her hand to the wall as the side doors opened and three giants strode down the ramp. Even Prassan stiffened beside her. They were struck dumb as they took in the size, the speed, the inhuman bulk of the Black Templars.

All of them stood eight feet tall, clad in black power armour, their pauldrons marked with a white cross on a field of sable.

Bendikt started down the steps to greet the Black Templars and his breath caught in his throat. He felt as though he were a prey animal, fed to some great beast, and stopped halfway down the stairs so that he could look the foremost Space Marine full in the face.

The warrior was something more than human, something otherworldly, with his square jaw, bony brows and a lurid fresh scar running down his overlarge forehead.

'Greetings, General Bendikt,' the Black Templar said, his voice a deep rumble. He bowed his head. 'I am Marshal Aleksus of the Black Templars. I bring you a gift.'

One of the accompanying warriors stepped forward. In his arms was an iron-bound chest. He leant forward and placed it on the step underneath Bendikt, then returned to his full height.

'Thank you,' Bendikt said. 'And we thank you for your martial prowess. Is your work here done?'

Aleksus stared at him from under heavy brows. Bendikt had no idea what the Space Marine was thinking. It was like looking at a statue. 'It is,' he said at last. 'We were there. I fought at the Cadian Gate before it fell.'

'Thank you,' Bendikt said. 'I am sorry that we failed.'

The Black Templar said nothing for a long time, then replied, 'Our defence of the Cadian Gate dates back through many lives of men. To the days of our first Chapter Master. Long before your people came to Cadia.'

There was a pause. 'We failed,' Aleksus said. 'Like you.'

The blunt words took Bendikt aback, but the Space Marine did not wait for a response. 'Farewell,' he said. 'The heretic has fled. We shall hunt him down.'

IX

Bendikt was feeling very pleased with himself. He was humming 'Flower of Cadia' to himself and was starting to feel distinctly upbeat as Lesk was brought to him again.

'Ah!' he said. 'I'm glad we caught you before you return to your unit.'

Minka made the sign of the aquila. Fed, washed, rested, she was ready.

Mere came forward with the news of another objective seized. He stood over the map as a Cadian counter was moved across the chart.

Minka had the general's eye view for a moment. Those trenches she had fought over were just lines on their maps.

'Is it going well?' Minka said.

'It is,' Bendikt said. 'Look!'

He pointed to the charts of Cinnabar's Folly, and then to the charts on the wall.

'Across the whole sector. This is a chart of the local systems. We are driving the Scourged back on every front. Look!'

Minka only had a vague grasp of the Gallows Cluster. She knew the places she had been to. Potence, Grunn and Cinnabar's Folly. Those battlefields were seared into her soul, but the rest were just names.

He pointed to where they were. Cinnabar's Folly lay on the spinward front of the Ghost Nebula. Further out were the lost worlds of the Brutal Stars. On the other side were a string of smaller planets all marked with red. Bendikt drew Minka closer as he stepped up to the wall.

He was strangely animated as he pointed to the planets that they had fought on, from Potence to Malouri to Cinnabar's Folly. 'This is our battle group,' he said. 'We have pinned the Scourged down here and here.' He pointed to the worlds of Grunn and Cinnabar's Folly. 'And this is where Warmund has broken Drakul-zar.'

'He has beaten him?'

'Yes,' Bendikt said and took a long breath. 'We just heard.'

'Is Drakul-zar dead?'

There was a long silence.

'No. He escaped,' Bendikt said at last.

'Where to?'

'We don't know.'

There was another silence.

The warp routes were etched in dotted lines on the charts. He could have taken any one of them. 'So, where next?' she said.

'That is for the Warmaster to decide.'

Minka nodded. It looked impressive enough.

'Now,' he said. 'Come and look at these.'

On a sideboard a black cloth covered a row of skulls. Bendikt pulled them aside. 'The Black Templars brought these to us. These are the skulls that were mounted upon the trophy rack of the traitor?'

A cold sweat started to bead in the small of Minka's back. She regretted eating so much. She nodded dumbly and coughed to clear her throat. She looked at them, and an involuntary shudder went through her. She took a breath. 'Yes, sir. As far as I can tell.'

Bendikt smiled broadly. 'Thank you!' he said and appeared delighted. 'You're sure these are the ones?'

Minka nodded again.

Bendikt nodded. 'Thank you. You may return to your unit.'

Minka looked about as if she expected someone to explain what was happening. 'That's it, sir?'

'Yes.'

Mere steadfastly refused to look her in the face. She turned and caught Prassan's eye, but he looked away. The silence became uncomfortable. At last Minka said, 'Glad to have been of help, sir.'

'What the Throne is going on?' Minka whispered as Prassan closed the door behind them. He made a motion for her to be silent and the two of them made their way along the main corridor to the top of the grand staircase.

The banisters were polished bloodwood, broad and heavy and solid. They were reassuring under Minka's hand as the stairs curved down to the opening hallway, where statues of the ruling family stood in marble niches.

Prassan waited till they were out of earshot of the guards at the general's doorway. 'The heads you found... Two of them are from units that were fighting in the Ghost Nebula. Bendikt has a theory. The traitor did not take the banner-pole from Cadia, but from the Ghost Nebula. He thinks that the Eighth might have fought their way through the warp and come out in the Brutal Stars.'

Minka stopped. 'You mean, he thinks that Creed might still be alive?'

Prassan nodded.

'Still fighting?'

Prassan nodded again.

Minka paused. Wouldn't that be something? she thought. But it was a long way off and a long way away, and she was dead tired.

'It's time I got back,' she said. 'I need to be with my troopers.'

Prassan offered her one of HQ's Centaurs.

'I'd feel daft,' she said.

Prassan looked about. At the service doors there was a supply corps Chimera heading towards the front. Prassan hailed it and spoke to the commander. The man pulled his earphones off one ear.

'Sure!' he said, and waited, promethium smoke puffing from the rear-mounted exhausts.

Minka caught one of the rungs of the metal ladder, put a hand to the track-wheels and pulled herself up. She found a spot on the tank's armour, as the commander shouted down to the driver to add the 101st's billets to their trip.

'Don't get too fat,' she called back.

She took in a deep breath as the palace fell away behind them. It was as if a vox-horn had been blaring away in the background, and had finally been silenced. Her shoulders relaxed as the Chimera swung out to point along the main drive.

The commander did not talk to her, and she enjoyed the solitude as the Chimera rolled through the defence lines and swung round towards the front.

Ahead of them was dark with battle. She could see the flashes seconds before she felt the thunder. But her battle was over. The 101st had done their job, and now the mopping up was for the others.

She brought the image of the star charts to mind. She wondered where they would be going next. Would Warmund forgive Bendikt?

The fate of the 101st depended on it...

The closer they got, the busier the roads. Earthshakers were being hitched to their transports as the batteries moved forward.

'They've outpaced the guns!' the tank commander shouted.

Minka nodded.

She looked down on columns of local riflemen stumping under their heavy packs, lines of Rough Riders heeling their mounts forward.

Minka's eyes watered with the wind and blew her tears back across her face. She felt exhausted and emotional. And worst of all she felt alone.

Just as she had been as she stood in the trench, with that traitor towering over her. In a moment she was there, again. Standing before it.

Her body was rigid. Her fingers were white on the tank's straps.

'You all right?' a voice said.

A hand grabbed her. It was the tank commander. She looked about. The Chimera had come to a stop at the side of the metalled bahn. He pointed across an open stretch of craters and deeply gouged tank tracks, filled with water and mirroring the flat grey sky.

'We're here,' he said.

She tried to speak, but her voice failed her.

He pointed again. 'Camp A-Forty-Three,' he shouted.

She nodded, and slid down the side of the tank. The Chimera's tracks skidded as they started up, and it splashed forward in a cloud of gritty brown promethium smoke.

Minka stumbled back from the road as columns of tanks and supply trucks rumbled past. There was a rutted track leading to the sunken Cadian camp, a low earthwork topped with a rock-crete palisade.

From the dark firing ports of the pillboxes she could feel the heavy bolter crews lining her up in their sights. She made her way into the camp, saw the sentries' helmets appearing above the firing step and lifted her hands to show that she was unarmed.

A lone sentry stood and hailed her.

'Lieutenant Arminka Lesk,' she shouted. 'Second Platoon, Seventh Company.'

There was a pause as her idents were checked, then the sentry walked out towards her. He had his lasrifle slung over one shoulder, tri-dome helmet pulled low over his head.

When he was close enough he nodded to her, rather than speaking. She reached inside her jacket and pulled out the tags.

He was one of the Fifth Company. A veteran, with a black goatee cut short. He came close enough that she could smell his breath. He held the tag. It matched the name that she'd given him, and he nodded again, as if to say that she could now approach.

She fell in step with him. He wasn't very curious, but at last he said, 'Injured?'

'No.'

They stumped along in silence.

'In the attack?'

'Yeah,' she said.

There was another pause.

'Shame about Baytov.'

Minka nodded.

'They caught the sniper. Strung them up.'

'I heard,' Minka said.

There was a wooden gate that let them through a dogleg of

razor wire. He pulled the gate open for her, and closed it behind them. 'Someone found the banner of the Eighth.'

'I heard,' she said again.

Next morning, Minka took a ride on the back of a Samaritan Chimera. She had a location scribbled on a piece of paper, clutched in her hand.

When she arrived at the medicae facilities she showed it to the guards, who waved her along. The medics were busy working their way through the wounded. She had seen scenes like this before. Wards and corridors overflowing with stretchers and injured Guardsmen, the moans of men and women who had been sedated, and the grim lines of troopers too badly injured for any help and who had been left heavily anaesthetised to slowly die.

It took her nearly an hour to find Jaromir. He was sitting up, a book in hand, frowning. She saw the bandaged stump of his left arm, amputated just below the shoulder.

He forced a smile as she came towards him. His stump moved as if he was going to pat the bed. She sat on the edge of his bed, careful not to sit on his feet.

'Lieutenant.'

'Sorry, I meant to come earlier...'

'It doesn't matter,' he said. 'Was I dreaming?'

'No.'

'It's true?'

She nodded. 'And you carried it.'

He forced a smile. 'I did...'

He looked like he might cry. He'd been a big, handsome man once, till he'd taken a bolt to the head. Didn't go off. Glancing blow, so he'd been told, though he remembered nothing about it.

He looked at the stump of his arm. 'Those bastards have been trying to retire me and it looks like the Scourged have finally done me in.' He sighed. 'All I wanted to do was die on the battlefield.'

Minka didn't know what to say. 'You never know.'

He forced a smile. 'I do know. They'll try to have me training Whiteshields on some bloody backwater. Do you think they'll let me stay with the regiment?'

'I'll put a word in for you.'

'Thank you,' Jaromir said. 'I lost my tattoo.'

He lifted his stump. The Black Dragon of his old regiment had gone with his arm.

'Get another one,' she said, 'and put the 101st on it as well.'

He half smiled. 'I will.'

'I mentioned you in dispatches,' Minka said. She had recommended posthumous awards for Jeremias and Krail, and the Eagle Valoris for Jaromir, for valour and courage in the face of extreme odds.

'Thanks,' he said. 'It'll be something to hold on to when I'm old.'

X

Two days later the 101st were pulled back for redeployment.

It was unceremonious. The job was done, and it was time to move on to the next one. Minka hoped there'd be time for them to at least lick their wounds before they were thrown back into hell.

'Where are we going?' she asked Colour Sergeant Tyson.

'We're being pulled back to El'Phanor.'

'El'Phanor?' Minka said. 'So Warmund has forgiven us?'

Tyson pulled a face. 'Refit and reorganisation.'

'Sounds ominous,' she said.

Tyson nodded.

'He wouldn't disband us, would he?'

'He's the Warmaster. He can do whatever he likes.'

'He can't,' Minka said. 'Not after Traitor Rock.'

Tyson laughed humourlessly. 'Oh. Better let Jaromir know that he should spruce up for the parade tomorrow.'

'I will,' Minka said.

* * *

The *put-put-put* of distant cluster munitions drifted on the breeze as the 101st paraded for the last time on Cinnabar's Folly. The mopping up would take months, but they would not be here to see it.

Minka stood at the right-hand corner of her platoon, with Sparker in front of her. The banner-pole of the Eighth had been hung with a Cadian banner. It stood next to their own, behind Lord General Bendikt.

He stood at an aquila lectern, his voice amplified across the vox-system.

This might be the last time they paraded together. Despite the victory, this fact hung over them all like a shadow. Bendikt tried to sound full of confidence and bravado, but his enthusiasm seemed a little overdone.

Minka found her mind wandering. She could not help but notice how much less space the regiment was taking up on the parade ground. She could not help but think of the men and women who had sacrificed themselves upon this moon, and those who, like Jaromir, had fought their last.

As Bendikt went on she realised that she missed Baytov. He would have found the right words, she thought to herself. It would have been a short speech, but it would have done what it needed to do.

On Malouri the whole regiment had been awarded the Star of Cadia. She'd also been given the Steel Skull for her action in taking Tor Tartarus.

'You're bound for great things,' Baytov had said to her, and those words had stayed with her.

In the corner of her eye, Minka could see the white of Jaromir's bandaged arm. She pursed her lips as Adjutant Mere read the honours out. Posthumous awards were announced first. The name call went on and on, and Minka heard the names of

Jeremias and Krail and was pleased. She could feel her whole platoon, the whole Seventh Company, swell up with pride.

At the end came the major awards. They started with the First Company and worked their way along. When it came to Seventh Company, Captain Sparker was the first called out, for the Silver Skull.

Minka was pleased for him, and then it was her own name, being called out with Jaromir as well. She snapped to attention and marched forward, then turned along the front of the regiment, to where Bendikt stood.

She waited as Bendikt pinned the medal to Sparker's chest and then marched forward and made the sign of the aquila.

'Lieutenant Lesk,' he said. 'Very well done. We are all very proud of you.'

'Thank you, sir.'

She stood as he pinned the medal to the left of her chest, then made the sign of the aquila, and marched smartly to her place.

As she waited, she realised she had been so surprised that she had not heard what medal she had been given. It was only afterwards when they had turned out, that Minka saw that she had been given the Silver Skull with Scarlet ribbon. And Jaromir had been given a Silver Skull.

She felt prouder of his award than she did of her own.

'Well done,' she told him. 'You saved me out there.'

'I did not,' Jaromir said, and she laughed.

'True. But you came when no one else did.'

The Cadians were ferried straight from the parade to the loading fields. Lines of Munitorum lighters stood waiting as promethium tankers refilled them.

The nearest was a weathered old craft, its Munitorum livery streaked with rust and the black of multiple planetary entries.

At the back of the craft, a conveyer belt was loading containers into the hold. All their kit and supplies, and their dead as well.

Minka stood to watch her platoon inside, then followed them in. She paused at the doorway to take one last look at Cinnabar's Folly, and thought of all the planets she had spilt blood on.

She had felt strongly about some worlds. But this moon she was glad to see the last of, and turned inside without a word or gesture.

Seventh Company were seated in rows in the underground hangar. The lighter smelt as though it had been used to ferry armour to the planet. The whole chamber stank of holy unguents and there were promethium stains on the floor, coated with sawdust, while the walls were obscured by piled-up heaps of webbing and rachet straps.

When they were all there, the companies had marched in and taken their places, then the ramps were lifted and sealed. The rear third of the chamber was empty. The dead were packed into containers in the hold.

As the engines began to warm up, the mood among the Cadians lifted. They were still alive, after all, and they were leaving this place behind.

Minka swapped words with Blanchez as she made her way to where Captain Sparker stood, his water bottle in hand.

He slapped Minka's arm. 'Well done, Lesk,' he said.

'Thank you, sir.'

'Another successful campaign.'

She nodded. 'Do you think it will be our last? The Hundred-and-First, I mean.'

'Possibly. Who knows what high command will do? Either we're in for a refit, or we'll be broken up and assigned to new regiments.' He stopped and looked at his flask, and took a long swig. From his breath she realised it was filled with amasec. 'Either way, I've enjoyed serving with you, Lesk.'

He offered her his flask. She took a sip. The fierce bite of amasec was just what she needed.

'They wouldn't really disband us, would they?'

'Yes,' he laughed. 'I'm afraid they would.'

Minka looked away as her emotions got the better of her.

Sparker slapped her on the back. 'Don't worry so.'

'But the Hundred-and-First,' she said.

'I know.'

She wiped her tears on the back of her hand. 'We've been in the thick of it on over half a dozen warfronts. It was us that kept Potence in loyal hands. It was us that broke Traitor Rock. And it was us that smashed the stalemate here!'

'I know. But we're just troopers. We do what they command.'

Minka nodded.

'Listen. Shand asked me to speak to you. Those rumours of the Eighth. High command have asked us to keep a lid on them for the moment.'

'I'm not spreading them.'

'I know,' he said. 'I know. Still, if anyone comes to you, just play it down.'

'I only ever answered questions, sir.'

'I know,' Sparker said. 'We all did. But let's not talk about it. It's political,' he added. 'Bendikt is worried about stepping on Warmund's toes. It might mean we are broken up, if Warmund thinks we're undermining his authority.'

Minka said nothing.

'From now on,' Sparker continued, 'discussion of this matter is *forbidden*. The future of the Hundred-and-First depends on it.'

'Understood,' Minka said.

PART II

I

ESPAH'S FORGE, THE BRUTAL STARS

Promethium rigs hung like a cloud of metal mosquitos over the oil-rich clouds of the gas giant Quence. Steel proboscises stabbed hundreds of miles down. Standing guard over them all was the Guild of Hostmen, who had maintained their thousand-year watch from the fortified moon of Espah's Forge.

The cratered lump had been hollowed out by thousands of years of human settlement. Once, the guild had held Imperial warrants. They had dealt directly with the ambassadors of the Munitorum, but since the fall of Cadia, the order of the Brutal Stars had broken down. Now the Hostmen allied themselves to the local power brokers. Their court was a sycophantic collection of spinward traders, promethium gangers and attendant hangers-on – and the main power broker of this tract, the Scourged.

Today, the court waited with bated breath as the embassy approached.

The lighter was typical of this range of wild space: the old livery of orange and black guild colours giving way to rust and battered metal, the voidship's stubby form blunt with slabs of welded ceramite. Its nose and waist turrets bristled with weaponry.

Slaved sentinel-guns tracked the approach of the embassy lighter, targeting matrixes keeping it within their sights as it approached the landing bay. Its vector thrusters kicked up curtains of dust and grit as it balanced for a moment then slowly descended, extended landing gear creaking as the craft settled.

There was a tense air as the engines whined down and the ramp lowered with a hiss.

Like everything in the spinward tracks, this facility had seen better times. The walls were pockmarked with the scars of old gunfights and there were rockcrete and spooled razor-wire barricades about the entrance.

There was a long pause before a figure appeared from the landing craft. She was a lean warrior, dressed in an ill-fitting suit of carapace armour, stitched and welded about her wiry frame. Following behind came a barefoot slave-child.

The child looked old beyond its years. Its skin was sickly yellow, its shaven head oversized and its face shrivelled, as if it had been cursed with years beyond its lifespan. There was a hand upon its shoulder: that of a blind penitent.

The child led this penitent, and the penitent led another, and it another till there were three of them, all dressed alike in cowls of rough sackcloth with rope belts hung with bones and esoteric trinkets. They shuffled forward with one arm upon the shoulder of the other, like sightless beggars.

The newcomer shouted across the landing platform, revealing a grin of filed teeth, needle sharp. 'I am Marŝal Baab. I invoke the right of parley.'

Baab looked like any other pirate or ghulam existing along the fringes of habitable space that plundered, exhorted and terrorised the worlds that had once been within the Imperium, except for one detail. Her left arm was bare, the skin puckered and scarred by whip and blade, and about her wrist she bore a plain manacle, a token of her servitude.

The Scourged commander stood in brigandine and mail, eyes glaring out from his dull iron bascinet. About him his war pack stood in tense silence, visors pulled low over their faces, hack-blades strapped to their legs, lascarbines gripped in scarred hands.

Baab made a show of pulling her pistol from its holster. It clattered to the floor. He waved her closer. As she reached the bottom of the ramp, he nodded two of his warriors forward. She held her arms out as they searched them all – even the barefoot child.

'They're clean,' the trooper called out.

Only then did the Scourged captain pull his helm from his head, revealing a boxer's face: broken nose, bull neck and a bald skull, swirling with black-inked heretical texts. His speech was distorted by the tusk-like snags of tooth that jutted from his lower jaw.

'You may enter, slave,' he said.

The Hostmaster's audience chamber was a baroque display of wealth and power. The black marble vaulting was edged with gold gilt, and the soaring panels of plaster were covered with ancient murals that detailed the glorious past of the promethium guilders. The dark paintwork glimmered in the light of flaming torches set along the walls.

Marŝal Baab stood and took it all in before she turned to the Hostmaster.

He sat on his marble throne at the end of the guildhall, chain of office laid over his fur-lined robes, his own liverymen ranked up about him in uniforms of heavy, embroidered silk, bronze armour gleaming in the torch flames.

The Hostmaster was the 812th to have held this position. Portraits of his predecessors were hung on the wall behind his dais, their stern faces staring down in disapproval. Any token of loyalty to the Golden Throne was now obscured with dark cloth.

Before all stood an honour guard of Scourged warriors. Their commander squared up as Baab stepped towards him.

'I am here to speak to the Hostmaster,' she said.

'You want to speak to him,' he replied, 'your words go through me.'

Baab paced forwards, leading the blind behind her. She stopped ten paces from him. The tension grew. The Scourged commander said, 'I ask you again, what would you speak of?'

'Your deaths,' Baab said.

The whole company of Scourged laughed. Their commander laughed most ostentatiously. 'Your threats are cheap.'

'So are your lives.'

'You have no right to talk like that, slave,' the commander said.

'The Scourged are not as mighty as once they were.'

As she spoke, the sickly child came forward, wide-eyed and ghastly.

Baab stepped closer. 'I am one of the Thrice-Bound. A servant of Hel.'

'And who is this "Hel"?'

Baab did not answer his question.

'What are they?' the commander demanded, as the child led the penitents forward.

'They are my masters,' Baab replied.

He put his head back and laughed. His laughter ended with a

strangled gasp as he tried to give the order for his pack to attack. But he could not move. And nor could his warriors.

The three blind figures stood behind Baab, their child-guide trembling as the Scourged were forced to their knees. The commander's eyes bulged. He struggled against the invisible force that held him as a gentle snow precipitated about them. It was fine and hard, like hail, but fell gently to the metal grille at their feet.

One of the stewards – a tall, thin man, leaning heavily upon his staff – hissed at her. 'You swore a parley!'

'I swore that I would honour the peace,' Baab retorted as she made her way to where the commander still stood.

His face was fixed in a rictus of horror and pain as Marŝal Baab stepped behind him and kicked his knees from under him. His hack-blade was strapped to his thigh. She reached down and pulled it from its human-skin scabbard.

The iron was stained and pitted, the long edge honed to a fine silver blade.

It would do, she thought, as she took his chin in one hand and pulled it back against her hip.

She could feel the stubble on his face, the sweat of exertion, the tremble of life under her fingers. His eyes were fixed in a stare. She moved so that he was staring into her face.

'I am a servant of Hel, and I am Thrice-Bound. I do not serve you,' she told him, and hacked down.

The gout of blood was hot on her hand as she sawed the blade in deeper. It took a moment for her to find the joint between the vertebrae of his spine, and then she was through. His bald head came away from his body, slippery with its blood.

'This is how we will deal with Drakul-zar when we find him.'

Baab let it fall to the floor and started upon the next.

The Hostmaster's guards stood watching on in horror as she

went along the line and hacked the heads from the Scourged warriors. It was bloody, but she had learnt her trade in the Brutal Stars, which had been lawless long before the fall of Cadia.

'Hostmaster,' she said at the end, 'you are now under the protection of Hel.'

II

EL'PHANOR

The Cadian 101st, 'Hell's Last', were berthed on the ninety-fifth deck, deep in the guts of the Lunar-class light cruiser *Lord Gisburn the Valorous*.

The space was divided into neat compartments, one for each company. There wasn't much privacy, only what a blanket slung along a bunk could provide. In order to keep herself sane, Minka maintained a strict routine. Exercise. Drill. Unarmed combat. Firing practice. When she was done, all before ten a.m. ship-time, she went to the shower blocks and scrubbed herself down. Conscious that the future of the regiment lay on her shoulders, she kept herself to herself, saying nothing about Creed or the banner. But Hontius was there the whole time, black uniform popping up like a bad smell.

Many of the 101st refused to be put off. Strangers waited for her in the mess or on her way to the latrines, but the commissars were always there, haunting her steps.

'Not spreading rumours, Lesk?' Chief Commissar Shand said

as news of their approach to El'Phanor was broadcast over the vox-grilles. His pink scar tissue twitched under his baleful violet eyes.

'Of course not, sir,' she said.

'We've got three troopers in confinement.'

'Not me, sir.'

'Good,' Shand said. 'I've read the dispatches from your action on Cinnabar's Folly, and we wouldn't want to blemish your record.'

'I think my record stands for itself, sir.'

Shand seemed to enjoy her spirit. 'Yes. Very commendable.'

Minka glared at him. 'Just serving the Emperor.'

Shand smiled. 'As we all are.'

Six months after the fighting on Cinnabar's Folly they entered the El'Phanor System.

On the last day before berthing, Minka came out of the shower block dressed in canvas trousers and Cadian green vest, towelling her hair dry. The female changing room was one of the few places she was safe from the commissars.

'Lieutenant!'

It was Blanchez. She pulled her sleeve up to her elbow to reveal a transparent layer of counterseptic cloth laid over her forearm. It was stained with blood and ink in the pattern of the Cadian crest, inset with '101st' and the regiment's nickname, 'Hell's Last'.

Minka smiled. It was good to be part of a regiment. And it might serve as a reminder, if they were broken up.

'So, El'Phanor...' Blanchez said. 'What is this place?'

Minka saw Hontius at the end of the hallway, peering towards her. Her cheeks coloured. 'New Cadia,' Minka joked. 'Well, one of them... It's where Lord Militant Warmund commands.'

'And we're joining him?'

'Apparently,' Minka said. 'At least that's what Bendikt hopes.'

Blanchez looked at her new tattoo and blew on it. 'What's he like?'

'The Warmaster? A bastard, but one of our bastards,' Minka said. She paused. 'Word is that we're being reorganised.'

'You think Bendikt would let them?'

Minka gave her hair a final rub, then she slapped the towel over her shoulder.

'Not sure he has much choice. He killed some Praetorian bigwig way back in a duel. That's why we got sent to Malouri. If we're lucky, cutting the siege short to the tune of a few decades has won Bendikt back some sway. Knowing Warmund, though, maybe not. Maybe he lost too many at the Battle of Joalara and he needs to refill his ranks.'

'They wouldn't break up a successful regiment?'

Minka shrugged. 'It's the Imperium of Man. They do what they like.'

Minka regretted being so blunt. Blanchez had spent her life as an orphan, kicking around barracks and void-stations, dropped and picked up like a piece of unwanted luggage.

'Frekk,' Blanchez said. 'But I've just found you all.'

Minka nodded. She could have expressed herself better. And it was how she felt as well.

She saw Hontius still hovering at the end of the dorm. She took Blanchez by the arm. 'Come with me.'

'Where to?'

'I don't know,' Minka said. 'Let's just go somewhere else.'

They hurried out into the corridor and Minka heard Hontius coming after them. She grabbed Blanchez's elbow and pulled her down a side corridor and then another, past a hangar where Father Keremm was leading the devout in prayer.

Their ranks were thicker than usual. Worship was a relief from the tedium of travel. Minka and Blanchez hurried past and found themselves at the bottom of the lifts to the viewing decks.

'Lieutenant Lesk,' a voice called. Minka froze, yet it was not Hontius but Yedrin. 'Are you going up to the viewing deck?'

'Yes,' Minka said quickly, and grabbed him and pulled him into the lift. As they stood waiting for the doors to close, Hontius appeared, his black-clad shape disappearing as the doors clicked shut.

Minka let out a long breath.

The viewing deck ran the width of the bridge-tower, with viewports that overlooked each aspect of the ship. The centre of the deck was taken up with the lift shafts and service ways, but there was a corridor that encircled the perimeter, offering views all around the craft.

They did a circuit of the deck, which took about an hour. It was largely deserted.

The view backwards, over the massive curved mass of the plasma generators and engine fans, showed the darkness of the outer system. As they walked along they looked out to either side, over the gun batteries, to where the rest of the fleet lay at void-anchor. The ships were vast. They bristled with weaponry, and about them were the bright traceries of void-craft.

They ended up at the forestation, looking along the spine of the cruiser, the huge armoured prow hidden behind the superstructure.

'Throne,' Yedrin said, a number of times.

Blanchez was harder to impress. She'd grown up as a camp-rat, and she'd spent a lot of her childhood, if that was the right word, kicking about on tugs and transports and void-waiters, which helped guide the bigger ships to their orbital docks.

El'Phanor had been slowly growing for a week, from a bright light, like a star, to the size of a moon, and now it was so large that they could see colour. But it wasn't El'Phanor that held their gaze. It was the *Imperial Heart*, the Ramilies-class star fort that hung in space like a moon of steel and adamantine and ceramite. The station was surmounted by an armaplas cathedral, its great gothic windows lit from within by a pure, blue light, while the facets of ten thousand pinnacles and buttresses made it glitter in the absolute cold of the void.

At the speed they were travelling, it appeared only an hour or so away, but it took over three hours to arrive, and with each moment the size of the thing grew and grew, until it filled the viewports.

Even Blanchez was speechless. It was large enough for the Lunar-class cruiser to draw alongside. The *clunk-clunk* of anchor chains sounded through the whole craft; arms reached out and secured the cruiser, with mag-locks holding it stern and aft, and then drew it slowly in. Bit by bit, the viewing deck started to fill.

'Ah, Lieutenant Lesk.'

Minka froze. She turned and saw Adjutant Mere. He was alone.

'Last time we were here, the planet was just a bone-strewn husk. But look at it!'

She did. There were bands of green across the equatorial reaches, and patches of blue water sitting on the surface, while the massive ruins of the Kromarch dominated the Arabor Plateau, their angular shapes standing out against the blackened landscape.

He caught her eye, and said simply, 'They're building a mausoleum. For fallen Cadians.'

'So that's where we'll all end up.'

Mere laughed. 'I suppose so, yes.'

The cruiser creaked as it was hauled sideways. Mere checked

his chronometer. 'Looks like we'll be disembarking soon,' he said.

Minka nodded. 'I'd better pack.'

Minka's platoon gathered their packs and lined up for final inspections like clockwork. She did the basics, checking that the sergeants had done their job, and Commissar Hontius led the inspection.

He went through each of Seventh Company's quarters, using his stick to dig for evidence.

'What's this?' he said, lifting up a mattress. 'Look!'

Captain Sparker looked.

'Well?' Hontius demanded.

'Graffiti,' Sparker said.

'Yes!' Hontius said. He threw the mattress aside.

The words had been carved. *Creed Lives.*

His face coloured. He looked to Minka as if she were responsible.

She felt herself reddening even as Hontius spoke to Sparker. 'Get this cleaned off! A regiment is judged by how they leave their barracks! Has this been recorded in the regimental log?'

Sparker turned to Colour Sergeant Tyson.

Tyson's eyes narrowed. 'I will make sure it is.'

Hontius stayed to ensure the offensive words were painted over, then went along, turning more beds over, banging lavatory doors open. The whole company was tense as he made his way to Jaromir, who stood in the third row, chin up, shoulders squared, looking like a statue of a Cadian Shock Trooper, except for the arm. He didn't move a muscle.

Hontius paused before him. 'Was that graffiti?'

'No, sir.'

Hontius used his swagger stick to inspect Jaromir's kit. The whole company were watching him. They felt the same way as Minka. They'd die for Jaromir. And they knew that he would die for them.

As Hontius picked at his belongings, Jaromir's stump twitched and Minka felt her heartbeat rising. She was in the trench again. It was Jaromir who came to save her. She tried to remember the moment that he'd appeared. Her sight turned red. It pulsed with her heartbeat. Red, and then black. A wave of nausea rose through her again. She had to grit her teeth to hold the horror down.

There was a voice in her ear. 'Lieutenant,' it said. There were arms under her armpits, and she was pulled aside.

'You all right?' Yedrin said. Minka pushed his hand off and pushed herself to her feet. Everyone was looking at her.

'I'm fine,' she said, even though she was a little unsteady upon her feet. 'I'm fine.'

'Sure?'

'Sure,' she said, and blinked her eyes. Her vision was clear. Her heart had calmed. The sweat was cold upon her skin. 'I'm fine,' she said again, and made her way to her position in the parade.

'Report to the medicae once we are embarked,' Hontius said. 'And make it quick. Top brass are going to want to speak to you.'

'About what, sir?'

'The matter.'

'Which matter?'

'You know which.'

'But I am not allowed to speak of it,' she said as she made the sign of the aquila and turned smartly upon her heel.

IV

As Bendikt stepped onto the Ramilies-class star fort, its scent took him back to his last time here, just after the fall of Cadia. His anger had been on a hair-trigger, and it had exploded one evening when some prig of a Praetorian had mocked the Cadians. The Praetorian was by far the better bladesman, but there was more to fighting than your skill with a sword. And Bendikt was Cadian, and Cadians were all about winning.

It didn't matter how. He'd lost his arm, and he'd disembowelled the man.

All this came back to him as he stood and smelt the ancient war-station. He rubbed his arm where the flesh met the augmetic.

'What was his name again?' he asked Mere.

The adjutant didn't need to ask who he was referring to.

'Lord General Reginald Monstella de Barka.'

'Ah,' Bendikt said. 'Yes.'

A groundcar was waiting. They climbed in and it set off. Bendikt was silent for a long time as the vehicle drove them along the interior highway, between cargo loaders with flashing yellow lights and tech-priests rolling past.

'A fine duellist,' Bendikt said at last. 'A good servant of the Emperor.' He paused, thinking. 'I rather regret killing him.'

'Do you?' Mere asked.

Bendikt nodded. 'Yes. Of all those that I have killed, and, to be honest, I have long since lost count, I regret Sir Reginald most. He would have served the Emperor far better on a battlefield.'

'But he slandered the Cadians.'

Bendikt nodded. He thought back to that moment, when the fall of Cadia was so fresh.

His anger was less sharp now. Less cutting. But back then he was prepared to die or kill for it.

He took in a deep breath.

'He did,' he said at last. 'You're right.'

When they arrived at Bendikt's quarters, there was a man waiting inside.

'A General Janka is here to see you,' Prassan said.

'Janka?' Bendikt said.

Mere took barely a moment. He put his hand to his mouth. 'He was a major then… ' he said, dragging the details up from his memory. 'Cadian Eight-Hundred-and-Fortieth. He was in your draft…'

Bendikt stood up. 'Janka!' he said, starting to pace up and down. 'That old bastard. Where is he?'

Deck by deck the *Lord Gisburn the Valorous* emptied its belly of troopers and tanks. As they passed through the docking ports, they could feel the cold of the void pressing in. Their breaths steamed, and the vast empty space echoed with the clang and clatter of tanks and loaders.

The Ramilies was as big as a moon. Its interior hummed with grav-generators. They marched for hours, passing ammo-lifts, mess halls, barrack yards. Five hours later they had reached their berth. Deck 297, Lower Quadrant C.

They had marched through thoroughfares large enough to drive ten tanks abreast, with intersections that slanted up and down, and a hundred lesser passageways heading off in every direction. The vastness of the place forced the Cadians together.

By the time they arrived at their sector, they were just getting a sense of the size of the thing.

'What happens if you get lost?' Yedrin wondered. The thought made him sick. You might spend your entire life wandering about this place. He wanted to get to his berth and to close the door behind him and to stay there.

Jaromir found his bunk, and threw his kit-bag down with the air of someone savouring the last times.

He had to keep himself busy. Little things were a challenge for him. He took his battle-knife out and wedged it under his leg as he ran his whetstone along its length. He had scrubbed it, sharpened it with grindstone and smoothed the raw metal with a leather strap. The steel blade shone with a cold blue light. He turned it over in his lap, letting the light fall on the surface.

It was mesmerising. Perfect.

'Heh!' a voice said. Jaromir felt the shadow fall over him. There was a tall, thin man standing over him, dressed in Cadian drab canvas trousers and a knitted drab top.

It was Viktor. He had a bundle of summonses in his hand. He gave one to Jaromir.

The big man took it and put it down on the bed next to him.

You are required for medical assessment. 'Thanks,' he said, his voice barely a rasp. 'Looks like my time is up.'

General Janka came through the door with a roar of recognition. 'Bendikt!' he said, arms open and gathering the lord general in a hug.

Janka was older, a little stouter, than Bendikt remembered, but he had the same air of gritty determination about him, the same steel plate filling in his fractured skull. But as he held Bendikt at arm's length, Bendikt saw that Janka had developed a twitch.

'Sorry!' he said, gesturing to his skull-plate. 'The medics keep asking me to come in and get this replaced, but there are battles to fight. You know how it is.'

'Of course,' Bendikt said and shook Janka's hand with his own augmetic. 'As you can see, none of us are untouched.'

Janka's smile was cut short by another twitch. It started just above his upper lip, and tugged it up in a snarl as it pulled his eye down at the same time. Bendikt forced a smile. 'I hear you were on Joalara.'

Janka slapped Bendikt's arm. 'You have never seen such a thing.' He paused. 'The battle raged across the whole continent. They came on in columns a hundred miles long, with crawl-tanks firing into our ranks. We harried and hammered them, but nothing slowed them. By the time they reached the foothills of the hive, I thought we could never break them. But Warmund had put all his Cadians together. There were a hundred thousand Cadians lined up. Each way you looked, all you could see were tri-dome helmets. It was magnificent. It made me feel as though I was on Cadia again. That was when Warmund threw everything at them. Guns fired down from every level of the hive. But still they came on!

'We only had two miles of defences left when Warmund

launched his counter-attack. We fixed bayonets and charged. As one. Shouting Creed's name. The earth shook as Warmund led us down the hill...'

Each detail was like a blow upon a bruise. By the end Bendikt felt like weeping. He had missed that moment. It was something that he would bear through life.

At last Janka paused. His face twitched again and he changed the subject. 'You were on Cinnabar's Folly?'

Bendikt's voice was a bare rasp. 'Yes. Scourged, under one of Drakul-zar's lieutenants, Drakul-vaahl.'

After Janka's speech, Bendikt had no heart to explain. It wasn't that Janka would not believe how hard the 101st had fought; the truth was, he wasn't very interested. What was Cinnabar's Folly but a minor sideshow? A skirmish, a minor altercation, a distant brawl.

The Felhkom family had been appalled when they saw the paltry force that Warmund had sent. A single regiment, and a lord general. But they had not realised what Cadians could do.

Bendikt inherited a poorly led and poorly motivated army. Within months he had turned them around, till they were a formidable offensive force.

With each little victory Bendikt had bolstered their confidence, while the 101st showed the enemy how fighting was done. Within a year of landing, Bendikt had finally trapped their finest troops in the Tribulation Salient, and crushed them.

'We won,' he said.

Janka smiled. 'I look forward to reading the dispatches...' But there was a change in the tone of his voice. It was enough to warn Bendikt of what was coming next. 'Warmund sent me. He said that you found an object of interest upon Cinnabar's Folly.'

Bendikt tensed. 'We believe so.'

Janka twitched again. 'Warmund wants it.'

'Does he?'

'Where is it?'

'Under guard.'

'I like you, Bendikt,' Janka said. 'You did well on Malouri. But don't cross Warmund. He's not a man who takes kindly to being thwarted.'

Bendikt smiled. 'Mere,' he said. 'Please ask Chief Commissar Shand to come.'

There was a pause. Janka made brief conversation about the battle on Joalara, and back, even further to their days on Cadia, and recalled a few stories about Creed. Bendikt let the other man talk. As Shand stepped inside, the general's twitch flared up.

Shand listened in silence. 'I am afraid that the lord general put the item in my care,' he said.

'Warmund wants it,' Janka said. The implication was clear. What Warmund wanted, Warmund got.

'Listen,' Bendikt said. He took a deep breath. 'I am prepared to hand it over. But I want two things in return.'

'What?'

'The Cadian Hundred-and-First. I know you're debating whether to reinforce them or break them up. I want them reinforced.'

'And the second?'

'I've got an inkling where the banner came from. I want to take the Hundred-and-First in that direction, and free rein to follow it up.'

Janka nodded. 'I cannot promise anything, but I will do my best.'

Bendikt smiled and put out his augmetic hand. He gripped Janka's own. 'I'm glad that we have an understanding.'

It had been a long time since Minka had seen medicae facilities as fine as these. She could smell counterseptics long before she got to the top of the stairs and turned down the broad corridor.

Into the wall were set servitors, each one chanting prayers of healing through their grille-mouths, and the walls were inlaid with golden calligraphy which exhorted the ill and the wounded to lift their hearts to the God-Emperor.

Bear your scars with pride, one read. *Each is a mark of your courage.*

The devout are untouched by plague or disease, no sickness can blight the pure of heart.

And across the wide doorway read, *Fight on! Death does not want you yet.*

There was a square hallway, with corridors leading off on either side.

Minka stood and looked about for someone to speak to. Suddenly a figure appeared. It was Father Keremm, with another priest, dressed in the same penitential robes but without his full beard. As they came forward, Minka saw that the other priest was a tall, dark woman, with hair braided tight to the front of her scalp. The braids were hung with Imperial icons.

'Blessed Throne!' Keremm said. 'This is the one I was talking about.'

'You've been talking about me?' Minka said.

Keremm stopped, and put his hand to the shoulder of the woman next to him. She was barefoot, dressed in the heavy wool robe of the Ecclesiarchy, but while Keremm's robe was plain and unadorned, the other woman's was stitched with holy symbols, scraps of parchment and illuminated pages of books. Her face was narrow, her round, violet eyes intent.

'This is Confessor Talbeas,' Keremm said. 'She's been assigned to the Hundred-and-First to help me in my ministry.'

Minka put her hand out and shook Talbeas'. The confessor's grip was suitably firm, her manner calm and assured. Talbeas smiled. 'I need to thank you. I hear it was you who found the banner.'

Minka nodded. 'Commissar Hontius has forbidden me to speak of it. Confessor, were you on Cadia?'

Talbeas nodded.

'Which kasr?' Minka said.

'Tyrok,' the other woman said.

Minka did not ask more. Cadia had been the kind of place that tested your faith. You spent every waking moment with the Eye of Terror staring down at you, and you learnt to resist the maddening glare of that lurid orb. It was a trial you shared with everyone on your world. You didn't have to talk about it. You just knew. And your faith was honed to a fine blade. Minka nodded. Confessor Talbeas had passed all the tests. Minka knew that the woman would serve on the battlefield.

'It's a pleasure,' Minka said to Talbeas, then turned to Father Keremm. 'I didn't know that we were taking up so much of your time.'

Keremm laughed then leant forward. 'I've been praying that the Hundred-and-First is not broken up,' he whispered. 'I took the Tarot this morning and... it looks good.'

'Thank the God-Emperor!' Minka said. 'So what will it mean if we are reconstituted?'

'What I have heard is that Warmund is bringing regiments back to full strength. Combined arms.'

'Armour, artillery, the works?'

'Scouts, Kasrkin, everything. I think Warmund will forgive Bendikt,' he added, and winked. 'I think you helped him out a little...'

Minka's cheeks coloured. 'We all serve,' she said.

Talbeas said, 'I have prayed upon this matter. We are all servants of the God-Emperor. This is a great relic. But you are honoured. He has singled you out.'

Minka didn't know what to say to that. She stammered, 'Thank you.'

'This is His message to us. He has sent this item to us. He

wants us to remember our vows. We swore to never give in to the heretics. We swore to keep fighting. The God-Emperor has sent Creed's banner to us to remind us of that.'

Minka nodded. She remembered her vows. Her father had lifted her up when she was a child and she had shouted at the Eye of Terror, the dreadful warp-bruise that had filled the Cadian skyline.

The vow then had been 'Never!' But never had come to pass.

Talbeas stared at Minka. 'We think in the terms of our own lifetimes. But the God-Emperor is all-wise, all-seeing. Cadia has fallen, but it does not mean that we cannot take it back.'

Minka nodded. 'I wish I had your belief.'

Talbeas smiled. 'I will work on you.'

Minka almost laughed. She had never had a member of the Ecclesiarchy take such an interest in her, and it left her uncomfortable. 'I'm just a trooper,' she said, but Talbeas tutted.

'No. You are a weapon in the hands of the God-Emperor. And it's clear that He has great things in store for you.'

Minka's smile stiffened. That was what Baytov had said to her. 'Thank you,' she said. 'But listen, I'm looking for Banting.'

Talbeas held her hand for a long time. 'Go. Find the medic. And remember the Emperor is watching you.'

Minka took the long, broad corridor deeper into the medicae. The steel walls were inscribed with holy texts. Her fingers trailed along their surface, feeling the sharp edge of the letters. There were symbols etched there too. Skulls, aquilas and familiar words of High Gothic caught her attention. She saw the name of Scarus, and realised it was a prayer for the defenders of the Cadian Front, and then the names popped out at her. A roll-call of worlds and systems that had supported the Cadians. Scarus. Belis Corona. Agripinaa. Scelus, and above them all the symbol of the Cadian Gate.

At one point a fresh votive candle had been placed in a small shrine niche. The flame glowed within the red glass casing. The inner walls were covered with inlaid gold, and within was an icon of Saint Josmane, her face framed in the Cadian tri-dome helmet, her bayonet fixed, her violet eyes staring out in grim defiance.

Minka held the saint's gaze for a moment, then nodded, one trooper to another, pursed her lips and carried on.

The corridor curved away around one of the ventilation shafts and Minka caught a range of scents, drifting through the miles of superstructure: tallow-fat from the galley kitchens, the warm smell of the plasma generators, the chem-tang of recycled air. She passed a pair of troopers walking the other way. They had the snake-and-winged-skull badge of corpsmen embroidered onto their sleeves. They made the sign of the aquila as they passed.

She forgot at times that she was a superior officer. At times she still felt like the Whiteshield who had cut her teeth in the ruins of Kasr Myrak.

A servo-skull hung outside the medicae's doorway, a mecha-dendrite arm plugged into one of the wall data-sockets, the data-point's light flickering over its metallic face. As Minka approached, it retracted its arm and swung in the air towards her before drifting back along the way she had come, anti-grav generators whirring, vestigial spine trailing.

In one chamber there was a vox-servitor droning out prayers of healing and purity through a vox-grille muzzle. Above it, a picture of Creed hung on the wall. The Lord Castellan's bullish face stared out from the gilt frame.

His grim visage offered nothing but struggle and war.

Three medicae corridors branched out. Each was empty and deserted, with brightly lit wards opening off on one side. Minka picked one, passed another servo-skull. More empty wards appeared on either side, neat rows of freshly made beds, white sheets folded down, ready for any casualties.

Her boots creaked on the scrubbed flooring. Everywhere smelt of counterseptics, everywhere looked clean and organised. She found Banting standing in the fourth bay, his white coat unbuttoned, his hands on his hips as he talked to a group of corpsmen.

The chief medic looked up as Minka darkened the doorway. 'Ah, Lesk,' he said. 'I thought you might be coming to see me.'

Minka stepped inside and the corpsmen made the sign of the aquila. She gave nothing away and Banting dismissed the troopers to their duties, then motioned to her to sit down on the plain bed.

The freshly starched sheets creaked as she sat, worn leather arm and leg straps hanging loose around her. Banting folded his arms and lifted a bushy black eyebrow. 'So,' he said. 'What's wrong?'

Minka gritted her teeth for a moment. 'Nothing much.'

'No?'

She shrugged. 'I got dizzy.'

He looked up at her. 'Happen often?'

'No.'

'Lie down,' he said. The blood pump whined as it started to warm up. 'Roll your sleeve up.'

Minka exposed the inked symbol of Kasr Myrak – its Mikel Gateway silhouetted under crossed carbines. The motto-scroll wrapped beneath it with the words: *Cadia Stands*. She had cried when those words were inked under her skin. It had been done by a burly man in a leather apron and augmetic focal. But it wasn't the pain that had moved her. Pain was easy to deal with. You gritted your teeth and endured it.

Loss and failure were much harder for a Cadian to suffer.

Minka lay back on the cot as Banting looked for a fresh needle.

He took her arm, pulled his chronometer from his breast pocket, placed his fingers onto her wrist, counted the beats.

When he was done, he slipped a rubber tourniquet about her upper arm, tapped a finger onto her inner elbow, and lifted the blood-gun. Three pipes hung from the heel of the handle and disappeared into the pump. Its cone head ended with a sharp metal needle. Banting tested the sharpness on the end of his finger. He tutted with disapproval.

'This will hurt,' he said.

Minka looked away as he plunged it into her vein. There was a sucking sound and the pipes gurgled. The machine hummed as the tests were run.

'Got enough?' Minka said at last.

'Hmm,' Banting said as he pulled the needle from her arm, slipped a wad of sterilised cloth over the wound, and folded her arm back on itself to hold the cloth in place. 'I hear Jaromir is doing well.'

'He is.'

'Hell of a mess,' he said. 'Never like burns. They're a killer. Loss of blood and heat. Hypovolaemic shock. And then the infection. Massive inflammation shock. Organ failure. Death... But he was lucky.'

Minka thought he was joking, but Banting didn't laugh. 'Plasma cooked his arm,' he said as he waited for the machine to start working. 'Dry gangrene. Non-infectious. But next time, get anyone like that evacuated back.'

'I will,' Minka said. She pulled her sleeve down and stood to wait.

At last the machine started to shudder as stimms ran through it, and after a pause, a scroll began to roll out. Banting read it and let out a sigh. 'You appear fit and healthy,' he said. 'But your commanding officers – I'm not saying who, so don't bother asking – are concerned about you.'

'It was just a dizzy spell,' Minka said. 'I don't know. Maybe it was lack of breakfast. Or something.'

Banting looked at her and shook his head. 'If there is anything medical, I can help.'

She got to the door before she stopped. 'I hear some troopers are being sent for medical assessment. What's the test?'

Banting shrugged. 'The usual.'

'And what is that, specifically?'

'Physical. Medical. Mental.'

'I'm thinking about Jaromir.'

'Ah,' Banting said. 'Then you'd better pray.'

'I want to put him in for an augmetic upgrade.'

'He's not suitable.'

'Why not?'

Banting laughed. 'He was already borderline. But now... I don't think he would pass the examination. Even if you could put him forward.'

'Why can't I?'

'He wouldn't pass. He's just a common trooper.'

'What if he wasn't?'

'Who's going to promote Jaromir?' Banting asked.

Minka had nothing to say to that.

'Off you go and stay out of trouble.'

'That's it? No pills?'

He shrugged. 'You're fighting fit,' he said. 'Now get out there and stop malingering.'

Sparker laughed when Minka asked for Jaromir to be assigned for augmetics.

'I've got a queue of troopers asking for augmetics, and I can assure you that Jaromir is bottom of that list.'

'Sir. He's a fine warrior.'

'*Was,*' Sparker said. 'Was. But now...'

'I've seen him fight. He's one of the best warriors I have.'

Sparker stifled another laugh. 'Listen, Lesk. I like Jaromir. But this is a regiment, not a social club. You can't let your emotions get in the way. Sometimes you have to make tough decisions.'

Minka was furious, but it was her powerlessness that hurt the most. She did not want to see anyone, and went to the training hall. She worked till she was dripping in sweat, her arms trembling, and she had vented her fury.

V

Minka found Jaromir in the canteen. He was balancing his tray one-handed as one of the serving men spooned carb onto it.

'I've heard,' he said. He pointed with his chin to the medicae summons.

'I spoke to Banting,' she said. 'But he doesn't think he can help.'

'Thank you, sir. For trying. I didn't expect anything else.'

'I'm sorry,' she said. She didn't have other words she could express, and patted his arm and squeezed his hand and then turned away.

There were wide, shallow trays of food. Squares of fried slab. Carb mash. Soggy green piles of stewed algae. She took a chipped enamel plate and loaded up.

The far end of the canteen was the quietest, so she went to the far corner, slid her tray down, stepped over the bench and sat down, pulled her spork from her breast pocket, and started to cut the slab into chunks.

The carb was a little raw. She tried to break the lumps down into bits she could swallow. In the end, she picked the lumps out and pushed them to the side of the bowl, then finished the rest. The reconstituted slab had bits of gristle in. She chewed those down and swallowed.

She was about to leave when Confessor Talbeas sat down opposite her.

'Confessor,' Minka said by way of greeting.

Talbeas smiled. 'Do you have a few minutes?'

'Sure,' Minka said, putting her tray back down.

Talbeas made small talk. The getting-to-know-you kind of crap. Minka sat through it. She believed in the God-Emperor, but she had always put more faith in a lasgun and a grenade than she had in prayer.

'You killed the Heretic Astartes.'

Minka leant back and folded her arms. 'No,' she said. 'I did not.'

'No?'

'No,' Minka said. 'Confessor. You must get troopers telling you personal things.'

Talbeas nodded.

Minka sat forward. 'Then, to be frank, I was shit-scared. I froze. Nothing glorious about it at all. Listen. We both grew up on Cadia. The first word I learnt was "never". Each day, each night, the Eye of Terror stared down at us. You know.'

Talbeas nodded.

'But they don't know.' She pointed down the rows of tables to where the Whiteshields were sitting. 'We can try to tell them. But seeing it on a data-slate is not the same as looking up at it. That unholy scar. Of course you can tell them that when you looked at it, you could feel a pain in the back of your eye. Sometimes your nose bled. It made you nauseous. Sometimes you could see shapes in the patterns. Sometimes they were a roiling hell of uncolour. But how can they understand?'

'I'm not sure I understand what you're trying to say.'

Minka closed her eyes for a moment. 'Have you ever seen an Astartes?'

'Yes. At the victory parade on Scolap.'

'How close?'

'Half a mile.'

'He wasn't trying to kill you?'

Talbeas shook her head.

Minka put her open palm right up before Talbeas' face. 'I've been this close. Brother Skarp-Hedin of the Space Wolves Chapter. He was loyal to the God-Emperor, but he scared the shit out of me... On Cinnabar's Folly – that bastard was twice as big and he was trying to kill me. I froze.' Minka stopped. 'What did you just do?'

Talbeas said, 'I just engaged my recording unit.'

'Why?'

'This is important.'

'Do you record all confessions?'

'No. But this relates to the relic.'

'It's just a frekking staff.'

'You're wrong,' Talbeas said. 'It's Creed's banner. It is a relic. It has power.'

'You think so?'

'It's been verified by the savants, and you've seen what it's done to the regiment. How they've reacted to it, what it's meant to them to have some hope again.'

Minka took one of the lumps of carb and chewed slowly. She made a point of not speaking until she had swallowed, and rinsed out her mouth with another swig of water. 'So here's the truth,' she said. 'It's the truth I've told every time, though it doesn't seem like anyone wants to hear it. I didn't kill it. Space Marines of the Chapter known as the Black Templars put a melta shot straight through it. It was all I could do to stay conscious. Gore leaked out of its hissing wound. The stench was terrible. I thought to myself, what are the chances? I mean. What are the chances?'

Talbeas didn't understand. Minka swallowed. She felt sick again. 'What are the chances?'

'I don't know what you mean.'

'What if it's not real? What if we are being led on... Or being misled.'

'What could be wrong with hope?'

Minka smiled humourlessly. 'Do not hope, for in hope lies despair.'

Talbeas said, 'Ursarkar E. Creed.' And Minka smiled.

'Good,' she said.

When Minka got back to the barracks most of the troopers had gone off to explore their deck. But Dreno was sitting polishing his boots, lho-stick hanging from his bottom lip.

'Ah. There you are.' He took the lho-stick out. 'Someone's here to see you.'

'Who?'

He shrugged and took another puff. 'Don't know. Told him to wait inside.'

Minka saw him as soon as she came into the barrack hall for Seventh Company. He was leaning against the doorway, a mug of recaff in one hand, lho-stick in the other. Broad, muscled, augmetic eye gleaming red from a face lined with years of experience.

'You're still alive,' he said.

Minka was rigid. It was as if she had seen a ghost.

'Holy Throne!' she said.

The man paced towards her. Drab canvas trousers, Brimlock kukri lashed to his thigh, greenskin belt marking him out as a veteran of the war for Armageddon. He had lost none of that menace.

'Rath Sturm!' she said. 'Where did you come from?'

'I've been waiting for you.'

'You knew we were coming?'

He laughed as he lifted her off the floor. 'Well. I knew the Hundred-and-First were coming,' he said. 'But I didn't know if you were still with them.'

At that moment Minka saw Hontius's black silhouette appear at the end of the barracks. She grabbed Rath.

'Don't ask,' she said. 'He's haunting me.'

She dragged him away and they ended up in one of the reserve stairwells. The blast doors swung shut behind them and she let a long breath out.

The metal stairs were dimly lit with reserve lumens, set at regular intervals along each flight of steps. A broad staircase zigzagged down between the floors.

'What's up?' Rath said.

Minka shook her head. 'Commissar being officious.'

Rath nodded. He knew the problem.

They descended to the next level.

It was a good place to sit and talk. They leant against the wall, and he took a bottle from his belt. It was strong clear stuff that burnt a track down your throat and into your belly.

Rath took out a pack of lho, sniffed as he pulled out a wrapper, and sprinkled the cut leaf along its length. Then he rolled it halfway, licked the paper and rolled it tight.

'Want one?' he said, offering the lho-stick.

She took it and waited as he rolled his own. Then he took his igniter out and flicked out a flame, lighting both. She inhaled, feeling her lungs fill up with the sweet smoke. He leant back and pursed his lips, and blew long blue cones of smoke up into the darkness. She joined him. He knew how she felt.

'You're the one who found Creed's banner,' he said.

'I'm not supposed to talk about it.'

He laughed. '*Everyone* is talking about it.'

'I didn't do anything. It was on the back of a Heretic Space Marine. I just saw it.' There was a thoughtful silence. 'I still have your blade.'

She took it out. He laid it across his lap and turned it over. She'd taken good care of it. The blue steel was etched with the name *94th Kasrkin*.

He looked down. There was a long pause.

'Brothers of Death,' he remembered. He took another swig from the bottle and then handed it to her. 'Doesn't exist any more.'

They sat in silence for a long time, and after a while he reached inside his jacket and pulled out a folded sheaf of papers. The corner staple was in the shape of the aquila. He unfolded the pages and looked for his place. 'I keep this list with me. No one else will remember them.'

He carefully folded the papers and slipped them back into his pocket. Sturm's regiment of Kasrkin had manned the salient strongpoints of Kasr Myrak during the Battle of Cadia. They had died to a man, leaving only Sturm to lead the survivors in a determined resistance.

Minka nodded. 'I remember looking up to them. We all did.'

Rath smiled. 'Good. If I get killed, you'll keep my list?'

'I will.'

He stretched his legs out.

'Do you remember Taavi?' she said.

Sturm paused. 'No.'

She turned. 'Sergeant Taavi. He dug me out of the rubble...'

'Was he the skinny guy?'

She shook her head. 'No. He was short. Broad.'

Rath frowned. It wasn't coming. He remembered the battle. They had inflicted a high price upon the enemy. But in the end it didn't matter. Cadia had been destroyed. Minka had been holding them back, but at last tears started to flow. Rath put his arm around her shoulders.

They sat for a long time. He took the occasional swig to pass the time as he held her. There was a long silence. Was it ten minutes, an hour? He didn't care. He had faced the worst the galaxy could throw at him, and he was still alive. But the grog had done its work. He relaxed and stretched out.

'I froze,' Minka said. 'Before that traitor. I could not move. I was terrified.'

She didn't say any more. She didn't have to. He understood.

'The Emperor understands,' he said at last.

'Do you think so?'

Sturm nodded.

They were sitting smoking when Blanchez pushed into the stairwell. She had her primer open in her hand, her mouth moving soundlessly as she committed it all to memory.

'Oh,' she said. 'Sorry, lieutenant.'

Minka smiled. 'No worries.'

Blanchez forced a smile, and carried on past them, continuing up the stairs.

'So that's a youngblood?' Rath said.

She felt the animosity in his voice.

'She's good,' she said. 'Very good.'

'They're not Cadian.'

Minka sat up. 'You can't say that.'

Rath pulled a face. 'It's true.'

'Listen,' Minka said, 'I've fought with them and they're good.'

'I'll believe it when I see it.'

'Good,' Minka said. 'Because you'll get the chance to.'

VI

It was late in the day-night cycle when Minka finally found her bunk. It seemed that she had barely put her head down when a voice sounded.

'Lesk. You're summoned by high command!'

Minka thought she was dreaming at first, but Tyson shook her shoulder, and she jerked awake.

'You're late!' he repeated.

Minka rolled out of the cot. Her mouth was dry. Her head throbbed. She felt as though she had swallowed an ashtray.

'What for?'

'They didn't tell you?'

'Tell me what?'

'Bendikt's flyer is waiting. You're going to see the Warmaster. Hangar Seven.'

The water came in thin spurts. It was ice-cold, which at least dulled the taste of counterseptics. Minka splashed water on her face, brushed her teeth with a fresh Munitorum-issue brush, but the charcoal paste did little to remove the taste of the night's grog. She swilled it out, grabbed a piece of fried slab from the canteen, and was buttoning up her jacket as she hurried towards the landing bay.

Hangar Seven was a wide, empty space and for a moment she thought she had come too late, but then, at the far end, she saw the distinctive blunt-nosed shape of an Arvus lighter. It was not much more than a passenger compartment with wings, and a pilot cabin welded onto the front.

Minka paced across the hangar bay. The Arvus was painted in Cadian drab and had the Cadian Gate emblazoned upon it, along with the green laurels of the high command and the twinned lightning strikes that were Warmund's personal badge.

There was a bay clerk in an open office. 'This for General Bendikt?' she called.

He nodded.

'When's it leaving?'

He shrugged.

Minka sat with her back against the wall. A servo-skull sailed across the hangar and disappeared into the darkness. After an hour a fuel bogie pulled under the wing, yellow light flashing. Minka ran her tongue around her gums. She could taste lho-stick and the gummy taste of Sturm's grog.

After another half an hour a tech-priest crawled across the plating like a metallic spider, mechadendrites moving out of sync with its legs. As it woke the machine-spirit, coolants hissed from the stabiliser systems, and then an Imperial Navy pilot appeared at the far side of the hangar, raw leather jacket hung on one shoulder, goggles pushed up onto his forehead, oxygen mask hanging free. He carried his hard helmet under one hand, battery pack in the other. She watched him stride up to the pilot's cabin and lift the door open.

The clerk handed him the flight plan on a data-slate. Minka watched the pilot stop at the fixed console as a servo-skull appeared from the doorway she had come from and floated at head height across to the opposite side, and then out of sight.

He came over to her. She saw from his eyes that he was Cadian. He put out his hand. 'Esting,' he said.

'Minka Lesk. Know when we're leaving?'

Esting shook his head. 'They don't tell me that kind of thing. All I know is top brass need taking.'

He made his way back to the lighter and checked the craft. Minka watched him. She could have still been in bed, she thought. Frekkers.

She'd been waiting nearly two hours before Bendikt appeared, deep in conversation with his aides. Minka stood up and straightened, remained smart as Bendikt crossed towards her.

'Ah!' he said. 'Lieutenant Lesk. I'm glad you can join us.'

She made the sign of the aquila. 'Thank you, sir.'

The passenger compartment was not much bigger than that of a Chimera. There were metal folding seats along either side, unadorned and plain, stencilled instructions sprayed onto the wall above Bendikt's head. And there was a prayer as well. A general one, that could serve all manner of religious purposes.

Bendikt and his staff took their seats, and Minka stood until everyone else had sat down.

The engines started to warm up, and a flashing light signalled that the ramp was about to close. The hydraulics hissed as it dragged the heavy plasteel ramp up. It closed and there was a pause as the void-seal locked before the engines started to roar.

The whole craft rattled with the din. She felt the Arvus lift off the floor, and then there was the change as they passed the void-gates out into space.

Prassan leant over to her. 'You know where we are going?'

'The Warmaster.'

He seemed disappointed that she knew. 'He is going to want to question you.'

She nodded. She was too hung-over for this. 'What should I tell him?'

'The truth,' Prassan said.

'Great,' Minka said. That was simple. It was all she'd been doing since this whole mess started. But now she needed to sleep.

It took two hours to reach the Warmaster's personal deck on the *Imperial Heart*. Minka felt almost human when Prassan nudged her awake. She was alert to the sounds of docking: the clang and scrape and thud as they finally touched down.

The ramp lowered, and Bendikt led them out.

Minka stood back, letting all the others go first. They were met by an honour guard of Kasrkin. They were well drilled, efficient. The kind of troops you wanted next to you in the battle-line.

They were frisked down, and Minka let them take her kukri. She stood as Bendikt and Mere were shown inside.

'Time to wait,' Prassan said.

She nodded. She had not seen anywhere so finely ornamented. The corridors were lined with wooden panels, the door handles were brass, and the soft sound of gently chanting hymnals came from vox-grilles. Prassan looked nervous, and he started to make her feel edgy as well.

A pair of Kasrkin stood guard at the door, chests out, gaze fixed, as still as statues. She tried to catch their eyes, but there was no luck. She and Prassan stood waiting. Neither of them spoke.

The minutes stretched into hours. Minka could hear a rumble from within. It was the Warmaster. She had been standing for nearly two hours, when the door cracked open, and an attendant called, 'Lieutenant Lesk.'

The guards remained ramrod straight as Minka passed between them and through the great doorway.

The magnificence of this place took Minka's breath away. She was within the very heart of Cadian high command, a vaulting circular chamber with walls made entirely of plex-glass held in place with iron ribs, and she could feel the power and deadly seriousness in the air about her.

There had to be a hundred officials and officers inside. Almost all were Cadians, their violet eyes staring out through the bars of medals and gold braid. On the walls were fifty feet of portraits hanging in columns, one from the other, on brass chains. The faces were grim, their eyes hard.

The attendant motioned her to take a place at the side, and she stood with her back to the wall as figures moved about before a great holo-chart.

Their faces were washed with a thin green light.

The planet of El'Phanor filled the upper quadrant of the domed chamber with swathes of green and blue. The thought of the planet hanging above her disorientated Minka for a moment. She had the odd feeling that she was standing upside down as she took in the rest of the chamber.

Crystal chandeliers hung from the ceiling on long brass chains, and sandalwood smoke gently fell from vast brass censers that swung above her. There was a bank of servitors, their quills scratching away, scrolls of vellum unravelling before them. A cogitator's fans whirred in the background, but Minka could only take these details in within a few seconds, as her attention fixed upon the dais before her, where Lord Militant Warmund paced before his throne.

He was more than a brick. He was a rockcrete wall. Blunt, brutal, with heavy brows and a curly mop of black hair over stone-hard violet eyes.

The minutes passed as sweat dripped down Minka's back. At last, Lord General Bendikt was summoned forward.

Warmund's voice boomed out. 'Your people have confirmed it?'

'Correct,' Bendikt said.

The lord militant took the banner-pole from him and set its base-spike into the floor. He looked at it and shook his head. His battlefield-enhanced voice was so deep Minka felt the lord militant's growl go through her innards.

'My savants believe it is real, as well,' Warmund said.

'I knew it the moment I saw it,' Bendikt said. He turned and found Minka among the crowd. 'This is the lieutenant who recovered it.'

Minka's breath caught in her throat. She stepped smartly forward. Her whole body trembled with the deep timbre of Warmund's voice.

'You are she?' he said.

'Yes, sir,' Minka said, coughing to clear her throat. 'Lieutenant Lesk, Cadian Hundred-and-First, Hell's Last.'

'Ah!' he said. 'I remember you. You fought at the fall.'

'Yes, sir.'

'One of our last Whiteshields. Your name was mentioned in dispatches. I've been following your career.'

'Thank you, sir.'

'You're a true Cadian, Lesk. Now, tell me how you found this sacred relic.'

Minka told him in brief. As she spoke, he turned away from her and held the banner-pole in one hand. At the end he said, 'The Black Templars. Why were they involved?'

'I do not know, sir.'

Warmund looked at the banner-pole again. He turned it in the light, so that the gilded mount glittered.

At last he turned to Minka and said, 'Do you think Creed is still alive?'

'I do not know, sir.'

'What do you *think?*'

Minka paused. 'I have never been so inspired as I was on Cadia. Before the fall.'

Warmund nodded. 'Yes, but if he was still with us, why haven't we heard of him? If he is still alive, then where are the battles, the counter-offensives?'

Minka had nothing to say. It was Bendikt who spoke. 'The Black Templars commander said that the heretic who carried this banner, his warband came from beyond the Ghost Nebula, on the fringes of the Cicatrix Maledictum.'

Warmund considered. 'It is possible, but it would take a great many assumptions and conveniences. Why would he have ended up here, and why would we have never heard of him?'

'Sir,' Bendikt said. 'The Archenemy would hunt him to the ends of the galaxy, and do all it could to keep us from finding him.'

Warmund thought about this. 'We must remain alert. Victory is at hand. We are driving the forces of Drakul-zar back, and their retreat is turning into a rout. Soon we will have captured him and brought him to justice. My savants have listed the Hundred-and-First for disbanding...'

Bendikt started to speak and Warmund smiled. 'But I shall countermand that order. I think your regiment have proved their worth. I have issued an order to the Munitorum. I am assigning the Hundred-and-First a full refit. Cadians, transplants from other regiments – the best of the rest – and a full complement of Whiteshields from the training world of Karnak. Top-notch, by all accounts.'

'Thank you,' Bendikt said. He started to go on, but Warmund put his hand out to shake that of the lord general.

'Welcome back,' he said. 'Once you have been brought back to full strength, the Hundred-and-First will be transferred planetside with due haste. When your regiment has been judged to be battle ready, I will consider future deployment.'

He spoke quickly, his tone implying that Bendikt was now dismissed, but the lord general remained standing before him, even as one of Warmund's attendants tried to shoo him away.

'Sir,' Bendikt said, 'I request that the Hundred-and-First are posted to the front lines as soon as we are brought to full strength.'

'Refused,' Warmund said.

Bendikt did not move. 'I do not want anyone saying that the Hundred-and-First are battle-shy.'

Warmund's expression hardened. 'No one doubts the courage of the Hundred-and-First. Nor yours, Isaia. Nor indeed your commitment to Cadia.' There were chuckles from the back of the room, where Minka stood. She felt the tension rise as Warmund's voice rumbled through them all. 'Your troopers need a rest. When you have bedded in the reinforcements then we shall consider.'

Bendikt's cheeks coloured. 'Sire. I petitioned–'

'Yes!' Warmund boomed suddenly, stunning them all. 'I know you did, Bendikt! I know. I know.'

The lord militant stood and paced up and down from one side of his dais to the other. Warmund made a sound in his throat that was like the rumble of a lion. 'Use your time well. We shall call upon you when the time is ripe.'

His words were spoken with such emphasis that Minka felt the air humming about her. She feared that Bendikt would speak again, but Mere stepped forward and the lord general understood.

'Thank you, sir,' he said, and made the sign of the aquila, and Minka followed them out of the chamber.

No one spoke as Bendikt led them back along the ornate corridor to the hangar. Minka came at the back of the file. The backs of Bendikt and Mere, and their guards, filled her gaze as Prassan slipped back to walk beside her.

'How did it go?' he mouthed.

Minka pulled a face. Not well.

In the broad thoroughfare, they passed an embassy from the Munitorum. The ambassador's robes reached down to his felt boots, and his augmetic eyes gleamed with a fierce red light that seemed to run over each of them in turn, like a targeting augur.

The ambassador and Bendikt nodded to each other, but no one spoke until they got to the hangar, where Arvus lighters were waiting to return legations back to their quarters.

Mere stepped forward to engage the officer in charge. He pointed to the Arvus they had come in.

'This way,' he said.

The ramp was open. Minka noted that they had been given a new pilot. She was already making her way out from the mess hall, leather helmet in hand, comms wires looping under her arm from her augmetic earpiece.

Bendikt stepped inside, one hand on the ceiling crew rail. One by one they took their places along the benches. As they settled inside, Mere pulled a canvas bag from under the bench.

'Good news,' Mere said as he handed round the tin mugs. There was a bottle of amasec as well. Arcady Pride.

Bendikt said nothing until he had drained his beaker. He put it out for a refill and nodded.

'Creed is out there. I know it. I can feel it here!'

He punched his chest.

Minka took a sip and felt her headache easing.

Bendikt was already on his third drink as Mere eased him off the topic of Creed and onto the reconstitution of the regiment. Bendikt nodded. Yes, it was great news. The regimental refit, armour, Whiteshields – the might of Cadia deployed once more.

Minka's interest faded. Facing Warmund had taken its toll. Her eyelids grew increasingly heavy, and she could no longer keep them up. She could hear them making plans as she dozed, and Bendikt fretting about them being on-planet, waiting for another engagement.

'It could take months, years!' she heard him say as she switched position and dozed once more.

The noise of docking woke her with a start. She straightened up and wiped her mouth. Bendikt waited for her as they dismounted.

'I wanted to thank you,' he said.

'There are no thanks needed,' she said. 'I just did my duty, sir.'

'You did indeed. Very well. Sparker has spoken highly of you. In fact, I need you to step up. We all need to step up.' She looked at him, not quite understanding what he was saying. 'I need you to lead one of our companies, Lesk. I need troopers I can rely on.'

He took her hand and pressed something into it. 'Congratulations, Captain Lesk.'

She felt the colour drain from her face as she stared down at a captain's badge. 'No, sir,' she started. 'I'm not ready for this!'

'Many years ago, Creed said to me, "With faith and courage and good leadership, anything is possible."'

'Yes,' she said, 'but…'

'Trust me,' Bendikt said, 'we are never ready for the command that is thrust upon us.'

Minka forced a smile. 'Thank you, sir.'

As news spread, Sparker was one of the first to come and congratulate Minka. He found her in the canteen, and made his way to where she was sitting. 'Seventh Company will be in good hands.'

Minka felt guilty taking his company off him. 'Where are you going?'

'Eighth Company. Armoured. Don't worry. You'll be fine. I'm giving you Tyson.'

'Ah…' Minka said. 'Isn't there someone else?'

Sparker laughed and slapped her arm. 'Yes, but I've got him.'

Minka stood on the command deck as Bendikt made a short speech, introducing the newcomers.

'Who's that?' she asked Sparker. She pointed to a tall, angular-featured man standing on the dais next to Mere.

'Can't remember his name. Sanctioned psyker.'

'I've never fought with one of those before,' Minka said.

'I have,' Sparker replied. 'Scared the shit out of me.'

Bendikt introduced the man, in the end, as Valentian. He carried a staff that bore the symbol of the Adeptus Astra Telepathica. The same motif repeated across his uniform, and it was inked into his cheek.

'Greetings,' Valentian said. His voice was deep, and Minka found herself drawn to him. Commissar Salice stood just behind him, with two Kasrkin.

The psyker was handsome in the manner of a marble statue – it was a cold, hard, chiselled beauty, but with the guards behind him he looked more like a prisoner.

As she watched him, he turned and caught her eye.

Yes, the look seemed to say, *if I lose control of my powers, they are here to execute me.*

'Can he read minds?' she whispered.

Sparker shook his head. 'I don't know. I'd just stay away from him.'

Sturm had been announced as the commander of Second Company. Minka could barely believe she was to serve with him again, and he sought her out at the end and slapped her on the shoulder.

'I hear they made you captain,' Sturm said. 'Which company?'

She told him. He nodded. 'Who's the colour sergeant?'

'Tyson.'

'Is he good?'

'Scares the shit out of me.'

Sturm laughed. 'Good. That's exactly what you want.'

Next day everyone was supposed to move to their allotted companies' quarters.

Colour Sergeant Tyson was already in the Seventh Company office when Minka arrived.

He stood and put his hand out. 'Welcome, sir,' he said. 'I am proud to be serving under you.'

He held up the roll-call of Seventh Company. 'We've done pretty well. We kept our core. Got Viktor and Orugi. But we also got Dreno. And some arse named Octavian Grüber.'

Minka didn't know him.

'Met him this morning,' Tyson said. 'His uncle was Maximus Octavian Grüber the Third. Died on Faith's Anchorage. Best thing he ever did. And this one is his grand-nephew.'

'Right.'

At that moment there was a knock on the door, and a figure

pushed in. He was tall and slim, with deep-set eyes and an angular nose.

He put his hand out. 'You must be Minka Lesk. I am Octavian Grüber,' he said. 'My uncle was...'

'Maximus Octavian Grüber the Third,' Minka said. 'And it's *Captain* Lesk.'

He was a good-looking man, and on his chest he wore the Eagle Merit medal. The steel caught the light and it suddenly struck her.

'I see you have heard of him. Good, now I would like some of your time...' Grüber said.

'I'm sorry, lieutenant. Something has just come up. Tyson.' She pulled the brown cardboard file out of the chest of drawers, found the form she was looking for. 'Colour sergeant. Can you help Lieutenant Grüber? I have an urgent case.'

Tyson's face was dark. 'Sure. Where are you going?'

Minka was already halfway through the door.

'I have an augmetic request to put in,' she said.

VII

The next few days were hectic as fresh troopers found their new companies, and new officers and sergeants found their feet.

'The stripes. How are they feeling?' Sparker asked her as she finished her breakfast and slid her mess tray into the kitchen window.

'Good,' Minka said. She had stitched her captain stripes on the night before and, of course, they did not feel right. The thickly woven cloth was stiff. She felt its resistance every time she moved her arm.

He slid his own tray into place beside her and then felt in his breast pocket for a lho-stick. He offered her one and she shook her head.

'Leading a company. I don't know how I got here. I keep thinking someone is going to catch me out,' she said.

Sparker laughed. 'I think we all feel that.'

'Not everyone,' Minka said.

Sparker looked to see who she was talking about.

Lieutenant Octavian Grüber stood out from the crowd. His voice had a braying quality. 'Ah, yeah. Sorry you got him.'

Octavian felt their gaze and looked up.

'I saw Jaromir this morning,' Sparker said. 'On the way to the medicae.'

Minka smiled. 'Yes. How was he?'

'A little shocked.'

'Hmm,' Minka said. 'I'll go and see him later.'

'I don't think he will be conscious till tomorrow. That was quite some plan you pulled. An augmetic for an ordinary trooper is a stretch, but a trooper in a company command squad? That held a lot more weight.'

'Yes,' Minka said. 'I got Prassan to help me. He's being made our quartermaster, so he worked out an upgrade.'

'Let's hope he's worth it.'

'Oh, I think he's proved that already.'

The morning was taken up with company business. She and Tyson met her platoon commanders one by one.

'First up,' Tyson said. 'Lieutenant Sargora. Catachan. Highly decorated. She's broken someone's arm already.'

'Who?'

Tyson shook his head. 'Some prat called Caspian.'

Minka had never met a Catachan before, but she had heard stories and when Sargora entered, Minka was not disappointed – the lieutenant was short and squat, with the muscles of an ogryn. She had been lieutenant in her previous regiment, and clearly thought she should have been promoted.

Sargora squared off against Minka. 'You're young,' she said.

'I am.'

Sargora nodded to herself. She was clearly reserving judgement.

'I hear you've broken someone's arm.'

'Yes,' Sargora said. 'He challenged me to an arm wrestle. I pretended to let him win. My hand was an inch from the table when I pushed his hand back...'

Tyson was listening closely. It was clear that Sargora was missing out some of the details he thought important.

'He was a Kasr Tyrok lad. Set his boots on the floor, hitched his trousers up. Thought he was in for an easy win...'

Sargora had a strangely humourless manner to her. 'Torsion,' she said. 'I've seen it happen before. The upper arm bone cannot endure such stress. It snapped straight through. To be fair, he barely let out a moan.'

Tyson laughed. 'And Lieutenant Sargora looked about and said, "Anyone else?"'

'Want to prove yourself?' Sargora said.

'No,' Minka said and slapped the lieutenant's arm. It was like slapping rock. 'I'm delighted to have you leading my First Platoon. Look at you! You don't need to prove anything.'

Elias Orugi had been promoted to lieutenant leading Second Platoon, and Viktor to Third. Neither man said much, but they were clearly taking their promotions very seriously.

'It doesn't feel right,' Viktor said, looking at his badge.

Minka smiled. 'I know. But the Emperor expects. Your platoons will be working with Sargora.'

'We've met,' Orugi said, running his hand over his freshly shaven scalp.

Viktor paused. 'Are you expecting any difficulties?'

'She's a bit prickly,' Minka said, 'but she seems solid enough.'

Once she had met her platoon commanders, Minka skipped lunch to go to the medicae.

Vasily was at the door talking to two of the nurses. He didn't pay her much attention, and she waited till he looked up.

'Can I help?' he said, in a *why-are-you-here?* kind of way.

'I'm looking for Trooper Ostin Jaromir.'

Vasily paused. 'He's just come out of theatre.'

'I know. I just want to see him.'

Vasily didn't say anything, but his manner said that she should follow him.

'How did it go?' she said.

'We'll find out when he wakes,' Vasily said.

Vasily left Minka at the doorway.

Jaromir's was the only bed inside. The room was quiet, apart from the low slush of the blood pump. Minka walked across to where he lay. The stump was wrapped in bandages, with tubes to syphon off the inflammation.

Prassan had promised her something good, but she looked down at Jaromir's new arm and didn't know whether to laugh or cry. There were many grades of augmetics, from simple metal claws, to ones that perfectly mimicked human musculature. Prassan had done Jaromir proud. This was a fine Militarum model, with exposed pistons and a crude, three-fingered hand.

'It might be second-hand,' Prassan had warned her, but it did not matter. This arm would keep him fighting.

After a long while she stepped closer and rested on the edge of the bed. Jaromir's blond hair had fallen over one of his eyes. She brushed it away, her fingers touching the steel plate that covered his scalp.

She sat, listening to the blood pump churn away, as Jaromir's breaths came slowly in and out.

'Don't worry, you will fight again,' she said softly as she took his good hand in hers, and held it.

It was a rare moment of stillness. She hadn't thought of Dido for a long time – her lieutenant, when Minka had been a sergeant, unsure of herself and lost to the prospect of command. Without Dido, Minka did not know where she would be. And now, she was gone. It was easier to not remember, sometimes, and if there was one person she could have saved from death it would have been her.

She sat as the blood pump swished back and forth. It sounded like waves on the shore of the Calcuades Sea. She wept a silent tear, and then, on an impulse, she bent over him and kissed Jaromir's forehead.

'Cadia stands,' she whispered, and she stood a moment longer, cheeks dried, before closing the door behind her.

When Minka got back, a small man was waiting outside her office. She saw his rank and suddenly remembered. 'Lieutenant Senik,' she said. 'I'm so sorry. I had to go to the medicae. Have you been waiting long?'

'Don't worry, I had nothing else to do,' Senik said, pushing himself off the wall as she opened the door to her office. 'Just kicking around.'

'You're new, yes?'

'To the Hundred-and-First, yes,' he said, stepping inside and looking about the room. 'I came from the Nine-Hundred-and-Seventeenth. There weren't many of us left by the end… I hear you did well with Lieutenant Sargora.'

Minka laughed. 'Did I? Where did you hear that?'

Senik scratched his cheek. He was missing the smaller two fingers on his right hand and a large chunk of his palm. 'From Lieutenant Sargora,' he replied.

'Oh,' Minka said. 'Good. Just as long as she doesn't break anyone else's arm.'

Senik laughed. 'Yes. We'll all be grateful for her aggression. I'm sure of that.'

Senik had the violet eyes of a Cadian, but his accent was not one that she knew. 'Which kasr were you from?' she asked.

'Kasr Gehr. Though the city elders would turn me away, if they still lived.' He pulled his sleeve up. About his wrist was an entwined tattoo of thorns. And above it a number. *D-3376540.*

'St Josmane's Hope?' she said.

He nodded. 'I was a shit of a kid. Got into the gangs. Smuggling and that kind of stuff. Was caught. Got sentenced. Thirty years. That was a death sentence. No one lasts thirty years on Josmane's Hope.

'Each night, in our barracks, we were subjected to voxed prayers. It was like battering against a rockcrete wall. But one night something made me think. And I understood. I had been given the chance to join the finest fighting force in the Imperium of Man and I had frekked it all up. I could have been a shock trooper, and here I was in a penal camp, cold and hungry and bitter. I could have wept. I had been so stupid.'

He pursed his lips. 'After that I was the best convict there ever was. I did the work of five men and one day they brought me in and gave me the enforcer badge. Tossed it across the table to me. Just in time...

'Six months later the revolt broke out. It spread so fast we could not stop it. The convicts were mad. I did not know whose side any of them were on. We were just shooting all of them. And we were running out of hard rounds. We had already started falling back when Creed ordered Exterminatus. It was panic then. The Emperor had given me a second chance and I was not going to die on that frekking world. Nothing was going to stop me getting onto that evacuation lighter.

'Nothing.' He laughed. 'Throne. I had two home worlds blown up before me in the space of a few months.'

'I'm sure the Hundred-and-First will be a breeze after that,' Minka said and shook his three-fingered hand. 'Welcome to the Seventh Company.'

'How long have we got?'

'Before we're assigned? I don't know. HQ reckons Drakul-zar has fallen back to raise new armies. As soon as he lifts his banner, we'll be there to smash him down.'

As Senik left, Orugi arrived. He shook hands with the other man and waited for him to leave.

'Sir,' he said. 'I have a request. When we are on the planet, I'd like to visit the Mausoleum of the Fallen Cadians. My brother is there and I'd like to go and pay my respects to him.'

'Of course,' Minka said. 'I didn't know you had a brother.'

Orugi nodded. 'His name was Jacul. After my father. He was killed five years ago. Clearing of Sporehive Slum City. On Gilgamesh.'

'That would be an excellent idea,' Minka said. 'In fact, I think we should all go. Pay our respects.'

VIII

Three days later the reinforcements were complete and the Cadian 101st were readying for disembarkation to the planet's surface. Mere's staff officers of the 101st had acquired lodgings at the southern pole, and their armour, repainted in ice camo of fractured white and blue and grey, was already loaded up for transfer to the planet's surface.

Prassan had been appointed regimental quartermaster, and he felt as though he had barely slept for three days. Food supplies were the last thing he had managed to acquire after a tussle with the Munitorum's lord quartermaster, who seemed to think that it was his job to never give anything out at all.

Each night he weighed the responsibility upon his shoulders, he had the sense of logistical vertigo. What if there were no boots or powercells or hostile-terrain suits?

The worry kept him up long after the day cycle had ended. He checked his own staff's work but could not find fault. They had done more than was expected of them, which was pretty much what he expected of them.

In those three days the barracks and canteens were busier than they had been for years. The 101st had been brought back to full strength for the first time since the fall. There were so many new faces to put to names. Minka found it all exhausting.

'Everyone does,' Colonel Sparker said to her the day before embarkation. They were in the drill hall, and there was barely space to throw down a mat. She let the bolter magazine drop for the last time. It hit the ground with a solid thud.

She pushed the sweat and hair from her face with the back of her arm. 'It's the admin that is getting me,' she said as she pulled a hand towel from the rack. 'If I want to get my morning drill in, I have to get up an hour earlier.'

'So, how did you do it?'

'What?'

'I saw Jaromir's new arm. That's not a trooper's upgrade.'

'Ah,' she said. 'Jaromir is a decorated veteran with the Silver Skull, and part of my command squad. Banting didn't even blink. Approval went straight through.'

Sparker shook his head. 'You're good,' he said.

'I hope so,' Minka told him.

That afternoon, Minka had just finished addressing her platoon commanders when Prassan arrived. He hung at the back of the room as she addressed questions. Sargora wanted to tell her what she thought, and then there was Octavian Grüber as well, who said, 'How long will we be training on El'Phanor for?'

'I don't know,' she said, 'but you can trust high command. It will be enough.'

'I've got a lot of youngbloods,' he said.

'Lucky you. They'll be ripe for training as you see fit,' she told him.

As the officers filed out, Prassan came forward. 'Come with me.'

'Where to?'

'I can't tell you...' Prassan said. 'There's an old general wants to see "the lieutenant who found Creed's banner".'

'This is not a good time,' Minka said.

Prassan smiled. 'You won't regret it. Promise.'

Prassan barely spoke as he pulled her through the corridors to one of the main access routes, where he had a staff car waiting.

They climbed into the back. It was an hour's journey on the spinward orbital. They passed all manner of internal traffic. Mostly cargo-12s ferrying supplies throughout the great craft. But there was also a column of unpainted Leman Russ tanks, fresh from the forge world, awaiting their logos and numbers.

'Here,' Prassan said. He pulled over into a slip road that read *Sector 9A*.

'Who is this general?'

'I can't tell you.'

'But he wants to meet me?'

'Yes.'

'I might be a bit of a disappointment.'

'Come on,' Prassan said.

When they arrived, a servitor let them through a heavy blast door. The groundcar was stacked into a parking bay, as Kasrkin guards showed Prassan and Minka into a side chamber.

'The Archenemy have tried to kill him a number of times,' Prassan said as he removed his sidearm.

Minka followed suit. She tipped out her pockets, slid her battle-knife onto the tabletop. One of the Kasrkin picked it up.

'Not bad,' he said.

The other Kasrkin frisked her legs and the small of her back, then along her arms, and then signalled that they could both go inside.

Prassan pulled her through a doorway into a dark chamber. There was no light, only the flicker of candles set before a wall-shrine. The scent was a musty mix of old uniforms, incense and counterseptics.

'Lord General Creed,' Prassan said in a low voice. 'I have brought her.'

'Come,' a voice said. It crackled with age. Minka was trembling. It took her eyes a moment to grow accustomed to the darkness. There was the wheeze of a blood pump, a figure sitting in a wing-back chair, an army blanket pulled over his knees.

It was a man, shrunken with age.

One of his eyes was augmetic, but even its red light looked wan and pale. It flickered, like a faulty lumen. 'Come closer, child, where I can see you. What is your name?'

She knelt before the old man. 'Arminka Lesk.'

'You are the one?'

She nodded.

'Creed's banner.' There was a long pause as the ancient general patted her hand. His skin was thin and cool. 'We weren't related, you know. I wish I could have been there…' In the darkness a carriage clock struck the half-hour. He let the chimes fade away before he said, 'Three hundred and twenty-eight years and I've never been back. But it's all there! Clear as day. There are times I can barely remember what I had for breakfast. But I remember Cadia. Oh yes! Left when I was just fifteen. Never went back…'

He sighed and seemed to forget what he was saying. Minka thought she should remind him, but then he said, 'I should be dead by all accounts. Of course, they keep me alive.' He wet his lips. 'I met him, you know? Ursarkar E. Creed. We had lunch together. He was on his way to Cadia. He said he had been dying to meet me his whole life. Him wanting to meet me! Can you believe it?'

He paused as he tried to regain his train of thought.

'I served well, but it was a mediocre career. I wanted to die in battle. But I kept surviving. Maybe I should have been bolder. I never wanted to grow old, and now look at me – they won't let me die!'

Minka could feel Prassan standing behind her.

'Both of us were from the same kasr,' the old man said. 'I guess that we could have been related. But I had no one to ask. People say I look like him.'

Minka nodded. Perhaps, she thought, trying to put the bull-necked image of the Lord Castellan through three hundred years.

Perhaps.

'We were on Katak. It was a training world. He emptied it. Took every healthy trooper we had. "It is the hour of need," he said to me. "Only by our full strength can we hope to win." I begged to go. Appealed against the decision that I should stay. I gave him a bottle of amasec. The very best stuff. I'd been given it as a gift and kept it for years. He drank the whole lot. Would have knocked out a grox. But he was on good form. Barely slowed him. At the end he slapped my arm and bade me farewell. Know what the last thing he said to me was?'

Minka shook her head.

'He said, "Don't worry. We won't let it fall."'

The general let out a long breath.

'Alas, he was wrong.'

Minka nodded again. She didn't have anything else to say about that.

There was a long pause.

'What is your rank?' General Ursarkar Creed said.

'Captain.'

'How long for?'

'Three days,' she said.

He half laughed, half choked. 'How is it going?'

'So-so.'

The old man leant forward. 'It's simple. Get the best troopers promoted. You'll need good sergeants. And they need troopers ready to fill their place.' He seemed to forget what he was going to say and patted her hand. 'I hear they're letting non-Cadians join. I don't approve,' he said. 'It's not right.'

'We had to,' she told him. 'It was that or die out. The new recruits have proved themselves.'

The old man made a sound in his throat, as if he was about to disagree, but the words and the noise died away.

'They ask me to make speeches, you know? To stir up the spirits of our Cadians. That is why they keep me alive...'

'We all serve as we are asked.'

He nodded. There was a scratch at the door. Creed said, 'I'm needed. Thank you for coming. You'd better go.' She started to stand, but he held on to her for a moment longer.

'The Emperor is watching you,' he said and wagged a finger at her. 'He has great plans for you. Remember that!'

When he let go, Minka made the sign of the aquila.

'Cadia stands,' he said.

'Cadia stands,' she answered.

It was a quiet journey back.

Eventually, Prassan broke the silence. 'A great man,' he said.

'I feel like I've been in a museum,' Minka replied.

'Why?'

Minka paused. 'He's the past. All of it. Cadia. The kasrs. How long till the last of us is dead? It's all going to fade away.' She sighed. 'To be Cadian is something else now.'

'And what is that?'

Minka thought for a long time. 'I don't know. It's up to us to define it. We can be more than Cadians. "Get the best troopers promoted," he said. You know who's one of my finest? Blanchez, and she never even saw Cadia.'

She fell silent. At last she said, 'To be better than those who went before us. *That* would be the best tribute to Cadia.'

Next morning the 101st made their way to the embarkation hangars. The procedure went smoothly enough, considering. Seventh Company finished half an hour ahead of schedule, which seemed like a good start for Minka.

'All aboard?' she said to Tyson as the colour sergeant paced towards her, hands clasped behind his back.

'All correct, sir.'

She took them all in – hundreds of troopers sitting with their packs, waiting on her command as the ramps started to rise and the tech-priests and Navy ratings made their final checks.

The ramps closed as the lighter's engines reached a crescendo, and then they took off. Minka closed her eyes.

The Cadians fell quiet. Most slept. A few wanted to see Jaromir's new arm. His stump was still bandaged, his new limb hanging across his body in a sling.

At the far end, Dreno pulled out a pack of cards from his breast pocket. They were worn and roughened, with a rubber band holding them all together. He looked around for someone to play with. He caught Minka's eye and she half smiled, then shook her head.

In the end Baine joined him. 'Come on, you cheating bastard,' he said.

An hour passed. And then there was a change in the tone of the engines.

Minka sat up. Throughout the compartment the other Cadians were doing the same. Dreno caught her eye again over his hand of cards.

There was the whining sound of landing gear being lowered, and then a *clunk* as they settled onto the deck. They could not be on the planet so soon, but where were they?

Tyson shook his head.

There was a hiss as the ramp seals broke. Minka was on her feet at once.

'Keep them calm,' she shouted out. 'I'll see what's happening.'

Three hours later, the 101st had disembarked into the hangar of a void-craft. They could hear the clangs as packed containers were loaded into the craft's belly, hear the hum of plasma generators starting to be lit.

The vast bulk of the Ramilies-class star fort filled the portholes, and behind it was the planet itself, with its clear blue water and bands of green. No one seemed to know why they were here and not planetside.

'Cock-up or frekk-up,' Baine said. That was the explanation for most things, but no one knew, and if they did, no one was telling them.

Dreno stood looking out at the blue bands of water, glistening in the light of the system's star. 'I was looking forward to breathing clean air again.'

Orugi nodded but said nothing.

After three hours, Minka came back. Her platoon commanders gathered round her. 'So this is what I know,' Minka said.

'We're on the Overlord-class battle cruiser *Cypra Probatii.* And she's due to lift anchor in six hours.'

'Where to?' Grüber called out.

Minka shook her head. 'I don't know.'

IX

The chains were already being hauled in to anchor the Arvus Lighter down as Bendikt stepped out and into the hangar. The whole regiment watched him as he spoke to Ostanko and Sturm. His movements were animated, excited. Minka felt the atmosphere change as a fuel loader was drawn up so that Bendikt could address them all.

The companies of the 101st crammed about it, and at last Bendikt climbed up and put his hands out for silence. 'Brothers and sisters, thank you for your patience! I have come from an audience with the Warmaster himself…' He let those words sink in. 'This is embargoed information, but I know that I can trust you all!'

There was laughter.

Bendikt waited for silence. 'You know that Drakul-zar was defeated at Joalara and that he had fallen back to raise new armies of heresy… Word has reached us that Drakul-zar has been assassinated.'

The Cadians greeted the news in stunned silence.

'The Scourged are crumbling. The whole battlefront is like a rotten door. All we have to do is kick it in.'

Bendikt put his hands out and the cheers died away.

'The Warmaster has entrusted us with a great opportunity. Our mission is to strike deep into the heart of the enemy and seize the world of Telken's Rest. Our orders are to raise the aquila upon the world and to garrison it and hold it for the God-Emperor of Mankind! We shall turn their retreat into a rout.'

They greeted that with a cheer as Bendikt helped another man up onto the back of the fuel loader.

All eyes strained to see as the old man was brought forward, and then Bendikt announced the speaker. 'Lord General Ursarkar Creed!'

At that name the whole regiment fell silent. Minka's skin goose-pimpled.

'Cadians!' The old man's voice rang out, stronger and more forceful than the one that Minka had heard in his private quarters.

'I was born in Kasr Gallen, over three hundred years ago.' His words echoed from the bare walls of the hangar and every Cadian bent forward a little closer as the old man went on, his voice growing in purpose.

'Since that time I have fought shoulder to shoulder with the finest men and women that the Imperium has ever seen. I wish I could fight still. It would be an honour to take my place alongside you all. I would bleed and die with you. When your moment comes, thank the God-Emperor that it is upon the battlefield. For there is no greater honour than to die in the service of the Emperor. I know. Look at me!

'You do not want to suffer the indignity of old age. Far better to fall in battle.'

Minka's eye fell on where Jaromir stood. He frowned with concentration as his three fingers opened and closed.

'The men and women of the Imperium – they all sleep well because of you and your sacrifice. Shadows are always plotting our destruction.

'Heretic, xenos, alien, traitor. *Your* duty is to fight that which threatens the Imperium of Man. And remember what my namesake said.

'"Cadia stands!"'

Bendikt's eyes were glistening as he stepped down from the fuel loader and caught Mere's eye.

The cheers were still echoing as the *Cypra Probatii* slipped its berth and began to move towards the Mandeville point. Ursarkar Creed remounted the Arvus and returned to the *Imperial Heart*, and one by one the companies marched off to their berths.

Bendikt watched them pass before him with pride. He was exultant. 'The Brutal Stars will be ours. He's out there, Mere! The Emperor has chosen us. I can feel it. And we will be the ones to find him!'

PART III

I

TELKEN'S REST

Ukara Khond sat whetting her blade upon the broken stalactite. Each sweep of her knife filled the cave with the rasp of cold steel. As the slave was dragged towards her she held the blade up, brushed the residue away and turned the edge to the light to see the gleam of the freshly honed steel.

The warriors holding the slave kicked out his knees and pulled his arms up behind his back to force him into a kneeling position. The chanting rose to a fever pitch as she took the man by the hair, put her boot into the middle of his back, and yanked his head towards her.

The low chant of the Kukulati went on, but the rest of the room was silent. Even the gods stopped to watch as she put her war-blade to the man's neck, and then cut down.

She held him as he kicked and writhed, as if she wanted to soothe his ending. But the truth was, the ceremony was not yet over. As his death throes ebbed, she walked around him, put her boot upon his naked chest and ran her blade across his belly.

The thin membrane of muscle peeled open, the tangled entrails spilled out.

'Haruspex!' she hissed.

The soothsayer was a hunched, mutant figure, crawling towards her. He stopped at the edge of the blood and two of his hands wrapped one onto the other, while the third tugged his hood forward. 'Oh, terrible one!' he hissed, his voice sibilant through his sharpened teeth.

She pointed at the dead man's entrails.

There were two heads within the mutant's hood. His breathing came fast and excited as Haruspex reached into the warm entrails, pushing and lifting as he searched for the messages hidden within.

Two hands pulled the guts aside as the third lifted the liver clear. It was blotched and pale, hard yellow lumps forming on its surface. The mutant turned it in his hand, examining its shape, and then dug his thumbnails in and tore it open.

The break was ragged and bloody, the texture within was hard.

'The toxins make it hard to read,' Haruspex whispered from one mouth as the other muttered to itself.

Ukara stood as the sibilant voices went back and forth between the two heads.

'It bleeds too freely,' one voice said.

'You tore it too soon,' said the other.

'He is not yet dead,' the first one decided.

The fragments of conversation continued as Ukara waited.

'What does that mean?' she said at last.

'They are coming,' one voice said.

'The blind man speaks, but what does he say?' returned the other.

Finally the heads fell silent.

Ukara demanded, 'What does it say?'

Haruspex's heads sucked their teeth as they tried to understand the meaning within.

'Here,' they said as one. 'He is here, on Telken's Rest.'

'And will we find him?' Ukara demanded.

The two heads murmured to one another as they turned the halves of liver over and over. She demanded so much of them and the gods were never clear.

At last one of them spoke. 'Yes. You will find him. But beware the blind man. You must cut out his tongue. The blind man speaks.'

II

The journey through the warp took three weeks.

They arrived in-system without opposition and made straight for Telken's Rest. Scout units landed first of all, at Pyre's Gate. Minka was with the company commanders as Mere ran through the final intelligence.

The holo-projector showed the planet. It was a dirty ice ball on the spinward fringes of the Brutal Stars. Its only importance came from the fact that it lay on one of the most stable warp routes across the Ghost Nebula. Warmund had sent them deep into hostile territory to seize this world and cut off retreating units.

Minka watched the psyker, Valentian, as Mere ran through a series of details. He kept his eyes closed, as if listening for something.

When Mere said, 'Here is the major space port facility, Pyre's Gate,' Minka willed her gaze away from the psyker to the holo-map. It showed a dirty little sprawl of stilt-habs and factorum districts within an encircling ice wall. 'City is divided into gang territories,' Mere continued. 'We're going in hard.'

'How should we deal with gangers we come across?' Sparker asked.

Mere said simply, 'With extreme intolerance. This world has spent a decade lost to the Imperium of Man. We are returning it to the Emperor's peace. And that means peace.'

The adjutant went through the orders one more time.

'Are you sure there's no resistance?' Sturm called out.

'Correct,' Mere said. 'Intelligence suggests it has not been garrisoned for a number of years. There're signs the place was shored up and defended once, but now there doesn't seem to be anything waiting down there for us.' He pre-empted any questions. 'We don't know why they left.'

Talk went on for a little while longer, and at last the intelligence briefing came to an end.

Minka walked out thinking that she had not learnt much.

'So that was the intelligence,' a voice said. She turned and saw Sanctioned Psyker Valentian. He had that way of looking right through you. She didn't like it and she didn't trust it.

'Seems a bit thin,' he said. 'Let's hope they're right. About the lack of a garrison, that is.'

She nodded.

He fell in step beside her. 'You're the one who found the banner.'

'Yes,' she said.

'Bendikt has talked of nothing else the entire trip. He thinks Creed will be here.'

'Well, my orders don't say anything about Creed.'

'Keep your eyes open,' Valentian said, very seriously. It was only afterwards, when she replayed that conversation in her head, that she couldn't tell if he had been joking or not.

* * *

That evening she went through the charts with her platoon commanders.

'We're here,' she said, 'in the Western Habs. Orders are to pacify. We're not expecting much resistance.'

'Who is looking after that flank?' Grüber said, pointing to the factorum district to their south.

'Drookian Fen Guard,' Minka said.

'Drookian thieves,' Grüber said.

Minka ignored him. 'Senik, you'll be on this stretch of the ice wall. Sargora, you will take the north.'

'What's out here?' she asked.

Minka shrugged. 'I don't know, lieutenant. Grüber, I want your platoon along the inner circuit.'

'In reserve?'

'No,' she said. 'Until the town is secure we have to assume that nowhere is clear. You will also be in charge of the supply dump. I want it fortified.'

There were endless questions, of course. Minka was not the only one coping with new responsibilities and she had to leave each of them believing that they could deal with whatever this planet threw at them. Senik, Viktor and Orugi took it all in their stride, but Sargora didn't like the plan. She had all manner of tales about the jungles of Catachan that she needed to tell to exemplify her point.

Minka was dead tired. 'Listen,' she said at last, 'if you survived that then Telken's Rest will be a breeze.'

Sargora was easy compared to Grüber.

'What is wrong with him?' Senik asked, afterwards, when she had finally answered all his statements and questions.

'He's an arse,' Minka said.

Jaromir was waiting for her as she came out. 'Banting has cleared me for service,' he said. 'Told me to be careful with the scars.'

He lifted his arm to show the range of movement. The scarring was livid and red, the flesh still puckered where the stitches had held it together. 'They screw the augmetic onto the bone. It's heavier than my old arm. But shouldn't take me too long to get used to that.'

'You're sure?'

'Yes.'

'You can carry your heavy stubber?'

Jaromir nodded. 'I've been training with that in mind,' he said.

'Good,' she said. 'I can put you in the reserves until you're ready for the command squad again.'

He answered with a look that said it all.

'All right, all right. You'll be with us.'

'I will,' he said. He flexed his metallic fingers, opening and closing them as one and then individually.

'Get some sleep,' she said.

Minka had about four hours' sleep before they had to land. She slept like the dead, and was up the moment the klaxons began to wail.

She pulled on her combat boots, yanking the laces tight, and then the three layers to her frigid-environment suit. Her flak armour lay at the end of the bed. The whole lot went over her head. She rolled her shoulders to get the pauldrons into place, and then she buckled on her belt, webbing and power pack.

This took bare minutes. Last of all, she checked and double-checked her kit – magazines, grenades – and then she was out.

Seventh Company's armour had all been loaded the night before and now the troops were heading down to the landing craft. Pilots were making their way to the cockpits. She recognised one of them. It was the man who had flown her to the audience with Warmund back on the *Imperial Heart*. 'Heh!' she said. 'Esting.'

The Arvus pilot stopped and put his hand out.

'Lesk,' she said.

He smiled. 'I remember.'

'Flying Arvus?'

He nodded. 'We're ground support.'

'I'm in the Western Habs. Keep an eye out for me,' she said.

He laughed. 'Will do. Wave when you see me.'

Minka's command squad were waiting for her, each one dressed in Cadian fatigues enhanced with frigid-environment survival undersuits, with ice world camo. Jaromir had the butt of the heavy stubber on the floor, Blanchez was leaning on her sniper rifle, her face painted with streaks of blue and grey, and Bohdan was already sweating.

'Only turned my hot-suit on for a few minutes. Just to check it was working,' he said.

They paired up to make sure everyone's power pack was plugged into the hot-suit cables.

She did Jaromir's, and he checked hers.

'Sorry, sir,' he said, as he fumbled with his metal hand. 'There,' he said, after a moment, 'got it.'

Only Tyson was missing. Minka didn't worry about him; she could hear his voice as he went along the platoons getting everyone ready.

'All good?' she said, when he appeared.

Tyson nodded.

Minka gave the order for them to deploy into the lighters. No one spoke. They were all braced, thinking of what was coming next.

Ten minutes later they were falling towards Pyre's Gate.

Scout units secured the space port as the first companies came down.

Ostanko's was the initial landing. He travelled in the lead Chimera, as First Company took the main road from Pyre's Gate and seized its spires without resistance. They used their dozer blades to set up a defence perimeter as other companies landed.

They were dug-in within the hour; the wind whipped in over the ice wall, skimming snow off the flat white surface, and sending it hissing and whistling over the edge.

Sturm's Second Company swooped on the main genatorium, a hulking square block half-buried in snowdrifts, adjacent to the merchant palaces along the side of the port. Gangers held it and his lead units came under fire as they approached. They cut their way in with meltaguns and lascutters. There was a fierce firefight. Sturm's Kasrkin did not bother asking if they were heretics.

Sturm led the main columns into the large genatorium chamber, under the roof of steel ducting, his hellpistol flaring in the half-lit gloom. Tech-serfs were spared, but the armed insurgents were wiped out with fusillades of hotshot lasgun fire. Within fifteen minutes the chamber was secure.

Sturm voxed confirmation as he kicked one of the dead bodies. The gangers had shaved heads, apart from a tuft at the forehead, which was greased into a stiff spike. The bare scalps were covered in gang symbols. 'Heretics,' he voxed. 'Neutralised.'

Once he had ended the vox-link, he looked about to where his troopers were dragging the dead onto a loader.

'Get rid of them,' he spat, and the bodies were tipped into the flames of the genatorium.

Third Company, under Captain Irinya Ronin, landed in the middle of the uptown area, her orders to seize the administrative buildings that towered up on either side with palatial grandeur.

The roads were deep gullies, with cliffs of dirty snow rising on either side. Her squads set about securing the main intersections and surrounded the governor's palace, a lonely spire on the equatorial outskirts of the city.

A brown pall of pollution hung overhead. The air tasted gritty in the mouth, the snow-banks pale bellies of light under the thick cloud of dirt, reagents and gutter mulch. On either side, tunnels had been dug into the wall of snow, the doorways shored up with scavenged flakboard and beaten metal.

It was as if humanity had broken down to a level of barbarism. A few lumens flickered with a sickly yellow light, but the majority of habs were burnt out, abandoned and broken. And everywhere were signs of old battles.

Bodies lay entombed in the ice, exposed flesh blackened, the snow about them stained a lurid red. And everywhere were scraps of wind-blown plastek, empty ration packs, dirty carb sacks, tins of slab crudely cut open and discarded.

Ronin's guards stamped back and forth on the main thoroughfares, keeping themselves warm as the wind whipped snow from the tops of the high drifts, tugged at the frozen scraps of plastek.

Ronin demanded news. One by one her squad leaders came back with negatives.

No sign of life.

Ronin led the approach to the governor's palace. The feet of the gothic buttresses were buried in snow, their heads covered in ice and icicles as long as a man. The wrought-iron gates had once carried ornate aquilas, but these had been cut out, the gates fortified with flay wire, broken down and bent out of shape, and then buried in ice.

A Leman Russ tank had been driven through the gates. Its burnt-out remains were halfway along the approach, its turret blown open and lying alongside it, the paintwork peeling and blackened by heat.

The lower floors of the palace had been gutted by flames. The snow about it was grey with soot. Under the coating of ice and snow, the walls were stained by fire.

She strode inside. The stairs had once symbolised Imperial power. The dead bodies might have been members of the palace guard. It was hard to tell: they were shrunken with age and cold, the frozen tissues dehydrated by the lashing winds, their clothes torn away by ice, their bodies plundered for armour and equipment.

An hour after landing Captain Ronin confirmed that the palace was secure.

Minka heard the news as Seventh Company descended towards Pyre's Gate. She was plugged into the vox-chatter, listening to the reports of scattered resistance, Ronin's confirmation that the palace was secure, and then Sturm's confirmation that the genatorium had been captured.

The lighters carrying Seventh Company hit the ground twenty minutes before schedule. The assault ramps slammed down and the armour moved out in column. Chimeras first, followed by her squadron of Leman Russ tanks, their tracks kicking up snow from the buried roads.

'This is it,' Minka thought as she led the armoured column out. Scout Chimeras went first, with Minka's Chimera right behind. Her view from the cupola was of a crashed Lightning and the burnt-out skeleton of a cargo-12, half-buried in snow.

The cityscape was dark. There was no moon, and precious few street-lumens still working. The only natural light came from the noxious nebula that lit the sky with a deep ruddy light. It silhouetted the metallic frames of the port spires, gantry rigs and cargo lifts that towered over the whole settlement.

Minka flicked her heat-see goggles down. It was all blue and purple. She could feel the frigid-environment suit kick in automatically, her hot-suit inflate with circulating warm air.

'*We expecting anything?*' Sargora voxed.

'Always,' Minka said.

Sargora laughed.

Minka's new driver was Anastasia. Sparker had tried to make off with Breve, but he had refused until he knew that his replacement had what it took. Anastasia's integration seemed to be going well. 'She has a way with machine-spirits,' he'd said. 'Any machine-spirit.'

Anastasia was a thin, dark-haired Cadian with lho-stained fingers. She smelt constantly of lho-sticks, and now she sat in the front of the Chimera, peering through the viewslit.

First and Second Platoons went straight along the main thoroughfare. Minka was behind them as flanking forces went around either side. Jaromir lugged the heavy stubber onto his lap, pulled the loading bolt, and the thing let out a satisfying sound.

Here and there, gangers were resisting the return of Imperial law.

Gunfights were breaking out across the city as Minka led her company across the algae farms. Their domes were cratered and broken, vats empty, sewage pipes leaking effluent that had frozen into long brown streams of sludge. On the far side the Western Habs rose up, dark against the dull sky.

The wind was whipping in across the tundra, sending storms straight up the main thoroughfare. Ice had brought down the tram wires. The carriages themselves were half-buried in it. The windows were broken, the insides filled with snow.

There was a ganger roadblock as they rumbled towards the Western Habs, flakboard shelters on either side. The lead Chimeras fired as they moved forward, their multi-lasers flaring out in the darkness, and then the Leman Russ tanks fired.

There was no return fire.

One of Sargora's squads went out to mop up any resistance, but the position had been abandoned. There was no one there, and the shelters were still burning when Minka's Chimera rolled through.

It was only now that she had a sense of the height of the Western Habs. They rose like a wall before her, each slab standing on rockcrete stilts, the towering edifices blackened and frosted, the broken windows hung with icicles and the pockmarks of missile impacts.

They were all dark, the panes broken, their interiors deserted.

Minka started to order her platoons.

Grüber's territory stretched along the inner perimeter of

Seventh Company's territory, away from the ice wall, with the factorum at the southern end of his range, the algae farms along the eastern flank.

'You need to keep your men ready,' Minka told him. 'We don't want any starving gangers looting weapons out of our supply dump.'

Grüber didn't like being here. 'I have no doubts about your fighting ability,' she told him. 'If there are any gaps, then I want my best commanders ready to plug them.'

Minka's platoons spread out to their allotted posts. Each reported in as they reached their positions around the habs and along the ice wall, and then spent the next hours digging in.

'Drookians aren't here yet,' Senik reported.

Minka nodded. They should have moved into place by now. 'They won't be long,' she said.

She went out, making her way around the habs and along the ice wall.

Senik came out to meet her. 'All quiet,' he said.

The factorums had been burnt out; their metal frames were stark against the glowing sky. 'It's like being on Cadia,' he said.

She nodded.

He looked about. The landscape was frozen, icy, still.

'What's wrong?' she asked him.

He shook his head. 'I don't know. It looks peaceful, but I don't trust it.'

She felt the same. There was something wrong with this place. It had all the stillness of a mantrap, waiting to be sprung.

Grüber had barely picked a base when the cargo-12s began to arrive, loaded down with containers of food and supplies. He set out a rough perimeter and had his squads fortify it with strings of razor wire and sandbagged pillboxes.

As soon as the trucks were unloaded, he sent supplies off to each of the platoon HQs so they all had an ample supply of food and ammunition.

As another cargo-12 rolled out of the fortified perimeter, he caught sight of someone crawling towards his lines and drew his pistol.

'You!' he commanded. 'Come here!'

The figure rose. It was a Drookian Fen Guard, who saw the Cadian officer and the drawn pistol, and lifted his hands as he came forward.

'What are you doing here?' Grüber demanded.

'I was lost, sir.'

'What's your regiment?'

'My clan is Mordaunt,' the man said. 'My tribe is Grindel. We are the warriors of the Southern Fens!'

'There are no fens here, Drookian.'

The man stopped and looked about. 'Ah!' he said. 'There.'

Grüber called out to his driver. 'We're taking this one back to where he came from.'

A minute later the Chimera was rolling south, with the algae domes on the right and the factorum on the left, the towering slabs of the stilt-habs falling behind them.

There was no sign of the Drookians, until a man ran suddenly out of the rubble before them and waved them down.

At that moment, warriors sprang up on either side and behind them. Grüber saw at least one plasma gun and a melta. If this were a battle, then he knew the Chimera would not have stood a chance.

He motioned for the Drookian to dismount. The man slid down the side of the Chimera and embraced his fellows.

A large woman pushed forward. Her straight black hair was bound into thick plaits and hung with tokens, apart from the fringe, which was cut square across her brow.

'I am Grawnya of the Grindel!'

'He is one of yours?' Grüber said. 'I caught him crawling into our supply camp.'

The woman stared at him. 'I will punish him.'

Grüber slapped the top of the turret and ordered the Chimera to reverse. 'Good,' he shouted. 'And make sure you keep out of our territory.'

Her eyes narrowed at that. 'Who are you to order me?'

'I am Lieutenant Octavian Grüber.'

'And I am Grawnya Ironbrow of Clan Mordaunt, foremost fighters of the Southern Fens!' she shouted after him. 'Your name means nothing to me!'

Minka's team set up a command post in the basement of stilt-hab R-67 as her platoon commanders made wide defensive sweeps, then established their own strongpoints. They used their Chimeras' dozer blades to scoop out scrapes, before they dug in as bastions, turrets panning for targets.

An observation post was set up on the upper floors of a building across the way. From there, the sniper teams could look east over the broken domes of the algae farms, south to the burnt-out factorums, and out west to where the ice wall was a clear, dark line that marked the edge of the city.

Blanchez's sniper post was higher up in the building. She came down as one of the other snipers took over and made her way into the command post. Jaromir handed her a mug of recaff. She held it in her cupped hands and took a sip. She drained it before it cooled.

'All good?' Minka said.

The wind had died down; the snow and ice reflected the purple bruise that stretched across the night sky. Blanchez looked up at the roiling heavens.

'Is that the Cicatrix Maledictum?'

Minka nodded. The sickening feeling was familiar. None of them could take their eyes off the sight.

'Reminds me of Cadia,' Jaromir said.

On the floor below, Jaromir had already set up the heavy stubber, ten feet back from the window, with a barricade of sandbags about him, the gun set upon its tripod, the ammo crates open and the belt of ammunition loaded.

Bohdan had the vox-unit up and working. Minka made her way up as her platoon commanders started to vox in.

Orugi had found a family living in the basement of one of the habs. *'Sent them into HQ,'* he reported.

Viktor voxed in that his sector was peaceful. *'Checking habs as we speak. Deserted.'*

'Same here,' Senik said. *'What happened to the heretics?'*

'I think they heard Sargora was coming,' Viktor answered.

Minka laughed. A watchful silence set in.

The stilt-habs cast a long shadow over them all. They stood above the permafrost on rockcrete columns. They were dark and lifeless, broken windows staring out, ice and icicles hanging from the eaves. Minka's Cadians scrunched across the snow, their breath steaming about their faces.

The circuit took them slowly around to the factorum district. It stretched south for miles, full of the dark skeletons of iron girders, patches of roof clinging to them.

The other side of Minka's territory was bounded by the ice wall – a thick parapet that circled the city, with watchtowers rising up every two hundred yards. Each of the platoons had occupied the command posts. Sargora took the northernmost, and Senik the centre.

Grüber's platoon were strung out along the factorum's edge.

He greeted Minka smartly. 'I've set up a guard, sir. Any of those thieving bastards come over here...'

Minka stopped. 'Listen,' she said. 'They're on our side.'

Grüber's silence was marked.

'Come with me,' Minka told him. She walked a little way off and waited until they were out of earshot of the other troops.

'Lieutenant Grüber. You have a fine lineage. Not just the Cadian Shock Troops, but also the men and women of your family who served the Emperor. Some might think that you have a lot to be proud of, but not me. I judge you not by your name or ancestry, but by your actions. And that is how the troops will judge you too.

'So cut the crap. The enemy are out there.' She pointed out across the ice wall. 'Who knows how long we will be on this planet. Your life might depend on the Drookian Fen Guard. Keep relations cordial. Understand?'

Grüber nodded.

Minka returned to where the other troopers were standing.

The Drookian Fen Guard had arrived about an hour after Seventh Company. They were dark shapes, cutting foxholes out with picks and shovels. 'Come with me,' she told Grüber and walked out across the wasteland in between.

The Drookians stopped to watch her approach. They were rugged warriors, with tribal plaid hanging over their flak armour; their helmets and weapons were a motley collection of military surplus. But it was all maintained to a high standard. Bendikt had clearly picked a good regiment to accompany them onto the planet.

Minka felt Grüber's reaction as they crossed the last few yards. The Drookian commander came across to greet her. He was a big man, with a shaggy beard plaited into heavy locks. There were beads and brass clan tokens woven into the plaits. They rattled against his flak breastplate.

His skin was dark, his eyes blue, his handgrip firm. 'Cadian,' he said. 'I am Captain Corandiac.'

'Captain Lesk,' Minka said. His grip was firm. He tried to pull her off balance, but she held her ground and beneath his beard she could see the flicker of a smile.

'This is Lieutenant Grüber,' she said. 'He is holding the ground here.'

The Drookian shook Grüber's hand. Grüber was not ready for the trick of pulling him off balance, and he fell forward. The Drookian slapped his arm. 'Welcome, Cadian!' He looked about at the ice and waste and laughed. 'Cold, huh? Where are the enemy? Have you found any?'

'They're around,' Minka said. There was the distant patter of an automatic weapon rattling across the frozen landscape.

Corandiac smiled. 'We are the warriors of Drook! We want battles to fight. Not trenches to dig.'

'No one doubts your courage, captain.'

He smiled, as if this was all the affirmation he needed. Minka looked to the woman who stood behind him. 'This is Lieutenant Grawnya,' he said. 'She is the war chief of Clan Mordaunt. She holds this territory.'

Grawnya stared down at Minka, arms folded. Minka put her hand out. The giant woman paused, as if considering whether to take it.

After a long pause, she did. There was no tugging or attempt to pull Minka off balance. But the handshake was as hard as any Minka had been given. She returned it, but the other woman had the stronger grip, and once this was established, they smiled and let go.

'Grüber, this is Grawnya.'

'We've met,' Grüber said.

Grawnya smiled. 'We have indeed.'

The two of them squared off. Minka saw Grüber's jaw tense as he tried to match the Drookian's handshake. She could hear the crack of knuckles and joints as they battled. It was hard to tell who had won.

Minka waited until they had let go of each other's hands. 'Good,' she said. 'Now, down to business.'

The settled the line of control, watchwords, vox-bands to call for.

By this time the Drookian clansmen had gone back to work, digging trenches and foxholes with picks and shovels. 'I can send a Chimera to help you dig in?' Minka said.

Grawnya said, 'No. We do these things with our hands.'

'Fair enough. And the supplies are in?' Minka asked.

'They are.'

'If you run short, let me know.'

'We are neither thieves nor beggars,' Grawnya said.

'We who have had the honour of fighting alongside the Drookian Fen Guard would never think such a thing. But I would not sleep well at night if I knew my troopers were eating and such fine warriors as yours were not.'

Grawnya pursed her lips. It was as if she was looking to find offence but could not.

Minka took her moment. 'Captain, lieutenant, it has been a pleasure. I hope we both find enough heretics to fight.'

The Drookians made the sign of the aquila, before Grüber and Minka picked their way across the ruined factorum.

'They're barely trained,' Grüber said, his words laced with disgust.

'Have you fought with the Fen Guard before?'

He shook his head.

'Well. You should see how well they fight before you pass judgement.'

Grüber snorted.

'Your uncle, Lord General Grüber, spoke highly of them,' Minka said.

Grüber paused and took a deep breath. 'I will bear that in mind.'

'The God-Emperor has many weapons to wield,' she told him. 'We Cadians hold ourselves up as the paragon of discipline and ruthlessness. But there are times when He needs a regiment like the Fen Guard. In the meantime, make sure your best sentries are out there.'

'I thought you said they were not thieves,' he started.

Minka paused. 'The Drookians would steal your moustache, lieutenant, if they thought they could get away with it.'

IV

Orugi's platoon made their way along the habs, flushing out gangers.

Minka joined them. She used the auspex to scan the habs before her. The towers were all of the same type. Stilt houses, each one devastated and broken. The windows of most habs had been blown out. Debris had fallen onto the forecourts – the glass, rubble and metal window frames now covered in snow – and there were holes blown in walls where missiles had impacted them.

The wind played the ruined hab like a vast panpipe. Minka felt Tyson judging her as she led the search.

At one hab they approached a stairwell. The porch doors were wedged open by drifts of snow and ice. Jaromir covered the doorway with the heavy stubber. Yedrin went first, pilot light hissing on his flamer. Water from a leaking pipe had frozen, the iron banisters buried down at ankle height, the surface smooth and slippery.

'This one is frozen too,' Yedrin reported.

Minka ordered them forward.

'Can you hear that?' Jaromir voxed.

Minka and Tyson exchanged looks but neither of them spoke. Jaromir stood back, heavy stubber braced. Yedrin advanced, his flamer ready.

They pushed inside. The fierce cold had cracked the plaster and rockcrete. 'Someone's cut steps into the ice,' said Yedrin.

He went first, crampons crunching as he started up the stairs. The first floor was deserted. It was a pitiful place to live. In better days, this block had housed factorum workers. The painted hallway and stairwells were scratched, stained, chipped and chiselled with initials and angry comments, the lumens coated in white rime. Now it was a deserted shell.

Yedrin and Tyson ran along the corridor, checking each hab.

'Nothing,' Tyson said.

The wind moaned through the empty building as Yedrin led them up to the second floor. Minka thought she could hear words in the noise.

They pushed up the stairwell. There was traffic to one of the doorways. They stopped before it. Bohdan stepped forward, lasrifle ready. Yedrin moved to cover him, as Bohdan pushed the door.

It creaked as it swung open. Inside the tiny hab, the windows remained intact. They were covered with an inch of moulded ice that turned the outside world into a confused blur, but the sky was lit with the red flashes of las-fire.

Bohdan pushed forward, lascarbine raised.

'Civilian,' he called.

Minka came at once.

It was a bearded man, wrapped in plastek and scraps of fabric. A length of rope served as a crude belt. There was a cloth bound about his eyes and an icicle of frozen snot hung from his nostrils. He was rocking back and forth on what looked like an old bed.

'Only by our strength…' he said. 'The hour of need…'

'I am Captain Lesk of the Cadian Hundred-and-First. We are here to liberate you.'

The man kept rocking. 'Cadia!' he hissed. 'The planet shall not fall!'

'What's wrong with him?' Bohdan said.

Minka nodded. 'Check him for weapons.'

'Clean,' he said after a brief check.

'What's your name?' Minka said to the man.

'The claw opens… We shall stand… It is the duty of all our people.'

'What should we do with him?' Orugi asked.

'Send him over to HQ. Father Keremm. Confessor Talbeas. They'll see to him.'

Anastasia was half-buried in one of the Chimera hatches when the locals were brought to her. Yedrin called across. 'We've got to take this man to the medicae.'

'Where's that?'

'The second port buttress.'

'You know where it is?'

Yedrin looked at the port spire. It looked fairly self-explanatory.

Anastasia let the hatch slam closed. 'The far side?'

Yedrin nodded. Breve called to Galm. He was doing repairs round the back. 'Found it!' he said, holding up a length of wiring.

'Hold on,' Yedrin said. 'I'd better get my rifle.'

At that moment there was a vox-call. Yedrin cursed. 'We've got two more. Mother and child.'

Viktor brought them in. They had the same beggarly appearance as the man, a similar manner – of beaten dogs desperate to avoid another blow.

Breve pulled a face. 'You think they're trouble? You're not going to be trouble, are you?'

The woman shook her head. Her son clung closer to her side. The blind man was mumbling something.

Yedrin stopped him. 'What did you just say?'

The blind man said nothing. Yedrin looked at Breve. 'He just said something about Cadia.'

'Get him inside,' Breve said. He ushered the blind man into the Chimera troop compartment. 'Don't touch the metal. It'll freeze. Understand?'

Breve didn't know if the man understood or not.

'He said "Cadia"!' Yedrin told him.

'Don't speak of our world,' Anastasia said. 'Have some respect.'

V

The starport was probably the most secure place on Telken's Rest, Esting thought, as he stepped outside the warmth of the pilot's shelter. He took a last drag and flicked his lho-stick out into the ice.

There was a brief hiss as its embers were extinguished.

He shivered. The cold was so intense it was like icy water.

As he stood, tracer fire arced up somewhere across the cityscape. It didn't bother Esting. The ground teams had been working all night – they had the auspex towers up and the aerial defence systems were armed and loaded, antennae-discs rotating steadily, sweeping the airspace above Pyre's Gate.

A squadron of Thunderbolts had just come back from a sortie. They had settled away to the left. Fuel trollies were rolling forward as loading trucks stood ready with missiles. His Arvus lighter looked like a dumpy old woman in comparison.

Esting yawned. He'd landed only an hour or so before, and his ears were still popping as they adjusted to the new planetary air pressure. A yellow light flashed as a Sentinel Powerlifter stalked forward and started loading one of the Arvus lighters.

Esting stepped back inside the pilots' mess. It was a plain room, with a single solid heater, folding table and chairs, and a tin-samovar of recaff gurgling in the background. The other pilots were standing around, clutching their press-metal mugs.

He poured himself another recaff and was blowing on it when a servo-skull came in, trailing a sheet of paper. Everyone watched it float across the room to the noticeboard. It hung there for a moment as its claw arms pinned the paper in place.

Harker stepped forward. 'That's you.'

Esting took a quick gulp of recaff as he checked the flight itinerary. It looked simple enough. Supply run to the Western Habs. He checked his flight on the planetary chart.

'See you in an hour,' he said.

Blanchez watched the Arvus lighter. It came in low between the stilt-habs, swung round once as the pilot eyeballed the landing zone, then began its approach.

The twin rocket engines roared as it slowed and then the vector thrusters steadily lowered the craft as Maksym stood back, waving the craft down.

It settled onto its landing gear and the Cadians ran forward, pulling the cargo from the hold.

Esting flicked through the display panel as the lighter's hold was emptied. One of the Cadians approached and gave the lighter's body a double slap.

All good, the hand signals said, and Esting throttled forward. His craft shuddered as it lifted up into the air. He swung the snout round and had a great view of the district over the ice wall to the frozen flats beyond.

The only feature out there was a causeway, heading straight into the ice fields. He came in over it, stilt-habs to one side, factorum district on the other. The Cadians were small figures manning the wall.

Poor bastards, he thought, as he swung the nose of the lighter round and skimmed over the cityscape back to base.

'Generator,' Jaromir said as the team pulled the tarpaulin off. The generator sat on a flakboard sled, fifty feet from where it needed to be.

'I'll get it fixed up,' Anastasia said, as Jaromir attached the cable-tow to the sledge. 'You're getting good with that.'

The big man looked at his metallic fingers and nodded. 'My new hand doesn't feel the cold.'

Anastasia's Chimera dragged the sledge across to the base of stilt-hab R-67. In the lower floors they had set up a canteen, warm room and barracks, with Militarum quilting screening the windows.

By the time Minka had finished her circuit of her territory, she could hear the distinctive rumble of the generator. For the first time in years, warm yellow light glowed from the lower windows of the hab.

Esting was still in the air with a lho-stick in his teeth when the vox burst into static, and the voice of a staff officer broke into the cockpit.

'You're currently flying over the city?'

'Flying high,' he grinned. 'You want me to report as we're going?'

He could hear her unfolding a chart, smoothing it out. He checked his own readings on the auspex against what he had stuck up on the dash in front of him.

'These are the most up-to-date charts we have,' she said. *'What needs updating?'*

Esting put his finger to the paper as he sketched out his route. 'Well,' he started, eyes narrowing as the lho-smoke curled up into his eyes. 'Let me see... This whole area is ruins. Bridges four and five are down, but the others seem usable.'

She was silent, but he could hear her sketching in the details.

'And the algae farms are wrecked. Looks like they've been fought over plenty.'

He waited for her to note this down.

'And the habs look deserted too.'

'Right,' she said. *'Thank you. That should cover us for now – make one last sweep and then bring her back in.'*

Esting felt the bang from the engines. The Arvus lighter dropped suddenly. The whole craft shook. Warning lights flashed before him as black rain sprayed across his windscreen.

He cursed as he flicked his vox-bead live.

'Broken fuel pipe. Request urgent landing,' he said.

There was a crackle. He gripped the steering gears with both hands. He was dropping quickly.

The landing pad was marked out with flashing lumens. A trail of them showed where the other lighters were swinging in. 'Requesting urgent landing,' he repeated, a little stress entering his voice.

'Confirmed,' a voice said. *'Hold.'*

'Holding,' Esting said, but the shakes were getting worse. 'Situation getting worse.'

'Hold,' the voice said again.

'I'm frekking holding,' Esting hissed between gritted teeth. 'But can't for long.'

The fuel gauge was spiralling towards empty. 'Frekk!' he cursed as the craft flung him about.

'I'm bringing it in,' he voxed, but the truth was his craft was in freefall.

'We're clearing a landing zone.'

'Say a prayer for me,' Esting managed, as he pushed the fuel injectors forward and felt the remaining engine scream with effort, as the landing pad hurtled up towards him.

VI

The first night on Telken's Rest tested everyone's nerves. Minka made sure to visit each of her platoons and everywhere she went, the sentries were on edge.

'There's something wrong with this place,' Sergeant Pavlo said as he stood on the ice wall, looking out both ways, into the habs and onto the wastes. 'And it's not just the frekking cold.'

Minka stood and looked out. The ice sheets creaked and cracked, the sounds carrying in the bleak landscape from a great distance. There was so much noise, it was as if the sheets were alive.

'It's like they're crawling forward,' Pavlo said as the bergs ground against and under each other.

Blanchez woke in a sweat. She saw a shadow in the room, and felt for her knife, before realising it was Captain Lesk.

'Sorry,' she said. 'Didn't recognise you.'

'It's all right,' Minka said. 'I couldn't sleep either.'

She came forward, so close that Blanchez could make her features out in night greyscale. The generator stuttered, somewhere below. The scent of warming slab began to drift up through the hab and the Cadians started to wake.

'What's up?' Minka said.

'Nothing,' Blanchez said, though that wasn't true. 'You?'

'I heard noises,' Minka said. 'I thought I saw something out there.'

Blanchez slipped her jacket over her shoulders, drew the canvas sheath off her long-las.

'I'll have a look.'

As Minka's squads warmed themselves with their morning recaff, Bendikt's lighter landed at the port facility. He stepped out of the craft's side door, and from the top of the ramp he took his first look at the planet.

'I've seen worse,' he said as he looked round. But the truth was it was a Throne-forsaken place. He stood and breathed in the world's air, and felt a sense of excitement. Something was going to happen here, he could tell.

Senik voxed Minka. *'I don't want to worry you,'* he said. *'But I'd like you to have a look at this.'*

Senik was stationed just south of the ice wall gatehouse. It was a massive edifice, one hundred and thirty feet high, its surfaces inscribed with the old crests of the ancient mining houses. His platoon had occupied the main bastion on their stretch of the wall. A handful were on top of the palisade. There was a small antechamber where they had set up base. They had used sandbags to block up the viewports and hung a rough tarpaulin over the door, and the rest were sheltering inside, with hands spread out over a low brazier made from salvaged regimental ration tins.

'Where's Senik?' she demanded.

They pointed topside.

The bunker was set inside the wall. The middle level had taken an ordnance blast that had cracked the gun housing open. Snow had blown in. Senik had a heavy weapons team set up on top. Their autocannon had been freshly oiled; the ammo crates had been stacked against the wall, the spools sitting ready.

At the top was a heavy metal door that had been frozen open. Minka pushed through and found Senik.

'How are things?' she asked.

'Thank you for coming out, sir,' Senik said. 'It's been very quiet so far, but I'm concerned about the gatehouse.'

She looked out across the dirty snow, getting her bearings. A line of iron markers tracked the trans-track causeway. 'Looks pretty vulnerable.'

Senik nodded. 'Sparker's new lot are covering the gatehouse, so they might need a bit of help.'

She paused at the edge. The ice wall dropped about a hundred feet to the plains below. The snow had been blasted up against the rockcrete wall and formed a ramp to the parapet. No doubt it had been kept clear, in better times. But now... The ice wall's defensive quality had been severely degraded.

'The slopes have been mined?'

'Mines have not been issued.'

'I'll speak to Prassan,' Minka said.

She took out her monocular and scanned the landscape. Even the dirty grey snow threw back a dazzling light. But she saw what looked like a tunnel entrance, a low crescent, almost blocked with snow, icicles hanging down.

'What are they?' she said.

'Funeral mounds?'

Minka didn't know. In Cadia, as a Whiteshield, she had

camped out among the tombs. There were great mounds, where the dead of campaigns had been interred together. Ancient generals buried under rockcrete slabs, the tombs fashioned into heavy pillboxes, the name of the interred carved into the walls of the blockhouse.

She thought of that as she scanned the landscape then handed the scope to Senik. 'I would say that was a mine shaft,' she said.

On the way back, Minka voxed Sparker.

'Who's manning the gatehouse?'

'Bulger,' he said.

'What's he like?'

'Good,' Sparker said.

She didn't like to intrude, but she had served under Sparker.

'It looks vulnerable.'

'I'll go check,' he said.

'Thank you. And I've had a look. There's a hole out in the ice fields. Looks like a mine shaft. Seen anything your side?'

'Nothing.'

The connection went dead.

'Probably the habs,' Bohdan said. 'Big metal walls, plays havoc with the vox.'

As soon as she got back to her command centre, she sent Tyson to go straight to the quartermaster's office. 'We need mines. Ask Prassan to go over the maps of this quarter. See if he's got any leads. Maybe there were warehouses preparing charges for mining expeditions, out on the ice. They might have left us some munitions to repurpose.'

VII

Bendikt's command post had been prepared in the merchant hall of Vening, the most aristocratic of the old trading houses. It was set a short distance from the lines of merchant hangars, backing onto the row of warehouses that lined Pyre's Gate.

An Administratum detail had selected it as the most suitable place for the command centre, and staff officers had moved in the day before to clean the place up. They had swept, mopped, whitewashed and stuck Imperial posters over heretical graffiti, even as teams brought in the vox-systems and cogitators that Bendikt was going to need.

The place had a busy feel: officers were marching quickly from one station to another, the clatter of cogitators came from each room, and servo-skulls sailed past, their grav-generators humming, files or data-slates clamped in metal claws.

Mere led General Bendikt up the main steps. The statues that lined the block's façade had all been beheaded.

A Thunderbolt swept overhead as they walked towards a low rockcrete control centre.

'I've sent patrols out,' Mere said.

'Well done.'

The entrance hall showed much of its former grandeur. Herringbone tiles lined the floor and a broad staircase swept up and round the room's perimeter.

Mere led him along, up a set of plain rockcrete steps and into a first-floor chamber, where the command centre was located. The wide windows had been covered with flakboard. Cogitators were already at work here too, and cabling ran to the scribe station, where a servitor sat over a vellum scroll, ink quill ready. Plain matting had been laid over the cables to stop people tripping. A folding camp table sat at the side of the room, with a gurgling samovar and a row of mugs.

Bendikt poured himself a mug of recaff. He winced as he tasted it, and looked at the city charts pinned to the walls.

Mere went through initial reports. Ostanko had taken no prisoners. 'Eighty-three gangers killed in total.'

'And the void shield generator?'

'Secured, sir. By Second Company. Tech-Priest Daederhom reports that he is making good progress.'

Bendikt nodded. 'Good. Any idea how long it will take?'

'To get the shield active? Not long, I am sure.'

'Encourage him to hurry. I want to secure our perimeters as soon as possible.'

A few minutes later the air crackled with static. Mere went to check.

'The shields are up, sir,' he said.

Mere's staff had been working on the main charts.

'Red dots indicate hostile activity,' Mere said. 'Green is where we have found civilians.'

Bendikt took it all in. There would be patterns, he knew. Every action threw up its own, and part of a commander's gift was to recognise them before anyone else.

He nursed his recaff as the scribe's quill began to scratch out a message. He could not see any patterns yet. Not yet. But they would come.

He was already planning the next phase of the pacification. He pulled the map out which showed the planets of the Ghost Nebula.

'Any hint of the Eighth? Of Creed, or Cadians in general?' he said.

Mere stopped and looked at him. 'No, sir,' he said. 'But if there are, I will be sure to let you know.'

PART IV

I

TELKEN'S REST

Incense curled up from a brazier, but there was no hiding the foetid stink. It smelt of disease, of treachery and failure.

The mood within the dying band was grim. Without a miracle they all knew their time was short, and most of them had given up praying.

There was a cry of pain. It was like a moan ripped from a wounded animal. It was bestial, primal, without words. But worse was the psychic wave that washed over them. It struck a dread chill through them all.

Kurl froze until the shudder had passed through him. He pushed through the hanging cloths. Their master was prostrate within. The healers were chained to the bed, fretting and fussing as they administered stimms.

One of them caught Kurl's eye.

He looked strained.

As well he might, Kurl thought. His life depended on it.

The whole warband felt it. Their dream, it seemed, was ending.

And when it did, their lives would go as well. First the healers, then the serving men like Kurl, and lastly the Scourged warriors.

Kurl pushed through the curtain into the main cave. A bare lumen cast a thin, yellow light through the subterranean chamber. There were barely twenty of them left, a pitiful collection of bodyguards, warriors and the hangers-on, like Kurl, who had nowhere else to go.

Kurl sat alone, saying a prayer as he set the tin upon the embers.

The prayer was not for him, or the food. It was for his master.

Kurl had been with him for years. It had been a glorious ride of victory after victory. Defeat had seemed impossible, until the end.

When the prayer was over, he picked the hot tin from the embers. He used a rag to lift it clear and set it between his knees. His spoon was in his pocket. He fished it out and stirred the contents, raised it to his mouth, and blew the heat off.

Each member of mankind was allocated a single life, a single death. Kurl had imagined it many times. When his master was dead, he would open his veins and let his blood flow out, let his soul serve his master in death.

II

Father Keremm and Confessor Talbeas had come down in the same flight as Bendikt.

Unlike him, however, they had had to find their own lodging. One of the staff officers had suggested that they take up residence in the chapel wing of Bendikt's command centre.

'The palace's chapel is next door,' they said. Their tone said it all. 'It was desecrated. We will help you have it cleaned. But until then, here is the key. For you to look after it.'

Keremm took the key, and once they had brought their packs into the adjoining rooms, he said to Talbeas, 'Shall we bear witness together?'

Talbeas made the sign of the aquila as they stood at the locked doors. A chain had been passed through the handles and padlocked. Keremm took the key from his belt and unlocked it, drew in a deep breath as he pulled the chain free, and then pushed the heavy wooden doors open.

Talbeas had her prayer beads in her hand. Her fine features were set in a determined expression as Keremm stepped inside.

Neither of them spoke again till they had left the chapel and closed the doors behind them.

'No one else must see,' Talbeas said.

Keremm nodded. His eyes were closed as he tried to cleanse his mind of the things that he had seen. Such hatred, he thought. Such heresy.

'It will be burned away, and we will start again.'

Esting returned to the scene of the crash. It was three hours since and the remains of his Arvus had been pushed to the side of the landing zones. His craft lay in a half-frozen puddle of foam, heat-stained, wings crumpled.

A Navy clerk appeared from behind the craft, a servo-skull hanging in the air over his shoulder. He looked up as Esting approached.

'This is your machine?'

'It is,' Esting said. 'I landed that bastard. Can you believe it?'

'It is severely damaged,' the staff clerk said.

'So was I!' Esting said.

The clerk did not laugh. 'For the report. What happened, exactly?'

'There was a bang, and suddenly fuel was everywhere.' Esting stepped forward, looking for evidence. The metal was still warm. He climbed up. 'I could swear I saw puncture holes.'

The clerk looked at him. 'I have inspected it. No signs of external damage.'

Esting shook his head as he stepped back. 'Well. Ruptured fuel line.'

The man made some amendments to what he had written.

'How long till a replacement is found?' Esting asked.

'It is here already,' he said. 'Hangar Four.'

Esting stood by the side of his craft while the clerk returned to his office.

He'd flown that thing since Cadia. He stood in silence, as if he were at the grave of a friend. There was a piece of metal panelling that had broken loose. He picked it up.

He'd keep that.

Minka had just spoken to Senik, when he voxed again. *'Chief,'* he said. *'We've found something. You should come and see.'*

'Scourged?'

'No,' he said. There was a pause. *'I think you should come and see.'*

'The railhead?'

'Correct. There's a municipal office right in front. We're in there.'

Minka arrived ten minutes later.

The municipal office was a squat, rockcrete block, with sandbagged windows and doorway, and its back to the rail gate. Minka's Chimera came to a halt where Senik's own had dug-in behind the front lines. She jumped down as Senik came out onto the steps.

His carbine was slung over his shoulder, behind his back. His gloves were off and hanging from the wrist straps. He had fingerless gloves underneath and was pointing inside with a three-fingered hand.

He looked shaken. 'Sorry, sir,' he said, 'but I thought you should see this yourself. There's a heap of bodies inside. Looks like an execution.'

Drifts had covered one side of the entrance hall, and Senik's lot had cut a hole through to the doors with lascutters. There were puddles of muddy water starting to freeze, and one of the doors had been burnt through.

'This way,' he said as he led her into the main chamber. She followed him into a meeting room, filled with a long thin conference table. Its surface was rimed in ice, and had been defaced with carved slogans and initials. Paint hung from the high walls, pale shapes showing where portraits and the Imperial aquila had once hung.

'Here,' Senik said.

He led her to the far end of the room. The wall there was brown with splattered blood and dark scorch-marks and the pocking of hard rounds. At its foot, a pile of bodies lay frozen.

'Gunned down,' Senik said.

Minka nodded. Despite the layer of hoar-frost, the mail and brigandine were clear.

'These are Scourged,' she said. She stood in silence for a long time. 'No idea how long they've been here?'

Senik shook his head. They could have been here weeks, or years.

Minka looked about, but the room was empty. Just her and Senik, and the dead. She looked down at the frozen corpses and shook her head. She thought she saw a breath, but she had to have imagined it.

'Let's get them out of here. Then burn them.'

'Right,' Senik said.

She made her way along the rail gate to the ice wall.

The causeway had carried a rail link into the city. The rail gate rose up with arching platforms and loading bays. Rows of gantries hung waiting in frozen silence. There had to be so many worlds like this, places that had ground slowly to a halt once their links with the Imperium had been severed.

Security, industry, trade, whole populations. All had gone.

She voxed Viktor. 'Eighth Company is holding the rail gate. But if something does decide to come knocking, they're going to need backup. I've sent *Fire of Cadia* up there. Sargora is going to cover your territory. I want you to go there too and guard their flank.'

Viktor paused. *'Garrison the wall?'*

'Yes. Take the factorum end. Senik will push north. And if anything happens, I need you to hold it.'

'I understand.'

At that moment, there was the sound of firing. It was sustained. A rapid burst of las-fire.

Blanchez's voice came over the vox-bead. *'Looks like First Platoon.'*

Minka took the vox-set. Sargora's voice came back. She sounded rattled. *'Nothing,'* she said. *'First Squad got jumpy.'*

'Sure?'

Sargora came back in the affirmative, and she shut the line. A few minutes later she called back.

'This might sound daft,' she said, *'but this place is starting to feel a little odd. I just turned around and there were three people standing right behind me…'*

There was another burst of gunfire and Sargora sounded much more confident now.

'Augurs showing contacts,' she voxed.

'How many?'

'Dozens,' Sargora said. *'Block K-Seventeen. I'm pushing forward.'*

'Confirmed,' Minka said. 'I'll get reinforcements.'

Minka's squad clambered into their Chimera.

'All good?' she voxed Anastasia.

'All good,' the driver said as they pulled out in front of a Leman Russ Exterminator, *Lady Vengeance,* its twin-linked autocannons panning about for targets. In her earpiece, Minka could hear the vox-chatter of Sargora's units making their way towards the contacts.

She had two Whiteshield reserve units under Pahlor moving in as well. 'Get them round the back of Block K-Seventeen,' she ordered.

* * *

The wind was cold on Minka's face as her Chimera moved down the thoroughfare. Ahead, ice spun off the tracks of *Lady Vengeance*, ammo spools clattering as the tank's twin-linked autocannons loaded. The air rumbled and the Leman Russ ground forward, dirty brown promethium fumes hanging low in the cold air.

'We're going round the back,' Minka voxed Sargora. In the background she could hear the vox-chatter as *Lady Vengeance*'s crew made their last checks, as the tank's main guns were blessed, and the prayers of firing were chanted.

They were half a mile from the gunfight when the las-shot flashed.

Minka felt it before she heard it. It hit her square in the chest and she slammed back against the casing of the Chimera's turret. And then she heard the rattle of hard rounds echoing off the wall of habs, and Minka dropped into the transport.

'She's hit!' a voice called out. 'She's hit.'

Jaromir dropped the heavy stubber as he pushed forward through the Chimera, shouting for the medic.

'Captain,' he said. 'Where is it?'

Minka pushed his hands off. 'I'm fine,' she said. She thought she was fine. All she had felt was the punch of impact. There was no blood.

The medic, Olek, pushed alongside. 'What happened?'

'I'm fine.'

Blanchez's voice came over their beads. *'I saw the shot. What's happened?'*

'There's a sniper,' Minka voxed back. 'Find them and hunt them down.'

'She was hit, but she's fine,' Jaromir said even as he checked her out. Her armour was marked with the distinctive black mark of a las-bolt hit. She pulled her flak armour forward. He put his hand inside and checked. 'Didn't go through. She's fine.'

'Why is everyone saying "fine"?' Minka snapped. 'It didn't go through. Look!'

'Sure?' Blanchez voxed.

'Sure,' Jaromir said.

'Frekking bastard,' Blanchez said. *'I'm going after them.'*

'Be careful,' Minka voxed. 'There might be more.'

They were all on edge. Even Tyson looked rattled. Jaromir looked like he was going to cry. 'Stay calm,' Minka told him. 'I'm fine. I need you to back me up. Understand?'

He nodded slowly.

Minka looked about. Olek and Bohdan were ready. Maksym had his flamer hitched up. His face was very calm. Minka remembered what had happened to Jeremias in the trench.

'Stay calm, everyone,' she said. 'They got a lucky shot, that's all. The Emperor protects. And He's a bastard to His enemies.'

Jaromir shook his head. 'If anyone is dying here, it's me.'

'Heh!' Minka told him. 'You stay alive, damn you. What the hell would Banting say? I just got you a new arm.'

The Chimera's multi-laser whined.

'Suppressing fire,' Anastasia said. *'I'm getting as close as I can.'* Then, *'We're almost there,'* and she counted down from five.

Minka fixed Jaromir with a look. He met her gaze and nodded. He would stay alive, as best he could. No more talk of dying.

'No one is dying today,' Minka said, 'unless it's a heretic. Now, ready yourselves.'

'We're engaging,' Sargora voxed.

'I see them,' Anastasia called.

At that moment they could hear the sudden roar as *Lady Vengeance* opened up with its twin-linked autocannons and three heavy bolters. The outpouring of fire was deafening. It tore chunks out of the rockcrete.

'Ready?' Minka hissed.

On two the ramp releases clicked open and Tyson slammed the ramp down. He went one way, Maksym the other, as *Lady Vengeance* fired again, her turret armament tracking across the building.

Maksym saw something move and fired a sudden gout of flaming promethium through one of the windows. Las-bolts and heavy stubber shells tore chunks out of the masonry, as Jaromir set his feet square and looked for movement. He fired off a quick salvo, before following the others up the ice drift, throwing himself into the lower hab windows.

'Cadia stands!' Minka shouted as she led the charge up the snowdrifts into the lower hab.

She stumbled up the ice, caught at the top, and pulled herself over the windowsill. There were gangers, torn to pieces, lying on the floor. It was hard to tell how many. One was moaning something heretical. She put a bolt through him and kept moving forwards.

'We're in,' she voxed Sargora, 'moving forward.'

It was a deadly game of cat and mouse now, but Minka had cut her teeth in this kind of warfare during the Battle for Cadia. She had fought through every inch of her kasr, through pillboxes, chapels, streets and marketplaces. Each one had been turned into a bastion to hold on to. A foothold to retain.

She lobbed a grenade through a doorway, waited for the explosion and then ducked inside. Two gangers lay on the floor. One was crawling to safety. She put her power sword through his back, shot the other one as well, just in case.

She could hear Sargora's lot now, coming down the corridor, and felt a sudden exhilaration.

The stress of waiting was over; she was in battle again, with a Leman Russ behind her, and a squad of Cadians at her side – what could stand against her?

III

Blanchez had seen the sniper shot hit. Not properly, but in the corner of her eye. It gave her a rough idea of where it had come from. She settled in and waited. They were bound to move. She let her gaze relax as she took in the cluster of windows from the hab along the way.

It had been a good shot, which meant a good sniper. She rolled her shoulders to keep herself alert. Scrolled the range of her sights to roughly the distance.

She could hear *Lady Vengeance* opening fire. The frozen rockcrete rattled with the noise.

Come on, she thought. Out you come.

She waited nearly ten minutes before she saw him. He'd camouflaged himself well, obscured behind a cracked window. The reflected glare had hidden him until he moved, crawling backwards from the broken glass.

She had only a few seconds, but lined him up, guessed the

difference the distance would make, and fired a quick salvo of las-shots and then ducked back out of the way.

Blanchez crossed the road, keeping under the stilt-habs until she reached the bottom of the building. She crept forward to get a closer look. The drifts reached halfway up the window panes. The plex-glass had broken under its weight. She paused at the top then carefully slipped forward, falling soundlessly into what had been someone's bedroom, once.

The place was filthy. There were stains on the walls – she did not know what – and the bed had been turned over. A cardboard chest of drawers had got damp and half collapsed into itself.

Blanchez slipped across the room to where the shattered pressboard door stood. Something had smashed it open. As she avoided the broken glass on the floor, she stopped.

A child's doll lay in the corner – a Militarum doll, one eye missing, the stuffing coming out where one of the arms had torn free.

Blanchez had a sudden vision. This door had been barricaded. And something had smashed its way in. It all made sense now, and in her mind's eye she could see a child in there, terrified as the door was splintered.

She bent and picked the toy up, slid it into her flak jacket, and moved on through the hab. There were more stains on the walls. The smears a body made as it slid down.

The corridor was long and empty. A scrap of paper pinned to a noticeboard fluttered in the breeze.

Blanchez kept going, passing hab door after hab door, all of them smashed through.

The building seemed to have one stairwell. She paused there, listening, but she could hear nothing. She crept forward, and saw it. A drop of blood, glistening red. It stood out from the grime. She put her finger to it. Still warm.

She moved up to the banisters. Nothing. But on the landing below she could see another drop.

Blanchez shifted the long-las, started down the stairs. It was hard to stop blood, she knew, once it started flowing. The drips got closer together as she went down the stairs, which meant they were going more slowly.

The trail led her down to the lowest level, a windowless store chamber at the bottom of the hab-block. She slipped on her heat-see goggles, and very slowly slid through the doorway.

Inside, the goggles showed all dull blues and purples.

She slipped quickly down the stairs, looking for the blood trail. It showed up a faint orange, leading across the chamber.

The chamber had once been used to store sacks of carb. Some lay against the left-hand wall, the stink of mould rising from them, the floor piled high with grains of rat droppings.

Along another wall there were the remains of more sacks. These had been cut open. It was hard to tell if their contents had been eaten by vermin or humans. Hard to tell the difference between them here.

Blanchez scanned about the room, just to make sure. The heat-see lens showed purple with dots of orange leading to the end.

She crept forward, and there he was, lying pressed up behind a pile of sacks.

The red heat of a human, the blood showing orange where it was leaking out. Blanchez made her way towards the body, rifle stock pulled close into her shoulder. She could hear the rasp of breath.

She paused, alert as a wild animal, nostrils flaring, ears straining in the darkness. She pulled her knife out of its sheath. She had smeared it with oil and soot, but even so the surface caught the light.

As she came close, she saw him: a young man, his beard a thin mess of fair hairs on his chin and upper lip. She knelt over the body.

Lung-shot, the blood bubbling through the wound. He'd done well to get so far.

Blanchez wasted no time. Each dead heretic made the Imperium of Man a better place, but there was nothing saying they had to die quickly. She considered letting him bleed out slow, for coming so close to killing her captain, but she thought of the child, inside that room, so terrified as they'd clung to a doll of an Imperial Guardsman.

It was a swift job. One hand on the forehead, knee on the chest, the body stiffening as the blade cut through.

Blanchez wiped the blood off her hand onto the body. The man was dressed in furs. They were dirty and greasy, but they did the job. Underneath were military boots, chain-mail skirts and heavy brigandine armour.

A battle blade was strapped to the leg. A pistol lay next to the body. The gun was loaded, but the powercell was low on charge. And he had dropped a sack. Her fingers found it. Rough hessian. Heavy.

She pulled the bag towards her. Her mind imagined what could be inside, conjuring all manner of dreadful items as her fingers reached within…

There were scraps of ration packs, a few lumps of mouldy slab, and a lump of rock sugar.

She looked down and engaged her vox-bead.

'Captain Lesk,' she said, 'what's the intel on the gangers here?'

Minka told her the intel. Scattered gangers. Petty little cults of personality, squabbling over food and resources. Locals. *'Why?'*

'I've got the sniper,' Blanchez said. 'He's not talking any more, but he looks to me like he's a Scourged warrior.'

* * *

Minka came to see the man that Blanchez had killed. She stood over the dead body, crouched down as she inspected his kit.

She had first seen these shock troopers of heresy in the astropathic tower on Potence. They had been terrifying then, swollen with fierce belief in their dark gods. Even on Cinnabar's Folly, they had put up a stiff fight. But what did it mean to be Scourged now that their leader was dead, and their armies defeated?

She picked up the plundered laspistol. It looked so worn and battered that it could have come down through generations of warriors.

Minka took in a deep breath. 'I think you're right,' she said.

She remained crouching.

'Get picts of this. Make sure HQ know: Scourged elements within the city.'

IV

Colonel Rath Sturm jumped down from the Centaur tracked carrier and strode up the stairs. The Administratum District was packed with buildings such as this, which, from the signs, had once housed the administrative wing of the Planetary Board of Rites.

His Kasrkin stood taller as their commander took the stairs two at a time. He acknowledged each one with a brief nod and strode inside, to what had once been the greeting hall. The grandeur was apparent, despite the damage that the heretics had inflicted.

Captain Ronin had dragged the crates up. 'We found these,' she said.

One of the Kasrkin was picking through the contents. They were packed with paper folders and scrolls of vellum, and each was burnt and disfigured. The man put the file back as soon as he saw that Sturm had arrived, and straightened up.

Ronin went on, 'There were cases of these,' she said. 'Most

were ashes. There were some at the bottom which appeared to have survived.'

Sturm took the file that the other trooper had dropped, flicked through it and handed it to Ronin. 'Good, well done. Let's send them over to HQ. We'll give the pen-pushers something to do.'

As Imperial forces pushed out across the city, supplies continued to arrive at the starport. Prassan was running about, trying to keep track of it all as the wall of containers soared ten high, their worn paint starting to rime. Demands were pouring in from all the companies.

He passed Medicae Banting and had to double take. The man looked like he had been waiting outside for hours, hands thrust deep into his pockets, Militarum-issue overcoat wrapped tight against the cold.

'Sorry, sir,' Prassan said. 'I didn't recognise you. Has the medicae facility arrived?'

'No. It is late,' Banting said. 'They say it is going to be here.' He pointed to an empty space behind the command post. 'But there are wounded already coming in. We're having to triage them inside.'

'Wounded?'

'Accidents,' Banting said. 'Frostbite.' He nodded towards the command block.

Prassan was sympathetic, but he had other things to worry about. He was trying to find the urgent containers. At that moment, a lighter descended with Banting's medicae facility slung beneath it.

Lumens illuminated the landing zone as the wind whipped up, biting cold.

Banting stared silently. He could barely wait for the lighter to land. He was a deeply territorial man, and the medicae facility was his bastion.

The lighter hovered just above the ground, slowly descending the last few feet, till the prop supports of the facility took the weight and the magnetic clamps released it, leaving the medicae block behind. Banting swore at the Munitorum workers, gesticulating wildly, as levelling hydraulics settled into the permafrost.

'Not there!' he shouted. But it was too late. The lighter-lifter was free of the facility's weight and soared up, the roar of its engines fading as it climbed into the darkness. The Munitorum workers seemed perplexed by the bundled shape of Banting as he marched back and forth, shouting and gesticulating.

They had jobs to do and there was no way they could move the facility now, as they fired up the genatorium and lights flickered to life.

'It's working,' Vasily called out, and persuaded Banting to go inside. Banting left the workers with a final curse and headed to where the heaters were already kicking in.

The medicae staff were still setting the wards up as Breve's Chimera arrived. He couldn't see the access ramp and went around the block until he found it.

Yedrin helped the blind man down the ramp, one hand on his elbow as the mother and child followed behind.

There was so much noise from the cargo-8s, lighters and fork-lifts that he had to shout to be heard. 'This way!' he called, steering the blind man towards the medicae ramp.

Lumens lit the way up, and double doors at the top slid open as they approached. As they closed behind them, the doors sealed off the cold and the noise. Yedrin could feel the heat as the air-recycling units blasted at full power. He looked about, and a clerk appeared from behind a high desk.

'Yes?'

Yedrin stepped forward. 'I've brought these three for cleaning up.'

'Wait there, please,' the clerk said. A moment later Corpsman Vasily appeared through the doorway, still buttoning up his white overalls.

'Civilians,' Yedrin said, gesturing to his charges. 'For decontamination.'

Vasily did not move. 'Decontamination?'

Yedrin nodded. 'Tyson sent them.' That wasn't true, of course, but Tyson scared most people, and they tended not to argue with him.

Vasily cursed and shook his head. 'This is a medicae facility…'

Yedrin nodded. 'Right. HQ want them for questioning. Wouldn't want them infecting the top brass.'

Vasily sighed as he pulled on plastek gloves. 'Right,' he said to the three civilians. 'In here.'

As the three showered, Vasily looked at the heap of clothing they had left. It was crawling with lice. He swept it straight into a bag, and called the clerk.

He held it at arm's length.

'Incinerator,' he said simply.

Yedrin stood uncomfortably on guard as Staarki joined Vasily.

Once the mother and son had dressed in blue overalls, their heads were shaved, counter-lice powder was administered, and then they were injected with a cordial of stimms and nutrients.

Banting suddenly appeared. 'Who are these two?'

'Civilians,' Yedrin said. Banting paid him no attention. He walked across to Vasily.

'Malnourished. Lice-ridden,' Vasily said. 'I've cleaned them up and dosed them with vitamins.'

Banting nodded and picked up the data-slates and scrolled through.

Yedrin felt he had to explain. 'Captain Lesk sent them for questioning.'

'You're locals?' Banting said, raising his voice. 'Asha Kilgard. Rumann Kilgard.'

The boy's head looked enormous. His eyes were wide as he looked to his mother. They both nodded.

'Born here?'

Asha nodded again, then coughed to clear her throat. 'Yes, sir.'

'Does he speak?'

Asha prodded her son. 'He does.'

The boy's eyes were still wide, but he didn't say anything.

When the medicae were finished with Asha and her son, they were sent to a side chamber, where two trays of food had been laid out for them.

Vasily was finishing up the blind man. He took the buzz-shaver. Wet locks fell away as he started to remove the man's beard, kept going up and over his head. The man mumbled the whole time. His lips moved even as Vasily trimmed away his beard and moustache.

'Nearly there,' Vasily said as he dusted off his gloved hands, then injected him as well.

'So who is this?' Banting said.

No one knew.

Banting raised his voice. 'What's your name?'

The man's lips kept moving, but they were mumbling through words that made no sense.

'He's been like that since we found him,' Yedrin said.

Banting looked at the man. He put a hand to his cheek and lifted an eyelid.

The eyeball was milky white, like a cooked fish's eye. He lifted the other. The same.

'The skies are dark,' he heard the man say. 'Across the planet, mankind strives against the legions of the Archenemy...'

Banting felt a chill go down his back. He let go of the man and turned to Yedrin. 'He's clean.'

'The few stand alone against the many. The banners of the enemy are legion...'

'What is he talking about?' Banting said.

They listened a little longer. The words had a strange sense of portent.

'He's been through a rough time,' Vasily said.

'No doubt. Send them all for questioning.'

The three stood out, their shaven heads vulnerable to the cold as they waited to be told what to do. Yedrin pulled a piece of paper from his pocket. One of the medics had drawn him a rough map of where the regimental priests were. He turned it round in his hand, trying to get his bearings.

'Right,' he said, as he led them out into the cold, 'this way.'

Father Keremm and Confessor Talbeas had set up what they called the Pacification Office in the foyer of one of the merchant houses that lined the space port. The gothic exterior was stained with old fire damage, the broken windows were boarded up and they had hung cloth over the flakboard to act as curtains.

'It's meant to soften the place,' Talbeas said.

Keremm lugged the solid heater inside and turned the dial onto full. He stretched his hands out over it. 'Give it time.'

* * *

Cadians were standing guard at the top of the steps as a cargo-12 pulled up outside.

Kasrkin started to unload large crates of documents.

'Where are they going?' Keremm asked, concerned about whether they might take any of the rooms he had set aside for Ecclesiarchal business.

No one answered, and he followed them inside. The crates were being stacked within one of the front chambers. He appeared mollified.

The door was closed and locked, and a pair of Cadians remained standing guard.

Talbeas and Keremm exchanged looks. The crates were clearly important.

'What is that?' Talbeas said.

The guards did not know. 'Looks like papers to me,' one said, 'but HQ are very excited about it.'

Mere did not consider the documents important enough to brief Bendikt, but as the news was brought to him, the lord general turned.

'What is that, Mere?'

Mere's cheeks coloured. 'Colonel Sturm has found records from the Board of Rites. I have secured them within the palace.'

'What records?'

'I'm not sure, sir.'

'Have you assigned them for inspection?'

'They will take weeks to go through. Someone tried to destroy them with a flamer.'

'Even more reason to go through them!' Bendikt said. He calmed himself for a moment. 'What if there is important information?'

Mere nodded. 'I will see who we can spare.'

'Good!' Bendikt snapped. 'Good.'

'If there is anything,' Mere assured him, 'then we will find it.'

V

Blanchez liked to keep on the move, and as she had a feel for this district she wanted a perch with a better vantage point along the main thoroughfares.

It took an hour to find the right spot. She clambered up through a stilt-hab, looking for a window that would give her the best view. One half of the building had collapsed out into the street, but the ice wall corner remained standing like a turret. She climbed up as far as she could go, the ruin of someone's bedroom, and crawled through the broken walling, up to the empty window frame, pulling her lasrifle alongside.

This high up, the wind was like icy knives on her skin. She pulled her snood over her cheeks, turned her hot-suit up and moved her shoulders to get the blood flowing. She pushed her goggles onto her forehead so she could get a good view along the street that ran back over the algae domes, and north towards the railhead.

She settled in, scope pressed to her cheek. Ready, just in case.

She had to blink her eyes against the cold. Orugi's platoon were still going hab to hab, checking them for survivors. She could see the squads making their way along the streets, spread out, covering each other.

The dirty snow shone with an inner light. She watched figures slipping through the darkness. A Chimera idling at the end of the road. Looked like Breve sitting up in the turret.

She used her scope to pan along the buildings at the end of the street, then kept herself busy searching the windows in the habs opposite. When her eyes grew tired, she blinked to clear her vision.

There! she thought, but when she looked again there was nothing.

She blinked again, panned back with her scope.

There was movement in the corner of her eye. In the window of a hab across the way. She checked where Orugi's platoon were. They looked safe, she thought. She breathed slowly as she lifted the rifle, flipped the powercell charge onto full, pressed the butt of her long-las into her shoulder, readied herself.

But there was nothing there. Just a shattered window, and inside, an empty chamber.

She shifted her eye away from the gunsight, and saw it again – a face. A pale face, hands pressed against the glass.

She flipped to the sights again, and the figure was gone.

'Is it just me,' she voxed, 'or is anyone else seeing things?'

Chief Commissar Shand spent the morning dealing with three wounded gangers that Ronin's lot had brought in. Their wounds had been field-dressed, but there was no need for more care. Shand noted down all the information he wanted, then sent them to the Commissariat for execution and started on the non-combatants.

'Three of them Lesk found in the Western Habs,' Hontius said. 'Mother and son, and a blind man, though he's unrelated, apparently.'

Shand had the mother brought in first. He thought she'd be the most helpful.

Hontius led her in, sat her down on the chair, and mag-locked her hands behind her back.

Shand had removed his peaked cap to reveal the steel skull-plate. His pink scar tissue was taut as his baleful violet eyes stared down. 'Name?'

'Asha Kilgard.'

'Occupation?'

'I worked in the manufactoria. Agri-fertilisers. Before the war.'

A clerk sat in the corner of the room, stylus in one hand. He noted her answer down as Shand went on. 'And when did that work stop?'

Asha puffed her cheeks out. 'When the gang came.'

'Which gang?'

She paused, trying to remember. 'They called themselves Something of the Ninth...'

'Covenant of the Ninth Siren?'

'Yes!'

'And when did they come?'

She put her finger to her lip. 'It was just after... the rift appeared in the sky. The leader of the miners. He told us that he was going to bring order. But each time someone brought order, more chaos came. And then the Covenant came...' Asha shuddered at the memory. 'We thought they were good. There was order at first... But order did not help. The Covenant split. I don't remember the names. Syndicate of something, and the Pact of Flagellation. They kept splitting and fighting till there was nothing but looting and destruction. If you could, you got off-world. If you couldn't, then you fled out into the wastes. Some of them lived in the mineworks. Then the Scourged came.

'They stamped order onto all. They killed the other gangers, purged the lot. Everyone was in fear of them. They took my husband. The miners were taken, the factorum workers. We did not know where they went. Not until the ships took them away. To fight in their wars, I heard. Or act as thralls. There was no one left. We were forced to work. They formed us into slave-gangs. They took my eldest. They dragged them off. That broke me.

'So I fled to the Western Habs. It was quieter there. The Scourged did not come so often. And I had to keep my lad alive. He was all that was left to me.'

Shand was impassive as he recorded the details. 'When did the Scourged leave?'

Asha paused. 'They didn't, did they?' She wanted desperately to please. She let out a long breath. 'I don't know. There's been fighting for months.'

There was a knock on the door and it opened wide enough for Hontius to put his head around it. 'Sir,' he said. 'I think you should come and see this.'

Shand gave him a look. He nodded as if to say that it was of the utmost importance.

As Shand walked to the door, Asha spoke out. 'Will I see my son?'

'All being well, yes.'

Shand left the room and shut the door behind him.

Hontius pulled him a little way, and said, 'We've had this one brought in as well.' He led Shand to a doorway. 'Have a look. See what you think.'

Shand went in.

The man wore the same blue overalls as the woman, and his face had the same emaciated look. But his eyes were even more sunken, his lips moving in a constant mumble.

Shand felt his skin prickle as he stepped into the room and shut the door behind him.

The man's words were clear. 'It is the hour of need… Cadia must stand.'

Shand came out. Hontius studied his reaction.

'Listen to him. Doesn't that sound like the order Governor Marus Porelska gave before the Battle for Cadia?'

Shand paused. It did.

'And look at his eyes,' Hontius said, and then whispered, 'I think he is an Imperial astropath.'

Blanchez came back after dark. Bohdan was sitting by the vox. He had it on the open vox-web, letting the chatter wash over him.

'Where's the boss?' Blanchez said.

'On a circuit.'

Blanchez nodded but said nothing. She unslung her sniper rifle from her shoulder and pulled the powercell out. She sat down without speaking.

Yedrin came in and leant his flamer up against the wall.

'Heh,' he said. 'What did you find?'

'Nothing,' Blanchez said.

'You all right?' Yedrin said.

She didn't answer. He handed her a mug of recaff. 'Here,' he said. 'This will warm you up.'

Blanchez nodded. After a long time, she said, 'You ever seen a ghost?'

'No,' Yedrin replied.

'I think I just did,' Blanchez said. She clutched her mug with both hands. 'I felt someone watching me… There were three figures. They had hoods pulled over their heads.'

Yedrin paused. 'And?'

'And then they were gone.'

'Weird,' Yedrin said.

Blanchez nodded. 'I'm going to rest,' she said, and went to the corner. She laid her sniper rifle out on the bed next to her, rested a hand over it, and pulled the blanket over herself.

Senik's squad were three hours into the job of clearing out the bodies when darkness closed in.

Senik brought searchlights in. Frozen mist swirled in the blue-white beam of light. The bodies were dragged out and slid onto the back of a truck. None of them wanted to be doing this. It wasn't that they were dealing with dead bodies, but the fact they were having to clear out heretics.

But then one of the troopers called out to Senik. 'Sir. There's something else. You need to see.'

Senik stumped over. He stopped and looked down. 'Throne,' he said. He knelt and wiped the shoulder plate, so that the emblem was clear.

'Throne,' he said again, and made the sign of the aquila. 'How the hell did they get here?'

Minka was just returning to the Administratum office, when Senik's vox came through.

'We've cleared the bodies... and, well, I don't really believe what we've found. This is important.'

'What is it?'

'I think you should see for yourself. I think I'm going mad.'

Minka arrived at the office. A halftrack stood outside, the irregular shape of the bodies piled up in the back. Sergeant Frost was waiting to bring her inside.

'Captain Lesk,' he said. 'This way. Senik's keeping it all a little secret. He's rattled...'

Minka walked in. She shivered as she stepped inside. The room looked strangely eerie, illuminated by two searchlights. Senik's troopers were standing guard.

Senik looked pale. 'Sir,' he said. 'I didn't want anyone else to see this, but I think it's important.'

He led her into the room and flicked on his lumen. 'Here,' he said. 'Look.'

The beam from his lumen stabbed down. She looked and saw what he was pointing at. She knelt, making the sign of the aquila. 'Throne,' she said.

The dead man was wearing Cadian flak armour, and his shoulder plate was marked with the number eight.

She looked up and caught Senik's eye. 'Frekk,' she said.

He nodded.

Minka stood. 'Right.' She stopped to think. 'The Eighth. Here?'

She looked about the room as if there were clues. Then she remembered what the Black Templars had said, six months ago, on Cinnabar's Folly. About the dead heretic having come from battles within the Ghost Nebula.

Minka looked down. 'How many are there?'

'It's hard to say,' Senik replied. 'Once we've moved the Scourged out of the way, then we'll know. But there could be fifty, a hundred?'

'Keep working,' she said. She remembered the shrines inside the *Imperial Heart*, and the chapel where retired regimental banners had been placed. 'Dump the heretics, but bring the Cadians in. Warmund will want them for his mausoleum.'

VI

Prassan felt like he was drowning under the reams of requests and had not thought that his day could get any worse, but he had just come from Bendikt's office, where he had received a severe dressing-down.

The Cadians prided themselves on excellence in all things, and to fight, an army needed food and ammo above everything else. Plus mines, fuel and all manner of other things.

'And I have Banting swearing about the location of his medicae facility,' Bendikt had told him. 'What would Creed think? He might be out there you know, fighting, and you can't even get a medicae in the right place!'

Prassan took his reprimand stoically. When he came out of the room, he had the exhausted, irritable look of a man who had been caught in a mess beyond his ability to solve.

Of course, had it been up to him, he would have taken that six-month sojourn on El'Phanor, to iron out all these details. But he was learning on the job, and failure was a fine teacher. It was not something he wanted to experience again.

Prassan was in such a hurry that as he crossed the road before the palace, he did not notice Minka.

She called out his name.

'Oh,' he said. 'Sorry.'

'I've been trying to contact you. We need mines,' she said, and he put his hands up in an attitude of despair.

'We're working on it. Listen, Lord General Bendikt is very busy.'

'We all are,' she said.

He nodded. He had the air of a man overwhelmed. She didn't waste any more time. 'One of my lieutenants was clearing out some dead bodies. There were Cadians at the bottom of the pile.' The real news was even more impactful. 'Look. This is the shoulder badge. The Eighth.'

'The Eighth? Here?'

She nodded.

He paused. 'I'm sorry. You're right. We should show the lord general.'

'We?' Minka said.

'You,' Prassan said. 'He's a little Creed mad. Just warning you.'

'I didn't find Creed.'

'Shame. Listen, I'd better go. I'll get you those mines. Good luck with Bendikt.'

Minka was shown straight into the palace, and along a corridor to Bendikt's office. It reminded Minka of the Durondeau from Cinnabar's Folly. It had the same monumental scale, the same faded opulence, same sense of military necessity.

Bendikt was upstairs. She could hear his voice as she approached down the corridor.

As she entered, she made the sign of the aquila. Prassan's tone had given her enough warning. He turned to her.

'Lesk?'

'Lord general, I have found bodies, sir, wearing the uniforms of the Cadian Eighth.'

She held the badge out.

'Where?' he said.

'There is an Administratum building, just north of the factorum district. It appears to have been used as a place of execution. There were Scourged bodies on top.'

She showed Bendikt the point on the map. Mere marked the spot on the chart. Bendikt looked a little stunned. 'The Eighth?'

She gave him the shoulder pauldron. It was Cadian drab, with the single digit marking the regiment.

'Creed's regiment here?' He stood looking down at it. 'Mere. He is here, I know it. It's all starting to come together.'

Mere nodded but said nothing, at first.

'The Lord Castellan's Own. Here. On Telken's Rest.'

'We should bring the bodies in,' Mere said.

'You're right,' Bendikt said. 'These are Cadians! They should be honoured. Lesk, have them sent over at once.'

Two hours later the halftrack had already returned. A tarpaulin covered the bodies in the back.

Bendikt came down the broad steps to inspect them. The corpses were old. Their fatigues had faded in the cold and the wind, but the uniforms were unmistakable. Cadian drab, combat boots, reinforced flak shin-guards.

Bendikt pulled a frozen arm towards him and dusted off the snow and dirt. 'Look,' he said. 'The Eighth. How old do you think they are? The Eighth were never deployed here... unless they came after the fall. So they must have come in the last ten years.'

Mere remained silent, thinking. 'None of them look like Creed,' he said.

Minka shook her head. 'I never met him, but I saw pictures. None of them looked like him.'

Bendikt looked at the heaped corpses. 'Thank you, Lesk. We'll have them transferred to the morgue. Leave them with me.'

Keremm and Talbeas had worked all day, scrubbing the heretical filth from the chapel walls.

At times they were so moved that they broke out into prayer, calling on the God-Emperor to smite those who had turned away from Him. But after hours of labour, they retired to the room they shared.

There were two beds inside, set on either side of the room.

Keremm was exhausted. One of the Cadians had left a tray of food for them and all he wanted to do was start eating.

'Shall we pray?' Talbeas said.

Keremm paused. 'Yes, of course.'

Talbeas knelt and Keremm felt obliged to do the same. But whereas she pulled her gown up so that she was kneeling on her bare knees, he thought his age excused him this added discomfort.

He let Talbeas lead the prayers, and at the end, she made the sign of the aquila and remained silent, her eyes closed in lingering contemplation. At last she stood, and Keremm thanked the Emperor. He was starving. He lifted the cloth from the food, and set out the metal cups and spoons.

'There!' he said, pouring water for her and sitting down to eat.

As he lifted the spoon to his mouth, there was a knock at the door.

'Yes?' Keremm called out and stuffed the carb into his mouth.

It was one of Mere's adjutants, Manon. She was a charming young girl Prassan had picked up from Warmund's staff.

She was apologetic. 'Sorry, father. Confessor. Chief Commissar

Shand has asked you to take care of one of the locals...' She escorted the person forward through the door.

It was a child with a shaved head and deep-set eyes. Manon pushed the child forward. He half resisted and stood trembling before them.

'He doesn't speak,' she said. 'We're calling him Tyrok. We thought that perhaps prayer might help.'

Keremm was not at all impressed, but he did not have a chance to speak before Confessor Talbeas stood.

'Poor lad,' she said. She put her arm about the young boy's shoulders and pulled him in. 'Here, sit down, my child. Have you eaten?'

The child made no answer, but she decided that he hadn't.

'Here,' she said.

Keremm looked from Manon to Talbeas to the boy and back again, as Talbeas took his bowl and doled some out for the child.

'Welcome,' he said flatly.

Manon had a set of mag-cuffs hanging from her belt. She spoke in a bare whisper. 'Please restrain him if you sleep, or if you leave him.'

Keremm took the mag-cuffs and laid them on the table.

Talbeas fed the child herself. He took each mouthful and chewed it slowly before swallowing. When he had finished, Talbeas gave him half her own.

'Careful,' Keremm said. 'You might make him sick.'

She nodded and took her bowl back.

'We have come from the Imperium of Man,' she said, and held up one of the tokens she had slung about her neck. 'Do you know the Golden Throne?'

The lad stared at her with wide, sunken eyes.

'The God-Emperor?' she said to him.

The child said nothing. Talbeas took his hand and held it between her own, patting it reassuringly. 'Poor child. We shall teach you it all. The God-Emperor loves you. He loves you so much. He sits upon the Golden Throne, and His light shines out across the whole Imperium of Man. That is where we are from… All humanity follows Him. Only those who are heretics do not. The Scourged. They hate Him. There is nothing we can do for them. There is only one cure for heresy.' She patted the pistol at her belt.

Keremm let out a short sigh, and smiled thinly as he stabbed his three pronged fork into the last piece of slab. He put the food into his mouth and chewed slowly.

Tyrok watched him.

'I'm going to the chapel,' Keremm said.

'Alone?' she said.

He nodded.

'Are you sure?'

He nodded again, and took a deep breath. 'We have removed the worst of it.'

'I should come.'

'I'll be fine,' he said.

Keremm lifted the key from his belt, caught the lock in his hand as the bolt sprang free, and dragged the chain through the handles. He swallowed as the doors creaked open.

He felt a little sick, and took a deep breath as his hand felt for the lumen.

The wall had a sticky texture. He found the brass switch and pulled it down, and the lumens flickered on. Instantly, Keremm wished he had stayed in with Talbeas. He knew how much they had cleaned away, but there was so much left: bloodstains, foul graffiti, eyes picked out of holy icons.

As he stepped inside, he had the feeling that there was someone else in the room. He spun round, but saw that the room was empty. He kept turning, certain he could hear something in there. Someone said his name.

It was a bare whisper. A cold breath of air that made his hairs stand on end.

'Keremm,' the voice said.

Father Keremm made the sign of the aquila. He wasn't up to this. Not alone. Not today. He flicked the lumens off, rethreaded the chain through the handle, locked it and stood in the corridor, fingers fumbling as he lit a lho-stick.

He smoked three before his stomach calmed. He went back into their chamber and Talbeas looked up. The child was lying on Keremm's bed. The confessor had stacked their metal plates, and was enjoying a lho-stick of her own.

She caught the look in his eye. 'How was it?'

'I couldn't,' he said. He pulled a chair out and sat down. 'Maybe we should seal it up.'

'We have to clean it,' she said. 'That is the whole point of us being here. We're here to bring the planet back to the Imperium. We shall clean this world as though the break had never happened.'

Keremm nodded. Where to start? he wondered.

He rubbed his temples, and washed away the taste of ashes from his mouth with a glug of chem water. The boy looked innocent enough, lying with his eyes closed and the blanket pulled up to his chin.

'Did he say anything?' he asked.

Talbeas looked to see if Tyrok had heard. 'No. But he is a good listener. I told him of Saint Celestine, and how she smote His enemies with the Ardent Blade.'

Keremm smiled. He sat on the bed and patted Tyrok's head.

He wasn't very good with kids. It was a long time since he'd had to deal with one.

'Rest,' he said. 'Let the Emperor know that you love Him. Hush. Be still.' He stood and made the sign of the aquila. 'We will pray for you and your home world.'

Chief Commissar Shand steeled himself as he approached the room where the astropath had been placed. The Guardsmen had stuck religious images to the door, along with purity seals and icons of the Emperor, and Shand had taken precautions since last time he was here. There were wards on the door and a squad of troopers standing watch, led by Hontius.

Shand was a man of implacable faith, but he felt a shiver of apprehension go through him. He pulled his bolt pistol out of its holster, checked the clip, loaded with blessed bolts, and returned it to its place.

'Any sign of taint and I'm required to end his life,' Shand told Hontius.

'Is this standard procedure for dealing with astropaths, sir? Is there anything I should do?'

Shand paused. 'What do you mean?'

'I don't know. What's the protocol in these kinds of cases? If I need to speak with him, should I avoid exciting him?'

'We will know soon enough if he is corrupted. Are you ready?'

Hontius nodded.

Inside, the plain rockcrete floors and walls had all been painted a plain grey once, but the paintwork was chipped and scratched, and there were dark, damp stains and mould streaking the surface.

In the middle of the room the astropath sat in a restraining chair, cuffs closed about his wrists and ankles, a metal hoop about his neck and forehead, and a ball-gag in his mouth. His face was still stained with delousing powder, the skin pale under the line where his beard had been shaved. He was moaning and rocking forwards and back as they stepped in.

'I am going to remove your gag,' Shand said.

The milky blind eyes opened as the chief commissar stepped forward and unbuckled the straps. The gag came out, dark with saliva.

'I have been sent by the Imperium of Man. Your world has returned to the safety of the Imperium. What is your name?'

The astropath loosened up his jaw and cheek muscles, and spoke. 'I see the planet as a claw closes about it. A great shadow. You must return. Sons and daughters, you must return. Your homeland calls you…'

Shand and Hontius exchanged glances.

'What is your name?' Shand repeated.

The man kept talking the same doom-laden talk.

Shand put his hand to his bolt pistol, ready for any sign of corruption. 'You are a member of the astropathic choir.'

The man paused at those words, his white eyes looking about, as if he could see things in the air before him.

'You are a member of the astropathic choir. I am Chief Commissar Shand. Speak. Tell me your name.'

'You all must return,' he said. 'In His name, the battle comes to our door once more.' The man started to shake violently.

Hontius drew his pistol, but Shand put his hand up to still him.

'Cadia has fallen,' Shand said.

At those words the man's fingers tensed up. 'The enemy!' he said.

'Who?'

'He crawls out from his hole, from his refuge, and he comes for us.'

'Who?' Shand said, but he could not get the man to say, and at last the exertion overwhelmed him.

Shand put the gag back in place and walked out of the room.

'What have we learnt?' Hontius said.

Shand pursed his lips. 'I don't know.'

The halftrack was brought to the side gate of the merchant palace and Major Luka's Whiteshields were given the duty of carrying the corpses into the waiting morgue containers.

They arrived at the halftrack as the engine was cut off, and the whole thing rattled to stillness.

They pulled back the tarpaulin and took in their assignment. There were about thirty bodies, stiff with cold. Most had tri-dome helmets, a few did not. They were smeared with red, all of it frozen.

'Poor bastards,' Ankela said.

The mortuary containers stood in the yard behind the palace. Major Luka picked the end one. 'Take them there!' he ordered.

They worked in pairs. Ankela made sure she did not slow Skyrin down. She knew she was not as strong as him, but she was damned if she was going to let him know.

Juliar was teamed up with Thainne, who was almost giddy at the thought of imminent action. He kept talking about battle and injuries and troopers being ripped apart by shrapnel. Juliar was sick of it. He didn't like the dead bodies and there was something almost industrial in the amount of blood that had frozen onto the corpses they were carrying.

'Looks like they were eviscerated,' Thainne said.

Juliar said nothing. Their gloved hands took each corpse under the armpits and the heel, and they lugged them along. Thainne had the feet.

'Chainsword makes a hell of a mess.'

Juliar nodded. He was so tense about fighting, he felt sick.

'Hear there was a Space Marine on Cinnabar's Folly,' Thainne said.

'Can you stop?' Juliar said.

Thainne didn't speak again until the last body. He couldn't help himself. 'Took out half a squad before they killed it. Ripped them apart with its bare hands. Tore someone's head off and threw it at another.'

'I'm sure we'll see it all,' Juliar said.

Thainne backed into the chamber.

'On three,' he said, and counted, and on three they swung the body into place.

They started walking to the door and Thainne said, 'He moved!'

'Don't mess around,' Juliar said.

They stepped out and Juliar slammed the door shut.

'I tell you, he moved!' Thainne said, and put a hand up Juliar's back.

'For Throne's sake, Thainne – just stop,' Juliar told him.

They rolled the bodies up to the open doors and then carried them in by the feet and armpits and laid them at the far end. No doubt the Eighth would have a special place on El'Phanor.

They were laid ten across, three high in an uneasy pile of stiff arms and legs.

Halfway through, Chief Medic Banting arrived. A blanket had been thrown over the faces of the dead and he lifted it briefly. There was a reverential hush as he moved along the line, inspecting the frozen corpses.

Last in the line was a young man, his expression fixed, lips pulled back in a grimace in death. Banting let out a sigh as he stood up, threw the blanket back over the corpse's face, and wiped his hands.

Mere had arrived and stood at the door. 'What can you tell us?'

Banting took a breath as he considered what his professional opinion should be. 'Well,' he said, 'they're certainly dead.'

Mere nodded. He looked uncomfortable and spoke in a low voice. 'But are they Cadian?'

Banting puffed out his cheeks. 'There are tests, but nothing we could do here.'

'The eyes?' Prassan said.

'I'll give it a go,' Banting said. 'But membranes desiccate after death…'

Mere and the other Cadians stood back as Banting took a lumen from his breast pocket and shone it into the dead man's eye.

'Inconclusive,' he said.

Mere considered the news. 'We'll thaw them out and send them to El'Phanor, and let them decide.'

It was two hours later that Bendikt finished assessing the reports from the company captains, and the commanders of the other regiments on Telken's Rest. There were scattered reports of resistance. Irregulars. Gangers. But no sign of the expected heretics.

'Seventh Company reported a lone Scourged sniper,' Mere reminded him.

'Ah, yes. But it doesn't fit the other data.' He peered at the maps. 'I don't get a feel from this lot… I don't see a pattern. Something is missing.'

Mere looked at the pile as Bendikt flicked through one more time.

'Maybe they fled?'

'Where to?'

'Off-planet? Who knows what happened after the assassination.'

Bendikt paused. He said nothing for a long time. The silence stretched on, broken only by the scratch of the servitor's stylus. 'Drakul-zar, dead. His own men killed him,' he said. 'Whether as punishment for his failure, or to try and curry favour with the Imperium, who knows?'

Mere shook his head. Such ignorance. The Imperium would never forgive.

'Imagine if we found Creed!' Bendikt said. 'I always felt I had a connection to him. We were the same age, you know.'

'I know,' Mere said.

'We were both upon the *Fidelitas Vector*. A fine battleship. Creed sought me out personally.' Bendikt's chest puffed out as he remembered. If he found Creed, he thought, how they would turn the forces of heresy back! How he would stick it to Warmund!

'Any news about those bodies?'

'I had Banting look,' Mere said. 'The bodies are frozen. He was unable to say how long they had been there. I have ordered them to be transferred to the mortuarium.'

'Good,' Bendikt said, 'good.' He was so excited he could barely stand still. 'We must not get carried away, Mere. We have to focus on the job before us.'

'Correct,' Mere said.

'Maybe I should have a look at them. You never know what clues others might have missed.'

Mere started to object, but Bendikt had got swept up in the excitement. 'Creed! Here! What luck that would be.'

VII

Commissar Hontius found Father Keremm standing in the corridor outside the priest's chambers. The priest was smoking. He took a long drag of the lho-stick. He did not smile as Hontius approached.

'All well, father?' Hontius said.

Keremm nodded, but did not speak.

'I hear they made a mess of the chapel,' Hontius said.

'Yes,' Keremm said. He looked at the door, lips pursed.

Hontius had a feeling that there was something going on… but he had no idea what. 'Chief Commissar Shand has a request,' he began.

Keremm took another drag.

Hontius stood over the priest. 'We have another civilian who is in need of prayer.'

Keremm said nothing.

'His mind is a little disturbed. Shand thought that prayer might help. It is an astropath.'

Keremm dropped his lho-stick and ground it under his boot. 'And you want me to pray for him?'

'He appears disturbed. Prayer might help.'

Keremm nodded. 'I'll come and see.'

Chief Commissar Shand stepped silently into Bendikt's planning room, but his presence was such that everyone felt the sudden tension.

The chief commissar approached. He spoke in a low voice: 'Lord general.'

Bendikt spun round. 'Chief commissar.'

Everyone's eyes followed Shand as he paced into the middle of the room. His hands were behind his back as he looked up at the chart.

It seemed that the Imperial landing had gone very well. All their objectives had been met, the port facilities were largely intact, and the rest of the task force was free to descend.

'Forgive me for interrupting, lord general. There is a matter of some import that I wanted to bring to your attention.'

He paused. Bendikt turned his full attention towards the commissar.

'A civilian has been brought to me. I believe him to be an Imperial astropath. Perhaps the only survivor of this world's astropathic choir.'

Bendikt sat up.

'He has been traumatised by the heretical occupation. I have no idea how he is still alive, or how he avoided death by the Scourged when the world fell.'

'Where is he?'

Shand exchanged a glance with Mere. 'A clerk is recording his words. Father Keremm is with him, until we can get more specialised help. I thought that prayer might help soothe him.'

'Good,' Bendikt said. He tried to hide his excitement. 'Good. Thank you, chief commissar.'

Shand made the sign of the aquila.

As the second day neared its end, Minka set all her platoons to sweep their territories.

'Correct,' Minka said. 'I'm concerned about possible Scourged presence.'

'I thought they'd all left?' Sargora voxed back.

'That's what command seem to think,' she said. 'But Blanchez killed a possible Scourged warrior today. Let's assume the worst.'

There were two hours left of daylight as Sargora led her own squad through the habs and cellars. Senik's squads worked their way as far as the algae farms, where they looked out over the shattered domes amid the stink of sewage escaping from the broken pipes.

'Do we have to search those?' Baine asked.

'Of course,' Viktor said. 'Come, follow me.' He slid down and tested the ice. 'It's solid.'

His squads made their way along the half-empty piping. There was no sign of occupation, and nowhere for anyone to go.

As this was going on, Minka joined Senik's platoon as they picked their way along the factorum buildings at the edge of the ice wall. The Drookian Fen Guard lines were half a mile south, the smoke of their fires rising blue into the air.

The Cadians picked their way through the deserted buildings. The burnt-out ruins were stark against the grey sky. The roofs were broken, the machinery crusted in ice and rubble, and the soaring hangars had a depressed, gloomy feel as the wind whistled through them.

The factorums looked like they had been stripped, but here and there were disused machines, cogs, great iron wheels and ancient smelting vats hanging in the air.

Minka looked about. The whole place had a melancholy air. She thought of Cadia and let out a sigh.

Creed had done the impossible: he had beaten the enemy on the ground. The forces of the Archenemy had been broken.

If only the Imperial Navy had held, she thought, then Cadia would still stand.

Tyrok was snoring when Father Keremm came back, his footsteps echoing down the empty corridor. Talbeas looked up as he came in. She was kneeling in prayer, and stood to speak to him.

'Where were you?' she said.

Keremm slumped down into the chair. He looked in the tin mug, drained the last few mouthfuls, put it down again, and blew out a weary breath. 'There's an astropath. Shand wanted me to pray for him. I did my best. But he is a tormented soul. I do not know how well I did.'

He paused, despite his exhaustion, to think. 'I chose the Consolations of Agony.' He looked across to where the child slept on his bed. 'How's he doing?'

'Fine,' she said. The boy was lying on his back, one hand chained to the bedpost.

She pulled the blanket up to his chin, tried to cover his hands as well. There was a tenderness to her movements. A sympathy that spoke of her humanity, Keremm thought, which, ultimately, was what they were all fighting for.

'He must be worn out,' she said. 'Poor lad.'

Keremm nodded. 'I saw his mother. She is held in the cells, for now.'

He picked up the plastek jug, but it was empty as well. He sighed. He knew where it had all gone. She'd given it to Tyrok, he thought.

He set his hands on his knees and pushed himself up, took the jug and started towards the door.

'Think we should unlock him?' Talbeas said.

He stopped. 'No,' he said quickly. 'That would not be a good idea.'

'He's not going to wake,' she said.

'What do you mean?'

She blushed. 'Banting came. He gave him suppressants. Said it would knock him out for a while.'

'Then he won't mind being locked,' Keremm said.

She nodded. 'Poor lad,' she fussed again. 'Just think what he's been through.'

'Exactly,' Keremm said. 'Which is why he must be restrained.'

He stopped. He had spoken too harshly, he thought, and he tried to speak more kindly. 'Pray to him. The Catechism of Saint Gerstahl the Martyr. I have always found that a source of great help.'

Confessor Talbeas picked up her prayer book. It hung on a chain from her belt, the leather covers folding over the front. The latch was in the shape of a skull. She pressed it open, and took a deep breath. The Catechism of Saint Gerstahl the Martyr was a common text among the regiments who had defended the Cadian Gate, who looked to Gerstahl for conviction and inspiration. She chose Book II, Chapter Three, Verse XVII.

He knew it by heart, and closed his eyes as he brought the words back, and spoke with emotion. 'Teacheth thy hands to war, thy heart to faith. Bolster thy soul with ramparts against temptation, let the faithless be snared in the fanged coils of wire.'

She nodded. The book fell open to the beginning of Chapter Three, and it didn't take her long to find the place he had suggested. 'Yes,' she said. 'I will.'

She started to read, and he closed the door on her, as her melodious tones continued along some of his favourite lines.

Girdest me with ferocity in battle, subdue those that rise up against me; smite thy enemies with thy holy wrath.

Thy numbers only increase our faith. The flames of war shall engulf thy banners. Thy dead shall rise up as hills and mountains.

Bendikt stuck to recaff until night had fallen. But as the last reports came in, he poured himself a cup of amasec. On his third he sat down and stretched his boots out and relaxed.

Bendikt said, 'I had a dream, once, that Creed was still alive.'

Mere said nothing.

Bendikt sipped his glass. 'There's never been a body found.'

'That is true of many who have died for the God-Emperor.'

Bendikt didn't seem to notice the tone in Mere's voice. 'If Creed was in command, we would have cleared the Brutal Stars by now,' he said.

Bendikt poured himself another glass of amasec, and felt the tension ease as it slipped down to his stomach. He thought back on the years since Cadia had fallen. They had been a dark time for him. They'd almost broken him. But now… now it seemed to him that it had all been for a *purpose.*

He would find Creed and bring him back.

He nursed his glass, swirling the amber liquid. In his mind's eye he saw an image of Creed's body, lying on some hilltop, surrounded by his dead enemy. So close to fighting his way out to the Imperium, but conquered at the last.

The God-Emperor had strange ways of making His will known, Bendikt thought, and he felt a wave of warmth rise through him. His grace.

Mere nodded as he stepped up to the charts. 'The Drookian Fen Guard are in position. As soon as the troop carriers arrive, we can push out from here.'

Bendikt nursed his empty glass as Mere went through the details, but his mind kept going back to Creed.

What a blessing it would be if the Lord Castellan came back to them from the ruins of war. That would show the God-Emperor's beneficence at work!

'Those dead Cadians…' Bendikt said. 'You went through the bodies, yes?'

'Yes,' Mere said. 'I took Banting.'

'Do you think one of them could be him?'

'No. I went through them all.'

'Mere!' Bendikt said, suddenly standing. 'Why is it for me to ask these questions?'

Mere seemed shocked by his explosion of anger. Even Bendikt was taken aback. He spoke more gently now. 'I shouldn't be the one prodding you on like this. Creed could be out there. He could be anywhere.'

Mere's eyes went to the bottle of amasec.

'I'm not drunk,' Bendikt said.

'No, sir?'

'No.'

When Mere had gone, Bendikt finished his amasec and took his sword, Paragon, from the wall.

It had been carried by Saint Ignatzio Richstar in the days of the God-Emperor. Bendikt drew the straight blade from its scabbard. He felt the poise, the balance, the ancient pedigree of this pattern-welded sword.

He pressed the power stud, and a crackling webwork of voltaic energy rippled along its edge. Why would the God-Emperor have brought this sword to his possession, unless He had great things in store for him?

He sheathed it once more and set it next to his shrine, and then, hands cupped on the hilt, he knelt down, steepled his fingers and took in a deep breath as he tried to feel the will of the God-Emperor.

Through them he could see the icon of Creed. The gold leaf shone out with a pure yellow light, textured with the minute creases of the gossamer-thin plate. That bullish face. Indomitable spirit. Strategic genius.

Bendikt closed his eyes and prayed with a passion he had not felt for years.

It was deep in the middle of the night when one of the staff officers came to Mere's chamber.

'There are contacts on the auspex,' he said.

Mere pushed himself up and rubbed his eyes.

'I wanted you to see before I woke the lord general.'

Mere nodded and let out a sigh. 'I will come see.'

It wasn't far to the command centre. A skeleton staff were there, working in silence, with cups of recaff to keep them awake.

Mere looked at the chart. The augur was picking up signals out in the ice wastes.

He yawned and frowned. With each circuit of the augur display, the contacts showed up.

Mere took a sip of someone else's recaff.

'Shall I wake Bendikt?' the officer asked.

Mere shook his head. 'Is it meteorological?'

The officer blushed. 'Not sure, sir.'

Mere checked his chronometer. It was two hours till dawn. He had seen electrical storms cause ghost traces like these, but better not to take risks. 'Get some flyers out there. I want visuals before we bring the general up to speed.'

'Yes, sir.'

VIII

Esting could not sleep. There wasn't anywhere to go, so he ended up at the pilot's mess, where the night lights glowed out and the samovar gurgled to keep itself company.

He poured himself a recaff, but left it to cool as he leant against the mess table, letting the last day sink in.

Death was a constant companion for them all, but it kept its distance most of the time and he could ignore it. But every so often it reached out to brush your sleeve, or tap you on the shoulder.

He puffed his cheeks out, glad of the solitude.

He'd been there for an hour or so when Mesina came in.

'Heh,' she said, letting the door swing shut behind her. The wind held it open so she pushed it closed, until the latch clicked.

She came across to the samovar, took a clean mug and poured herself a cup.

'Couldn't sleep?' Esting said.

She shook her head. 'We're going out on patrol.'

'Are we?'

'You weren't told?'

'No,' he said, though the truth was he'd been here already. They'd probably gone through the barracks waking everyone with the news.

Mesina stifled a yawn and shook herself awake. 'HQ wants us to help out with the search. Fighters are heading further out and we're combing the near territory.'

'For what?'

She laughed. 'I don't know. The enemy?'

'Surely they'll come and find us.'

She took a sip of the recaff and winced, but she took a second cup. 'That was you, yesterday?'

He nodded.

'I didn't think you'd walk out of there.'

'Nor did I!' Esting laughed. He patted his leg. 'Landed nose first. It crumpled.'

She nodded and poured herself a third mug of recaff.

At that moment one of the Navy staff officers walked in.

He didn't say anything, but pinned the latest orders to the wall, then unfolded a large chart and pinned it alongside. The pilots nursed their recaff as they walked across to see. The area beyond the ice wall had been broken up into a series of sectors. Each one had been initialled. The order sheet was clear. Patrol each sector and report any sign of life to HQ.

Start time was half an hour from now.

Esting took in a deep breath.

'Time for another recaff?' he said as two more pilots came in, a gust of cold blowing in behind them.

It was still dark when Minka finished her nightly circuit. She picked her way north to where her Chimera was waiting. Jaromir refused to say so, but he was starting to flag.

Minka signalled to Yedrin to help him out.

'I'm fine,' Jaromir said as he lugged his heavy stubber up.

Yedrin nodded, and said nothing.

Blanchez was following behind them. The Chimera was starting to loom up out of the gloom when she tapped her vox-bead.

Minka's squad dropped at the warning.

Minka looked about but couldn't see anything. Blanchez was pointing.

'There!'

For a moment Minka thought she saw it. A shape – or was it three? – hurrying under the stilts of a hab. She lifted her hand to warn the others, when a las-bolt flashed out in the gloom.

The stray shot seared against the dark skies, staining the belly of the clouds with a brief, ruddy light.

'Senik?' she voxed.

They could hear voices calling. Everyone seemed to be confused as to what was going on.

'Who fired?' Minka demanded.

It was Senik who answered. His voice was very calm, which immediately alerted her.

'Sorry, captain. I think we stumbled into something.'

The factorum shell was lit from within by the strobing light of a savage firefight.

The flare of the las-fire was so intense that it reflected off the edges of girders and the icy exteriors of stilt-habs. Minka led her squad towards them at a run as the firefight grew in intensity.

'How many?' she voxed Senik, but he was busy trying to order his troopers.

'Frekk knows,' he said.

Minka voxed Bohdan. 'Alert the Drookian Fen Guard that hostiles might be coming their way.'

* * *

Minka reached Senik in the middle of the main factorum block.

The enemy were down in the southern corner, where the walls still stood. He gave her a quick briefing. Two squads were pinning them down, while his other three were working their way around either flank.

'They're putting up a hell of a fight,' he said.

'Gangers?'

'I don't think so,' he said. 'They've got a lot of firepower.'

Minka nodded. 'I'm going forward,' she said.

She crawled along to find Sergeant Frost. 'They have heavy weapons,' he shouted over the thunderous din.

Minka risked a look over the parapet. Whoever they were up against were dug in along a rough barricade of flakboard and machinery. The enemy had triangulated the approaches with hails of suppressing fire.

Minka knew in an instant that the enemy were good.

She voxed her Chimera driver. She was moving down the side of the factorum block.

'I can't see where it's coming from,' Anastasia replied.

Minka snapped, 'Just keep their heads down! The Drookians are sending reinforcements.'

A few moments later the Chimera's turret laser fired a quick salvo of incandescent bolts. They streaked in from the right, over the enemy's position and disappeared into the gloom of the factorum. Then another fired from the other side, a panning salvo that hit lumps of old machinery and exploded with fountains of molten sparks.

Minka crouched down, trying to work out what was happening. There was a pause as a hail of hard rounds pinged against the metal casing of a vast crucible, hanging fifty feet above her head, and then a voice came across a personal link.

It was Blanchez.

'Captain,' she said, her voice calm and quiet. The kind of voice someone used when they had their prey in their sights. *'Scourged.'*

'Sure?'

'I'd bet my mother's life on it.'

Minka voxed back to HQ. 'Suspected Scourged in factorum.' The message was passed along through the squad. They kept the enemy's heads down as the flanking squads finally got round the side of their position. A melta blast glared out.

There were shouts of alarm. Grenades were thrown. The flash was seared on Minka's retinas. She couldn't see what was happening, but she could feel her squad with her. She drew her own power sabre as multi-laser shots lit the factorum with strobing light.

'Let's go!' she told her squad, and they clambered up over the barricade.

Shouting 'For the Emperor!' she started the charge.

The enemy were pinned as multi-laser shots hissed overhead.

Minka was twenty feet from the foe when the earth before her lifted. It was as if the world were shrugging its shoulders. Minka was thrown backwards. She fell back as a fireball rolled up and over her. Everything was rising up, the factorum floor and walls and roof, and then they started to fall, and girders and roofing slabs started to rain down in a shower of deadly debris.

Prassan arrived at a rush. He did not want to speak over the lord general, but Mere could see that he had urgent news.

'Lord general,' Mere said, gesturing to Prassan.

Bendikt spun round. 'Ah!' he said. 'Speak, man.'

Prassan nodded. 'Apologies, lord general. There have been contacts. Lesk's company. She believes it is Scourged elements.'

But at that moment there was the sudden bang of an explosion, and the lumens flickered and then went out. Prassan leapt to his feet, stumbling for the door, already reaching for his sidearm.

Alarms started to ring out across the HQ block.

'Lock down,' Mere snapped. The order went out, and the palace was secured.

Bendikt stood at the window, looking south to where the explosion had come from. 'What's happening out there?' he said.

Esting walked awkwardly as he pushed out from the pilot's mess. He reached his new Arvus. His leg had stiffened and he had to swing it into the cabin. He slid down into the seat and pulled his belt across him as the ground crew slammed his cabin hatch closed.

Esting posted his flight plan onto his dashboard. He went through the standard checks: fuel, weight, flight path. The engines started with an enthusiastic roar.

He flicked the vox on and signalled that everything was okay. He tried not to think of his last flight. Lightning doesn't strike twice, he told himself as the engines growled, and he pushed the fuel chart forward. It was sharper than his old craft. It lifted off with a jerk and he took a few moments to steady it.

Soon, though, he was getting the feel of this new lighter. He wiggled it from side to side. 'We'll make a great team,' he told the craft. 'With time...'

Mesina's Arvus was rising to clear the factorum and he swung his round onto the correct bearings.

Father Keremm was jolted awake. He lay in his cot, working out where he was. He could hear Confessor Talbeas' gentle snoring, and the thin, hissing breath of Tyrok.

He'd been dreaming himself back on Cadia, on the night he was made a priest, praying in the chapel, as something clawed at the door. He paused for a moment. It was that sound that had woken him. He tried to work out if the sound had been in his dream, or real.

He turned over and tried to sleep, but his mind had been startled. He lay in the darkness, alert to any noise.

Father Keremm had trained as a shock trooper before his spiritual bent meant he was selected for training for the priesthood. He had lodged in enough barracks and battle camps to know that each barrack block and prayer hall had its own personality, its own quirks – the midnight scratches and sounds.

It was nothing, he told himself, and said Saint Gerstahl's Prayer of Banishment. It was a real warrior's prayer, one that did not shy away from the tests they faced, but it only left him feeling more awake. He was halfway through when the scratching sounded again.

Father Keremm felt that there was something out there in the corridor. He thought of the chapel and a cold fear spread through him. It started in the middle of his back, and rose up to his forehead, and his bald pate shrank over his skull.

His pistol was under his pillow. Cadian issue. Its worn stock was comfort to him as he stood. The floor was cold under his bare feet. His robes flapped against his legs. He checked the powercell and safety clasp with his left hand, slid the bolt back, and turned the handle as quietly as he could.

The door opened with a creak. Outside, the lumens were set low. He slipped out, stood in the corridor, listened carefully. He could hear all the normal noises. The background hum of the generator. The muttering voices of prayer servitors. The hiss of atmosphere recyclers maintaining oxygen within habitable limits.

The scratching sound came from inside the chapel.

Keremm crept closer and put his head towards the door. A

voice said to him that he should go back and tell Confessor Talbeas, but he could have been a shock trooper once, before the God-Emperor called him. This was a personal test that he would face down.

His mouth was dry as he took the key from his belt. He holstered his pistol and worked the key in the lock.

He slid the chain through the handles, pulled the heavy door open. The cool air washed out towards him. It smelt of counterseptics, and the cleaning fluids.

The candle-lumens were flickering in the heavy darkness.

There were three figures standing in the middle of the chapel.

'Who are you?' Keremm said, and as one, the three figures turned.

Minka was lying on her back.

She wasn't clear what had happened.

She was looking up at a bruised sky through the broken iron ribs of a monumental building. Her goggles were crazed. Something was pressing on her chest. She twisted and turned, but she could not move. Her impulse was instinctive. She was filled with sudden fury, but she could not lift the weight from her chest, could not find purchase, and she cursed and snarled with anger and frustration.

All she could hear was a whistling sound inside her left ear.

A torrent of memories flashed through her. She tried to squirm out from under the debris as the past decade came back to her in a rush of images. The fall of Cadia, the Evercity, sergeant stripes on her arm, the weight of responsibility as she stood and looked at her company. She had to get up. She had to fight.

Someone was pulling her up. It was Jaromir, his face lit by the flickering glow of fire.

His mouth was moving, but she couldn't hear anything but

the constant whistle. She pushed and shoved. The debris on her legs slewed to either side as the weight lifted from her chest.

As suddenly as it had gone, her hearing returned: sudden and alarming. The sound of agonised voices, and the panicked shouts of troopers trying to staunch the blood loss from catastrophic wounds. Senik shouting the names of his squads.

'What happened?' she said, as she staggered up.

'You all right, boss?'

'I'm fine,' she said, her own voice sounding strange in her ears. 'What went off?'

'I don't know,' Jaromir said. He was clearly in shock as well.

Minka pushed her goggles up. It took a moment for her to get her bearings.

'You're bleeding,' Jaromir said.

She put her finger to her nose and it came away red. She nodded as she stood.

'I'm fine,' she said. 'Honest. Just a few bruises.'

IX

The flames took an hour to die down. It gave them time to pull the dead and wounded from the debris. Fire was still licking through the ruins as Anastasia's Chimera ground forward. Its turret-mounted searchlight stabbed a blue-white beam into the gloom of the factorum.

Scraps of burning roofing fell about Minka as she picked her way forward. Melting ice hissed and spluttered into the flames, and smoke and steam curled up through the bar of white light.

Dust and fumes hung thick where the enemy had been. Minka's left leg ached as she limped forward. Her head was ringing, there was blood in her mouth and the air tasted of ash. The lip of the crater was taller than she was. She picked her way up. The rubble was sharp and unstable. Within the debris she could see the remains of sandbags and lengths of flakboard that marked where the enemy had been. There were scraps of ration packs and a water bottle, malformed by the explosion.

But no bodies.

Jaromir followed her up, and Bohdan after. The three stood on the lip of the crater looking down.

'I don't see any,' Bohdan said.

Jaromir nodded. Minka felt as if she doubted her own sanity, but there were no bodies.

Ten minutes later Blanchez came from the right, long-las carried under her arm. Minka was sitting on the side of the crater.

'I bagged one,' Blanchez said.

Olek laughed. 'Sure?'

'Sure.'

'Well, he ain't here.'

'I bagged him,' Blanchez said, again, more forcefully.

Olek pulled the medi-pack off his back. 'I'm sure you did.'

'I'm fine,' Minka said. Her head was ringing, and she dabbed her nose. The blood was starting to scab. Olek sprayed coagulant into her nostrils. She shook her head as he wiped the blood away, then stood. 'Frekk,' she said. 'That stings.'

She blinked away the tears. 'They're here somewhere. They didn't fly away.'

Minka called Anastasia in. The Chimera made slow progress through the ruins, but at last it reached the rubble field, its dozer blade scraping the debris aside. There was the blast of a grenade from under the rubble, and Jaromir stepped forward and used his metal hand to pull lumps of rockcrete away.

It was slow work as the heaps of debris and iron bars grew.

It was an hour later that Blanchez put her hand up and shouted, 'Hold on.'

She picked forward. A boot was sticking from the rubble. Dust swirled up in the bright searchlight. The light was so intense it turned everything to light and shadow.

She pulled a piece of rusted metal aside, hauled lumps of rubble away.

'Said I bagged one,' she shouted out.

One by one the Cadians came to see. The Scourged warrior lay on his front. The back of his head had been blown away, and dust clung to the exposed gobbets of brain.

Blanchez was triumphant. It had been a hard shot.

'Keep digging!' Minka shouted to Anastasia. The Chimera surged forward, the tracks grinding as the dozer blade shoved the dead body into the growing mound of rubble.

Minka stood, intently staring down as the dozer blade kept scraping. 'Stand back,' she said, as the blade went in again.

At last she put an arm up and started pulling rubble away by hand. There was a metal hatch set into the rockcrete floor.

She cleared the last of the debris.

It took two of them to lift it. 'Careful,' Minka said as they peered down.

There was a sandbagged tunnel, scrap-board ceiling held up with iron pit-props.

Minka called out to Senik. 'I want three squads ready to go. Now!'

The squads arrived at a jog. They were going in fast and light. Just the necessary kit: heat-see goggles, lascutters, flamers, stun grenades.

Blanchez had gone in already to check for demo traps. She came back with a handful of trip-wires.

'See anything?'

'There's a rail track the entire way, and a big chamber about a hundred yards down.'

Minka nodded and signalled her force forward, and squad by squad the Cadians crept off.

* * *

This tunnel had once been accessed by a ramp. There was a monumental archway set under the ground. It was thirty yards across, and just as tall, and had once been closed with heavy metal doors that slid sideways on iron tracks.

The doors had rusted open, the great panels broken and bent. The entrance had been fortified at some point. Roofing panels had been piled up, and inside there was a narrow walkway, between a heap of frozen rubbish and tumbled ore. And under it all was a thick layer of black dust.

Blanchez led them in.

In some places there were falls of rubble that reached almost to the tunnel roof, but through it all narrow, well-trodden tracks had been worn, winding round the larger pieces of debris, finding the easiest way up the roof-falls.

'Reminds me of St Josmane's Hope,' Senik said.

Blanchez said, 'I thought they blew that place up.'

'They did,' he replied.

'Frekk,' Blanchez said.

Senik nodded. Last lighter off the planet. Frekk about summed it all up.

There was a set of massive iron tracks set into the rockcrete floor as it headed downwards. Stalactites of lime reached from the ceiling as Blanchez led them towards a deep shaft that plunged into darkness. It looked like a winch station. Winding cogs soared over them, the teeth thickly smeared with dark unguents.

The steel cable hung straight down. It was as thick as Minka's thigh, the cabling made up of a thousand plaited lengths of steel. Set along it were carriages, positioned at regular intervals. Minka didn't know what they had hauled up from the depths, but there was a thick black dust covering everything.

'Mine shaft,' Senik said.

'Sure?' Minka said.

'Looks like it. I'll go first.'

Minka stood at the lip as he rappelled down into the darkness.

She followed Senik. The shaft plunged three hundred feet down. It went through granite. The stone still bore the scars of the boring behemoth's adamantine teeth. Water had dripped down and left a pale crystal residue on the hoop reinforcements. They glowed with a faint green luminescence.

At the bottom there was an intersection. Two bore tunnels led off in different directions, each one with hooped reinforcements and iron props set at regular intervals.

Heat-see goggles turned the world into shades of dull red, fungoid growths showing yellow in the lenses' spectrum.

There was evidence of foot traffic in the thick black dust. Minka nodded. The air had the dark, damp breath of the underhive. The foetid stink of benighted places.

She thought of Viktor. She wished he was here. They'd gone into Markgraaf Hive together, burrowing into the underhive packed in Assault Termites. That company had been as tough as any other she had ever fought with.

Cadian veterans, slamming deep into the dark, polluted guts of the hive.

It had been ferocious fighting. The casualty rate reflected that. It was a time when emotions about their home world were still running high.

Minka let the memories rise through her as she waited for the last few troops to arrive.

Within twenty minutes, there were three squads at the bottom of the shaft. She stood with Senik and Bohdan, weighing the options. Bohdan had grown up on the hive world of Macharia. If anyone could make sense of this labyrinth of cold, dark tunnels then it would be him.

'What do you think?' she whispered.

Bohdan smelt the air, getting his bearings.

'This way,' he said, pointing towards the tunnel heading out towards the ice wall, 'is blocked.'

'Sure?'

He sniffed and nodded again. 'Sure. The breeze is coming from the other direction.'

Minka looked about. She could not feel a breath of air, but she trusted him, and the order was passed along the line.

They left a guard at the intersection and headed away from the ice wall. Blanchez went first again, heat-see goggles pulled down, feeling the faint breath of air flowing into her face.

The darkness was absolute. After ten minutes they stopped.

Minka pushed forward. 'What's up?'

It was Bohdan who spoke. He had gone ahead. 'There's a fall-in,' he whispered. Minka paused. Now he had said it, she thought that she could make it out. Her eyes had grown accustomed to the darkness, and she could see the edges glimmering, the figures before her blocking the light out.

Bohdan spoke so quietly it was almost like a breath of air. 'Smoke,' he said.

Minka couldn't smell it, but she believed him. 'From the explosion?'

Bohdan paused. 'Possible.'

But as they pushed on, the scent of smoke grew stronger and it was not the stink of fyceline.

They moved forward as warily as ever, the only sound the gentle scuff of boots on grit, the *drip-drip-drip* of surface water splashing into a puddle, the low moan of the wind passing over the top of ventilation shafts – like a trooper whistling over the top of a grog-bottle.

Bohdan touched Minka's arm. 'There's light ahead.'

She could hear the gentle clicks of safety catches being flicked off as Blanchez crawled forward.

She came back ten minutes later. She made a hand signal: *Scourged standing sentry.*

Minka puffed her cheeks out. They had to engage, and surprise was their only hope. It was going to be a tough job if they were attacked. It would get messy very quickly.

Esting felt each buffet as his craft dropped and slowed and was knocked sideways by the gusts and eddies. The wind was swinging in from the south, but the habs were throwing it all over the place.

The city was diminutive from this height. He could see far out, across the plateau, to where the mountain range thrust up from the ground. He looked for a visual reference point, picked one of the jagged peaks, and flew towards it.

He checked his bearings, flight plan, and pulled himself northwards as he passed over one of the main thoroughfares. Ice was forming on his windscreen. It was gathering in the corners, and in the lee of the steel struts. He engaged the wipers, but they only cleared the front of the screen.

Within a few minutes Esting passed over the ice wall, and the whiteout was sudden and blinding. The wind suddenly gusted, and the Arvus dropped violently.

He pushed the thruster forward, and it rattled violently as he ran head first into the wind. The engines... He couldn't tell if it was his imagination, or if they were sounding strange. All he could see was the sparkling grey of the ice sheets.

'You see anything?' he voxed to the others.

'Negative,' Mesina said.

* * *

Blanchez went first, pressing herself into the edge of the tunnel as she crawled slowly forward. She was alert to every breath of wind or drip of water as she paused just a few yards from the enemy, barely daring to breathe.

The sentry stood before a heavy curtain that screened the rest of the corridor, but a thin light fell through to illuminate him. He had a tin of recaff in his hand, a lasrifle thrown over his shoulder, his dull mail glimmering in reflected light. He sniffed as he sipped, cleared his throat, spat into the darkness.

Blanchez was close enough to smell him. He was big. Much bigger than she had expected, the brigandine and chain mail glimmering in the thin light. She could not believe that the sentry had not seen her as she weighed her options.

The armour ruled out a stab to the heart. It would have to be the throat. Which meant she would have to get behind him. She moved so slowly it took what felt like ages for her to draw her knife, the blade held in a reverse grip as a second Cadian joined her.

It was Bohdan. His eyes were intent as she turned to look at him. She signalled the plan. It was his job to restrain him, her job to silence him.

A simple plan, but not at all easy.

Blanchez touched five fingers upon Bohdan's arm to get his attention, and then tapped them down one by one.

At four, she was up in a silent rush. Bohdan could barely keep up.

Esting had been flying for nearly an hour, his Arvus tilted so that he could see over the windscreen ice. 'You guys seen anything?' he voxed again, over the crackle of static.

The answer was still negative.

He kept going, weaving up and down, till his fuel gauge was

three-quarters empty. This would be his last circuit. There was nothing beneath that you could get your bearings from.

'Heading for home,' Mesina voxed.

One by one, Esting heard the other pilots turn back. He pulled the nose of the Arvus round. He had enough to get back, and a little bit more. He saw something in the corner of his eye and tried to look back over his shoulder, but it was hidden.

'I just want to check something,' he said, bringing the lighter about and dropping closer to the ground.

In the snow, in the ice, shapes began to resolve. He descended further and saw figures crouching in the snow. A handful at first, then he realised there were hundreds of them, rising up as his lighter swept over them.

He reached for his vox-bead, when he saw a light flash past his cabin.

Over the roar of the engine, he felt the thud-thud-thud of automatic fire and his craft juddered.

'Holy Throne!' he said as tracers flashed by the cockpit, flicking the vox-link to live. 'Hostiles!' he voxed as the windscreen before him shattered.

Bohdan's hand slammed into the heretic's face as his other found the man's mouth. He drove his fingers in, could feel lips and teeth and tongue, stifled the man's cries as the sentry bit down hard. Bohdan snarled with pain and fury, punched again, knocking the man's hands away as Blanchez caught his head in an elbow-lock and plunged in her knife.

The tin clattered to the floor. Hot slop fell on Blanchez's hand. There was the suppressed sound of curses and snarls. She staggered against the rock wall as the dead weight fell against her. She held the sentry as he bled out.

Bohdan looked at the chewed mess of his hand, as Minka

brought her squads up in silence. They stood, waiting, fingers on triggers, the heavy blanket hanging before her.

A voice sounded from the other side of the curtain. A mailed fist took hold of it and pulled it aside, and Minka stood face to face with a Scourged warrior.

His expression turned from astonishment to fury and alarm. He pulled his laspistol from his belt and swung it upwards. Minka fired first.

Her bolt-round slammed through his rusty brigandine and exploded within his ribcage as her power sabre cut through his collarbone, his flesh cooking with the heat of the blade.

Tyson was right behind her, his chainsword roaring as he cut the legs from the heretic. He stamped on the man's head as he stepped past. Olek was on Minka's other shoulder, firing from the hip as Jaromir jostled for a clear shot, braced himself and fired.

The roar of his heavy stubber ricocheted about the stone chamber.

The air was full of rounds. The weight of fire cut through armour, sending up a spray of blood and flesh as the enemy dived behind stacks of sacking, barrels and heaps of ore. Within seconds the room was filled with fyceline mist, which hung blue in the room. The Scourged littered the ground, dead and dying, as the others fell back, laying down a furious counter-fire.

Minka pushed forward, firing and cutting at the surprised enemy. Las-bolts lanced towards her, flashing in the corner of her eyes as beams hissed about her head. Stubber fire slammed into the ground about her. Minka threw herself behind a metal table. The frame was bent, and the metal grew hot as las-bolts crashed against the other side.

Tyson and Olek were next to her. Blanchez dragged herself into cover behind one of the dead Scourged. Here and there,

Scourged warriors were squaring up to the attackers. Blanchez fired rapidly, las-bolts knocking each of them back.

'Jaromir!' Minka shouted.

'Here,' he called back. Minka couldn't tell where he was, but she could tell that he was reloading the barrel magazine. Olek unpinned a spare heavy stubber mag and slung it across the room. The action set off a flurry of las-bolts. They hissed through the air, leaving the burnt stink of ozone hanging about them.

'Got it,' Jaromir called back.

He'd taken a las-bolt to the belly. She could see where it had burned through the harness of his flak armour, and the growing red stain. The pain did not seem to stop him from sliding in the fresh magazine.

'Cadia stands!' Minka called, and every Cadian stood and fired.

The chamber was lit with the sudden flare of las-bolts as Minka led them in another charge. The enemy were sheltering behind impromptu barricades: upturned beds and tables, sacks of carb, the bodies of the dead.

Throughout the chamber the enemy were fighting with berserk fury. There was an insanity to their temper. They did not flee and they would not die, even though they suffered terrible wounds.

Minka fired her pistol point-blank into a Scourged chief's face. He was a huge, hulking man with slab-vat muscles and went down like a stunned grox. But there was another right behind him. A woman, but just as large with vat-grown musculature. One hand gripped a laspistol, the other clad in a gauntlet set with a brutal spike, honed to a razor edge.

She swung at Minka's face. The spike slammed into Minka's helmet as she ducked, but the back-swipe scored a deep gouge across her flak armour.

The woman's metal teeth were fixed in a snarl of fury. Minka barrelled into her, but the woman barely budged. Her power and speed were terrifying. Minka dodged as the fist-spike slammed into her gut. The slab-hanced muscles drove the razor edge through the plates of flak armour.

'Cadia!' Tyson shouted. He was at Minka's shoulder and hacked down at the giant woman's arm. His chainsword threw sparks off the chain armour as the Scourged warrior caught him with one hand and drove the blade up into his gut.

It burst out of his back.

Tyson grunted with pain as he came off the ground.

Minka's power sword cut the woman's arm off. The blow didn't slow her. She backhanded Minka and caught her helmet strap. She dragged Minka so close she could smell the woman's foul breath.

'I can taste you!' the other woman hissed, as inch by inch she dragged Minka closer – her bloody stump hooked behind Minka's neck. Minka drove herself forward. Her tri-dome helmet smashed into the woman's face. Minka kept headbutting till the woman's grip relented, and Minka pushed herself to her feet.

She held her bolt pistol with both hands and fired a series of shots into the woman's stomach. The heretic was still reaching for Minka even as her torso came apart from her legs, and she fell in a wet mess.

Minka pulled her bolt pistol round, but the magazine was empty.

She rushed to Tyson's side. The spike was still embedded in his body. She caught his shoulder and pulled him over.

'Stay with me,' she hissed as Tyson's head fell, limp.

She called Olek over. When he saw it was Tyson, he came at a run.

He pulled his pack off his back and knelt at the sergeant's side.

'Stay with me,' Minka said again, lifting Tyson's head. His

eyes had rolled up into his skull. 'Quick!' she snapped as Olek fumbled for the stimms.

'I've got it,' he said. He ripped off the foil and pressed the dispenser to Tyson's neck as Minka searched for a pulse, giving the sergeant a double shot of stimms.

'Stay with him,' Minka ordered, standing up and turning to the battle.

The Scourged were dead but they had fought furiously. The chamber was a scene of dreadful slaughter. Their massive corpses lay on the ground, bleeding out their last.

Minka had lost almost half her troopers, but they were going round finishing off the heretics.

'Save one,' Minka shouted.

'There's one here,' Blanchez said. She stood over the dying heretic. He had taken a string of Jaromir's rounds to the gut. They'd stitched across him and punched through, cutting a fist-shaped hole in his stomach.

Minka came over and knelt at his shoulder.

'You are the Scourged. Were you on Joalara?'

He spat back at her.

Minka stood and gave Blanchez the signal.

Blanchez put her long-las to the side of his head.

The las-bolt flared briefly and the heretic lay still as a curl of smoke rose from the wound.

Tyson rallied long enough to crack a joke.

His voice was thin. 'I survived nine years with Sparker... but look what you did to me, Lesk. That bastard Sparker was a slacker.' He coughed. 'Tell him that.'

'You tell him,' Minka said.

Tyson laughed. The action hurt him. He winced and stopped. 'I will,' he coughed as the stretcher team lifted him up.

Minka took a moment to catch her breath.

This camp looked like an old pump station. Dirty stalactites hung from the fissured rock and amidst the filth on the floor were the remains of ancient rail tracks, each a foot wide, the iron caked in grime. Dead Cadians were covered with scavenged blankets, steadily reddening. The heretics had been dumped against the far wall, one atop another, and the puddle of blood beneath them grew larger.

Stretcher teams were already taking the most seriously hurt away. The wounded were being patched up. Olek's pack had been emptied of bandages and stimms, but he bound up Bohdan's fingers.

Minka took a deep breath in. She needed to speak to HQ, but she was stuck in an old mine tunnel, buried somewhere under the factorum district, without a direct vox-link. The ground blocked everything.

'Senik,' she said, 'send a runner, at once.'

'There's another room,' Jaromir called out. He sounded fearful. 'Boss. I think you should come and look.'

There was a beehive service chamber and standing in the middle was a chieftain's yurt. It was an incongruous object, more suited to the wild steppes of a feral world, with heretical symbols stitched into the felt.

Waves of dread emanated from it, along with a stench of rot and festering flesh.

Minka checked her bolt pistol, checked her power sabre, took a deep breath. Her Cadians came up behind her, but she had to go first.

A chill ran through her as she pushed forward.

'Cover me,' she said to Jaromir.

She stepped to the entrance of the tent, used her sword to lift the flap.

It was as if she were in the trench again, in the presence of utter evil. But she forced her nausea back. The heavy woollen cloth had a rancid stink mixed with the scent of unholy incense.

The interior was lit by flickering flames. She pushed in, her teeth clenched.

In the middle of the room was a bed. A giant lay upon it. His gene-hanced muscle slabs were covered with suppurating sores, and a stench of corruption flowed towards her as a blood pump gurgled in the background.

Before it crouched a few miserable, twisted and half-starved things, with knives clutched in their hands. Behind the bed stood three healers.

They looked as terrified as she felt. As they moved there was a jangle of metal, and she saw that they had been chained to the bed.

'Put your weapons down!' Minka ordered. 'Down!'

The mutants hissed at her, but the giant on the bed signalled to them, and the weapons rang out as they hit the stone floor. Minka kicked them away, her pistol held up as the giant let out a snarl of pain.

'Back!' Minka snapped, waving them aside.

The giant let out a moan. It was an inhuman sound that sent another wave of shock through her, left her feeling sick. 'Who are you?' she demanded, but the giant was wracked with pain that lanced through him.

'Who is he?' She grabbed one of the servants. 'Speak!'

The middle medic spoke. He was a tall, thin man, dressed in filthy whites. There was a sore about his wrist, where a chain had worn away the skin. His eyes were sunken, and he was shaking.

'He is the master,' he said, his voice a bare rasp.

'The master of who?'

The medic looked down with dread as the figure on the bed

started to move. The cloth covering him fell away and Minka saw flesh, green with corruption.

'In the name of the God-Emperor,' she hissed.

It was all gene-hanced, augmented, corrupted, and the face was barely recognisable. The bull neck and huge and malformed face turned towards her. The head was hairless. The body was swollen and bloated with decay.

As the eyes opened, she clenched her jaw against her horror. They were red, with black slits staring out.

The giant licked his lips, and spoke again, despite the tusks that grew from his lower jaw. His voice was deep and sonorous.

'They are looking for me. You cannot let them find me.'

The giant closed his eyes. His nostrils flared as another wave of pain spread through him. 'Please,' he said. 'Help me.'

'What are you?' Minka said.

'I am Lord of the Brutal Stars, Commander of the Faithful, Chieftain of the Scourged. Chosen Son of the Emperor.' The final title was upon the tip of her tongue as the warrior spoke once more. His face straining with the pain.

'I am Drakul-zar.'

PART V

I

TELKEN'S REST

'Right,' Minka said to her squad. 'Let's get in there and bring that bastard out.'

Minka ordered the medics unlocked, and the bed wheeled out, and there was a winching team at the vertical shaft. It was tough going along the tunnel. They had to carry the bed, with four along either side, lugging the wounded giant over the rockfalls.

Someone found a servo-hauler used for carrying ammo crates. They positioned the bed on top and let the hauler take the strain of Drakul-zar.

'I'll catch you up,' Minka said. 'Bohdan, come with me,' she ordered as she took Yuriv's squad with her.

Keremm was a man who fearlessly faced battlefield horrors, but at that moment his face was white, his hands were trembling.

'I saw them,' Keremm said. 'In the chapel.'

The psyker listened silently, his minders standing behind him, their carapace armour creaking as they adjusted their stance.

Valentian was a good head taller than the priest. He did not doubt the priest's words. He stared down and said nothing, listening to things that Father Keremm could not hear. That no one else could. The ether, swirling about him.

He had come as soon as he felt the disturbance. The empyrean about him was unnatural. It was like standing in a wood where all the birds had fallen silent. There was a sense of watching and waiting, of potential danger.

Father Keremm pointed towards the chapel door.

'There were three of them,' he said. 'In the middle of the chapel.'

Valentian signalled one of his minders forward. The Kasrkin opened the door with the barrel of his hellgun, stepped half inside the doorway, looked about.

'Looks clear,' he said.

'I saw them!' Keremm said, frantic. 'They were there!'

Valentian stepped forward, and looked into the chapel. The candle-lumens were flickering. They illuminated scrawls of heresy.

Valentian paused. He could sense the warp. The watchful stillness. The taint of evil.

He called the Kasrkin out. 'Close the door,' he said. 'You have a key?'

Keremm edged forwards. He stood at arm's length, his fingers fumbling as he handed the key over.

Valentian nodded. 'I will take that,' he told his minders.

He locked the room, and turned. Beads of sweat were glittering on his forehead.

'This chamber is forbidden,' he said. 'I will keep the key until it can be destroyed.'

* * *

Bendikt's office was moved to the basement of the palace for security reasons. Important reports had come in overnight, and the staff officers had been there throughout, responding to reports from the fleet, Naval patrols and stacks of logistics.

Questions had been building up. Only Bendikt could answer them and they waited for the lord general to appear.

'Any idea where he is?' Mere demanded.

He sent an officer to Bendikt's chambers. They returned without him. At last, one of the Kasrkin came back and said, 'I found him, sir. He wanted to inspect the bodies. The dead Cadians. He is coming, presently.'

Mere cursed as he paced up and down.

As he stood waiting, a report came in. The vox-officer was sitting along one side of the room, his desk facing into the chamber. Mere could tell from his demeanour that the news was bad. A clerk brought the note to him.

'Arvus shot down, sector Q-three. Hostiles. Number unclear.'

Mere stared at the map. Q3 was a large stretch that ran from Sparker's territory in the north right down to the factorum district, where the Drookian Fen Guard had been stationed.

'Get Lesk,' he said.

There was a pause.

'I can't raise her,' the vox-officer said. 'She was engaging Scourged elements in the factorum.'

Mere cursed. 'Then get Sparker.'

A few moments later the vox-officer had the contact.

'Sparker?' Mere snapped. 'There are hostiles out beyond the ice wall. They've shot down an Arvus. I can't tell you how many because I don't know.'

At that moment the vox-officer put up a hand and then signalled to Mere. 'Sir,' he said. 'Message from Lesk's company just came through. She thinks she has found something. She says it is urgent. She wants to speak to you or Bendikt. Directly.'

Mere took the handset. 'Yes?' he said, and frowned. It wasn't Lesk he spoke to, but one of her lieutenants. At that moment, Bendikt came in.

'Hold please,' Mere said. He took a deep breath. 'Sir. There are hostiles along sector Q-three. They have shot down an Arvus lighter. Number unknown. I have alerted Captain Sparker.' He took a deep breath as Bendikt nodded. 'And I have just spoken to one of Lesk's lieutenants.' He paused. 'She has a high-value prisoner. She did not want to say who. She is bringing him in.'

Senik took the lead as they picked their way along the tunnel. It was in a worse state than the others. After ten minutes they reached another intersection, with the rail tracks connecting.

The rockfall had slid sideways across the tunnel. Minka climbed up a little, and paused.

She took a breath. 'Can you hear that?'

Bohdan nodded. 'Tunnelling?'

'I think so.' She remembered Markgraaf Hive, and the journey packed inside the Termite. She would never forget the sound of the teeth cutting their way through rock. It sounded like the metallic grind of tank tracks. Or winding gear...

There was a pause. None of the others could hear it. Minka paused again. She put her hand to the stone, but could not feel anything. As she listened now, she could not hear anything either. She might have imagined it.

Bohdan looked back the way they had come, and said, 'We must be under the ice fields.'

Minka paused. She wanted to go further, but there wasn't time, and now she knew there was a network of tunnels that stretched beyond the wall.

'This is enough,' she said. 'Come. Let's get back.'

They retraced their steps and when they reached the vertical shaft, Minka said, 'Yuriv. Get this place wired. I don't want anything following us up out of here. We need to be ready to blow the place.'

Lieutenant Sargora looked out across the frozen flats as she marched along the ice wall.

Sergeant Dreno came out to greet her. He'd been playing cards in the guard-chamber, and stamped his feet and rubbed his hands as the squad hid evidence of the game.

'Sir,' he said, by way of greeting. He kept back so she wouldn't smell the grog on his breath.

'Where are the guards?' she demanded.

He pointed to where he had stationed his heavy weapons team.

'That's it?' she said.

Dreno started to speak, but Sargora didn't have time. 'Listen, sergeant. I grew up on Catachan. You learnt that danger could come from anywhere, any time. And if you didn't, you died. Didn't matter. Something got you.'

Dreno tried to speak again, and again Sargora cut him off. 'What are you waiting for? Get them out on sentry. Now!'

Sargora went along the line and Ordell had only half his squad out on duty, while the others kept warm. Her orders had been clear. Every pair of eyes on watch. Sargora was in a foul mood, but Ordell tried to stand up for himself.

'They've been out for two hours. They need a break so they can stay fresh.'

Yuriv watched as Minka's squad picked their way back up over a rockfall and disappeared. There were puddles in the mine-works where meltwater had dripped. Their surfaces were glassy, reflecting the last light of the troopers' lumens, which gradually receded till his squad were left in almost total darkness, feeling the breath of the tunnel rise into their faces.

A single lumen had been left on, to cast a low glow where they were standing.

Baine found a place to lie down, and Hwang lay next to him.

'Frekking great,' Baine said as he felt for his lho-sticks. 'Sign up with the shock troops. See the Imperium of Man.'

II

The Drookians had watched the Cadians fighting.

'Should we help?' one of the clansmen said.

Grawnya nodded. 'We will. If we are needed.'

She led her troopers forward towards the line of her control. As they reached it the explosion went off. It knocked some of them to the ground, as debris rained down among them.

Grawnya pushed on. They could see the lights of the Chimeras, searching through the ruins.

'Ask if they need help,' she told one of her scouts.

Her troopers watched as the Cadians took control of the factorum. They kept a picket just in case any of the enemy tried to slip past.

As dawn started to lighten the skies, one of her clansmen was scavenging through the factorum. He saw the traces of blood, gleaming out in the dawn light, frozen but red enough to still be fresh.

The trail led south, taking the easiest route, which made him think of a wounded animal, crawling away to die. The trail led to a collapsed storeroom. The walls and roof had fallen sideways, forming a rough bivouac. He bent down and peered in, and he could see a boot. Two boots.

Five minutes later the sun was cresting the ice wall when he returned with Grawnya and some others. They looked together, walked around the bivouac, certain that there had to be a booby trap of some kind.

'If there is then I'm a goat,' Grawnya said at last.

'So, what do we do?'

'We pull him out,' she said. 'Go in and get him.'

'He's mighty big.'

'So,' she said, 'get a rope.'

They looped a rope about the wounded man's foot and hauled him out. He was clearly a warrior, from his boots, metal shin-guards, mail skirts, and the heavy brigandine. As soon as his arms came free, they were seized and pinned down.

Grawnya stood over him as her clansmen searched him. The wounded man was pale and shivering. His belly was smeared with scabbing blood. All he had with him was a knife and a powercell.

'Clean,' they told her.

Grawnya stared down. 'Who are you?'

The man did not answer, but it was clear from the tattoos on his face that he was a heretic, and the Drookians had no time for such.

'We should kill him,' one of them said, drawing his knife.

Grawnya wanted to kill him herself, but she relented. 'It is one of the Scourged. We shall take him to the general. He will reward us.'

* * *

The psychic prodding had been going on for hours, and Marŝal Baab was the first to wake. She shook like a leaf. Her skin was white and wet. She put her fingers to her cheek, and found fragments of ice.

She wiped them off. But there was no warmth in her hands or her face. She lay for a long time, as pain spread down each of her limbs. She stood, long before she could feel her toes. It was hard trying to keep her balance. She went along the bodies, dragging the top layer away.

Some of them were moving. Twitching fingers. Mouths opening. Arms flexing slowly. She knocked the ice from them. Puddles were spreading under the bodies, the blood and ice mingling on the metal floor.

Waking was not a pleasant experience, Baab knew. Her clothes were sodden. Her heart thundered as it struggled to get her body up to temperature. She was bound, and would not die here. Not while she was called to higher purpose. Not while her masters needed her.

As warmth returned, so did pain.

But pain was a sign of life, Marŝal Baab told herself. And life meant that there were battles yet to fight.

Viktor's platoon stood in the factorum, alert, as the servo-hauler brought the wounded giant out into the light of day. Anastasia's Chimera stood idling nearby. They manoeuvred the hauler into the back of the vehicle, then the ramp was brought up, and locked.

'Who is it?' Viktor said.

'Enemy commander,' Minka said as she swung around the back of the tank. 'I'm bringing him in for assessment.'

At that moment there was the eruption of another firefight. It was louder and closer.

Minka scrambled up into the commander's turret hatch, and slid down into position. The rest of her squad clambered up alongside. None had wanted to go in with Drakul-zar.

There was a hatch into the rear cabin. 'Keep an eye on that bastard,' Minka called down to the crew. 'Anything happens, let me know.'

Mauger was the front gunner. 'Confirmed,' he said.

As they swung out, the Exterminator-pattern Leman Russ *Ironside* pulled up behind them. Minka was taking no chances with this one. The convoy drove through the Western Habs; fighting was breaking out along Sparker's stretch of the ice wall.

Minka listened to the vox-traffic. 'What's happening over there?' she demanded.

There was a long pause before Pavlo answered.

'Hostiles are attacking the ice wall in force. Armour. Infantry.'

'Grüber,' she voxed. 'Make sure you're ready to reinforce as needed.'

As they rolled through the algae farms, Minka tried to get through to Bendikt's office, without success.

She tried Prassan, and got nothing there either, till finally she managed to raise Sturm.

'What the hell is going on?' she demanded.

'It's a shutdown,' he said. *'Insurgents have infiltrated the Administratum District. We're shooting on sight.'*

She paused. She didn't want to communicate this on a vox-channel she was not certain was secure. 'Rath. Listen. I need you to alert HQ. I passed a message along, but I've heard nothing back. No orders, nothing. I have a high-value prisoner that I am bringing in. Make sure Bendikt knows.'

'I'm on my way,' Sturm said.

The vox-link ended, but those words brought Minka more

reassurance than anything she had heard that day. She felt her shoulders relax, her tension start to dissipate. She trusted Sturm more than any other man alive.

Las-fire flared up from the ice wall. Sparker had to take command of her company. She spoke to Sargora and Viktor and Orugi as well. 'Stand by,' she told him. 'Orugi – get your platoon to the ice wall. Grüber is on stand-by. Sparker is in command until I return.'

They were crossing the algae farms when Minka finally got Sparker on the vox. She couldn't tell him what was happening, apart from she had to get to HQ.

'I need you to take command,' she told him. 'I've spoken to my platoon commanders. You have Viktor, Sargora, Senik and Grüber.'

Sparker laughed. *'Don't worry. Nothing I can't handle.'*

He sounded like he was ending the conversation. Minka wasn't done. 'Listen, Sparker! The ice wall. It's not defensive. There are mining tunnels all over this place.' She could tell what he was thinking. 'This position is not at all secure. We're garrisoned the perimeter, but the middle could be as leaky as a sieve. The enemy could be anywhere.'

Lieutenant Grawnya of the Drookian Fen Guard stood in the back of the halftrack as it rode north with the factorum district on the right, and the broken domes of the algae farms on the left.

The tracks skidded along on the hard-packed ice. She had the warriors of Clan Grindel standing about her. As the halftrack approached the Cadian checkpoint they fell silent.

Grüber's squads had thrown up a dogleg of tank traps between the stilt-habs. The driver had to slow right down to slew the vehicle round the obstacles. As it came to a halt, Grawnya saw that the Cadians had left nothing to chance. She counted six weapon emplacements in the hab above her, the gun-barrels all trained on the roadblock.

One of the Cadian sentries marched forward.

'Papers,' he said.

The driver motioned to the open carriage and the sentry looked up. The Drookians stared down in silence as he picked Grawnya out.

'Papers,' he said again.

She pulled her tribal plaids away to show the Imperial aquila embossed upon her flak armour. 'Where is Grüber? Ask him if I need papers.'

The trooper nodded, and Grüber appeared after a few minutes. He marched over and tried to make conversation. 'There's a lockdown,' he said. 'Just in case. Perimeters are no longer secure.'

Grawnya said nothing as he waved her through. The wounded Scourged lay in the middle of the crowd. They had done nothing to help him, but wrap him up in sacking and plastek sheets that they had pulled out from the snow and dirt. They checked on him only to reassure themselves that he was still alive, as the halftrack swept along the edge of the algae farms before crossing over the causeway.

'Which way is it?' the driver shouted back.

Grawnya only had a rough idea.

They turned right, towards Pyre's Gate, and through a number of checkpoints, where the Cadians made cursory inspections of the troops.

It was only as Pyre's Gate swung into view that they were flagged down. This dogleg was of rockcrete palisades; the Cadian officer waved them sideways into a separate area, and signalled for the driver to turn the engine off.

The vibrations ended as the machine-spirit fell asleep.

'Where are you going?' he called out.

'I am Lieutenant Grawnya,' she said. 'I am on my way to see your master.'

'I still need to see your papers.'

'These are my papers!' she said, putting a finger to a scar that ran along her cheek. 'I have bled for the Golden Emperor.'

The sentry sighed. He exchanged looks with his companions. 'Papers. We're locked down. Or you will have to turn back.'

'I will not. Look! I carry the same icon you do. The aquila of man.'

The man did not budge, so Grawnya took out the papers that she had been given. They were official, stamped and sealed with Coriandoc's own signet. 'Here!' she said.

The man took the sheet, and said, 'Wait here.'

'Why?'

'I need to get confirmation from HQ,' he said.

Grawnya checked on the Scourged warrior. He was still breathing, which meant he was still valuable. She felt the mood of her clansmen. They were as stubborn as she was, and they would wait here till the lord general decided to come out and meet them.

The sound of battle rose as Minka's convoy swung towards Pyre's Gate. She could see las-fire in the Administratum District, and over her shoulder there was smoke rising along the Western Habs.

Minka's Chimera was waved through the checkpoints as it rolled towards the space port. Only at the last one was the Chimera ordered to slow down, and then as soon as the guards saw that it was Captain Lesk, they cleared her to continue.

The port itself was held by First Company, under Ostanko. It was much busier than it had been when she had landed. Then it had been an icy waste. Now walls of containers, tall as Titans, loomed over her.

Poor bastard, she thought, imagining Prassan's workload. She'd rather sit in a trench getting shot at than try to manage all that.

As the Chimera rolled towards the merchant palaces, one of the lighters on the landing zone lit its thrusters. The rockets blasted downwards and Minka felt her armour vibrate as the vast craft lifted up, dwindling as it powered back to orbit.

The Chimera turned along the line of palaces where First Company were barracked. The Kasrkin were running to their Chimeras, engines idling as they loaded up. A few of them saluted Minka, but they were focused on the job ahead.

Minka readied herself for meeting Bendikt as the Chimera slowed. She hated leaving the Seventh in Sparker's command. All she wanted was to get back to her company.

Nothing bonded commander and troops better than battle.

Baine was still stretched out in the tunnel, arms folded over the lasrifle lying across his chest.

They'd been here hours. Long enough to be relieved by Yuriv, and then sent back.

Hwang paced up and down.

'Are you not bored of this tunnel?' Baine said.

Hwang made a non-committal noise. He was bored of Baine most of all.

Baine fumbled in the darkness with the lho wrapper. He held it in one palm as he sprinkled the leaf along it, then licked the tacky side and rolled it closed.

Hwang gave him a look. 'I know!' he said. 'No smoking on duty. But the minute I get out of here...'

Hwang paced up and down the width of the tunnel. He ground the grit under his feet. He had passed that black, glassy puddle of water a hundred times, and it had always been still. But now... there were faint ripples. He didn't think anything of it the first time, but the third time he paused, thinking that his footsteps had caused them.

He stood still, and yet the ripples went on, trembling across the surface of the water.

Hwang looked to Baine. 'Do you feel that?'

Baine was pretending to be asleep. He opened one eye. He said nothing, which was confirmation that he did. A second ripple.

Baine pushed himself up. 'What is that?' he said.

Hwang had his hand up for stillness as he lifted his head. The ground was shuddering. 'It's artillery,' he said.

Baine frowned. Surely not? 'Maybe it's a lighter taking off...' he said.

Neither of them were convinced.

'There're no Titans on Telken's Rest?'

'I think we would have spotted one...' Baine laughed.

'Then it's artillery,' Hwang said. 'Or tanks.' There was a pause. He shouted back to Yuriv and the rest of the squad. 'Heh. Do you lot hear that?'

'Yeah,' Yuriv said. 'Something is kicking off up there.'

Baine looked pleased. 'Well thank the Throne they're dealing with it and not us. Let Captain Lesk earn her stripes!'

Lieutenant Sargora spotted the enemy troops first, creeping forward through cracks in the ice-pack. She had handed the scope to Captain Sparker, who was making his rounds. 'Look!' she said.

It took him a moment to see them, then he said, 'Throne!'

He panned round. 'Where the hell did they all come from?'

'What are your orders, sir?'

Sparker paused. He didn't want to have to go after them, out on the ice. 'Let them get to three hundred yards away. Then open up with everything you have.'

* * *

Minka's Chimera slowed as they came closer; HQ was busy with running attendants.

There was a sudden boom from across the city as a fireball lifted into the air. Minka frowned. It did not look good. 'That was something big,' Blanchez said.

She had her scope out to try to see, but whatever it was was hidden behind the stilt-habs.

They passed through the void shield. You could always tell the line. The air was full of static, and there was a thin crackle along the tank's armour as it breached the field.

There was another explosion. A missile, Minka reckoned.

Her Chimera slewed into the last checkpoint at the front of the palace. Kasrkin were on station, Ostanko's lot. Their sergeant came forward.

'Where are you going?'

'HQ,' Minka shouted.

'Impossible,' he said, and waved her aside.

Minka jumped down, and had to run to catch him up. 'I have a prisoner that must be brought to HQ. Urgently,' she said.

'Sorry,' he shouted over the din. 'I have my orders from Ostanko.'

'Where is he?'

The man didn't know, and he wasn't giving in. Ostanko was senior to Minka in all degrees.

Minka cursed. The road before her was blocked with parked Leman Russ tanks. The Kasrkin were waving her sideways. Minka clambered up and dropped into the cupola. 'Go left,' she shouted down to Anastasia.

The Chimera swung round on the spot and went left along the side of the building.

There were troops lined up, waving them along a long wall. Minka ordered the Chimera to take the first gateway. There were guards manning a barrier. They saw Minka's rank and pulled the barrier back. They had First Company markings, but they were not as officious as the men out along the front.

Minka shouted down and Anastasia pushed through. Minka slapped the roof of the turret as they reached the right spot. The Chimera stopped, and Minka slid down the side of the tank as *Ironside* pulled up behind them, the Leman Russ taking up a defensive position around the entrance.

Minka suddenly realised where she was. It had looked so different before all the activity, and it had been fortified as well. There was a halftrack with a detail of Whiteshields unloading bodies. Dead Cadians, from Fourth Company, by the looks of it.

The Whiteshields came forward with officious concern.

'How many bodies?' they asked.

'None.'

At that moment Major Luka limped out. 'Captain Lesk!' he called. 'Sturm told me you were coming. You have a prisoner of note.'

'Correct.' Minka looked at the freshly dead. 'What happened?'

Luka didn't know. 'They keep trickling in. The longer we're here, the more casualties we're taking.'

Minka's command squad slid down to guard the prisoner as Anastasia lowered the ramp with the hiss of hydraulics. The stink billowed out, and Minka heard the groan of the man inside.

No one else wanted to bring him down. Jaromir stepped up and put his hand to the servo-hauler.

'Frekk,' Major Luka said as he saw the body upon the pallet. 'What the hell is that?'

'Possible heretic commander,' Minka said. 'Found him hiding in an old mineworks.'

'Scourged?'

She nodded.

'Do they know about this?' Luka said. He pointed towards the HQ post.

'Yes,' Minka said. 'Well, I hope so.'

There were loading doors that slid sideways on metal tracks. Minka pushed the servo-hauler inside. The room smelt of urine and mouldering sacks. There were empty wooden pallets stacked against one side.

'You're guarding this place?' she asked.

'Correct,' Luka said.

Minka nodded. 'No offence. I'm going to leave a guard here.'

'You're welcome,' Luka said.

The tank commander, Rogg, made the sign of the aquila. He clambered up the side ladder, lowered himself into the hatch, and pulled his headpiece on.

A moment later *Ironside* swivelled as the tracks moved in opposite directions. There was a pause as the driver swung it round, checked his bearings, and then the tank backed up through the warehouse door till it was almost touching the inner wall, its turret pointing at the entrance.

'Blanchez, Jaromir,' Minka said.

The two nodded. Nothing would get past them.

Lieutenant Sargora paced up and down the parapet of the ice wall as the troopers of First Platoon crouched and waited. She did not speak to them. She did not need to. Her physical presence was such that they felt her anger and her venom.

It was so still you could hear the creak of the ice sheets as they buckled, one against another. At the moment the enemy came within range, Sargora stepped forward. 'For Cadia,' she shouted, 'fire!'

The troopers threw themselves against the parapet, lined the enemy up in their sights, and fired a devastating las-volley.

Minka tried to get hold of Prassan, but there was no one who could locate him. She tried for Manon as well, and got through. *'Hello?'* Manon voxed.

'It's Captain Lesk,' Minka told her.

'Who?' Manon said.

'Lesk,' Minka shouted over the din. 'I've brought a high-level asset in. They would not let me bring him to the front. I'm at the morgue with Major Luka. It's urgent that he is assessed. Is someone coming over?'

'I don't know,' Manon said. *'This is a busy time.'*

'No, you can't fob me off. Manon, where is Bendikt?'

'He's not here.'

'Where is he? Is Mere there?'

'No.'

Bohdan checked the vox-link. Bendikt wasn't responding.

'Let's find him,' Minka said.

Showers of ice and snow rained down upon the ice wall and the troopers on it. Sargora stood as artillery shells started to land among them. She had her pistol in hand. But her contribution was her personal aura.

She had grown up on one of the Imperium's most deadly death worlds, and even though the enemy assault was ferocious, she was confident. The initial volley had thrown the heretics back in confusion. Now her squads were taking their time, picking their targets and firing. It was hard to make the enemy out amidst the glare of the snow, at times, but precise las-bolts stabbed out and the snow was littered with the dead.

'I've killed at least ten!' one of her troopers shouted.

'Good! Maybe we'll make a death worlder of you yet!' Sargora told him.

The enemy started to pull back; she called her squads to stop firing.

Sergeant Karni repeated the order along the line. Her left arm was an augmetic claw. It clamped together as she reholstered her pistol. 'Probing attack,' she said. 'They didn't push the assault.'

Sargora nodded. 'Sergeant. I want one of those bodies brought back. Pick two of your troopers.'

Karni didn't want to have to pick. 'I will go,' she said.

'No,' Sargora said. 'You are a sergeant now. This is a job for the troopers.'

Karni read the expressions on their faces. None of them wanted to go. 'I need two volunteers?'

Five Cadians stepped forward. They didn't want to go, but they sure wouldn't let someone else take the glory. Karni picked two. 'Nathanial. Lyrga.'

Lyrga took a bandolier of grenades and threw it over her shoulder. She slapped Nathanial on the back. 'Time to earn your pay.'

Baine was standing, alert to every sound, when Hwang put a finger to his arm and tapped it. Baine started to speak, but Hwang's expression said it all.

Stay silent.

Hwang signalled to the heat-see goggles. Baine pulled his down and peered into the shaft.

'I don't see anything,' he whispered.

Hwang pointed again. 'There were two. They just ducked back.'

'Frekk,' Baine hissed, flicking his safety off. 'We're supposed to blow this tunnel... What are the orders?'

Hwang wasn't sure. 'I'll stay here. Tell Yuriv.'

Baine nodded and made his way up the tunnel to where the rest of the squad had made a small camp at the bottom of the rockfall. It was hard going in the darkness, and he cursed every turn of a stone, every tumble of rocks.

'Yuriv!' he whispered. 'Hostiles in the tunnel.'

'How many?'

'Hwang saw a couple, but who knows – there could be hundreds moving through behind them.'

Yuriv stood. 'The charges are set?'

The demo team were already standing. 'Yes, sir. Three hundred yards back along the tunnel.'

'Right,' Yuriv said. 'No messing around. We set the fuses and fall back.'

There was a sallyport at the base of the ice wall, an arc of bare ground where it opened inwards. Rockcrete stairs set into the wall led obliquely down to the bottom.

They disappeared into drifts of snow, blown into smooth concave depressions by the wind.

There was a noticeboard on the wall by the door. The plastek screen had been shattered, the inner cavity filled with snow, the information notices bleached.

Karni paused in the doorway. 'I'll stay here,' she said, 'just in case.'

Nathanial peered out. The landscape seemed empty. He looked to Lyrga.

This place gave her the creeps as well, but she slapped him on the back again. 'Come on. Let's get this over with.'

Lyrga went first, her grenade launcher loaded and braced against her shoulder as she dropped into the drift. The crust was thick enough to hold her weight, but here and there her boot went down as deep as her hip. As the drifts levelled out, there was a broad stretch of snow before the ice sheets began.

Each footfall was a deep scrunch. It was heavy going. From the top of the wall the plains had looked flat, but now they were down at the bottom, Nathanial could see that the land sloped up to a low ridge and the ice sheets had bent and buckled, one upon the other, making the way treacherous.

It also offered ample cover if any of the heretics were still here.

'Stay alert,' he said, carbine ready.

Lyrga didn't answer. She pushed forward, waiting till they reached the top of the ridge, but when they did, she stopped and looked about. She couldn't see any dead.

'Didn't we shoot some of them?'

He stood and spun about on the spot, searching for any sign or footprint, but there was only the glare of ice.

Lyrga nodded but said nothing. She started forward, looking about to either side. She tapped her vox-bead. 'I don't see any,' she said at last. She turned to look at the ice wall and checked her bearings. She looked for someone to point her in the right direction.

She tapped her vox-bead again. 'Sure you killed some?' she said.

It was Sargora who answered. Her tone was implacable. *'Keep going. They have to be out here somewhere.'*

Hwang and Baine stood guard as the sappers set the fuses. They worked quickly and as soon as they were done, Yuriv voxed, *'We're done. Pull out.'*

Hwang acknowledged, but at that moment there was the hiss and clang of a rappelling wire, fired up the shaft. Hwang threw himself sideways, tapped the fuse of a grenade and lobbed the whole satchel of them over the edge.

He saw the satchel fall as he stood on the parapet and fired full-auto. He would make them think twice about coming up here until long after the fuses blew.

'For the Emperor!' he shouted, the las-bolts strobing the deep shaft with red flickers of light. He kept firing, panning about the chamber until the grenades exploded like a bag of firecrackers, staccato blasts ripping out.

But even as the enemy were fragged, more grappling hooks were fired up with the distinctive pop of pneumatic charges.

Hwang felt one bounce off his shoulder, and a grappling wire caught his leg. He tried to kick it off, but he was suddenly dragged forward.

Baine was crouching at the top of the rubble. 'Get the hell out of there!' he called.

Hwang dropped his carbine as his fingers scrabbled with the grappling hook. It had snagged his boot, and he was being pulled towards the lip of the fall.

Baine ran back and seized his arm. 'You stupid bastard!' he hissed as he looked for purchase. Something to stop their slide.

'Go,' Hwang told him through gritted teeth as he tried to pull the grappling hook towards him, to free it from his boot.

'Believe me, I'm tempted,' Baine told him, but he found an old chain that was embedded into the wall and grabbed it. It snapped taut, and they both stopped sliding. But there was nowhere they could go, and the fuses were lit, and they could hear the shouts of the hostiles as they clambered up the grapple ropes.

'Let go,' Hwang hissed.

'I'm going to let go,' Baine said. 'I need you to hold on to me. Promise you're going to hold tight.'

Hwang didn't understand, but he grabbed Baine's webbing with both hands.

'Got me?' Baine hissed.

Hwang's face was strained. He nodded.

Baine used his free hand to reach for his knife as one of the chain links began to bend under their weight. 'It's going,' Hwang said, and Baine heard the creak of the old metal. He cursed as he reached as far as he could, to where Hwang's boot was taking the strain.

The wire cable was never going to break.

Baine took barely a moment to make up his mind.

He said, 'This will hurt.'

IV

Minka hurried along the frozen remains of palace gardens. Statues had been defaced. Dead bodies lay buried in snow, and here and there a window was pockmarked by gunfire.

The sentries at the palace rear door recognised Minka's rank and let her through. She had the air of someone on important business as she strode along the ground-floor galleries, and up the stairs, into the southern wing of the merchant palace.

Her boots echoed off the tiled floors. She marched along a suite of empty rooms, the only sound her own passing and the faint din of tanks and shouted commands outside, and she immediately regretted not asking for directions.

At the end of the long corridor she turned left. Another, equally empty. She set off, a sense that something was very wrong growing within her. There were sounds from one of the rooms. She pushed the door open, and found a group of attendants standing in a tight circle.

They turned.

'Where is Bendikt?'

They didn't know. She saw their insignia. Logistics.

'Prassan?'

One of the men came to the door and pointed. 'Up the stairs,' he said. 'Second on the right.'

Minka started up the stairs, taking two at a time, her hand on the banister helping her up at pace. Through the high windows she had a view down into the courtyard. The Chimeras were pulling away. One casement was broken, and a heap of snow had blown in. She looked about and saw no one. She was slightly breathless as she reached the door, knocked and pushed inside.

It was an old bedchamber, with strips of hand-blocked wallpaper hanging from the plaster. The remains of a four-poster bed were stacked against the far wall. Thrown over it were bedsheets, mouldering carpets and what looked like velvet gowns; someone's portrait had been casually slung onto the pile, the canvas slashed through.

She had a brief impression of a void-craft and stars, and the golden robes of an Imperial trader. But she didn't have time for that. 'Prassan?' she called. There was an antechamber with folding metal desks and metal chairs. All Munitorum grade, looking plain and municipal.

The room was empty and quiet, apart from the whirr of a cogitator, the twitch of a servitor-scribe.

She tried the next door.

Another room littered with signs of occupation, but currently deserted.

She cursed and lengthened her stride as she paced along the corridors. An officer came out of a doorway and walked away from her. She shouted out to him, but he did not hear. She slammed through a door and broke into a run.

'Holy frekking Throne!' she said. 'What is wrong with this place?'

At that moment she heard voices along the corridor behind her. She spun about and saw Valentian, with Commissar Salice and two Kasrkin.

Valentian's staff tapped the floor as he came towards her. His eyes stared at her in that way that made her feel as though she were as transparent as a pane of glass.

'Captain Lesk,' Sanctioned Psyker Valentian said. 'Shouldn't you be with your company?'

'I just brought the prisoner in,' she said.

'What prisoner?' Salice asked.

'He claims to be Drakul-zar. Where the hell is everyone?'

Valentian stopped and turned his full attention onto her.

'Drakul-zar?'

'Yes!' she said. 'He's at the morgue. Nobody is answering the vox.'

'The morgue?' Salice said.

She nodded, furious. They were dream-walking their way into oblivion and it felt like she was the only one awake. 'Where the hell is Bendikt?'

Major Luka picked out twenty Whiteshields.

'I am sending you to the ice wall,' he told them. 'You will operate under Captain Sparker's command. This is your chance to earn promotion.'

Each tri-dome helmet lined up before him had the distinctive white stripe from the crest down to the rim. Under the steel rims, the young faces were eager and nervous as the cadets clambered up onto the top of the Chimera, their lasrifles in hand.

'Not all of you will make it back,' he continued, 'but some of you will return as troopers. Whatever the God-Emperor has in store for you, I want you to know that I am proud of each and every one of you.

'Cadia stands!' he called out, as the Chimera started off and the Whiteshields answered.

The ones who had been left behind looked like they were in mourning.

'Don't worry, you will get your chance soon enough,' Major Luka said. 'Next call, you lot are going into action. Now, we're moving the bodies of Creed's Eighth to HQ.'

Thainne said, 'Sir. We don't have to carry them again, do we?'

Luka half laughed. 'No. There is a cargo-8 coming. You will be the honour guard that goes with them.'

One of the Whiteshields said, 'You won't forget about us, sir?'

'What's your name?' Luka asked.

'Juliar, sir.'

Luka stepped up to him. 'No, Juliar. I will not forget you. In fact, I am coming with you.'

They stood waiting for the cargo-8 to arrive. It swung into the courtyard. The driver reversed until he was alongside the container in question, then he jumped down and clambered up onto the back. Stabiliser legs lowered along the side of the truck, as he swung a mag-lifter arm down.

It moved with stiff jerks. The Whiteshields stood watching as the mag-lifter's claws closed with a clunk and the arm took the strain.

Clouds of brown promethium smoke billowed up as the container started to lift. It swung over the cargo-8. The driver moved it slowly as he lined it up, and then it started to descend, and settled with a hiss of released hydraulics.

The stabilisers lifted and the suspension creaked as the wheels took the weight.

Luka waved the Whiteshields forward as he limped to the cabin, and pulled himself up.

Jaromir watched the container being loaded.

'They're going to HQ,' he said.

Blanchez looked at him.

'That's where the captain was trying to get to.'

Blanchez nodded.

'So,' Jaromir said, 'shouldn't we go too?'

He was right, but Blanchez didn't like to disobey orders. 'I'll take responsibility,' Jaromir said. He called out to Luka.

'Major! You are going to HQ? Hold up. We'll bring the prisoner.'

Luka waited as Bohdan and Yedrin pulled the servo-hauler into the back of their Chimera.

They turned right around the back of the palace, with the flat expanse of the space port on their left. The supply dumps were like stilt-habs made not of apartments but tiny squares of colour that picked out each individual container.

Jaromir shook his head. 'Prassan is in charge of all that.'

Bohdan didn't know Prassan.

'Served with us on Potence,' Jaromir said. 'He wasn't up to much, but he read books all the time.' Jaromir laughed as he remembered. 'Was born on the wrong planet. Should have been born on an Administratum world. He'd have done well there...'

'He has done well,' Yedrin said. 'He's quartermaster!'

Jaromir looked at Yedrin as if the other man was stupid.

The ideal of any Cadian was to live as he did, as a Cadian Shock Trooper – the finest soldiers in the Astra Militarum. It seemed obvious to him, despite his injury. 'Yes,' he said. 'But he doesn't get to fight.'

* * *

No one spoke after that. They watched the columns of black smoke rising from the Western Habs, saw the Hydra batteries on the edge of the void shield, the augur-emplacements slowly revolving as they scanned the skies.

There were walled gardens behind the palace, but now they looked at a mess of broken plastek and dead vegetation, sticking up from the thick bed of snow.

They swung into a narrow access track. The rear façade of the palace was not as grand as its front, but the mass of the building reared up before them as they entered a cobbled square behind the block. There had been a statue there once, but the plinth was empty and only the legs remained, lying disconnected amidst the snow. On one side was a line of containers, stacked two high, and a disused Skyshield landing pad stood on the other, its armoured side-flaps hanging dormant. The container was wheeled to the end of the stack, and then they lifted it down.

'Careful!' Luka called out. 'There are heroes of the Imperium in there!'

The driver lowered the container as gently as the machinery would allow, and made something of a salute as he climbed back into the cabin.

As the cargo-8 swung back along the track, Luka started organising the Whiteshields with him. 'Juliar and Ankela. Congratulations. You're on guard here.'

Juliar and Ankela saluted.

'Skyrin. Round the back. No one comes or goes without your say-so. Understand?'

'Yes, sir!'

Blanchez covered them as Jaromir went in to get the servo-hauler.

The opiates seemed to be wearing off. Drakul-zar was starting to moan, and each time he did there was a sickening feeling in the pit of Jaromir's gut.

'Let's get him out,' Jaromir said. Bohdan took the other end of the hauler.

Yedrin looked about. 'We should take him inside.'

They walked towards the nearest doorway. Where the palace cast a shadow, the ice was piled high, but the paths had been swept mostly clear, and someone had spread grit. They followed the tracks to a doorway. No one was on duty.

'I thought they were locking down?'

'Looks like they're locking down somewhere else...'

They looked at each other, and Yedrin held the door open as they pushed inside.

There was an empty corridor before them.

Jaromir looked to Blanchez.

'This way,' she said.

Minka and Valentian marched side by side.

'Something is wrong,' she said. 'There's no one about.'

'Bendikt has a hunch about Creed. He has sent Ostanko out to search the Administratum buildings. Just in case there are more dead Cadians. He has become rather obsessed...'

Minka's vox-bead crackled. It was Jaromir. *'We've got inside the building,'* he said, but his voice was fading in and out. *'Looking for HQ.'*

'It's moved to the basement,' Minka said, with a glance at Valentian. She had not spent so much time so close to a psyker before.

On Cadia the sanctioned psykers led a lonely existence, exiled from the rest of the community. No one wanted to be around them. Life this close to the Eye of Terror brought nightmares enough.

Ostanko should not have left Bendikt so undefended. Her platoons were engaged, and besides, they were too far away. She flipped her vox-bead onto Sturm's personal channel.

'Minka,' his voice said.

'Something is wrong. At HQ. Bendikt has sent Ostanko out. I can't find anyone.'

'I'm nearly there,' he said. There was a pause as someone in the background spoke to him. *'Yes,'* he said, and then carried on talking to Minka. *'I couldn't get anyone on the channels. I've just passed half of First Company. Is anyone left there?'*

'Rath, there's no one.'

There was another pause as Sturm spoke to his driver.

'We'll be there in three minutes.'

'I'm going to see Bendikt. Meet me there!' she shouted, but the line clicked and she didn't know if the message had got through.

They had gone further from the ice wall than they liked, when Lyrga and Nathanial found a dead hostile. He lay face down, his shins wrapped in rough puttees, and they dragged the body back across the snow.

He did not have the heavy armour of the Scourged. This warrior looked wilder, with crazed tattoos and ritual scarring.

'Ganger?' Lyrga said.

Nathanial didn't know. 'Let's get back. I feel like we're being watched.'

She nodded but said nothing. They took a hand each and hauled him along behind them.

Lyrga didn't want to waste her breath on conversation. She felt it, the sense of eyes on her, but the going was heavy and she just wanted to get back to the wall. All she could hear was the crackle of her vox-bead, her own breath, heavy in the cold air, and the crunch and swish of snow.

Someone shouted as they drew closer. She didn't hear what they said. She assumed it was a friendly hail, and then her vox-bead crackled.

'Leave him. Hostiles returning.'

Lyrga looked up. She couldn't see anyone, but she wasn't going to wait.

Nathanial was looking over his shoulder as well. 'I don't see them.'

'Frekk it,' she said and dropped the dead man's wrist. He lay, splayed out in the snow beneath the wall. They waded through the snow, back up the slope of the drift.

The metal door was shut. Lyrga hammered on it.

'Where the frekk are they?' she hissed.

After an interminable wait a bolt slid open and the door creaked wide.

'In!' Karni said. They bundled through and Karni slammed the door closed.

At that moment there was the shriek of a missile booming overhead, a whole salvo of them, some roaring over the ice wall and slamming into one of the habs behind, others striking true and blasting the parapet apart.

Masonry fountained out as smoke and flames started to lick upwards.

This did not look like the start of a mere probing attack.

Sargora had moved along the ice wall to Dreno's squad. Karni voxed her.

'They said he didn't look Scourged.'

Sargora relayed the information to Sparker.

'If they're not Scourged then who are they?' he said.

'Don't ask me,' Sargora said. 'That's what HQ are for.'

Sparker laughed at that, and Sargora ended the vox-call. As

she straightened, a las-round flashed past her face. The others ducked. But not Sargora. Life on Catachan had taught her to expect the worst.

But it had come from inside the wall, not without.

'Lieutenant!' one of the troopers called out to her. She made a big target, but Sargora stood full square, looking for the source. A second las-bolt flashed towards her. She liked being a target. It was a feeling she had grown up with.

'There!' she pointed. 'Stilt-hab, halfway up.'

Her heavy weapons team scrambled to get their autocannon round. Within a few seconds, the gun barked out, and spent brass shell cases rang on the frozen rockcrete.

'You frekking bastard,' Hwang snarled as he hopped along, one arm over Baine's shoulder.

Baine nodded. It was a tough thing to have done to you, but it was better than being dead.

'Just keep going,' Baine told him. The shouts of the enemy were echoing up from behind. They knew they had been found and they knew that this was now a deadly race against time.

Hwang stumbled and fell. He was losing too much blood.

Baine flicked one of his chest pouches open. The tourniquets were at the bottom. He pulled out his packet of pre-rolled lho-sticks and tossed them away. The shouts were growing louder as he found the end of Hwang's shin, and tugged the plas-tek band tight. The bottom of Hwang's trousers were wet with blood. Baine put his boot onto Hwang's leg and pulled tighter.

Hwang cursed in pain. 'Bastard!'

Baine nodded. Yup. But he was keeping Hwang alive.

Baine discarded his own pack. 'I'm going to carry you,' he hissed as he used his knife to cut the shoulder-straps of Hwang's. 'Help me.'

Hwang was growing weak, but he did his best as Baine dragged him up by one arm, and bent down and threw the other man over his shoulders.

'Frekk me,' Baine said as he took the weight and a las-bolt hissed past his left side.

'I'm coming!' he shouted. He didn't want Yuriv blowing the tunnel with him in it. He hadn't done all this to get crushed under a megaton of frozen rock.

'Quick!' Yuriv shouted.

I'm trying, Baine thought as he stumbled along, but the combination of weight and darkness made it treacherous. He could hear Yuriv and the rest at the end of the tunnel urging him to go faster, as las-bolts started to streak around him.

'I'm frekking trying,' he snarled. He staggered along, hearing Hwang's heavy breathing in his ear. He couldn't tell if Hwang was conscious or not.

'You hold on there!' he ordered the other trooper. 'I'm not dying for you unless you hold on.'

The sounds of battle had been growing steadily. Major Luka could not bear to sit still. Perhaps he should have sent more Whiteshields to the front, he thought, as he started to where he had sent his cadets as guards.

'What's happening, sir?' Cadet Skyrin said as Luka limped towards him.

'Looks like we've flushed out the heretics!' Luka said, stopping and turning back to see the billowing plumes of smoke rising across the city. 'Battle will soon be upon us!'

Skyrin grinned nervously. 'Do you know if the others are in combat yet?'

'I have not heard,' Luka said. 'But don't worry, your time will come!'

Whiteshields were not promoted to Cadian Shock Troopers until they had killed in battle. Skyrin kept grinning. He hovered between elation and terror at the thought of earning his spurs, or dying before he did.

Luka smiled. 'Don't worry, lad, we'll get you into the front line when the time is right, and you'll do fine.'

The old man had a way of making the average trooper feel like a veteran.

Skyrin made the sign of the aquila. 'Thank you, sir.'

Skyrin watched Luka limp off back to the main square, then put his shoulders back and paced up and down, his eyes turning westwards whenever there was a low boom, or when a new pillar of black smoke started to rise up on its own heat.

He remembered his training. Remembered what his parents had said to him when he passed selection: that they would pray to the God-Emperor that he made it to trooper, and more than that, that he would have a long and honourable life, fighting for humanity against the enemies of the God-Emperor.

'I made a little shrine,' his mother had said as she showed him the place where she had put a pict of him in Whiteshield uniform in front of a print background of Kasr Tyrok. An unlit candle stood before it.

'I will light it when I pray,' she told him.

He had set off thinking that his life would be one of adventure and comradeship. It was better than the drudgery of his parents' life. He would escape the factorum, and go out and see the Imperium of Man. But he also understood that he would probably never see his mother, or father, again.

Skyrin was thinking of his mother, the way she made their slab and carb, and the sores on her hands from the job she had in the ammo factorum – fyceline wore away at the skin, and no matter what she did she could not stop it peeling.

There was another low boom from the west. He saw the lightning flash of a lascannon, streaking out across the cityscape, and then another. The livid bolts disappeared behind the palace bloc. He puffed out his chest, pulling his carbine strap high onto his shoulder.

He would be worthy, he told himself, and some day he would return to see his mother's shrine. He had to have that hope. The chance to prove himself to his parents. The moment of return. He was thinking on this when he turned and fumbled for his carbine, and shouted, 'Stop!'

The four figures came towards him. They were led by a sickly child, those following with one hand upon the other, like blind beggars.

He lowered his carbine, pointing it at them. 'Hold, I said! You can't come this way!'

Except he could not speak. He was frozen and his mouth would not move. Nothing moved. Not even the heavy las-bolt that was frozen in the sky above him – a glowing bar of red light.

The child stopped, sunken eyes wide, as one of the blind penitents came towards him. As it approached, Skyrin saw that within the hood was not a face, but a diabolical thing of tentacles and inhuman flesh.

Skyrin wanted to curse as it stepped close, and the feelers reached out and closed about his head, pulling him forwards.

In the vast ruins of the factorum, Senik stood at the mine shaft head, the ploughed pile of rubble overshadowing him, and counted his troopers out.

Yuriv and the rest of his squad came at a run. 'Where's Baine?' he asked.

'He's bringing Hwang.'

'What happened?'

'I don't know,' Yuriv said, standing at the entrance to the tunnel. 'It should have been simple.'

They stood waiting as the seconds dragged like days. One of Yuriv's lot was crouching in the opening.

'Are they through yet?'

Sergeant Frost had his hand on the detonator. He had wanted to blow it five minutes ago. Senik didn't mention that to Yuriv. He felt their moment slipping past.

Senik looked to Frost. The other man's lips were pursed. He was getting increasingly tense. He didn't seem impressed, but then Frost hadn't been impressed since the day they landed, when he found out that he was serving under a man who had once been sentenced to St Josmane's Hope.

There were flashes of las-fire in the tunnel.

Senik's voice was tense. 'Any sign?'

'No,' Yuriv said, and then, 'I see them! They're past the charges.'

'Shall I blow, sir?' Frost said.

Senik paused. He wanted to ask if Baine and Hwang were safe. But the truth was that none of them were safe. Even less safe if the intruders reached the charges and dismantled them.

He took a breath. 'The Emperor protects,' he said, simply. Then, 'Frost. Blow the tunnel.'

'I'm coming!' Baine shouted as las-bolts slammed into him. He could feel the impacts like punches into the small of his back and thanked the God-Emperor for his flak armour.

One bolt found a gap. He didn't feel it, but suddenly his leg went out from under him and he crashed down, Hwang on top of him.

So close, he thought to himself. The end of the tunnel was only fifty yards away.

He cursed, pushed himself up, determined to drag Hwang the rest of the way, when the charges went off.

It suddenly struck him what Yuriv had been shouting. *Get down!*

You should listen to your superior, Baine told himself as he felt a blast of heat on his exposed cheeks. It was a sudden hot wind, that then whipped up like a dust storm blasting over him. It was so strong it lifted him and tossed him like a rag along the corridor. Flame and dust and smoke roared along the tunnel, then everything went silent as he came to rest on his back, with dust and rock pouring down over his outflung arm and chest.

He pushed himself up, spitting out a mouth full of grit.

His goggles had come off in his fall. He could not see a thing. 'Hwang!' he tried to say, but his throat was dry.

'Hwang!' he tried again, and his own voice sounded distant, as if it were being shouted through water. Someone grabbed his arm, and he tumbled sideways. He had dropped his carbine and reached back to grab it.

Someone pulled at him again and suddenly his hearing returned, and he could hear coughing and cursing. A three-fingered hand seized his webbing and hauled him back.

'The roof!' Senik shouted. 'It's going to fall.'

V

Whiteshield Juliar needed the toilet. He was out along the track that led to Pyre's Gate. He had been watching the containers being unloaded hundreds at a time, upon huge void pallets. It had been mesmerising. Awe-inspiring, to see a job done so well.

'Maybe you should have worked for the Munitorum,' Ankela said.

'Maybe,' he laughed, though his nerves were starting to get the better of him. After a pause he said, 'Know where the latrine is?'

She shook her head. 'You could do it round the back.'

He looked up at the palace windows. 'What if Bendikt was watching me?'

She understood the feeling. 'There's bound to be somewhere inside.'

He nodded, and said, 'I won't be long.'

He walked along the track towards the palace. There had to be a latrine somewhere.

One of the other Whiteshields was walking back to their post.

'See the latrine?' he called out.

'There's an old potting block,' the other said. 'I did it in there.'

Juliar passed the row of containers. He slapped them as he walked along. They gave an empty sound.

He found the potting block. There were a few frozen lumps of crap and scraps of paper. He did his business, buckled his belt and made his way back to the doorway. Another explosion lifted up a column of black smoke.

It couldn't be long, he thought. He had one last trial to pass. He walked, tapping his knuckle against the metal containers. They echoed back their dull, full notes till he reached the last one.

Juliar stopped, thinking he had imagined it.

He tapped again, a double note, and paused.

The sound came back, from the inside. Juliar looked about, thinking there was someone tapping the container from the other side.

'Help!' a muffled voice said.

Juliar did not believe it. 'Stop frekking with me,' he said, but no one else was there. He was quite alone. He gripped his rifle, flipped the powercell to live, rested his finger next to the trigger. 'Who's in there?'

There was a muffled voice. The sound of fingers scratching down the inside of the metal chamber.

'If that is you, Thainne...'

The knock came again.

'If that's you I'll kill you,' Juliar said as he put his hand to the bolt and pulled the door open.

Jaromir guided the servo-hauler along the empty corridor. He was so close he had a good look at their enemy. The protruding lower jaw, the blunt stumps of tusk jutting up from the heretic's mouth, the ribbed subcutaneous piping that gurgled with sickness.

Jaromir felt almost complete, despite the metal skull-plate and his metallic arm.

Drakul-zar's red eyes blinked. 'Where are we?'

Blanchez and Jaromir exchanged looks. 'At command,' Jaromir said.

Drakul-zar swallowed. 'I can feel them.' His fingers gripped the side of the pallet as if he wanted to push himself up.

'Don't try that,' Yedrin told him, even though the heretic was bound down.

'I can feel them,' he said again. 'They are coming for me.'

'They're not here,' Jaromir said. He sniffed. It seemed completely fitting that an enemy of the Imperium should end up like this, strapped to a gurney, in abject fear of his foes – and awaiting the judgement of the God-Emperor.

'What did they do to you?' Jaromir said.

Drakul-zar was sweating. 'Gene-toxin,' he said, as if Jaromir would understand.

They passed through another doorway, and heard the sound of running steps behind them.

'Who are you?' a Kasrkin demanded.

Jaromir answered. 'Command squad, Seventh Company. We're bringing the prisoner. As ordered.'

The man seemed reluctant to let them through, but he saw the Silver Skull pinned to Jaromir's sleeve, and the quality of the augmetic. Only the finest warriors were honoured so and he nodded and shouted back to his companions, who had spilt out of a guard-chamber.

'I'll take you there.'

They turned along a subterranean corridor. Warm air flowed out of the cellar doors, where cogitators were whirring away. They passed a tech-priest, talking to himself in binharic cant – or he was talking to the servitor, Jaromir couldn't tell. But the guards at the end of the corridor were not willing to let the three Cadians through.

'Who sent you?' the officer demanded.

'Captain Lesk. Seventh Company.'

'Not the lord general?'

Jaromir was never going to win a debate. 'No,' he said, feeling that he should have left the talking to one of the others.

Yedrin started, 'She is going to meet us here...'

'No she's not,' the officer said. 'Because you're taking this man back to wherever you found him.'

Drakul-zar let out a moan of terror. His words were so dread-filled that they stopped the conversation dead. 'You don't understand. They're coming. Where are your armies? You cannot let them take me.'

'Sorry,' the Kasrkin said. 'I can't...' His words failed as he felt a presence behind him.

'What's happening?' a voice called out.

It was Minka, with Valentian beside her.

She stepped up between them. 'What is the problem, officer?'

'I'm sending these men away.'

'They are here on my command,' she said. 'And on the express wish of the lord general.'

Sanctioned Psyker Valentian loomed, his violet eyes staring intensely down.

'There are protocols,' the Kasrkin sergeant started, already sounding more hesitant. 'You can't just come down here demanding entrance.'

'You are correct,' Minka said. 'I apologise on behalf of my troopers. But sometimes war cannot wait for the correct paperwork.'

'Let them through,' Valentian said.

The sergeant nodded, both chastised and mollified.

* * *

The sign on the door read *Planning Office*. Two Kasrkin stood guard, but they made no effort to stop them. 'Wait here,' Minka said to Jaromir as she pushed inside.

The meeting chamber had a hushed air. One of the attendants came to intercept her. 'Excuse me,' he started, but she pushed past.

Here were the charts and maps, and Bendikt's bottle of amasec standing on the side.

'Sir!' she said.

Bendikt looked up, surprised.

Mere intervened. 'Captain Lesk?'

He stood in her way, but she pushed past him as well. 'Lord general,' she said. 'I have been trying to contact you! Do you know what is going on out there?'

He put up his hand and gestured to the table, where there was a mess of sheets and reports. 'Listen. This is a matter of utmost secrecy. The astropath. It has taken us a while to work it out. But he is repeating the Order of Return. The order that summoned all Cadians to fight the Thirteenth Black Crusade. There are scraps of speeches as well. Some of them are the ones Creed made on Cadia…'

Minka met these words with silence as she quelled her anger. 'Sir. No one can get through to you. There are Scourged elements *within* this city.'

'Scourged?'

'Yes!' Minka said, her voice rising.

Bendikt frowned. 'Captain Lesk. The city is secured.'

'The city is not secure. Not at all! Are you aware of the mines? They go out beyond the ice wall. Whatever that is there for, it is not defensive. The enemy could be under our feet as we speak.' Her temper was rising. 'And do you know about Drakul-zar?'

Bendikt frowned. 'Of course I know about him.'

'Sir. He is *here.* On this planet, hiding. And he's *terrified.*'

Understanding fell like a stone. Minka grabbed his sleeve and led Bendikt to the doorway.

Bendikt felt the cold dread shed off Drakul-zar as the heretic's red eyes opened.

'They are here,' he said. 'You cannot let them take me, Imperial general. You do not know what danger we are all in.'

'You're safe here,' Bendikt said.

Drakul-zar laughed. 'You have no idea, Imperial... They are here. Within your palace! I can feel them. My armies marched, and they skulked in the shadows. You have walked, sleeping, into their trap.'

Bendikt stepped back. It was as if he had been struck. He reached for the glass of amasec, and found it empty. Mere turned his gaze away, Minka stepped forward. 'Sir! You and the Hundred-and-First are in grave danger. We need you. Your regiment needs you.'

She stopped before the word 'sober', but the implication hung in the air.

Bendikt turned away and rested his fists upon the chart table. The room was deathly silent. Minka could feel the tremble of the defence silos starting to return fire.

'Yes,' Bendikt said at last. 'I know. What can I do?'

'Recall Ostanko. You have sent his company away?'

'I wanted a sign,' he said. 'Of Creed. His troopers are here. Maybe Creed is here as well.'

Minka stepped forward. 'Sir. You cannot put your faith in the past. We have a future and it is for us to make it, without Creed.'

A whole wall of containers rose as the void-pallet was moved by a giant lifter, and slid into the wall. 'That's impressive,' Major Luka said, as he appeared limping across the ice.

Ankela had no idea he was coming, and smartened up, her cheeks colouring.

'All good?' he said.

'Yes, sir,' she said, saluting.

Luka looked about as the lifter reversed to line up a new pallet. 'Where's Juliar?'

'He went to the toilet.'

'And left you here?'

She nodded. Luka was not impressed.

The Drookian Fen Guard stood in the back of the halftrack, pulled their clan plaid over their shoulders, and hunkered down as snow began to fall.

Grawnya looked about. This was the first snow she had seen on Telken's Rest. It unnerved her. 'Heh! You have our papers!' she shouted. 'What you waiting for?'

At last, one of the Cadians came out. 'Here,' he said, and handed the papers back.

'That's it?' Grawnya demanded, but the Cadian signalled for the Leman Russ tank parked across the road ahead of them to move. The tank's machine-spirit woke with a cough of brown promethium fumes, and then it reversed, tracks spinning for a moment before they caught purchase on the snow.

Grawnya's driver was standing by the front cabin. He pulled himself up into the seat, took one last, long drag of his lho-stick, tossed it out of the window, and then started to wake their machine-spirit.

Damp or cold had got into the engines, but on the third go they sparked and he coaxed the vehicle to life. The promise of movement prompted her warriors to stand. The wounded Scourged remained huddled in the middle.

'Is he still alive?' Grawnya said.

One Guardsman bent down and slapped the wounded warrior's cheeks. There was a diminishing sign of life.

'He is.'

'Come on, you bastard!' Juliar called out as he pulled the container door open. He reached out with his boot and hooked it under the bottom of the metal, to drag it wider.

The frekkers had moved the bodies. 'You idiots, Luka's going to kill you,' Juliar said, and stuck his head around the corner.

A cold hand caught his collar. 'Get off, you idiot!' he snapped, as they dragged him inside. But it was not Thainne.

A Cadian stood over him. 'Who are you?' she hissed. He saw that her teeth had been filed to spikes.

Juliar didn't want to answer, but there was a blade pressed into his throat.

'Whiteshield Juliar, sir.'

The woman laughed. The Cadians all laughed.

'You're Creed's troopers?' Juliar said.

The woman smiled. 'Yes,' she said.

Juliar paused. He had to get out of here alive. 'We thought you were dead. Lord General Bendikt will be very excited when he meets you…' Juliar paused as he took in the faces of these troopers. His eyes flickered from one to the other. They did not have violet eyes, he realised, and he stopped.

The Whiteshield thrashed back and forth as they butchered him.

Marŝal Baab stabbed him in the mouth, to stop his dying cries; stabbed him in the eyes as well, so that his soul would not be able to identify those that had killed him; cut his throat, so that his struggles were over.

'They are close,' she hissed. She didn't need to tell them. They could all feel the presence of the Kukulati. It filled them with a sense of dread and of sacrifice.

Marŝal Baab took the dead Whiteshield's helmet, grabbed his lasrifle, engaged the powercell as she strode out, then slammed the bayonet into place.

The container was set in a deserted yard behind a large palace. She slipped down, the wet squelching in her boots, went straight to the next container and pulled the door open.

Ration packs. Stacked to the ceiling.

She went along the line. The containers were full of powdered starch and dried slab; boxes of boots.

At the last, Baab thanked the Chaos gods and whistled through her sharpened teeth. Her ghulam hastened to her. This container had what they needed. She handed out rifles and powercells. They had grown up scavenging an existence in the Brutal Stars. Many had never seen a carbine or powercell fresh from the factorum. Behind the cases of powercells were wooden crates of grenades.

Baab started to laugh. The Chaos gods had blessed them all. It was time to repay them for their many generosities.

The ghulam marched towards the generator block. Marching was not natural to them, but they tried to look like Cadians, going quickly but quietly towards the building.

The sentries stood, watching them approach. They were alert, but were not alarmed as the ghulam came towards them. One of them put his head in through the door.

'They're here!' he called inside.

'About frekking time,' one of the guards said.

The ghulam could barely believe their luck. They came forward, quickening into a trot. By the time the sentries shouted out with alarm, it was too late.

There was a crack of las-fire as the intruders rushed inside.

'Shut the frekking door!' another Cadian shouted, his face a snarl of fury.

The ghulam had the advantage of surprise. In just a few seconds the Cadians were dead and the ghulam locked the doors, and looked about.

The guard-chamber reeked of smoke and steam. There were a few chairs set around a ceramic heater, and a cup filled with the stumps of ash and lho-sticks.

'He's taking a long time,' Major Luka said as he stood at the end of the track.

It was almost imperceptible. A sudden pop in the air, as the pressure changed. Ankela looked up.

'Void shields are down,' Luka said. He looked towards the generator as the seconds ticked by. Sirens wailed. His concern grew. Ankela didn't know what was happening.

At that moment, Hydra platforms along the port's southern edge started to fire. The quad-mounted autocannons swung around, targeting matrixes scanning the sky.

Each magazine was loaded with five hundred hard rounds packed into spiralled belts. They put up a devastating fusillade, emptying within a minute of ferocious fire, clouds of blue fyceline smoke enveloping each as spent brass shell cases clattered down.

'What are they shooting at?' Luka said, half to himself.

The percussive thud-thud of the autocannons travelled over the frozen landscape. The lines of tracer fire pointed to the west, and he saw the contrails of a rocket streaking towards them.

A salvo had been fired. Each missile soared upwards, reached the apex of its flight path, and tilted down into the desperate hail of Hydra fire.

Ankela flipped the safety from her lasrifle, put the butt into her shoulder, and felt fear wash through her.

'Come with me!' Luka snapped, and started limping along the frozen track.

He was halfway along when the first rocket struck. One hit the southern wall of the palace and the blast came out of the north in a hail of glass and debris that rained over the deserted gardens. Another hit the wall of containers, and impacted in a burst of fire. Three more arced overhead. One struck the fuselage of a cargo-lighter that had just been refuelled. It went up in a series of explosions. The fuel bogie went up as well, and Luka could see dark contrails of more missiles climbing into the air far out past the ice wall.

Luka's augmetic leg hissed as he went as fast as he could, and Ankela hurried alongside, her lasrifle ready.

The explosion tore through the upper levels. Mere spoke to the Kasrkin outside at the door. 'I've sent them to find out what has happened,' he said as he came back in.

Bendikt looked pale. He glanced around. At Drakul-zar, Minka and Mere.

'Throne,' he said.

Minka nodded. It was bad.

'Who is close by?' Bendikt said, as another missile slammed down behind the palace.

'Sturm is on his way,' Minka said.

Bendikt put his hand out to steady himself.

'They are here, Imperial,' Drakul-zar said. 'You are Cadians. I was always told you were the best the Imperium had to offer!'

Minka grabbed the grav-pallet and shoved him towards one of the empty cellar rooms. 'Put him in there!' she told Jaromir.

The Kasrkin appeared. She looked at them, and her squad. 'Nothing comes down this corridor. Understand?'

Blanchez was checking her long-las. The powercell was charged.

She steeled herself for whatever came. Jaromir cursed. He had left his heavy stubber in the Chimera. He took a lascarbine, and engaged a powercell.

Minka threw a carbine to Mere. He caught it one-handed.

'They are coming!' Drakul-zar's voice rang out from the adjoining room.

Minka was ready to sell her life. 'Sir,' she said to Bendikt, 'you are in extreme danger. Stay within. We shall protect you.'

'I have failed,' Bendikt said.

'No,' Minka said. 'You have led us from victory to victory. I remember Potence. Traitor Rock. And the Tribulation Salient. You did that, sir. No one else could.'

Bendikt was pale as he gripped the table. 'Creed would never have walked into this trap.'

Minka took his hand. 'Sir! At this moment, what matters is how you get us out.'

He took a deep breath and nodded. 'I will get us out,' he said, half to himself. 'I will. I will set this right.'

Minka had no time to deal with him. 'Stay with him,' she said to Valentian.

The psyker nodded. The two Kasrkin exchanged looks.

She grabbed the vox hand-set, and put out a broadcast across all command bands.

'This is Captain Lesk at HQ. Command void shields are down. Suspected infiltrators. High priority. Request urgent assistance.'

VI

Sparker's troopers were coming under sustained attack. The earlier assaults looked like mere prequels as the enemy surged forward en masse. He voxed Sargora. 'How is it where you are?'

'We have it under control,' she told him.

She sounded confident. He did not ask any more questions.

Sargora ended the vox-link and took a moment to look along the line.

On Catachan there was a saying that you had to cut a man to see what colour his blood was. There was truth in that. You only got the measure of a trooper when they were in battle, and Sargora had the sense of her platoon.

They were very different to the Catachans she had grown up with, but she saw where their strength came from. The best steel had many ingredients, and the Cadians did not just have excellent training and skills, but also knitted seamlessly together.

The sharp crack of las-fire grew to a sudden storm as hundreds of dark figures rushed towards the ice wall, crawl-tanks among them, their heavy weapons blasting out.

Sargora roared out a warning that was repeated along the line. She had the Catachan belief that nothing and no one was as fearsome as the Catachan Devils. But she was impressed with the response of her Cadians. Theirs was not a death world, like Catachan, she reminded herself, but it had demanded everything of its people.

The Cadians had taken up positions along the wall and they were working in teams, targeting the enemy. Heavy weapons teams picked out the crawl-tanks, leaving burning wrecks littering the flats. They were facing enemies on both sides, an ordeal which would strain most troops, but they were remaining calm.

Sargora felt the tension rise. If they could just concentrate on the tanks. She called Grüber.

He was already leading his troops across the habs.

'I'll flush them out,' he said.

Sargora laughed, 'Not if I get to them first!'

She ran along the wall's firing steps, taking each third trooper with her. Her orders were brief. She crouched under the parapet and said, 'They think they have us within a pincer. You are the men and women of Cadia. We shall show them who is in the pincer. Grüber's platoon is coming up behind, we will drive the enemy back upon them.

'Are you ready, brave Cadians?'

There was a roar of assent.

Sargora grinned. 'With me!' she shouted, and started the charge down the rockcrete steps.

Gunfire was erupting through the palace.

'Better get inside,' Major Luka said, and sent Ankela back to take shelter. 'I'll make sure no one is left outside.'

He made his way back along the track to the cobbled yard behind the palace, and was approaching when he heard the crack of las-fire. It echoed off the palace walls as his White-shields came out of the doorway.

He read their body language. They were startled and alarmed. There was more las-fire. Thainne, he thought, and put his hand up to stop someone. Renie knelt and put his lasrifle to his shoulder and Ankela stepped into the cover of the doorway.

Thainne shouted again. Luka could hear his voice, though not the words, and then he heard the crack of las-fire and Thainne staggered back.

'I'm coming!' Luka shouted as he started to run towards danger.

Renie dragged Thainne back to the potting block doorway. He was bleeding and crying, 'I'm hit!'

At that moment Luka came limping into the yard, augmetic leg wheezing.

He fired shots across the cobbles and ducked into the doorway. 'What's happening?' he asked.

Ankela was startled. 'They looked like Cadians,' she said. 'But they shot at us.'

'They're working their way round!' Renie shouted. He could see them picking their way under the derelict landing pad.

A grenade landed a few feet away and Renie kicked it sideways, under the parked Chimera.

The blast went off barely a second later. The smoke and flames licked out from under the tank, and Ankela fired another salvo to keep the intruders under cover.

'Stay calm,' Luka told them. 'Well done! Cadia will be proud of you.'

The intruders had ducked out of cover. One of them made a dash to get closer, and Ankela fired a quick salvo.

'I got one!' she hissed. 'I got one! Sir, did you see that?'

Luka grinned. 'Congratulations, trooper!'

'Frekk me,' Renie hissed. 'You bastard! Ankela has made it. Wait till I tell Juliar!'

'Steady,' Luka warned, 'they're going to charge.'

Thainne pulled a lasrifle towards him, but he was in too much pain to hold it straight.

'Get him out of the way,' Luka said.

One of the other Whiteshields pulled him into the corner of the chamber.

There were ten cadets huddling inside. Luka kicked the double doors open. 'Two lines!' he ordered. 'Front rank kneeling.'

The Whiteshields did as they were told. 'Get your man,' he told them, 'and you can die a trooper!'

Ankela took in a deep breath. She sniffed away the emotion as she stood in the second rank, lasrifle pressed into her shoulder, her cheek resting against the butt, her gaze running down the length of the gun, through the sights.

'Hold fire,' Luka warned.

There were too many heretics. They lobbed grenades across the yard. Two of the Whiteshields fell, while the one next to Ankela staggered back.

'Hold,' Luka said as one of the heretics put his gun round the edge of the building and fired a wild salvo. It sprayed above their heads.

'Hold!' Luka whispered. He was proud of them as the remaining Whiteshields held their ground.

Luka shouted, 'Cadia stands!' as three heretics charged, their carbines firing full-auto. Two of the Whiteshields were hit. Las-bolts stitched back and forth across the cobbles.

The heretics came from savage worlds. They had struggled since birth to stay alive in places abandoned to heresy. They fought with grit and courage, the ferocity of their people revealed in the way they fought.

But there was more to hand-to-hand combat than personal courage and savagery. The Whiteshields stood shoulder to shoulder, a bristling hedge of bayonets stabbing before them. They drove the heretics back. The barbarous warriors stumbled away, tripping over the dead and dying.

'Charge!' Luka shouted, and led the way.

The Whiteshields did not hesitate. Bayonet work was the hardest way to kill another human, but there was no hesitation. They met the heretics with their own fury, stabbing their blades in, again and again.

Major Luka stamped down upon the head of one of the heretics, the clawed toes of his augmetic leg closing upon the skull and cracking it open.

'Cadia stands!' he shouted, as he had done many times, on many battlefields – bringing courage to the hearts of young Whiteshields facing the fear of their first battle. 'You shall all be troopers!'

All of a sudden, the fight was over. The heretics were down. One of them was clawing his way forward. A second was lying on his back, one hand moving to his neck as if to loosen his collar.

'They're wearing Cadian uniforms,' Renie said in disgust.

'A trick,' Luka said, 'they're heretics.' He marched forward, pistol outstretched. He fired down, the las-bolts hissing as they hit human flesh. He turned to his Whiteshields. Only Renie and Ankela were still standing. She was helping two of the wounded Whiteshields.

'Well done!' Luka roared, as he fired his pistol into a wounded heretic. 'I'm damned proud of you all!'

* * *

The upper floor of the palace was starting to burn as Marŝal Baab led her ghulam through the empty corridors. Staff officers were running about, trying to salvage documents. They were brought down mercilessly as Baab's team stopped at office doorways, threw grenades inside, and shot the survivors.

They left a trail of destruction. Pushing onwards, killing and moving.

Spreading terror ahead of them.

The sounds of fighting echoed down through the palace. There was barely a handful of defenders. They did not know how long it would take for reinforcements to arrive.

'Lock the door,' Minka told Mere.

He did so, leaving Minka and her squad outside. She stood in the doorway, and looked through to the next chamber; Jaromir and Blanchez stood over Drakul-zar.

She could feel the tension rising. Yedrin's face was a strained mask. Blanchez looked as though she was going to be sick. She caught Minka's eye, and it was clear that the sniper understood the enormity of the responsibility upon their shoulders.

The sounds of fighting started to draw closer.

Drakul-zar was cursing inside the cellar.

Minka could hear shouts of alarm and anger. As she paused, she heard Sturm's voice in her vox-bead.

'I'm almost there,' he said.

'We're in the basement,' she told him. 'Bendikt's planning room. They're inside the building. I have no idea how many of them there are. They're killing everyone.'

There was another explosion, so close that Minka could feel the blast ripple down the corridor.

'Nearly there,' Sturm said again.

He was going to be too late, Minka thought.

'Jaromir,' she said. 'If they get through, shoot him.'

Jaromir did not want to be left behind.

'Yes,' Drakul-zar said. 'Do your job.'

Jaromir turned pale. 'Don't leave me.'

'I need you here,' she said. 'Protect Bendikt. And kill the heretic.'

To her squad she said, 'With me.'

She did not look round; she knew that they would follow as she strode away from Bendikt's locked office. As she marched into the corridor, a squad of Cadians came around the corner. Minka shouted a warning to them just as some primal instinct kicked in.

'Traitors!' Blanchez shouted.

Minka drew her power sabre and charged, as Blanchez dropped to one knee and fired a deadly salvo.

Minka's bolt pistol barked as she ran. It was rapid, suppressive fire, many of the bolts missing. Her shells slammed into the lead heretics and punched them back into the path of those that were following on. The next was a brute of a man, with heavy brows and slashed forehead, the thick scars cutting his eyebrows into thin streaks of hair.

His mouth was a snarl of hatred. She more than matched it with her own. How dare these heretics wear the uniforms of Cadia? How dare they pretend to be the hallowed soldiers of the Cadian Eighth?

Minka met the brute midway along the hallway. Her upswing caught the big man in the shoulder. The blade crackled with voltaic power as it tore through skin and flesh and bone – the blood boiling away from the wound as the fine blade carved his arm, shoulder and neck.

Minka was already moving past him, even as the blood gouted from the massive wound, and the sliced sections of his body fell apart.

The downswing met the helmet of the next – the sacred tri-dome of Cadia – and cut it into two, the fat of the brain hissing as searing heat melted it into a thin grey lard that poured and cooled like dripping wax.

Minka barrelled into the third. She put her shoulder in low, and felt the shuddering impact as the man doubled over, swinging wildly with his rifle butt – it slammed into her back, and skidded off her flak armour. It was all she could do to hold on to her weapons. She elbowed upwards, and felt the satisfying crack of a jaw being slammed shut. Something wet splattered across her face. She had no idea what it was, had no way of knowing the heretic had bitten off the end of his tongue and heretical ravings were turned into choking gurgles as his mouth filled with blood.

Minka fired her bolt pistol into him, point-blank range. The shot went straight through him, and into another behind. She cut the leg from a third man, and ran the point of her blade through the guts of the next.

Yedrin and Bohdan drove after her, cursing and shouting.

But more of them were coming and Minka knew that she could not kill them all.

Blows fell on her. They were all around her. Knives and trench axes slewed off her flak armour, scoured lines down her shoulder plates, rang her tri-dome helmet like a bell. She did not cry out as the blades cut into her.

She did not care about her own life. She had to stop them. She had to hold them up until Sturm got here. She was a child of Cadia, and she would fight heresy with every last breath in her body.

'Cadia!' she heard Blanchez shouting, but Minka was stumbling as the blows fell upon her. She refused to go down till a heretic swung his lasrifle, and connected with the back of her helmet.

Minka staggered like a stunned grox in the butcher's yard, legs starting to wobble as she lost the ability to fight, and Blanchez stood over her, swinging the long-las like a club.

VII

Catachan Devils went to war with the ferocious 'Devil's Fangs' – as much swords as war-blades. But the Cadians had bayonets fixed, the cold blue steel honed to a vicious edge.

Sargora was keen to see if they were as deadly.

She led her troopers down the stairs as las-bolts stabbed up from the habs. The heretics were working their way out from one of the buildings. She could see their heavy weapons teams scrambling to drag their guns into position.

There was fifty yards of open ground. This was going to be messy, she told herself. But she knew that her Cadians would be right behind her. She started to shout a war cry in the Catachan manner, but the troopers with her did not wait.

The Cadians charged. Straight into the hail of fire, and Sargora cursed.

She did not want to be the last to reach the enemy lines.

* * *

Luka was so busy congratulating his troopers he did not feel the sudden chill. Did not see the rime on the walls crack as the ice set firm. He felt something about his throat, and tried to pull it away. But the grip tightened. It was like a hand grasping his neck. He pulled at his collar – but there was nothing there. Nothing he could feel with his hand.

'Throne!' Ankela said, as she backed off.

Luka saw the terror in Ankela's face. He wanted to turn, but he could not.

He could not move, he could not breathe. His windpipe was being crushed. It was as if the breath were being sucked from his lungs. Slowly, he was forced to turn. His eyes bulged as he stood transfixed.

A sickly child walked towards him, three hooded figures shambling barefoot along the track behind. They looked small and pitiful in the vast landscape, but a sense of terrible power emanated from them.

Nothing else moved, only the four figures. They stopped twenty feet off, and Luka heard his own throat croak as the air was sucked from him. The child stared from sunken eyes.

One of the hooded figures started to walk towards him.

There was nothing he could do. He could not run or shout or shoot. The waiting was the worst as the figure came so close he could see inside the hood, and wished that he had not.

It was nothing he had seen before.

Flaps of skin opened as grey tentacles reached out for his head. The tentacles closed over his face and drew him forwards.

'For Cadia!' Lieutenant Sargora roared as her Catachan Fang went through the heretic's chest. She punched the next enemy and threw him backwards, neck broken by the force of the blow.

Her Cadians were all about her. She singled out the heretics' leader: a big man with three heads slung from his belt.

'You're mine!' she roared, and cut one of the cultists down, backhanding another as she waded through the enemy.

The warrior was the embodiment of the feral tribes that inhabited the Brutal Stars, his serrated axe swinging at her head. She saw the astonishment in the eyes of her foe as she stopped his blow and threw him backwards. He spat at her, lank black hair whipping about his face as he swung again.

She stopped the blow again with casual power.

He realised that she was playing with him, and that sent him into a berserk fury. She parried a third blow and laughed in his face as she went onto the attack. She wanted to drag this out so that his whole warband saw his death. He struggled to parry her Fang, and Sargora took a stride towards him, driving him back. He stumbled as he tried to stay alive, and fell, quickly scrabbling to his knees.

Sargora stood over him. She lifted her Fang two-handed, and drove it down.

Her strength was such that the blade lanced through his chest and torso, spearing into the frozen ground.

Blood bubbled up as he died, fingers clutching for his blade.

Sargora kicked his axe away and stepped back, his head hanging forward, his dead body held upright, impaled into the ice with her war-blade.

The crack of las-fire sounded in the halls of the palace as Rath Sturm's Chimera rolled towards the entrance. He was riding on the top of the vehicle. He did not wait for it to stop, but leapt down and landed on his feet, bounding forward, leaping up the stairs four at a time.

His squad jumped down after him, hellguns ready. They ran

into the foyer, where dead Cadians lay in pools of blood. Flames were pouring out of the upper windows, and the top of the stairs were dark with smoke. The sound of battle led them straight onwards.

Sturm met a heretic who was throwing grenades into each of the offices. He fired as he ran, the heretic's head coming apart as the bolt exploded. Sturm followed the trail of destruction down to Bendikt's office.

He heard screams and shouts as he came around the corner, and he raised his power axe, carving into a heretic with his first blow. Voltaic energy crackled as he slammed through the dying man, into the next, with an upward swing that ripped through the flak armour as if it were carb mash.

His Kasrkin struggled to keep up with him. It was like trying to chase a whirlwind. But they showed their veteran status. Incandescent bolts from their hellguns knifed through armour and flesh. Fires started as stray bolts seared the walls, and Sturm beheaded a last heretic with another swing of his axe.

The weapon's head snagged in the heretic's helmet. He activated the power stud to help pull it free. Worms of energy crawled out over its surface as brain and gore and shards of skull were cooked on its edges.

He dragged it clear. Curls of dirty black smoke carried the stench of burnt flesh.

'Rath,' a voice said. 'You came.'

Blanchez was pale with fury, bleeding from a dozen wounds. But she had protected Minka with her own body, allowing her to struggle to her feet.

Jaromir was lying on his face. Minka stooped and pulled him over.

'You were supposed to stay back,' she told him.

He cursed, which was enough to know that he was still

alive. His trousers were wet with blood and his augmetic hand clenched and unclenched with his failing nerves.

Bohdan bent over him, looking for the wound, and pressed down upon it to try and stem the bleeding.

Minka looked to Yedrin. He had taken a bayonet to the throat.

'Stay with me,' she said, and he nodded. Or was his head just falling forward? 'It's not your time,' Minka told him, but he slumped towards her. She lifted his head up but his neck was limp, his eyes glassy.

'Throne. Yedrin,' Blanchez said. The blood was flowing in a torrent.

Minka cursed.

Not Yedrin.

She looked about for anything they could do, and she was powerless.

Not Yedrin. He was too young. He should have had years ahead of him. Minka could have wept, but there was no time for grief.

'Drakul-zar is here,' she said. 'Something dreadful is hunting him. We need to get the void shield up. We need to secure Bendikt.'

Sturm's Kasrkin stationed themselves along the corridor. Minka had dragged the wounded into the room with Drakul-zar, where she was trying to minister to them.

In his office, Bendikt was shaking, his augmetic hand tight on the hilt of his sword. Sturm went in. 'There are more Kasrkin on their way,' he said. 'We have neutralised the heretics.'

'Thank you,' Bendikt said. 'The walls must hold. Every traitor that tries to kill me here is another that does not break our defences. We... we will turn their trap against them, with my blood as the bait.'

* * *

Minka looked desperately around for something to stem Jaromir's bleeding as Drakul-zar started to shout.

'Kill me,' he begged. 'The Thrice-Bound Daughters of Hel! Don't let them take me.'

She could not see what was approaching, but in an instant she understood Drakul-zar's terror.

'They're coming,' she tried to say, as panic clutched at her throat.

There were two Kasrkin in the room with her.

One fell to the floor and balled herself up in the corner like a terrified child, hands over her head, knees drawn up to her stomach, eyes pressed tightly shut as if she could make this horror go away.

The other was trembling as beads of perspiration gleamed on his forehead.

Minka had never felt so sick. Not even in the trench, facing the Heretic Astartes. Not even on Cadia, when the dead had risen from the blasted earth, animated with unholy life. The presence of these things filled her with abject terror.

Part of her wished that she had not come here. She could be on the ice wall now, not stuck here. But the God-Emperor commanded them, and their lives were His.

Minka closed her eyes and made the sign of the aquila. She adjusted her footing and weight, held up three fingers and saw how her own hands was trembling.

She had to save Drakul-zar.

She had to stop them getting to Bendikt.

VIII

The halftrack came to a halt behind the palace.

Grawnya was first down. 'Bring him,' she said, and two of her Guardsmen lifted the Scourged warrior under the arms. His boots trailed on the ground as she led them forward.

The palace was burning.

'The shields are still down,' one of her troopers said.

'What's wrong with these Cadians?'

Grawnya could see the generator building and started towards it. Her troopers came behind her, dragging the Scourged warrior, as she paced along the line of containers.

She could see the dead Cadians lying outside and as she walked forward, las-fire stabbed out from one of the windows. Grawnya put her hand up for her clansmen to wait.

They took the situation in and made an instant decision on how to attack.

'What shall we do with him?' the two Drookians asked of the wounded Scourged.

Grawnya cursed. They didn't seem to lack heretics for interrogation. 'Kill him.'

One of her Drookians put his lasrifle to the back of the heretic's head and fired.

There was a hiss of steam and gore as he slammed down to the ground.

Grawnya sent half her troopers round to the left while the others laid down fire to keep the enemy occupied. It was a favourite Drookian tactic, and she led her troopers forward in short dashes to the next cover.

The flanking squad were almost in place as Grawnya shouted her war cry. The Drookians answered with their blood-curdling voices. Las-bolts stabbed out from the window as the Guardsmen charged.

A melta blast burst the front doors open, and the Drookians lobbed grenades inside. Smoke and flame billowed out of the chamber as one of the Drookians stood at the window, lascarbine firing on full-auto inside.

Grawnya was first through the door.

The room was full of dead Cadians, and she couldn't tell which ones were imposters and which were not. One had been fragged and there were bits of her spread across the inner chamber, while the larger part of her body was a tangled mess of fatigues and flesh. Another half sat against the far wall, one hand to his stomach, the other holding a pistol outstretched.

Grawnya laughed at him as the heretic fired.

His las-bolt went wide. He did not have a chance to fire another. She swatted the pistol from his fingers, and drove her boot into his face, and felt satisfaction at the sound of crunching teeth and breaking bones.

* * *

Valentian could sense the approaching enemy. They gave off a psychic stink of foul corruption and he knew he was the only person who could hold them off.

'Stay here,' Valentian said, in a low voice. 'There is something terrible coming.'

The psyker's words chilled them all.

'Stay with the lord general,' he said to the Kasrkin, and turned to Hontius. 'Will you accompany me?'

The blood had run from Hontius's cheeks. His voice failed him, but he nodded, drew his bolt pistol and stepped alongside.

'Close the door,' Valentian said, 'and do not come out, no matter what you hear, until I order it.'

Drakul-zar begged for death as Valentian and Hontius stepped into the corridor. They heard the sound of the door being bolted behind them, and turned to face what was coming towards them.

In the corner, one of Sturm's Kasrkin had fallen to the ground and was letting out a dreadful mewling sound. He crawled back along the base of the wall, so petrified that he did not even look up. Hontius's hands were trembling so hard he had to grip his pistol two-handed. His lips moved in a silent prayer.

Valentian braced himself as snow began to fall. The sanctioned psyker had trained for this moment, as the shock troopers trained for combat. His fingers turned into claws, his breathing grew deeper, nostrils flaring.

Witch-fire crackled about his fists as he summoned his powers.

Three hooded figures came around the corner and turned towards him.

Valentian felt a wave of hatred roll outwards from them, and his whole body tensed. It was not just their physical appearance, but their incorporeal forms as well. A foul combination of the human and the corrupt.

Hontius let out a gasp of pain. Valentian could not turn or look or do anything to help the commissar as he felt the vice-like grip tighten about him.

Veins on his forehead and neck bulged, and trickles of blood started to run from his nostrils.

Valentian could not speak. He lifted his hand and sent a stab of psychic flame at his enemy, but it parted on either side of them, and dissipated in swirls of white.

A moan escaped his own body, as he struggled with powers that were starting to overwhelm him. It was a long time since Valentian had faced psykers of such raw power. He summoned another psychic blast. A ball of flame, a crude and vicious thing, that singed him even as he brought it into being.

It was so fierce it filled the whole corridor with flame, engulfing the three figures in a violet conflagration. He heard the scream of pain as the creatures were hurt, but as the eldritch flames dissipated the three figures limped forward still, their robes falling away in burning patches.

Hontius let out a moan of horror as he saw their uncovered forms. They were a heretical blasphemy, limping towards him, their menace driving him back.

Valentian's violet eyes glowed, but his strength was spent. He felt their power starting to overwhelm him; it took all his strength to resist their choking power, and Drakul-zar screamed as the three figures paced silently towards the room where he lay.

Grawnya cursed as she threw the genatorium doorway open, and looked inside.

She pushed in as a fist slammed into the side of her head. She was knocked sideways, slamming her skull against the metal door-jamb.

Grawnya twisted as the assailant wrapped hands about her throat, felt the blade stabbing into her forearm as she tried to protect herself.

She threw herself backwards and felt the air go out of her opponent, dragged them round, felt her shoulder connect with the enemy's gut.

There was a hiss of pain and frustration as Grawnya got her knee up and pressed her enemy down.

It was a scrawny woman in Cadian uniform. Grawnya parried the knife with her bare hands. Her fingers were slippery with her own blood, but she was far stronger than the other woman, and used her strength and size to pin the knife-hand down.

Her assailant started to snarl and bite.

Grawnya put her knee upon the other woman's throat. Her forearms were lacerated and bleeding, but her weight was such that the heretic let out a strangled sound.

'Want help?' one of her clansmen said.

'No,' Grawnya hissed. She had no need to slow her enemy's death, but kept pressing as the other woman's eyes bulged, her face turning slowly purple.

At last Grawnya stood, blood pouring from her fingertips, and she stamped down upon the heretic's exposed throat.

The crunch was sickening. The heretic's body spasmed in its death throes.

Grawnya held her hands out, red and wet with her own blood. 'How the hell does this work?' she said, looking at the mess of the genatorium in bewilderment.

'They've blown the inlet,' one of her clansmen said. 'If we can get another power source, we can wire this back up.'

Grawnya said, 'Sure?'

The clansman laughed. 'Of course I'm sure.'

Grawnya didn't take kindly to his tone of voice. 'Then what the hell are you waiting for?'

Minka stood by Drakul-zar's bed. The giant was hysterical.

Blood poured from her nose. She fumbled with her bolt pistol as she tried to pray again, but she could not will her mouth and lips to make the right sounds.

All she could hear was the rattle of her teeth as she heard footsteps, saw a shadow appear in the doorway.

Blood was starting fresh from one of the cuts on her forehead. She tried to stop it dripping into her eye, but she did not dare to let go of her pistol. She felt a sudden chill. She tried to swallow but her mouth was dry. She willed her terrified limbs to respond and did not know if she was shouting or silent as the figures filled the doorway.

'Shoot me!' Drakul-zar begged.

Minka stood before him as something slid through the door. She had a brief impression of scaled skin, sinuous and boneless, and fired.

Her grip was so tense her shots skewed wildly, her shout stifled as something seized her by the throat and crushed the breath from her body.

The wet gurgle was her own voice, trying to say the prayer of Faith in the Face of Heresy as the creatures walked barefoot towards her.

Tentacles reached out for her. The touch was repulsive as the suckers closed about her head and tugged her forward. She saw what lay within the centre of the dreadful face – a rasping maw that drew steadily closer – and she willed herself to pull back, or pull the trigger, but even though her finger was so small and light, she could not move it an inch.

Tentacles pulled her so close she could smell its breath: a foul, rotting scent.

Her mind was suddenly full of images of Cadia. It was not the planet she had grown up on, but the tormented last hours of her home world. The sky was black, the earth was breaking, and the dead walked, slack-mouthed across the ruined landscape – and then her world started to break apart.

Despair! the vision seemed to say to her as the tentacles tightened about her. She wanted to weep, and felt the thing before her suck at her, as if it was draining her despair from her, and she felt her life going with it.

Minka thought of Yedrin, and willed her mind away from that moment.

She was a child again, standing on the parapets next to her father, who stood in his uniform.

The tentacles tightened about her, crushing her head in their leathery embrace, and the despair returned. Her teeth ground upon each other and she forced her mind to go back. She could see herself, a Whiteshield, barely out of childhood, crouching in the ruins of Kasr Myrak.

She could hear 'Flower of Cadia' playing in the back of her mind, and then Creed's voice came crackling as it had, across the vox.

'Brothers in arms,' he said. *'We face a monstrous evil with resolve, with courage, with the faith of the unconquerable Imperium of Mankind!'*

Minka took faith and resolve from his words, and in her mind 'Flower of Cadia' grew louder, till she could hear the words, ringing out.

It was the soundtrack as nightmare images ran through her mind. She saw the dead rise, Cadia break apart beneath her, the Eye of Terror reach out and swallow her home world, as the Cicatrix Maledictum tore a rift across the Imperium of Man.

But through this montage, 'Flower of Cadia' grew steadily

louder and she felt her heart lift and swell. Her heart filled with resilience, defiance, hope.

A single word built within her, bursting out like a geyser from her lips, and her pistol fired.

The creature let out an inhuman squeal. She watched its ribcage explode as the bolt detonated and tore it apart. There was a wail from its sisters as Minka knelt and fired again.

The shots rang out, over and over. She emptied her magazine into them, till at last the pistol clicked empty and Minka stood in a cloud of blue fyceline smoke.

She pulled the trigger, but it kept clicking.

'It's dead,' a voice said.

A hand rested upon her shoulder. She could not look away from the things at her feet. The bodies of the monsters were like a child's dolls, torn, misshapen and broken.

'They're dead,' Valentian said. 'They're dead.'

Minka swallowed. She did not trust herself to speak. At last she allowed him to pull her away. His eyes were bloodshot. 'They're dead,' Valentian said.

Minka nodded. A word rang through her. It would define her for as long as she lived.

'What do you want to say to the arch-heretic who wants to burn our world?' her father had once asked.

'Never,' she had told him.

Never.

EPILOGUE

Colonel Sparker met Lieutenant Sargora in the shadow of the rail gate. The fighting had been fierce. Columns of black smoke rose on both sides of the ice wall. Fires were still burning in the stilt-habs.

He put out his hand. 'Well done, lieutenant.'

Sargora smiled. 'You did well, yourself.'

Sparker half laughed. He wasn't quite sure how to react to a woman who was bigger and stronger than him. 'Thank you,' he said.

Grüber stood, waiting to be acknowledged. It took longer than he would have liked. His platoon had swept in and cleared the insurgents, and he felt that the whole victory could not have been won without him.

Senik limped up. He was the first to congratulate Grüber. 'Well done,' he said.

Grüber nodded. 'You too. It would have been much worse if you hadn't blown the tunnel.'

Senik pursed his lips. Who knew how many they had buried beneath the city.

It had been a busy day for Banting. He wiped his hands upon his medicae whites, and pulled the stained apron over his head.

'Another from Seventh Company,' Vasily said as Banting prepared himself.

The man was lying on his front. A bag of plasma hung from an intravenous drip. Vasily flicked the valve to make sure the opiates were mixing in.

'And what happened here?' Banting said.

'Severed foot,' Vasily said. 'And five las-wounds in the back.'

Banting checked the treatment that the patient had received. He checked the clipboard. Trooper Hwang. He snorted to himself. He was impressed. The man was lucky to be alive.

He moved along the line. 'Baine,' he said.

Baine smiled. 'Las-bolt,' he said, and turned to show the dressing on his backside.

'In the back,' Banting observed. 'Running away?'

'Kind of,' Baine said. 'I was carrying him.'

He nodded to the bed where Hwang lay.

Banting raised an eyebrow. 'Looks like he took all the las-bolts.'

Baine nodded. He had never believed that courage could be rewarded, but his faith in the Emperor had increased this day.

Last along the line was Jaromir. Banting lifted the clipboard from the end of the bed and let out a sigh. 'What are you trying to do to me?' he said. 'How many augmetics do you want?'

Jaromir lifted his metallic hand in a gesture of innocence.

'You're getting good with that,' Banting said.

Jaromir made a gesture with his augmetic, and Banting laughed. 'Very good. Cut to the leg?'

'Seven stitches,' Jaromir said. 'I think I can keep it.'

'Good,' Banting said. 'Well done.'

The palace was still burning as Colonel Sturm escorted Drakul-zar to the nearest lighter. The command centre had been moved, as Sturm stood with Mere to watch the heretic loaded into the transport for transition to the *Cypra Probatii*.

'We saved him,' Sturm said.

Mere nodded.

'What next?'

Mere paused. 'He'll be sent to Warmund, and then, I cannot say.'

Sturm half laughed. There were worse things than death, he thought.

Better to die than to live in captivity.

Mesina saw the wreckage as she swept over the ice fields. The Arvus had made a long scar of wreckage, and it was half-buried, wings torn free, its tail in the air.

She did another circuit, just in case there were any hostiles around.

Black smoke was billowing up from the palace as she brought her Arvus in to land. It was hard gauging how close the ice was, so she descended slowly, until she felt her landing gear grate upon the ice. The lighter slid for a moment, and then came to rest.

She pushed the cabin door open and slid down, her feet crunching on the ice.

Her flight boots were stiff, as she stumped towards the wreckage. The promethium tanks had ruptured. The whole place stank.

The Arvus had not caught fire. No doubt the cold had saved it that.

Mesina's breath was loud as she reached the fuselage.

She clawed the ice away from the cabin.

The screens were smeared with frost. She scraped and pulled.

The cabin was empty.

She cursed and looked about for tracks.

She crunched round to the back. 'There you are,' she said.

Esting pushed himself up. One of his eyes was swollen shut. It looked like his nose had broken as well. Scabbing blood hung from his nostrils, and his flight suit was covered.

He was shivering.

'You came for me?' he said.

Mesina pushed herself up into the cabin and put her hand out.

'My leg is broken,' he said. 'But I can crawl.'

Mesina let him crawl to the end of the cabin, and then helped him down.

'I didn't think anyone would come,' he said. He seemed in shock.

'Of course I'd come. We're Aeronautica, aren't we? Who else is going to look out for us? Those mudboots?'

Esting nodded. He closed his eyes and said a silent prayer of thanks.

'I heard shooting,' he said.

Mesina took a breath. 'There's been a hell of a shitshow. Lucky you missed it.'

Esting nodded, and started to laugh.

Fires were burning across the city outskirts as Minka came out of Commissar Shand's office. She stopped at the doorway and spoke in a bare whisper. 'I assume I have passed, sir.' She coughed to clear her throat. 'I am free of corruption?'

He nodded. 'Correct,' he said, closing the file before him and looking up. 'Otherwise you would not be here, speaking to me.'

Minka swallowed. Sanctioned Psyker Valentian had been inside her mind, and the experience had left her feeling nauseous.

'Lesk,' Shand said.

She stopped.

'You were with Lord General Bendikt during this time.'

'Yes, sir.'

'Was there anything different in his behaviour?'

'No, sir. He was in complete control at all times.'

Shand paused. 'Was he drinking?'

'He might have had a drink. I don't remember.'

'He wasn't drunk?'

She shook her head. 'No, sir. Absolutely not. He was in command of his senses at all times. And he led us all. He was admirable, sir.'

Shand nodded. 'Thank you, Lesk.'

She nodded and made the sign of the aquila, then stepped outside and closed the door behind her.

The void shield crackled above the city as the lighters brought down more troops to Pyre's Gate.

Yedrin had been taken to the morgue. His battle was over, she thought, but the other three were coming back with her.

One by one they filed into the Chimera's troop cabin. Bohdan helped Jaromir limp up the ramp. He sat with his bandaged leg stretched out, as Blanchez sat in the corner. Her eyes were fixed on the floor by her boots. She was rocking back and forth, her long-las clutched between her arms.

Minka knocked on the driver's panel.

'Let's go!' she called out as the ramp closed behind them.

The Chimera's engine woke, and it started to move through the frozen city.

Minka closed her eyes. There were a lot of empty places within her Chimera, but they would be filled with new Cadians.

She took out the paper she had been given. *Recently Promoted Troopers*, the title read, with a list of the companies they were being assigned to.

She looked down to Seventh Company and read the first name, *Ankela P.*

She thought of Major Luka, and her eyes strayed to where Blanchez sat. She had a child's doll in her hand. It looked like a Militarum doll, missing an arm.

Blanchez rubbed her fingers over it, and then slid it inside her armour.

Minka didn't ask her about it. Blanchez had taken Yedrin's death hard.

One young and one old, Minka thought.

Luka had died as any Cadian would wish to. He had fallen on the battlefield, and he had fought and bled many times. And more than that, he'd had that gift, she thought, of giving fresh recruits the belief they needed to succeed.

That they too could live up to the ideals that Minka had grown up with. That they too could graduate from Whiteshields to Cadians.

That they would keep the fight alive.

ABOUT THE AUTHOR

Justin D Hill is the author of the Warhammer 40,000 novels *Cadia Stands, Cadian Honour, Traitor Rock, Shadow of the Eighth* and *Pilgrims of Fire.* He has also written the Necromunda novel *Terminal Overkill,* the Warhammer Horror novel *The Bookkeeper's Skull* and the Space Marine Battles novel *Storm of Damocles,* as well as several short stories. His novels have won a number of prizes, as well as being *Washington Post* and *Sunday Times* Books of the Year. He lives ten miles uphill from York, where he is indoctrinating his four children in the 40K lore.

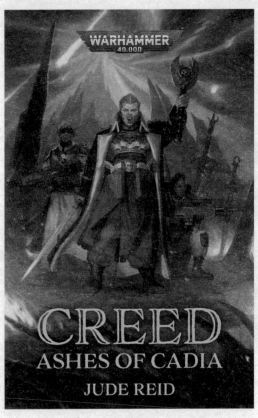

An extract from
Creed: Ashes of Cadia
by Jude Reid

'Lord castellan? They need you.'

The interruption came as she poured the second cup of recaff. The tentative knock at the door was as unwelcome as an ogryn in the mess hall, and as easy to ignore. It was followed by a nervous cough and underscored by the faint scuffling of feet, as if whoever was waiting there had a fair idea of the reception they were about to get.

Ursula Skouros, lord castellan of the lost fortress world of Cadia and commander-in-chief of the Tectora IV campaign, closed her book and took a hasty mouthful of the scalding liquid. The first cup had been purely medicinal, gulped down in a single shot without her noticing the taste, nothing but a jolt of rapid-acting stimulant to take the edge from days of sleep deprivation. Ten minutes of peace to enjoy the second had clearly been too much to ask for.

She sighed. 'Come in, Wilfret.'

The door opened. Lieutenant Wilfret Fletz – nineteen standard Terran years of age and the newest member of her staff – stood in the open doorway, an apology writ large in every hesitant movement of his spindly frame.

'My apologies, lord castellan.' Fletz looked abashed. 'We have a problem in the strategium.'

'What manner of problem?' Ursula rose to her feet, any lingering fatigue instantly dismissed by a fresh wave of alertness. The assault on the planetary capital was less than two hours away, and her strategy was planned out to the minute. Now was not the time for problems.

'I have no details as yet, lord castellan. Major Argent was quite insistent that it couldn't wait.'

Fletz was already moving through the cramped passageways of the Capitol Imperialis. A faint vibration through the deck plating underfoot was the only sign that the *Wrath of Olympus* was still in motion, rumbling towards the battlefield like the inexorable march of time. Speed wasn't one of its qualities, but the *Wrath*'s portable void shields, adamantine armour plating, Behemoth cannon and array of twin-linked heavy bolters provided adequate compensation, to say nothing of its entourage of Baneblades.

The strategium sat at the very heart of the vehicle, a vast chamber with a high vaulted ceiling lit by an array of sulphur-yellow lumen-globes. One wall was dominated by a huge viewscreen displaying a granular image of the ruined surface of Tectora IV, all detail rendered indistinct by the pre-dawn gloom and the driving rain. Every inch of space was jammed with data-looms, maintenance servitors, the platform's bridge crew and her own staff officers, all of them clustered around the room's focal point: the giant hololithic display of Redemption City projected above the war table in its centre.

'Lord castellan. Forgive the interruption.' Ursula's adjutant snapped a crisp salute.

'Major. Do we have a problem?'

'I fear we do.' Gideon Argent gave a rueful nod.

'Details.'

Argent moved around the flickering blue projection so that his hand hovered over a miniature Imperial tank division on the city's western approach. 'The issue is the Third Armoured infantry under Lord General Valk.'

Pyoter Valk should have been holding position. Instead, his armoured column was trundling forwards with his personal Stormlord in the lead, the battle group following like fawning courtiers in a royal procession.

'I see the general is moving early.' Ursula took a step closer to the table. 'Has he given a reason for that?'

'None. And no answer on the vox.'

Ursula settled back into her command throne and placed her right hand on the sceptre built into its armrest. A needle flicked out like a razor-sharp tongue, aspirated a drop of her blood, then retracted to deliver the sample to its cogitator array. The *Wrath* had a permanent crew of forty-five humans and as many servitors again, but its gene-locked machine-spirit answered to her alone.

She let her eyes rest on the hololithic battlefield. Assuming steady progress over firm ground, Valk's battle group would be in position to assault within half an hour, leaving the rest of the Cadian forces a full ninety minutes behind. Valk wasn't an idiot, which meant either he was moving in response to enemy action – unlikely, but not impossible – or he was enacting a plan of his own that had nothing to do with the overall strategy.

'Time for a word with the lord general,' Ursula said. 'Rho, open a holo-link to *Deus Imperator Vult*. Use my personal channel.'

With a silken rasp of well-oiled metal, the *Wrath*'s enginseer unfurled from between two data-looms and extended a slender mechadendrite towards the hololith.

'Certainly, lord castellan.'

There was a bright binharic chirp, and the hololith went dark, then flickered to life again in a two-dimensional display of the Stormlord's cabin.

'Lord castellan! What a pleasure to see your face.' Lord General Pyoter Valk brushed the fall of pale blond hair back from his forehead, all smiles and rakish charm, as if they were face to face at a high-society event and not thirty miles apart on a rain-soaked battlefield. Paired scars traced the high lines of his cheekbones, distinctive despite the poor quality of the projection. *'I trust all is well?'*

'I note you are moving ahead of schedule, general.' Ursula kept her voice flat. 'Is there a reason for that?'

'Of course, my lord.' Valk's infuriating smile didn't waver. *'My scouts identified an advantageous position closer to the city walls, a better vantage point to gain intelligence on enemy movements. Under the circumstances, it appears too good an opportunity to miss.'*

Ursula shot a glance at her adjutant. Argent rolled his eyes. His low opinion of the lord general had been an open secret for some time.

'Some effort has been made to acquire adequate intelligence on the enemy already, lord general. Resume your former position. We must hope your enthusiasm has avoided the enemy's notice.'

A burst of static rippled across the projection, and when the image and audio returned Valk was leaning forward in his throne, mid-sentence.

'...waste of time.'

'Kindly repeat yourself.'

'My apologies.' With the image in monochrome it was impossible to be sure, but she thought Valk's face was flushing red. His tone was urgent. *'Allow me to get into position. This opportunity*

could bring the battle to a close within hours. I have a hand-picked assault unit ready to follow me through the city's defences to disable its void shields from within. Once that is done, the rest of the division will be in position to force a breach and make its way inside.'

Ursula allowed a moment of silence to stretch out between them, as if she were actually considering the merits of his plan. 'No, thank you. A valiant offer, but one that will not be necessary on this occasion–'

'Lord castellan, may I have your permission to speak freely?'

'By all means.'

Valk was fond of speaking freely, and she was rarely glad to hear what he had to say. A dull sense of weariness crept over her. Right at that moment, she'd have given a month's stipend for a decent cup of recaff.

'Let me do this, and you can have Redemption City in your hands by noon.'

The worst thing was that he was probably right. The city would be hers for the taking, albeit with its walls shattered and the streets running with blood.

'Return to your position, lord general. Everything is proceeding according to the established battle plan–'

'Ah, yes. Your sacred battle plan.' Valk's thin veneer of charm slipped, exposing the raw contempt beneath. *'With a different strategy we could have conquered this planet in half the time. Instead we're taking it at a crawl and worrying over every shot fired. At this rate it'll be weeks before Redemption falls, when I could be in there right now getting the job done.'*

It was nothing she hadn't heard before. Ursula was perfectly aware that he wasn't the only one of her officers chafing in his harness, but that was a problem that was going to take months to sort, maybe even years.

'Your concerns are noted, general. I'll make time later to

discuss them face to face. *After* we've dealt with the matter at hand.'

'Your father understood what it meant to be Cadian.'

The strategium fell still. Cogitators hummed.

'Allow me to remind you that Lord Castellan Creed presided over the greatest defeat in Cadia's history. For myself I prefer victory.' Ursula closed her eyes, counted to three, then opened them again. 'You have your orders. That will be all.'

The enginseer voxed a binharic command. The hololith vanished, and the image of the battlefield returned.

Ursula shot a glare around the bridge. 'Does anyone have anything to add?'

The bridge crew were suddenly fascinated by their data-looms.

Argent shook his head. 'I don't believe so, lord castellan.'

Ursula watched the hololith, waiting for Valk's squad to make their move. For a moment she wondered if he had any intention of obeying her orders, until first the Stormlord then its trailing retinue began the laborious work of retracing their route back into position.

'Excellent.' She settled back into her command throne, and tried to loosen some of the tension from her shoulders. Valk's impromptu plans were becoming all too common an occurrence. This one could hardly have come at a worse time: yet another exhausting battle fought to a stalemate before the first shot against the enemy had even been fired.

Contrary to Pyoter Valk's grim predictions, Redemption City fell just before dusk. The city's void shields had crumpled at the first barrage of artillery, and a hurriedly voxed broadcast of unconditional surrender had followed, accompanied by a white flag wrapped around the key to the city and the former governor's freshly severed head. It had been a textbook conquest from start to finish. Tectora's cities had fallen one after another like an obedient house of cards, setting the planet – and by extension, the sector – on the road of return to full compliance after the isolation of the Long Night.

Ursula looked up again at the statue of the God-Emperor in the *Wrath*'s tiny chapel, and wondered if the uneasy sense of oppression she was feeling was the weight of His disapproval.

'Tell me if this is overstepping the mark,' Gideon Argent said. 'But generally I would expect the successful conqueror of a planet to be wearing a different expression.'

'And what expression am I supposed to be wearing, major?'

'Less disappointed. Less angry.' In public, her adjutant was the soul of deference, but in the privacy of their own company they could speak freely. Any real formality had long since been abraded to nothing by more years of service together than she cared to count.

'Why would I be angry?' Ursula forced a smile onto her face. 'See?'

'You're right. That's worse.'

Argent was right, Ursula thought. She was letting a treacherous sense of anticlimax rob all savour from her victory. Even if the fall of Redemption had been a foregone conclusion, the rebel governor's posturing nothing but a final vainglorious stand long after his people's thirst for war was slaked, that didn't make it any less important. Her plans had come together beautifully in the end, the victory a fitting reward for all her labours.

It still felt hollow.

'Maybe Valk is right,' she said.

Argent snorted. 'If he hears you say that he'll be even more insufferable than he is already.'

'I mean it. Plenty of the old guard are thinking the same. We could have had the conquest over months ago if I was willing to move quicker. Shed more blood. Reduce a few more cities to rubble.'

'Yes, another blasted asteroid is certainly what the Imperium needs. We should reach for the cyclonic warheads every time some idiot provincial governor decides they would be better off not paying their tithe.' Argent withdrew a compact flask from the inside pocket of his tunic and raised it in a toast. 'To your glorious victory. Even if you failed to shed quite enough blood for your generals' tastes.'

'Any fool can turn a planet to ash.' She accepted the offered flask, took a sip of Argent's foul-tasting rotgut and handed it back. 'Having something worthwhile left afterwards is the tricky part.'

The words hung in the air of the chapel like incense. Ursula could guess what her adjutant was thinking. There was only one broken planet that would have brought that solemn, thoughtful expression to his face.

'Between you and me, I suspect Valk has never got over not being there for the Fall.' Argent's voice was bright, but there was something brittle behind the words. Years might have passed, but the wounds left by Cadia's destruction still ran deep. 'To hear him talk, he could have fought the Despoiler and the whole Thirteenth Black Crusade single-handed. We'd all be in Kasr Myrak right now knocking back amasec by the pint. That, and he considers himself the rightful lord castellan of Cadia. If only the High Lords of Terra had seen it that way too.'

'Yes, if you listen to him the whole Guard is a hotbed of nepotism and corruption, and I only have the job because of who my father was.' She rolled her eyes. 'I would be insulted if I thought the man had a single original thought in that golden head of his.'